SILENT WHISPERS

UNLOCKING SECRETS AND SOLVING MYSTERIES

JIMELLE SUZANNE

Rev 10.21

PROLOGUE

BLUE VISION'S last chapter ended with Courtney's shocking discovery... the universe led her to her twin sister! Shortly after Courtney's birth Clyde and Clarissa Hammond adopted the new baby. They assumed she was an only child and as she grew Courtney had no idea that the visions that plagued her would lead her to find her twin sister. But once it happened Courtney felt an inner peace sweep through her being, it was as if Caitlin was exactly who she had been waiting for all of her life. The two are completely identical except for Caitlin's disabilities and as it turns out her physical and mental challenges fade to the background as her brilliance as an artistic savant glow in the forefront.

SILENT WHISPERS describes the journey of the two sisters as they work with their silent communication skills and together discover the path that their lives are destined to follow.

Before we rejoin Courtney and her newly discovered sister there is someone we must meet 'across the pond' in London to be exact. The first chapter of SILENT WHISPERS introduces Abigail Whiting. She is unusual, daring and at times unscrupulous and always brave. You may dislike her at times then suddenly laugh with admiration as she escapes a challenging situation. You will always wonder what she has to do with Courtney's story, but mark my words, she is an important figure in the lives of the Camdens and the Hammonds. Be patient. Enjoy the antics of Abigail and the adventures of Courtney and Caitlin then read DESTINY'S CIRCLE. The puzzles will be solved and the questions answered and the secrets will be revealed.

Life offers us surprises at every turn. Some can be frightening, challenging and rewarding but all will make us stronger.

CHAPTER ONE

London 1986

Adrenaline slammed into her body as fearful frustration threatened to explode her outwardly calm demeanor. She fought her rising panic with every breath as she covertly glanced at her watch again. The frizzy ends of her white blond hair floated in a halo on her head and around her face softening the bored harshness of the expression she wore to something akin to angelic, that is if one consumed enough alcohol while peering through the suffocating haze of cigarette smoke. Male patrons seated at crowded tables sticky with spilled spirits, labored to focus on the petite female perched on the barstool. She blatantly avoided all eye contact with any save the increasingly inebriated man who sat near her.

As the diminutive woman dragged deeply on her cigarette, several pairs of male eyes darted to the plunging neckline of her little black dress and openly admired the movement of her chest as she exhaled a long plume of smoke. She was well aware of their leering gazes as her blue eyes followed the undulating stream as it curled lazily above her head, and joined other slow crawling vapors floating on stale air currents which finally blended with the thick undefined sea of noxious fumes.

She drew a gold compact from her black shoulder bag and studied her reflection. Her eyes burned and she saw that the whites were shot with red angry veins. Her smooth provocative movements belied her inner agitation and pounding heart. This was not her first evening in the seedy pub but she fervently hoped it would be her last and if all went as planned she would never grace the bloody place with her presence again.

The bloke leaning heavily on the bar near her was a sure thing. He was the type to flash fat wads of money and buy rounds of drinks for everyone in the pub. She had investigated him thoroughly, following him and listening to him, and watching his drunken behavior. She was very good at finding the right investment. She considered all of her Marks as investments, after all it was an investment of time and cunning to put them in the right mood to uh, relieve them of the excesses that they surely would have no need of.

4

Her back was beginning to ache and the hard stool was an abomination as she squirmed to find a more comfortable position. If this wanker would just get tired of drinking and ask her to go home with him she could get on with her night. Her frazzled nerves were approaching a meltdown when she heard him mumble.

"So Blondie, waddaya say we go round t' me psflatt. I can show ya ah jolly good time." She grimaced when a fine spray of spittle showered her as he struggled to form spittle filled slurred words.

"I thought you'd never ask." Her spirits shot up and in a moment of overwhelming generosity decided to forget about the spittle spray as she gracefully slid from her stool and arched her back rewarding him with a look at her delectable curves. His eyes did indeed hungrily focus on her well-endowed chest, which was a big mistake. His foot caught on the rung of the barstool. His body lurched forward and he made a frantic grab for the edge of the bar as he fell heavily against his small companion. Other woozy patrons yelled obscene protests as their questionable conversations were interrupted by the rough jostling they received as the pair tried to prevent an unwanted tumble to the filthy floor.

"Ugh! C'mon Luv," she gritted as she attempted to steady the large man.

"Hey, yer purty strong ain'tcha, for such a wee lass!"

"Thank ya kindly," she chirped, clearly relieved that her plans would at last be implemented. She could afford to flash one of her dazzling smiles and charm him into delirium before she lifted his money and cards and anything else she could get away with.

A cold drizzle dampened the dark street as the couple emerged from the pub. Lights from other seedy establishments flashed garish colors through the mist. Trash tumbled out of over-filled containers and lay in stinking piles on the narrow sidewalks.

A group of toughs huddled in the dark doorway of an abandoned building. Their churlish voices silenced as the couple staggered near them. Blondie's heart skipped a beat as they passed. She tried to urge her drunken date to a faster pace. The men stopped their argument for only a moment then continued as though they had never been interrupted.

The temperature had dropped and white puffs of air floated from their mouths and nostrils as they labored on, fighting the effects of cigarette smoke and excess alcohol.

"How much longer do we have to walk in this bleedin' drizzle? My hair is blasted flat as it is and I'm freezin' my bloody ass!" Her mood had taken a down turn as his weight pushed down on her small thin shoulders.

"D'ya see a large red door just down there?" He flung his arm in the direction they were walking.

"I don't see a bloody thing. It's black as hell on this street!"

"Right 'ere…'ere," he lurched hard to the right and his shoulder hit the corner of the doorway. "Bugger!" His pain-filled grimace was unseen in the darkness. His cold hands fumbled as he felt around for the door latch. He shoved his weight against the heavy door. It banged open with shrieking hinges, and a rush of warm stale air assaulted them. At least it was dry. Both of them nearly fell again as his foot banged painfully against the bottom of the dark stairs.

"Don't anyone turn their lights on in this 'ere neighborhood?" Her patience was stretching thin as she realized this bloke might not have as much as she had first thought. She groaned inwardly as she realized this whole evening might turn out to be a terrible mistake. By the time they reached the top of the stairs she was shivering with cold, anger and apprehension.

Her eyes had grown accustomed to the darkness but she was gratified to notice a faint glow illuminating the musty hallway. She could just make out two doors on each side of the hall, but none of them had any identifying numbers or letters until they stood directly in front of the nearest one.

The man leaned forward squinting his eyes in an effort to make out the faded outline of the number four.

"Isss is it!" He announced proudly. He jammed his large hand deep into the pocket of his heavy coat and triumphantly produced a ring of keys. At last the door was unlocked and he stepped into the room flicking on the light switch as he entered.

"Ahh, Lovey this is nice, it is. We'll 'ave a good romp after all!" She squealed with undisguised relief. Her eyes took in the expensive and tasteful furnishings. She admired two beautiful paintings and the elegant light fixtures but her smile faded instantly as her glance found a dangerous leather whip leaning against the wall to her left. Handcuffs lay across a wooden chair and some sort of shiny black fabric lay in a tumbled heap on the floor.

She realized that her face must have mirrored the shock that had jolted through her. She refused to let him know how frightened she was. She need not have worried though because he misunderstood her expression thinking that she was just pleasantly surprised.

"Yer kind like's it a little rough anyway doncha?" He moved quickly for someone who had been drinking for most of the evening. His open mouth clamped down hard over hers as his hands pulled her into a smothering embrace. He grabbed at the top of her dress and prepared to rip it from her shoulders when something stopped him.

"Wha? Me eyes is goin' out!"

"And not a moment too soon!" She nearly cried with relief as she pulled back from his liquor-soaked breath.

"Wha'd you do you cheap bloody whore?"

"It's just a bit of sleepy powder in yer drink to make sure ya stay friendly Luv."

He was not ready to succumb yet and lunged forward. He put all of the strength he could muster into the fist he hoped would break her jaw and wipe that superior smirk off her face. She saw it coming however, and ducked well below his powerful arm. The forward thrust of his body knocked her back. Her arms flailed wildly as she fought to regain her balance. He knew he was losing consciousness and tried again to hit her. By this time their struggle had carried them to the wall, knocking over a wooden chair. Something hanging from the back of the chair clattered noisily to the floor. She was startled to see another pair of handcuffs, leather straps and a strand of leather with spikes protruding from it land in a tangled heap. In the midst of her struggle the chill of dread pierced her heart.

He pinned her to the wall and his huge hands were clamped around her throat. Instinctively she clawed at his hands leaving scratches from her long red nails. She was beginning to feel faint from the lack of oxygen as she savagely scratched at his face leaving long raw streaks through the stubble on his cheeks. She fought like a tigress trying to gouge his eyes but he was too tall for her. Then she kicked viciously at his legs and pumped her knees upward toward his groin. She refused to give in. She would not lose her life here like this. This decision had been a bad mistake that she promised herself she would never repeat, that is, if she lived through it. She was close to passing out, if only she could find a weapon. Her hands reached and grappled for anything she could use. Her fingers closed around something hard and she yanked it with all of her strength and shoved it into the midsection of her attacker. His grip loosened and she jabbed again and again until he stumbled back letting her go. She gulped in her first breath choking and coughing as her lungs greedily gulped in life-giving air. The darkness that had threatened to engulf her lifted. She leaned against the wall gasping for a split second frantically looking for a way to get around the stumbling bulk before he tried to grab her again. His eyes began to appear glassy then rolled back in his head. The drug was finally working. She was panting hard as she stepped toward him and shoved with all of her strength and he toppled back like a giant tree in slow motion. He crashed against a table and ricocheted onto a bookshelf then bounced against his exercise machine, scattering oddly shaped objects to the floor. Finally he lay still. A red spot appeared on the side of his head. Blood seeped from the wound and pooled on the floor under him.

"Bloody 'ell and damnation!" She rasped as she coughed and gagged trying to regain her breath. "I hope...you...rot in hell if you've died you bloody bastard! Trouble is I'll get blamed for killin' yer worthless bloody ass when I was only just tryin' to save my own life!" She knelt beside the prone man and touched his neck. She heaved a sigh of relief when she felt the weak but distinct pulse.

She moved a few inches away as she waited for her breathing to become less labored. For the first time she noticed several objects that had fallen to the floor during the struggle. Pliers, matches, a pair of tongs; "ugh! ", she shuddered as she realized that the exercise machine was something else entirely. Bile rose up in her throat as it dawned on her what she had nearly gotten into. She scrabbled away from the objects as if they might rise up and try to attack her as he had. She slammed into the wall and tried to pull herself up. Something tore at her hand as she pushed against the baseboard.

"What now?" A splinter protruded from the wood and the paint was slightly chipped where two boards met. She pushed one board and it wobbled loosely and she noticed that the two ends did not quite match up. Her senses were thrumming with something other than her frightening encounter. She pulled at the loose edge and the board easily pulled free revealing a hidden compartment. Something was jammed tightly into the small space. A soft cloth covered a rectangular object. She carefully dragged it into the light and discovered another one just behind the first. They were both wrapped identically and tied with a cord. She tugged the second one out and bent low to peer inside to see if there was anything else hidden behind it. Her eyes widened at what she saw next. She pulled out four tightly bound fat packets of American money.

"They're all bloody hundreds," she squeaked as her heart nearly pounded through her chest.

Her throat was still swollen and the fight had left her knees weak so she crawled over to her fallen handbag and grabbed the shoulder strap. She dragged it back to the baseboard. This was an opportunity if she ever saw one. She knew she had better act fast. She crammed the packages and money into her bag as quickly as her shaking hands could work. Then she searched the man's pockets and stuffed their contents into her bag with the packets of money. It was time to go. She wanted to get out straight away before he woke up.

"Ohhhh…mmmmpfh," he rolled his head slowly from side to side as he moaned in pain, but his eyes remained closed. She held her breath waiting to see if he would regain consciousness.

"I can't imagine you waking up this soon after your sleepy powder and that nasty crack on your noggin, besides the fact that you were drunk on yer ass to boot," She whispered incredulously, as she held her breath until he quieted down again. His breathing deepened and he made no further moves or sounds. Her ears were on hyper alert to the muffled noises of the building. Someone had turned the sound of the telly up and somewhere a door slammed. She listened quietly as fear drove her heart to a noisy thud in her chest, but she heard neither footsteps in the hall nor any other sounds that would indicate that the recent scuffle had alerted other tenants.

"Hunh, well obviously everyone is accustomed to the sounds of your depravity you sick bastard. I don't feel a bit of guilt by taking your hidden treasure. Fact of the matter is you probably stole it anyway. That's a comedy right there isn't it now, a thief stealin' from a thief!" For a moment hysterical laughter born of the relief from her narrow escape, threatened to explode from her bleeding lips, but she quickly regained her self-control. It was time to try to get out of the flat and she began crawling toward a chair with the idea of pulling herself to a standing position. Her throat hurt and it was still hard to breathe. She clutched the arm of the chair and pulled herself up. She leaned heavily on the chairback and took a tentative step forward. She clapped her hand over her mouth to keep from screaming as a hot stabbing pain tore through her leg and foot. This would never do. She dared not delay. Her safety depended on her ability to make a fast and silent exit immediately. Sweat beaded on her forehead and upper lip as she filled her lungs with air and her head with determination. Tears squeezed out of her eyes as she ground her teeth together and fought to cope with the pain. She told herself she could make it especially if there were no broken bones in her foot.

A door slammed in the hallway. In her state of anxiety, the sound was a thunderous echo. She froze as loud footfalls drew closer to the entry door. Little dots danced in front of her eyes as she held her breath waiting for someone to pound on the door. The footsteps passed the door and clumped down the stairs. She heard the grinding of protesting hinges as the outer door opened then banged shut as someone went out to the street.

Air whooshed out of her lungs with grateful relief. By this time her throat had become so dry she knew she could not have screamed louder than a whisper even if her life was depending on it. If she encountered any more blokes like the one lying on the floor she would surely have to work up some more fight and a scream to top it off. She continued to scold herself for being weak as she regained her composure and listened for any further noises in the outer hall.

The building had settled into a normal silence with the only sounds being the distant traffic passing on the street outside. She was ready to take her first halting step. She put out her injured foot and gingerly stepped forward. The pain was intense but she knew she would have to tolerate it. She took one hesitant step after another, but stayed focused on her progress toward the door. In the dim light she stumbled over one of the ghastly torturous objects that had fallen during her earlier struggle. She lost her balance and fell toward a brown overstuffed chair. Even through her pain she felt a familiar pull. There were precious stones here!

She slid her hand under the seat cushion. Nothing. She slid her hand to the side of the cushion finding an assortment of crumbs and the manufacturer's identification tag. She could not have made a mistake. She was as familiar with that feeling as her own breath. After all she had been following that pull for most of her life and it had never been wrong. She took a deep breath and stilled her thoughts. She felt it again. There was something here. She leaned as far as she could and her hand touched the back of the chair. She let her instincts guide her hand and shoved her fingers down between the cushion and the back of the chair. She gasped when she felt them. There were precious stones in a setting of some sort either a necklace or a bracelet. She tugged gently with her fingers but her prize was stuck. There was very little room and she was unable to ball up her fist to pull with more strength. She worked patiently and finally managed to pull it up a fraction of an inch. Then it would go no farther.

"Bleedin' bloody hell," She was losing her grip. Now it was a matter of pride, and stubborn determination as well as her obsession with jewels and the wealth that they would bring her. She heaved herself into a better position without putting too much weight on her injured foot. She yanked at the cushion only to find that it was anchored securely in place. The pain in her foot was forgotten as she threw her whole body into the task of pulling the seat cushion off of the chair. The sound of ripping fabric gave her added energy and with a final jerk, the cushion pulled free.

One hundred pound notes fluttered to the floor, as did a sparkling diamond bracelet and a gold compact. The items fell out of a woman's black silk evening bag and were now lying on the floor. She opened the bag and found a small bottle of expensive French perfume. There was nothing in the bag to identify the owner. A feeling of dread came over her as she looked at the items she had found. She was relatively sure that the owner of those things had met with some unfortunate circumstances. She knew that even a wealthy woman would not leave any of those things behind...intentionally. For just a few seconds she felt sorry for the unknown lady, but then self-preservation set in.

"Well, if she's dead, poor dear won't be needin' these things. I'll just take them along and put them to good use." She gathered everything up and stuffed them into her bag along with the money and the packages she had found behind the baseboards. It was time for her to seriously consider getting out of the flat. She dared a glance at the fallen man. He was not moving, but she could see the rise and fall of his chest with each breath. He was alive. The door was still some distance away and she started hopping on her good foot. Her shoulder bag was heavier now making her progress awkward and difficult, but she managed to reach the door without further mishap. She paused for a moment to catch her breath. Then she found the light switch and flicked it off before she opened the door a crack.

The hall was empty just as it had been when she and her companion had entered a short time earlier. There were fewer sounds now as the night deepened and most people were already asleep. She opened the door a little wider and peered into the gloom. Satisfied that no one was about, she hopped out into the hall. She closed the door behind her with great care. Thank the Lord for well-oiled hinges. She knew that her foot was swelling but she dared not take off her shoe. It was still raining and she knew she would have to walk some distance before she could find a cabby or an entrance to the Tube. She put her foot down and winced with pain but she made herself keep going. When she got to the stairs, she hesitated for only a few seconds, before stepping down with her hand on the wobbly rail. She was nearly crying by the time she reached the ground floor, but she refused to give in to her injuries. She pushed through the front door trying to ignore the shrieking hinges and at last she was out on the street. The cold drizzle was actually refreshing. Sweat was streaming down her back and chest. She lifted her face to the cool air and filled her lungs.

The street was deserted. She could hear her own halting steps echoing off of the silent buildings. She would seriously have to rethink her life. This was not the way she wanted to live. It was really time for a change. She knew that the world was changing and she was getting too old to continue these little back street adventures. The adrenaline rush was superb but these games she played were too dangerous. She decided that she should stick to a more normal activity such as just stealing jewels from under the noses of the very rich acquaintances that she had acquired. It was not so much fun but it was much healthier. Maybe she could even start a legitimate business of some sort like maybe selling antiques. She had always thought about having a little shop of her own some day. Maybe she could move to France or Italy or for that matter maybe the United States. They just love people with a British accent over there.

Her beautiful face was screwed into a terrible scowl as the pain in her foot worsened. Her eye was swelling shut. That was one thing she had no memory of. How could she have missed a bloody black eye? The rain was washing away her mascara and she was certain that it was leaving dark trails down her cheeks. Her foot throbbed and her throat was still dry and sore. Just when she thought she could not take another step, she spied an empty cab driving by on the cross street. She waved and the driver pulled over to the curb.

She nearly sobbed with relief. "Looks like ya been 'it by a double decker," The cabby regarded her suspiciously.

"Same as. I can pay," she flashed some of her newly acquired pound notes at him.

"Got no change. Where to?" He snatched the notes and stuffed them in the pocket of his rumpled jacket.

She desperately wanted to go directly home but being the careful thief she never went anywhere, directly. The cabby dropped her in front of a respectable hotel and when he pulled away from the entrance she engaged another driver to take her to her own cozy flat.

She eased herself down into a hot bath and scrubbed her skin until it was pink and glowing. She shampooed her hair and gently applied cleansing lotion to her bruised face. When she finally felt clean she climbed out and wrapped herself in a soft warm robe, then hobbled into the kitchen. She needed to find some ice for her throbbing foot, knee and swollen eye. She was formulating a plan for her new future. Her mind was made up. There would be no more dubious adventures to the dark side of London, chasing after sleazy men and their stash of goods. Her skin still crawled at the thought of the pincers, masks, whips and other apparatus in that bugger's flat. She was a talented professional. Gifted even. The jewels always spoke to her. That meant she was supposed to find them and give them a new home. Yes, she would stick

11

to what she was born to do and no more daft adventures. It was time to settle down a bit.

The first light of dawn silently crept through the windows and fell in soft glowing pools of light on the walls and furniture around her. She sat with her foot propped up on a pillow without moving for so long that her muscles were stiff and aching. She stretched and yawned hugely, praying she would be able to sleep now. She hobbled into her bedroom and sat on the edge of her bed. After some rest she could figure out what to do with the valuables she had taken. Some of them would require special handling. "But, after all, things do happen for a reason," she told herself. Her spirits lifted as she continued to plan the changes she would make in her life. It was important to think positive. Her rich discovery earlier in the evening was going to make it possible for her to be more than reasonably comfortable by anyone's definition. She was already quite wealthy, but her obsessive fear of loss and poverty held her captive to her equally powerful compulsion to find jewels to add to her growing collection of treasure.

Her beautifully appointed bedroom was filled with light and her sense of well being had fully returned. Now the sounds of people readying for their day brought comfort to her as she heard cars and buses passing on the street outside. Her eyelids were heavy with fatigue and she knew that the bliss of a dark slumber was near. She would not mind sleeping the day away at all. Maybe she would sleep for two days. She deserved the rest after everything she had just been through. Just imagine the nerve of that wanker trying to kill her. She only wanted to lift his wallet after all.

CHAPTER TWO

Charleston, South Carolina - July 1986

Courtney's eyes opened when she felt a soft touch on her cheek. Her heavy lids squinted shut after being momentarily blinded by bright golden shafts of light streaming through her bedroom window. How odd, she mused, she did not remember so much morning sunshine coming through the windows of her little studio apartment in Santa Monica.

The second pat was more insistent and was followed by a barely audible meow.

"Pavlova?" Courtney turned her head wondering what the elderly white Persian was doing in her apartment. It was not the blue eyes of the aging family pet that stared down at her.

"Oh you're Storm Cat!" She whispered as her sleepy disoriented mind suddenly cleared. She was no longer in her studio apartment in California. She was at Willows. The graceful plantation had been the home of the Camden family since the Civil War. Courtney rubbed her fists into her eyes in an effort to sort out the collage of images that struck her senses like shards of broken glass.

Yesterday she had been the happy adopted daughter of Clyde and Clarisa Hammond; granddaughter of the grand matriarch Esther Camden. Today she understood what the psychics of Hilton Head Island had told her. Their words rolled through her mind like echoes on a mountain wall, "Related by blood and by soul," they had said. It was true. She now knew that Camden blood flowed in her veins. She relaxed after a few moments of deep breathing and tried opening her eyes again. She told herself that everything was going to be just fine. Her parents were nearby and Hattie was in the kitchen making breakfast. She could manage to face whatever life surprised her with if she could just have a cup of Hattie's coffee.

Storm Cat had been patiently watching his charge as she slowly awakened. He was hungrily anticipating a nice bowl of milk and possibly some left over chicken. He knew Hattie would be unable to resist his charms but at the moment he had decided that the newest member of his household required his care and being the loyal sort, he could not in good conscience leave her alone after sensing such a deep disturbance in her the day before.

"I guess I've over-slept haven't I, Storm Cat. I smell coffee and I'll bet that the other heavenly aroma is Hattie's cinnamon buns." Her mouth watered.

Courtney sat up and stroked the soft gray fur of Storm Cat's back. "If I know Hattie, she has probably poured a bowl of milk for you and maybe if you sweet-talk her she'll give you some other goodies too like chicken from yesterday." Storm Cat licked his whiskers.

Courtney yawned and stretched her arms above her head. She felt a sharp prickling sensation on her skin. She twisted her arm around as far as she could in an effort to see the skin above her elbow. Fiery red scrape marks were the cause of the pain on her arms. She examined her other arm and found similar and equally painful scrapes there. She felt the same pain on the backs of her legs and discovered a series of the same injuries on each one. She should know what caused those scrapes but her memory was oddly vacant. She mentally pushed against the closed door in her brain. Small arrows of fear pricked at her chest. She pressed her hands to her forehead and willed her mind to find its way through the lost corridors. She remembered performing the ballet…but that was two nights ago. Yesterday morning she had taken her brother's finance', Michele and her best friend Latoia on a sight-seeing tour of Charleston. They had gone to Market Street for lunch and then walked through the open-air market. At this point her thoughts collided with a pair of blue eyes. The lightening bolt of illumination brought everything forward with such force that it nearly knocked her backward.

Yesterday in the Market place, she had made the most amazing discovery of her life. She had walked over to a display of watercolors. The artist had painted a series of seascapes featuring a young woman posed in a series of dance postures. Courtney had often visited the beach in Santa Monica and had been inspired to dance with the waves and seagulls on countless occasions. She remembered how her heart had begun to beat rapidly as knowledge exploded in her mind. Miraculously *she* was the subject of the artist's renderings. Her logical mind had battled furiously with what her eyes were seeing and what her heart was telling her.

She remembered pushing frantically through the crowds of people who stood in front of the other paintings. She was utterly stunned to find a picture featuring a lion and another with a young girl bound in a straitjacket. The most amazing work of all was the exotic face of Aeonkisha. The tribal queen was not a being with human flesh, but an ethereal vision appearing to Courtney and on one occasion actually intervening when Courtney was attacked and nearly killed. No one could possibly have known about the images that only she had witnessed with one exception. Hattie had seen many of the same events with the aid of her own psychic ability but Courtney knew that Hattie had not reproduced these beautiful paintings. Hattie could sing like an angel but painting was not one of her gifts.

14

Even now as Courtney sat comfortably on the canopy bed reviewing yesterday's stunning events, she grappled with the realization of what she had learned. Goose flesh rose on her arms as she remembered what happened next.

The display of art was the work of patients from a local institution. Volunteers from the medical staff of The Oaks along with a few of the patients themselves, were proudly exhibiting their artistic efforts as a result of a new outreach program that was being launched in Charleston. One of the patients limped her way through the crowd and stood directly in front of Courtney. They gazed into each other's eyes as mirror images. They were twins.

"Oh my God," she moaned as the memory screamed through her mind, "it really did happen!" Her voice rose to a high squeak, "I have a twin sister! I can't believe it! But I do believe it! God oh God, how could this have happened?"

Tears poured from her eyes and her long lashes clumped damply together. Her head pounded as she tried to fit all of her fragmented thoughts into a completed jigsaw puzzle. She rocked back and forth shivering as waves of realization swept over her. Childhood memories, dream events and the one she had always thought of as her other self were now explainable, at least to someone who understood such things. The other presence she had sensed so often had been her lonely frightened little twin.

They had grown up nearly three thousand miles apart and had no conscious knowledge of one another and yet bruises had often been transferred from one twin to the other. She also remembered waking up more than once with blood on her pillow and broken skin on the back of her head. It made an odd sort of sense now if you think about how an autistic child might rock and bang her head against something hard. At that very moment Courtney was unaware that she was mirroring the rocking motion that Caitlin favored as part of her every day life.

Storm Cat suddenly jumped onto her lap effectively startling her so that she immediately stopped rocking.

"What am I doing?" She sobbed softly, "Storm Cat you are right! I need to get out of this bed and into the shower. I can't figure all of this out right this minute. It's going to take some time to put everything together. I need some of that coffee that I smell."

Some of the tremors subsided as she whispered to the purring gray cat. She had been gripping her hands so tightly together that her fingers felt numb, and she shook her hands vigorously until sharp tingles signaled the return of her lost circulation.

"Everything is going to be all right," she told herself as she stretched her legs out straight and scooted toward the edge of the bed. Storm Cat leaped lightly to the floor and rubbed against her legs as she stood up. He meowed and trotted to the bedroom door, satisfied that she was up and would soon be starting her day. With one graceful leap, he pulled on the door handle and easily released the door so he could squeeze through. He wanted to see about breakfast and then head out to the garden for his daily routine.

Courtney made some phone calls and spoke with someone at the Oaks. The lady that she spoke to assured her that she could visit her twin but due to various routine medical evaluations it would not be feasible for the up-coming week. Courtney was disappointed but she knew it would probably be better anyway since she had guests in the house. She wanted to have complete freedom to visit and speak with her newly discovered... sister! The word sister was stunning to her! She had a sister! It would be difficult to wait a week before she could meet with her, but after all they had waited twenty-five years for this meeting. She felt she could just barely manage to wait another week.

* * *

Clarisa lay next to her husband Clyde as he slept deeply. It was three o'clock in the morning. She hoped that Courtney was still asleep and not wide awake like she was. So much had happened. Her life would never again be the same. Her thoughts were spinning around from the past to the present. She looked at her sleeping handsome husband as he slept and a rush of love and gratitude filled her heart. She felt so lucky to have met and married this remarkable man. She had often thought that some angel had taken pity on her and brought this man into her life to make up for all of the loneliness and loss in her childhood. She prayed that he would never be taken from her, but if *God forbid* that happened, she had at least lived in more joy and comfort for more years than she could have dared to hope for.

She knew that her mother, Esther Camden, would survive her most recent brush with death. It would be a lengthy recovery, but she should heal nicely with time and therapy. Her mother's misguided sense of honor and morality had, oddly enough, most likely been partly the cause of her stroke, which in turn had caused her to fall off of the dock and into the Ashley River. It's surely a wonder that she didn't drown and how she got from the water to the bank was nothing short of a miracle. Little did she know that it surely was a miracle brought about by Aeonkisha , who is a powerful spiritual guide.

Clarisa turned on her side as gently as possible so as not to disturb Clyde. Her thoughts raced on to her adopted daughter, Courtney. Of course, she never thought of her as adopted..."Oh God!" Clarisa whispered, as she relived the story that Hattie had told them after Courtney and the girls got back from the Market Place. Her own brother Charles had fathered a set of twins. He had seduced poor Tessa, the girl her mother had hired to help Hattie with the housework. When Tessa became pregnant Charles ignored her and moved on to other conquests. On the very day that Tessa went into labor Charles was joy riding in his sports car with one of his wild girlfriends. The car went out of control and both occupants were killed.

No one was home to help Tessa and she gave birth to twin girls on the kitchen floor. The young girl died before anyone found her. One twin was healthy but the other one was damaged during the birth and nearly died. Hattie had explained that she thought the baby *had* died after it was taken to the hospital. She claimed that Esther never mentioned the twin again and had sworn the housekeeper to secrecy. Then Esther had convinced Clarisa and Clyde to adopt the surviving twin. They did and named her Courtney. Clarisa sighed heavily as she thought about what her mother had done. She shivered though it was a warm July night, but her chills had nothing to do with the weather. The knowledge of the amazing almost other-worldly events caused her body to tremble forcefully for several minutes while she tried to sort through everything.

"So that means that Courtney, my adopted daughter, is actually what, my niece?" Clarisa mumbled shakily.

"Harmph, what did you say Lissa?" Clyde reached for her in his sleep. She cuddled close to him and tried to relax. Something was bothering her. A small but persistent tentacle of fear probed at her mind. A door had been tightly closed and locked. The seal around the secret chamber had grown stronger as the decades passed. Clarisa felt it there in her mind. Something terrifying lived behind that closed door and dread clutched at her heart. She gasped audibly when the intensity struck her midsection. No. She did not want to remember. That door had to remain closed.

"No!" She spoke aloud as she jerked to a sitting position.

"What Luv? Are you ok?"

"Oh darlin' I am so sorry to wake you. I think there's just been so much going on. I'm a little restless. I think I'll take some aspirin or maybe a sleeping pill. I just can't seem to settle down. You just go on back to sleep. I'll be right back." Clarisa spoke quietly as she reassured her concerned husband. He was only half awake, she noted, as she slipped out of bed to go in search of her medications.

***

Nearly a week had passed since the miraculous discovery of her twin sister and Courtney walked through her days in an automatic response mode. She communicated with her guests, Latoia, Raeford and her brother Shane and his girlfriend Michele. In another part of her mind, thoughts of her sister looped endlessly.

Courtney was immensely relieved when her mother announced that she would stay on for at least another two weeks. Clarisa wanted to spend additional time with her mother, Esther Camden, while she recovered from a massive stroke. Courtney's father, Clyde Hammond had to return to California due to pressing matters at his law firm. Shane and Michele left that day for a backpacking trip in Europe. Courtney smiled as she thought of them and how right they were for each other.

The old plantation house was emptying out quickly. A mysterious phone call had caused Raeford to frown deeply. The muscles of his jaw worked as his expression turned dark. He left abruptly soon after. Courtney was slightly amused by the look on Latoia's face when Raeford had told her good-by. They had not overtly displayed any affection toward one another and bid each other farewell as two friends. The heated glance that shot like a lightening bolt from blue eyes to brown...well, definitely hot! Courtney chuckled to herself.

It was late afternoon by the time Courtney finished teaching her ballet class and shopped for the items on Hattie's list. She pulled around the old plantation house and stopped near the kitchen door. The air was heavy with mid-July humidity and heat. Cicadas raised their vibrating call to each other. Magnolia blossoms covered the tree standing just a few yards away and the summer air was laden with their fragrance. Rows of Azalea bushes long past their blooming season grew in lush green obedience along the drive. Bees hummed as they diligently moved from Petunias to Impatiens. Courtney shifted her focus and heard the unmistakable sound of the Ashley River flowing restlessly just beyond the line of graceful old Willow trees.

"I am so grateful to be here in this beautiful place," she murmured to herself. Suddenly she knew what she had to do. She had to bring her sister to Willows. It was the right thing to do. If she was damaged then this place could help her heal. Being with her family would help her to heal.

Hours later after more telephone conversations with various officials including Doctor Baylor, it was decided that all routine medical evaluations were nearly complete and Courtney could visit her sister at the Oaks Mental Health Facility on the following Monday. Her sister. She rolled the word around on her tongue again and again.

"Imagine it," she kept thinking, "I have a sister." Another voice startled her as it loudly spoke in her mind, *"So do I!"*

"Hey baby, your momma's callin' from the hospital. Ms Esther is takin' a nap so she wanted to talk to you for a minute!" Hattie opened the screen door just as Courtney pulled her dance bag from the car. It was time to tell her mother about her plans.

"Well darlin'," Clarisa's Southern accent had deepened during her prolonged visit in Charleston. "You can, of course, do what you think is best, but I don't know if it is such a good idea to rush into this new relationship until you see her again and speak with her doctors. This girl has several mental problems and we just don't know how to uh, cope, with someone like that. Darlin' are you still there?"

Courtney was taken aback by her mother's words. She sensed some fear and almost, revulsion as Clarisa's feelings washed over her like toxic exhaust fumes. "This is my sister we are talking about. My own real flesh and blood sister, and I don't care if she has two heads! I am going to get to know her and

I am going to bring her to Willows and let her experience a real home for the first time in her life!" Courtney's voice grew shrill and tears welled up in her eyes.

"Of..of course, Honey I didn't mean to upset you, I'm really just tryin' to protect you from getting your heart broken and Honey I'm sorry, please forgive me for soundin' harsh and uncarin'. It's just that so many things have happened in such a short time. I just love you so much and I don't want anythin' else to happen that will disrupt the life you're makin' for yourself here in Charleston."

Courtney swallowed hard, "I know, Mom I'm sorry too. It means so much to me to get to know my sister," she paused and took a deep breath. "I understand what you're saying. Now that everyone has gone back home I want to talk to you when you get home from the hospital tonight. I think when you hear what I have to say; you will agree that everything is going to be just fine. Uh, how is Grandmother?"

"She is doing as well as one can expect. She is amazingly strong and of course, stubborn as all get out, so she will fight her way back to health no matter what," Clarisa chuckled softly. "Well, Honey I'd better get back to her room. I'll be home about six."

Hattie was bustling about in the kitchen washing vegetables and trimming them before putting them in the refrigerator. Courtney hung up the phone and turned to find Hattie holding out a glass of iced sun tea. "Oh, thank you Hattie, this is just what I need right now."

"Did I hear you say you goin' to bring your sister here?"

"Yes, at least for maybe a day, just to see how she likes it."

"Lord have mercy, baby it's about time things is set right. Have you asked the hospital about the permission and about any medication she might need?"

"I've spoken with Dr. Baylor. He thinks it's a great idea. I'm going out there on Monday to meet with him and to see, my sister. I'm going to find out everything then."

"You know Sugar, my granddaughter, Theresa, works out there. You want me to see if she can go with you? It's a big ol' place and it might come in handy to have someone show you around," Hattie sat on one of the kitchen stools and sipped her own tea.

"I would like that, thanks Hattie." Courtney sat on the other side of the butcher-block island sipping her tea and savoring the cold liquid as it slid down her dry throat.

"You know Hattie, Caitlin and I have been communicating telepathically for some time now. I didn't know who it was. I ...obviously didn't know about her so I thought it was me...some other part of me. Maybe that's actually true. She is another part of me." Courtney shook her head and sighed.

"Uh Hunh. You thought you were losin' your mind din't you Sugar," Hattie made clucking sounds when Courtney responded with a small nod. They sat in comfortable silence for a moment listening to the hum of the ceiling

19

fan. A smile twitched at the corners of Hattie's full mouth, then spread into a wide grin showing all of her even white teeth. Her shoulders began to shake and her deep hearty laugh rolled through the kitchen.

Courtney stared at her with a puzzled frown. By this time tears slid down Hattie's cheeks and she rocked back and forth on her stool laughing and sputtering as she tried in vain to speak.

"Oh Honey," she gasped, "We all probably out o' our minds if you think about it! Heee heee heee! You and your sister talkin' with your minds; us seein' a spirit with a feathered cape!" Her voice rose to a little shriek and she grabbed for a napkin to cover her mouth and wipe her nose and face.

"Not to mention a lion," Courtney's voice was lighter and her mouth slowly stretched into a smile.

"Oh..Oh…and how 'bout that little trip we took into a past life?" Hattie grabbed for another napkin as her laughter erupted in a fresh explosion of hearty guffaws, giggles and spittle. This time Courtney's merriment spilled into the mix. The two women slipped into the realm of mirthful release as they laughed at themselves and the strange collision between the worlds of the unseen and the density of terra firma. The kitchen had witnessed many events and moods in the long history of the old plantation house, but none made it glow as much as the laughter of two kindred spirits such as these.

Clarisa lay quietly alone in the large bed. The darkened house made her more aware of her husband's absence. She felt so alone. She missed his strong comforting presence. She wished for his arms around her so the world would stop spinning out of control.

They had met during her sophomore year in college and since then he had been a stabilizing force effectively stopping the aimless drift of her lonely life. Until Clyde, music had been her only solace. She treasured the experience of studying with the passionately dedicated professors in the music and art programs. Her mother had insisted that she be sent to London to study with the best teachers that money and influence could buy. The young Clarisa immersed herself in her studies but she was desperately lonely until she met Clyde. It was as close to love at first sight as any mortal could experience.

She allowed her memories to warm her as she followed the lovely days and nights she and Clyde had lived through during their early stages of falling in love. She thought of Courtney and the horrifying nightmare that her daughter had almost *not* lived through. Now this. Courtney had a twin and fate had managed to bring them together despite the plan that Esther Camden had put into motion. Clarisa's temper rose like the mercury of a thermometer. Her face felt red hot as she thought of her mother's deceptions. Her own brother had fathered those two girls. He was evil. Bile filed her throat and angry tears rolled suddenly out of her eyes and into her hair as she stared up into the darkness. Powerful emotions clawed her chest trying to burst from the dark storage vault where she had held them captive for most of her life. She thrashed in her bed and finally buried her head in the pillows to muffle the sobs while her fists pounded harmlessly on the mattress.

She was exhausted. Her tears dried up and her fists were no longer clenched. She could hear tree branches scraping against the roof as the wind picked up. The patter of rain followed. The summer storm was soothing to her exhausted mind. She was reminded of something she read once in the I Ching. The passage stated that in all of nature no storm could last forever. It would wear itself out and it would leave the earth cleaner and more refreshed. Maybe that would happen for her and her family. She drew in a deep shuddering breath as muted thunder rumbled in the distance. The rain stayed on and danced playfully against the house and windows, easing her troubled heart and bringing her a peace that would allow her to sleep.

On Monday morning Courtney's heartbeat quickened in anticipation of the meeting with her sister. This would be the first time since their dramatic fate-driven encounter at the Market Place.

Hattie's granddaughter, Theresa, was working a morning shift and had agreed to meet her at the reception desk in the main building. She would then show her to Dr. Baylor's office at nine-thirty in the morning.

The directions were easy to follow and Courtney was comfortable driving her grandmother's luxurious white Lincoln. She had been traveling for forty-five minutes when she finally saw the sign for The Oaks. She made a right turn and followed a winding entry road, bordered on either side by massive Oak trees, whose gnarled branches reached toward one another and formed an interlocking canopy. The lush foliage was so thick that even the intense July sun could only pierce the shadows with a few weak streams of light. The road dipped; then climbed up out of the dark shadows into the dazzling sunlight. Below her she saw the bright green lawns and large white buildings of The Oaks.

Shaded walking paths meandered near manicured flowerbeds bursting with colorful blossoms. Benches were placed along the paths where patients and visitors could rest quietly while enjoying serene ponds covered with green floating pads bearing enormous white flowers. Uniformed attendants pushed wheel chairs or strolled with patients across the lawn or along the pleasant walkways.

At first glance, Courtney thought the main building resembled an old plantation house much like her grandmother's. She followed the circular drive in front of the building and pulled into the designated visitor's parking lot. It was noticeably vacant so it was easy to find a parking place.

She stepped out of the car and stretched her back. There were birds chirping, a plane droning overhead and sometimes the voice of an attendant giving instructions to or just talking with a patient. Courtney was struck by the outward appearance of serenity here. She wished she could feel serene right now. Nerves jerked around in her stomach as she walked the short distance to the entrance and climbed the steps. Her heart pounded louder with each step she took. She paused before continuing and took a deep breath in an effort to calm her rising panic. She noticed the concrete planters on either side of the large doors. Lovely ferns and bright flowers spilled in a cascade of lush color creating the illusion of colorful waterfalls.

Despite the beauty around her Courtney felt ill. She shivered as though she was chilled even though it was a typically warm summer morning. She felt compelled to turn around.

She gasped at the sight that greeted her and then the breath whooshed out of her lungs like a punctured balloon. The landscape had transformed. The lovely walking paths were suddenly unkempt and cluttered with fallen leaves, branches and debris. The bright flower beds had been replaced by an ugly tangle of dried brown stalks that bore only sad shriveled remnants of their former colorful glory. A sharp gust of cold wind rushed at the piles of dry leaves and scattered them with angry dry whispers across the paved drive. Tufts of grass pushed stubbornly through any available opening in the cracked black top.

The vision held her in a breathless vacuum so powerful that she had to use all of her will to pull away from the sucking force of the wasteland of ruined gardens. She turned in slow motion then suddenly she was free. She gulped greedily at the warm humid air and panted with exhaustion as if she had just finished a strenuous allegro combination in ballet class. Her knees felt weak and she leaned against the door for support. The weight of her body caused the door to open unexpectedly and she stumbled into the building. She stood still for a moment trying to catch her breath and shake off the effects of the vision. It was comforting to see the normal busy hubbub of employees moving through the hallways as they carried out their assigned tasks.

She was grateful that no one seemed to notice her awkward entrance. She looked around for the reception desk and started walking in that direction but stopped when someone called her name. When she turned toward the female voice she saw a smiling young girl wearing white pants, a bright pink blouse and a white lab coat with a laminated picture identification tag clipped to the left front pocket. Her dark hair was pulled tightly back from her face and fashioned into a series of complicated braids that hung nearly to her shoulders.

Theresa introduced herself with a smile. "Things were pretty strange for you I'm sure," she said sympatheticly. Courtney nodded. " I don't mind telling you it was strange for all of us! It's still strange for that matter. You and C.C. are just the spittin' image of each other! Just imagine all these years and no one knew?" Theresa's smile was genuine and Courtney could feel the warmth of her personality.

"Yes that's right. It was such a shock to see her at the Market Place…I can't even tell you. I'm still trying to get it all straight in my head." Courtney's voice shook slightly and again she fought the stinging sensation of tears that threatened to overcome her. "Listen, thank you so much for taking the time to show me around. I am supposed to…"

"Meet with Dr. Baylor," Theresa finished for her. "Unh huh, ok I'll show you to his office. He's waiting for you, I just checked." Theresa smiled and pursed her lips as she looked at Courtney. She raised one eyebrow then turned and started down the corridor.

Courtney was puzzled by Theresa's tone and searching look but she had too much on her mind to think about it at that moment. She had a feeling that she was going to like Theresa very much.

CHAPTER THREE

Uniformed nurses and aides called out greetings as Theresa led the way through the maze of corridors that led to offices and patient quarters. She pointed out the directions to the cafeteria, common rooms and a therapy center. Courtney only half listened. She was distracted by the strange sounds that echoed occasionally through the halls. Frequent squeals and garbled words bounced from one wall to another making it impossible to discern their point of origin. A large man suddenly stepped from one of the doorways and stood directly in front of them causing the women to stop suddenly. His face was unnaturally round and his tongue protruded from thick lips. A small stream of drool shimmered wetly as it flowed in a steady stream from the corner of his mouth.

"Mackie, what are you doing out here honey? You g'on back in your room and play," Theresa spoke playfully to him as if he were a small child. Slowly he moved each huge leg as if he were an unsteady toddler and made his way back into the playroom.

Initially Courtney had been startled by his abrupt appearance but as she began to understand his situation her heart nearly burst with compassion. She sensed the injured soul living in his huge body. She sensed karmic implications of actions in a past life that might have caused him to want to undergo lessons of this nature. She looked around at others in the playroom. She could not imagine what it must be like for them to live a lifetime in such abject helplessness. Then she thought of Theresa, Dr. Baylor and all of the others who make it their life's work to care for those who were injured in body, mind and spirit. She decided that they are all true heroes.

"Uh, Courtney?" Theresa had stopped and touched her arm. "It's a lot to take in for the first time isn't it?" Courtney nodded silently as she swallowed back the tears that threatened to overflow. "I know I had a hard time adjusting for the first week or so. It touches everyone that way…at least the ones with a kind heart. Well this is Dr. Baylor's office. Are you ready to go in?"

Courtney cleared her throat and smiled her answer.

Theresa knocked politely then opened the door to Stephen's small office.

"Please come in. Thank you for showing her in, Theresa," Stephen spoke with as much friendly detachment as he could muster, but the truth was, he felt completely flustered in the presence of this beautiful young woman. He looked into her blue eyes framed by long dark lashes and felt his face flush.

He quickly averted his eyes and gestured to the chair opposite his desk. He noticed her slender figure as she sat gracefully and brushed back a curling wisp of auburn hair with long tapered fingers.

He stepped back and his foot caught one of the rollers on the leg of his chair. He lost his balance and the chair moved away from him striking the filing cabinet. A stack of files slid from their precarious perch and emptied their contents in a flowing cascade of paper, which fluttered all over the chair and floor.

"Well, I think those needed to be reorganized anyway," He chuckled in embarrassment as he bent down and began scooping up the folders and reports. He managed to bunch them up in an unruly clump then turned abruptly looking for an empty space on his desk. The sudden move caused him to knock over his partially filled coffee cup, spilling the contents on his desk blotter and staining the papers he had been working on.

"Here, I have some tissues! "Courtney leaned forward to help clean up the coffee.

The neck of her soft, cream-colored blouse gaped open revealing smooth sun-kissed skin as the blue topaz swung free on the gold chain.

The flustered young doctor gulped, "Maybe you would like to walk down to the cafeteria with me for some coffee. This office appears to be giving me some trouble today." He shrugged and grinned sheepishly.

She found his smile utterly disarming and decided that having coffee with him in the cafeteria would be exactly what she wanted to do.

They decided instead to have a glass of sweet tea after Dr. Baylor warned her that their coffee was "ferocious". Courtney asked endless questions about C.C. and what she might expect from her twin's behavior. The doctor explained that he knew very little of her childhood. He had gone through all of the files that were available and gave her as much of the relevant information as he could find.

"C.C. nearly died at birth. The umbilical cord was wrapped around her neck, according to the housekeeper who found her, uh you and her. The twins were delivered about three weeks early. Their…er…your mother was a young Cajun girl, who worked for the Camdens. She gave birth on the kitchen floor and began to hemorrhage. The mother managed to cover the babies in kitchen towels and remove the cord from your sister's neck. Sadly the mother was dead before anyone discovered them. Both babies were incubated for some time." Dr. Baylor paused as he sipped his tea and studied Courtney's face before he continued.

"You were the strongest one and obviously not injured. A private adoption was arranged as soon as you were healthy enough. Apparently the father had died tragically so there were no living relatives other than your Grandmother Camden. C.C. was considerably weaker and was not expected to live. She did, of course, and was put into foster care. The foster parents noticed that she was not developing normally and required constant care. She displayed behavioral problems at an early age. The tantrums and head-banging were just too much for most people to handle, so she was passed from one family to another and finally ended up here at The Oaks."

Tears glistened in Courtney's eyes, as she envisioned her sister's loneliness and physical problems. She almost felt ashamed of her own life of privilege, loving parents and extensive education. Her only real problem had been Antonio. She shuddered at the thought.

Stephen saw the chill pass through her. "I know that her story sounds cold and clinical, but your grandmother also sent money for her care and special needs. She has had the best medical care available."

"But she didn't have a family," Courtney's words were a barely audible whisper. "So my grandmother sent money for her care…all of these years…"

"Well as much as I can gather, there is some sort of trust fund for her that will take care of all her needs for as long as she lives, so your grandmother did care about her," Stephen spoke with a firm gentleness.

"She only cared about making sure the Camden's good name didn't get dragged through the mud! I doubt very seriously if that old crone even has a heart!" Courtney's voice was raised and several people turned to look in their direction.

"Miss Hammond, people just do the best they can. I'm not excusing what she did mind you, but I have learned that there are many ways to express family loyalty and caring and no matter how misguided it may appear, it is a good idea to take an objective look at all of the circumstances. If you would like to talk this out with someone I would be happy to make some recommendations."

Courtney was surprised at the level of anger that had surged up in her chest. She breathed deeply and fought to bring herself back to a calm reasonable state of mind. "I'm sorry. I didn't know that all of that anger was inside of me. All that emotion sort of took me by surprise. I'll think over your offer and let you know. Thank you."

"You're welcome. Now, I notice that you didn't ask about the paternity status. Is that something you are interested in knowing?" Stephen was unsure how far he should take the information. Under the circumstances he decided that the truth was needed in this family situation where lies had dominated everyone's life up to now.

"Actually I know about that. I know that my Uncle Charles is actually my father. He died on the same day that…we were born. I just didn't know I had a twin sister." Courtney felt her eyes tear up again. She was embarrassed at the roller coaster ride her emotions were on today but, she told herself, since the episode with Antonio her psyche was still raw. She realized that she had constructed some pretty thick emotional walls in order to cope with the dramatic turns her life had been taking. She was afraid some of those walls were starting to crumble. The anger and tears leaked out occasionally. Courtney took a deep breath. No, she felt as though she were growing stronger and more decisive because of the recent traumas. It was as though she had been sleep walking through the earlier years of her life and suddenly she was jolted out of that reverie into full alert.

Her outward appearance was serene but her heart and mind were rioting between panic and anger. Her face became flushed and her fists clenched in an effort to hang on to herself. A soft voice in her mind spoke *"Everything is going to be just fine. Don't worry."* She knew now that it was Caitlin. The thought of her sister and the sound of her voice in her head brought a sweet comforting feeling that seeped into all of the dark wounded places in her psyche. Courtney had never defined herself as being lonely. Her half brother, Shane was wonderful and they had always had a great relationship. She had friends. Latoia was her closest friend. Her parents were loving and supportive but, something about the words "twin sister" just made her feel complete as though she could take a deep breath of relief now. Maybe, subconsciously, she had been looking for her sister since the day they were separated.

Dr. Baylor watched Courtney carefully. He was sure that she was filled with conflicting emotions as he watched them register on her expressive face. She was extremely beautiful but unlike some of the beautiful wealthy women he had met, Courtney had a complexity about her that intrigued him and he was hopeful that he would have the opportunity to get to know her better. This situation was astounding and though not completely unheard of, it *was* exceptionally rare. It was absolutely his first encounter with anything of this nature.

The young doctor thought that C.C. was beautiful as well but he had not thought of her in any capacity other than a patient who needed his expertise. Courtney Hammond was a different matter. He felt the stirrings of a powerful attraction for the first time in a long time. There had been very little time for considering a serious relationship while attending medical school, working odd jobs and trying to maintain a high grade point average as well as his own mental and physical balance. He was not a loner exactly. He loved having friends and being around people, but he was also very comfortable riding for hours on his bike, alone, or sketching pictures of wildlife or landscapes. His gut told him something was changing.

"I have a large family myself and I am here to tell you that they are a lot of work. I have cousins scattered from one coast to another and parents who just love to put together huge family reunions," he smiled hoping to lighten the mood. "Every so often we run across a branch of the family tree that we didn't even know about. Sometimes I wonder if they're really just strangers that have heard about our big reunions and just decided they want to be invited, " he joked.

"Sounds like you had a full rich childhood and a wonderful family," Courtney smiled.

"Yes it was great. And the family is great. Along with their good qualities there is an assortment of neuroses, psychosis…in fact I have a second cousin that has been arrested for shop lifting so many times that she's on a first name

27

basis with the local PD. My grandfather was obsessed with cows and insisted on sleeping with the sick ones in the barn rain or shine. Then of course there is Aunt Laura who collects string and has storage shelves absolutely crammed with large balls of string and twine and rope of every description," Stephen rolled his eyes making Courtney laugh.

"I get your point."

"Oh, well I'm not even finished yet. The reason that one branch of the family was estranged from everyone else for generations was some sort of land dispute in the late seventeen hundreds. That part of the family split off and made their way to parts unknown. Out of sight out of mind, as they say. Subsequently they were forgotten as the years went by. Just ten years ago, my mother got a call from some sort of genealogy researcher and lo and behold we have twenty-five more people showing up at the annual reunion!"

Courtney burst out laughing at his comic facial expressions and gestures. She really was feeling better. She knew that it would take some time for her to work her way through the idea of her grandmother's terrible deception. That thought made her frown.

"Well I see you frowning again and I know that family anecdotes are not going to erase what has happened to you and your sister. I think a good thing to keep in mind is your grandmother was raised in a different time with different values impacting her decisions. Unfortunately there has been a stigma, a prejudice wrongfully held by a great number of people about mental illness of any sort. Up until recently there has been limited interest in funding for therapy research, partially due to the lack of awareness in the general population.

"I don't necessarily agree with her course of action, but I understand to a degree why Esther Camden tried to cover up the existence of your sister. She did make sure that you were adopted by a family member and as I understand it, during the years that Dr. Mann was alive, she was in constant contact with him and it looks as though she received monthly reports on C.C.'s health and general progress. She was responsible for getting the best care available for your sister. There isn't really very much known about autism from cause to treatment. There are lots of theories and there are some new therapies being tried but the reality is, there is simply not enough information about it yet."

"You're right of course. I studied psychology in college and in fact I had started the Masters program at UCLA. I remember reading about autism. I think if I go back into the Masters program I might consider doing a study on it."

"Well you certainly will have the opportunity to study it first hand. What made you stop your education?"

Courtney realized it was an innocent and perfectly logical question but it made her stomach lurch. She was still susceptible to the fears that her narrow escape had instilled in her. She knew it would take more than a few months and two thousand miles to make Antonio's actions fade into the background.

Stephen watched her face realizing that his question had upset her. He knew she was trying to decide how to answer. Whatever had made her stop her studies must have been another traumatic situation.

"You know what," he said glancing at his watch, "time has raced by. I have a long day ahead of me and I am already a little bit late. Are you ready for your visit with C.C.?"

Courtney took a deep breath. She was relieved that Dr. Baylor did not pursue the answer to that question. She was not ready to discuss it with anyone yet. Maybe she never would be. She smiled and nodded.

"Great. I have to dash off so I am going to have Kevin show you to the Common Room where she spends most of her time painting. Now if you need me for anything just ask one of the orderlies or nurses to page me. I am going to be busy in different parts of the hospital today but I will be happy to talk to you at any time."

"Thank you, Dr. Baylor, for your time and understanding."

"You are welcome," his heart jumped as she flashed her warm smile. His throat nearly closed completely as they shook hands. He was very flustered by his obvious attraction to her and he would be glad to get away and regain his composure.

CHAPTER FOUR

Kevin was friendly and open as he pointed out restrooms and directions explaining the general rules and functions of the facility as they walked together. Courtney tried to listen to his words but her mouth was dry as she followed him through the maze of halls and turns. Her heart fluttered nervously and she tried to swallow in vain.

"Here we are Miss Hammond. C.C. is always painting or drawing over by the window these days. You don't have to worry about anyone bothering you. Someone is always on duty in here if you need anything." He gestured his muscled arm toward a tall robust woman with graying brown hair that she wore pulled back in a low ponytail.

"When you're ready to leave just tell Angie there and she'll have someone show you out."

Courtney braced herself and inhaled taking in the artificially cooled air heavy with smells of antiseptics and sweat. She was suddenly reminded of previous visions. There was no doubt about it she had visited this place on more than one etheric occasion.

Kevin had walked over to Angie to let her know that Courtney would be visiting her sister. It was the talk of the hospital and Angie felt fortunate to be the one to witness the first meeting of the two sisters. She would have some stories to tell on her lunch break.

Kevin noticed the increased pallor of Courtney's face and hurried back to her side. "Are you okay Miss Hammond? Can I get you some water? Do you need to sit down a minute?"

"No. No thank you. I am just fine, or at least I will be." If the truth were known, she had no idea whether to laugh or cry hysterically or maybe jump up and down and run around the room screaming. She was about to meet her twin sister in the flesh. Face to face. Their 'chance' encounter the previous week had been far too shocking to form articulate words or thoughts. She had fainted on the blistering hot concrete during the street fair, right in the middle of the art display. Her sister's paintings were a chilling depiction of private moments in her life. Those moments were not shared by anyone else except her *dream self.* She now knew it was an actual person, her sister.

Courtney walked over to the girl who sat bent over the table. C.C. was rocking gently back and forth as she stared at the painting she had been working on. Time slowed. The chattering and babbles of the other patients faded until there was only the sound of her breath. Courtney's body felt so light that surely she could float up off of the floor.

C.C.'s rocking slowed as Courtney came to a stop near her. It took only seconds to understand the painting that her sister was working on. It was a picture of The Oaks. Instead of a brilliant blue sky, green lawns, flowers and giant Oak and Sweet Gum trees loaded with lush summer foliage, the sky was bleak and gray. The trees were dark spiked skeletons. Tall brown weeds grew everywhere even through the cracked asphalt of the circular drive in front of the entrance.

Courtney was shocked to realize that the painting mimicked the vision that Courtney had experienced just as she prepared to open the front door of The Oaks.

On the far right side of the painting a series of soft curving lines encapsulated another small scene. Two girls, quite obviously the twins, were depicted from the waist up, holding hands. They looked into each other's eyes while a golden light glowed around them.

The significance was profoundly obvious. Courtney had no problem understanding the message that C.C. was giving her. Words were not necessary to convey the desolation that C.C. felt before meeting her sister for the first time face to face. When they finally did meet, C.C. felt the warm glow of that golden light that families must feel when they know they belong to each other and no matter what happens to disrupt their lives they will always have the knowledge that the family encircles and supports their own.

Courtney pulled up a chair and sat near C.C. The normal sounds in the room had returned but she was feeling the disorientation that often followed the more intense visions.

C.C. turned and in a rare gesture, reached out her right hand and touched Courtney's cheek. A tear had slipped down her face and C.C. caught it on the tip of her finger. Similarly Courtney reached toward C.C.'s face and caught a tear escaping from her eye. No words were spoken as each balanced a tear on the tip of their index fingers. The tears sparkled in the sunlight that sliced through the spaces between the bars covering the window. They moved in a synchronicity until their fingers came together. The tears blended and dropped onto the picture of the two girls holding hands.

Unbeknownst to them Angie sobbed in the background and dug into her pocket for a tissue. Other employees had sneaked in to watch the meeting of the two sisters. They all stood in reverent silence. Those who would tell the story for years to come knew that they had been privy to one of the most unique events that they would ever see between two people.

The room appeared to shimmer around them and Courtney felt that they had entered the very bubble that C.C. had painted. It was in that rarified space that they would be free to speak unfettered by physical or mental impairments and they could enjoy complete privacy.

31

"Caitlin," Courtney spoke with her mind, *"how could this have happened to us? Can you hear me?"*

"Of course I can hear you," came the reply, *"I have seen you and heard your voice for as long as I can remember."*

Courtney knew it was true. She now realized that she and her sister had been catching glimpses of each other's lives since they were toddlers. She was deeply comforted to know that all of those strange visions could be attributed to someone real and tangible. It both thrilled and puzzled her. First knowing that she had a twin sister and then the fact that they had a psychic bond that was beyond anything she could have imagined. She felt connected. She no longer felt like a dangling loose end.

"I have so many questions about you and your life. I want to know everything! I want to know why we were separated until now! Do you know any of the answers?" Courtney's thoughts tumbled out forming the silent whispers that only she and her sister could hear.

A feathered cape whirled in front of them interrupting Courtney's muted flow of excited mental communication. A smiling Aeonkisha appeared.

"You are reunited in the Universal timing. Events on earth are often mistakenly viewed as accidents. There are no accidents.

You have both faced your challenges with courage and determination. Your choices have been correct and you have both learned valuable lessons. It has been important for you to have many experiences for the development of your soul. You have a great work to do and your lives up to now have prepared you for this work.

When you were first born as twins centuries ago. A terrible wrong was committed as you reached puberty. You have lived separate lives until now in order to nurture your best qualities and to learn to forgive yourselves. There is a story you must hear. Once this is accomplished you will have the information you need to accomplish your goals."

The powerful apparition opened her cloak and wrapped it around the girls.

Angie was unaware of what was happening to the twins but she noticed one of the patients in the corner. Avery was pointing to the girls. He was short with a medium build. Though he was unable to move very fast it was easy to see that he was highly agitated. He bounced up and down though his feet never left the floor. Avery's ability to speak was impeded by an abnormally large tongue and like many with Downs Syndrome his communication was somewhat limited.

"What do you see Avery. What's the matter?" Angie glanced at Courtney and C.C. as they sat quietly looking down at C.C.'s painting. They seemed fine and were engrossed in their own company. In fact it almost appeared as though C.C. were talking to her sister. That was impossible of course. Well who knew what had agitated Avery.

"Wook! Wook! Feddesh. Waydee!" A bit of drool was running down the side of Avery's mouth and spittle sprayed in every direction as he sputtered unintelligible words.

"I see Avery. I'm looking. Avery there *are* two ladies sitting there but I don't see a single feather anywhere. C'mon let's turn on the television and find some cartoons." She finally succeeded in distracting him and he plunked himself down in front of the television set in a pout. Angie studied the twins but could not detect anything amiss.

Avery had always been able to see beyond the physical world but his gift did not extend to his communication skills. He sat on the floor with one stubby leg tucked beneath him and the other one bent at an angle that allowed him to rest his elbow on his knee and cup his chin in his hand, from all outward appearances a petulant child. In truth he was nearly thirty years old. He had been institutionalized since the age of six when his parents discovered he would probably not progress any further as a Downs syndrome child.

Avery sat very still in the same position for a long while. The only obvious movements were the rapid blinking of his eyes as the cartoon characters cavorted and shrieked through crazy antics around the television screen. He really was not interested in the program. A large feathered cloak had enveloped him along with the twins. All of them listened and watched as the story of their ancient lifetimes unfolded, revealing possible answers to their present day circumstances.

SCOTLAND 1503

A dank thick fog gobbled greedily until the tiny village of Rogan Kincardin outside of Innes, Scotland had been completely swallowed into its cold gray belly. The residents were well acquainted with the mists that unexpectedly rose from the bog with creeping curling tendrils. In silent stealth it often surrounded each cottage dimming the glow of the cheery peat fires that burned on every hearth.

No one ventured out during the "dragon fog" as it was called. It was well known that those foolish enough to wander beyond the safe boundaries of the village could risk becoming lost or worse and perish in the bottomless sucking mud that lay just under the surface of the brackish water in Macdonough's Bog.

Amilee McIlry stumbled forward as the first sharp pain hit. It was too early for the baby to come and tears of fear and panic welled up in her enormous blue eyes. The next pain tore through her young body and she dropped to her knees. She fought to catch her breath and beat back the rising panic. She wanted to be strong and courageous. Her anger took hold and she cursed the forces of war that had taken her young husband so far from his home at this important time in their lives.

"Why the devil can'na these men live in peace," she yelled to no one in particular.

33

Amilee knew all too well the role of the village women in 1503. Daily life was cruelly demanding even with a good husband. Without one, a woman and her children were lucky to survive at all unless she received the help of family and friends.

She was essentially alone. Villagers said her mother died of a broken heart when Amilee's father was killed in battle. Her four brothers had left years ago to fight in the rebellion. She had no knowledge of their whereabouts or indeed if they still lived. The only blood kin she knew about was old daft Jerusa, her mother's sister. Amilee was a little frightened of the fierce wild-eyed woman, as were the other villagers. Old Jerusa lived alone. No one knew quite where except that it was far from the comfort of neighbors. She was given to fits of ranting and some whispered that she summoned spirits and hobnobbed with the 'wee people'. She was indeed by all accounts the most mysterious person any of the locals had ever encountered. But mind you, when someone fell ill or was injured, Jerusa would suddenly appear in the village and go straight to the home of the afflicted family. She always brought a goatskin pouch filled with precisely the healing herbs and balms that were needed. The villagers had long since forgotten when she had begun doing that or for that matter no one could remember a time when she had not been there to help them heal their ailments.

In God's truth everyone was more respectful of Jerusa than afraid of her. The only time she really struck terror in a man's heart was when she prescribed bathing as part of the healing treatment. She was unusually tall and muscular for a woman of that era and her dark heavy lidded eyes bore a look sharper than any warrior's lance. Few refused to follow her orders whether due to her compelling demeanor or her good results, none would confess. It was rumored that a man of strong stature had once refused her orders to bathe. He suffered from an itching affliction of the skin and Jerusa assured him he would be healed if he bathed in a solution of hot water and herbs. She never uttered a word so the story goes, but lifted the man fully clothed and dunked him in the tub of hot water she had prepared. There were reports of terrible screams coming from his home. His neighbors thought he had died. But when he was seen next his skin affliction was gone and he was very much alive for many years there after.

Amilee sighed with relief and exhaustion as the last pain released its crippling grasp on her swollen body. "Praises be to the Saints," she murmured as she looked thankfully at her full stew pot and a skin of fresh rainwater. With shaking hands she reached for the fire poke. Slowly she used it to pull herself to her feet. She was shivering as she worked to build up the fire before the next pain came.

A warm wet rush on her legs told her that surely a wee bairn would be coming soon. She lifted the coarse fabric of her skirt to dry her legs from the birthing water. She cried out in shock when she saw all of the blood. She would have to go for help. Surely she could make it through the damnable fog

34

without losing her way. Another pain ripped through her body before she could consider doing anything further. She was grateful to release herself into the dark dreams of unconsciousness where she would be free of pain. She saw her beloved husband Nicholas as he rode with their protectors the great clan Mackintosh. He marched with the others wearing his tartan proudly across his chest. His red hair gleaming in the sun made her sigh with pride. True to his heritage and the meaning of his surname he was a McIlry and that translated to son of the red-haired youth. Perhaps the wee one would too be a red haired son.

"Ahh now open yer eyes lassie 'an sup this tea bitters. There now t'will give ye strength for the work ahead. Would've been here a bit sooner but the vision showed me ye might be wantin' some extra potions for the arrival will be twice the trouble."

Amilee coughed and grimaced as the hot bitter tea was forced between her tightly clenched teeth. She had not known when her Aunt Jerusa had arrived nor how she had been able to find her way through the impossible mists, but she was flooded with a sense of relief and profound gratitude to hear the older woman's husky voice. The mind numbing pain receded. The tears on her cheeks sparkled in the firelight. Tallow candles flickered above the hearth and in other places in the room. Their combined light drove back the darkness and cast a golden warmth throughout the small living space.

"There ye be lass," Jerusa crooned as Amilee opened her eyes, "just lie quiet now while ye can. The herbs will ease you and you'll have an easier time. Just you rest yourself. Everything will be all right," the old woman soothed as she bustled around folding swaddling cloths, mixing herbs and building up the fire.

The young mother-to-be, relaxed while she watched Jerusa's sure quick movements as she completed her tasks. The pain was leaving her body and she felt lighter or was it her head that felt lighter? An odd humming reached her ears. Jerusa threw something into the flames and sparks exploded into fiery little stars that floated around the room. The contractions came again and forced a loud groan from Amilee.

"Here now sup this good hot potion. Sup it all there's a good lassie. Now listen to what I say. You will birth two wee bairns on this day." Fear raised the hairs on the back of Amilee's neck and arms. She knew that Jerusa meant that she would have twins. What an unexpected wonder that would be.

"Do'na worry tis yer fate and a good one it is. Ye'll bear two daughters. The first-born is to be called Belaine. The second is Begata. They will be blessed by the Wee People and expected to serve as healers and keepers of...the secrets, just as your great grandmother did.". Jerusa lowered her voice and released her words in a harsh hissing whisper as Amilee sank into a floating echoing world of burning stars and small gnarled women speaking a strange language. She felt her body working to give birth, but the pain was

35

gone. An angry cry startled her. Jerusa lifted a wiggling pink body for Amilee to see. A strange substance covered the face of the first twin.

"Your first born Belaine arrives and she is veiled. She will have the gift!" Jerusa cut the cord near the binding and handed the kicking bundle to a tiny woman standing nearby.

Another mighty push and Jerusa spoke again. "Your second born Begata arrives and she too is veiled as my vision foretold. Mmmm she refuses to cry but breathin' God's sweet air she is, as she watches all that transpires!"

Once again tears flowed from Amilee's eyes but this time she was so very happy. Her twins, praise the Saints, had lived and so had she herself. There was so much she did not understand. Questions struggled to form but her tongue was thick and her lips too numb. She only managed to mumble gibberish.

"No. No. No. Amilee lass, din'na try to speak now. Tis time fer ye to rest and sleep. There will be time fer yer questions later." The exhausted girl closed her eyes and was instantly swept gently into a healing slumber.

Birds sang and goat bells jangled as the first light of the rising sun crept through the cracks of the shutters and the front door. A thought pushed at the darkness in the back of her mind. Something amazing had happened last night. She could see that the sun was already up. She tried to sit up in a panic. She was late to milk the goats.

Just then the door was flung open and Jerusa entered carrying the bulging milking skins. At that moment an angry cry rose from the rocking bed and then another. A smile stretched across her mouth, she was a mother today. She had twin daughters!

"I see ye be feelin' better now lass. A fine thing it is too. Yer daughters are hungry!"

Amilee gazed in awe at her first-born, as Belaine suckled greedily at her breast. Jerusa held Begata and suckled her using a goat's teat stretched over a small cured skin that she had designed herself. The Wee People had taught her many things including the fact that wee bairns could drink goat's milk as well as mother's milk and survive to be healthy adults.

"Aunt Jerusa, what is this pouch you have tied about the neck of Belaine?"

"Let us finish feeding the wee ones and soon as they are asleep I will tell ye what ye need to know."

Finally the babes were asleep and Jerusa dipped out a large bowl of stew for each of them. While they ate Jerusa told Amilee of her vision and her secret knowledge of the future.

"This secret goes far back before the Wee People cloaked themselves from human eyes. There was a time when all creatures lived in harmony. So far from that have we come." Jerusa sighed sadly. Amilee snuggled deeper under her furs and waited for her aunt to open her eyes and continue the story.

"I din'na know exactly where the greed and lust for power came from. The Wee People may not know either. But come it did. The Wee People had

always shared the wealth of their realm with humans and glad to do it too! Whenever a human was ill or injured you could be sure to find one or two at yer door bringin' herbs and healing balms to make it right. If yer only milk goat died or yer wool-makin' sheep you can be sure that you would find others to replace what was lost. These would be gifts from the wee people o' course. Everyone lived nicely with warm cloaks, full bellies and a fire on every hearth." Amilee yawned but she was fully awake listening to every word. Jerusa rose from her wood frame chair to poke at the fire and add more peat. When she had the flame built up once again she returned to her chair. She took a minute to rearrange the furs that were thrown across the woven strips of hide that formed the seat and back. Satisfied that it would now be more comfortable, she sat down and continued her story.

"A discontent crept over the land. Humans drew together in groups whispering about one another. The neighbors no longer shared and instead began to hoard their food and animals. For the first time they were afraid there would be not enough for themselves. They gave up the old ways of leaving gifts by their doors for the Wee People and the fairies. There were bands of men trying to seek out where the Wee ones lived so they could steal their food and their gold. The evil hunters searched the great forests and cut down trees for t'was thought that they made homes amongst the roots of the oldest trees." Amilee's eyes had grown large and she grabbed her chest with one hand as she envisioned the destruction.

"Ahh," Jerusa sighed *"there was no help fer it. They simply had to go into hiding. They can see us mind ya and they know what goes on here but t'is us who are blind to their existence. They disguise themselves as a gnarled root or a spring flower or a cluster of butterflies. If ye look closely ye might see a wizened wee face peerin' from the knothole of a tree. Some say they've even heard a distinctive chuckle risin' above the gurgle of the water as it flows over the stones in the river bed."*

Amilee's eyes grew heavy as fatigue bore down on her exhausted body. She could no longer fight it off and was soon peacefully asleep.

"Sleep well," Jerusa whispered as she stood up, *"I will return soon."*

The sun's first light awakened Amilee even before her new babe's first cry. She felt joyous and refreshed. Her body only felt a little weak and sore. Jerusa was gone but there was cheese, goat's milk and a large portion of the delicious stew.

Jerusa kept her word and returned in two days bringing fresh herbs and healing balms. This was her habit throughout the childhood of Belaine and Begata. The twins thrived and grew more beautiful than any of the other children in Rogan Kincardin. They're hair curling in the morning mists and shining with golden highlights in the high noon sun fascinated every passerby. Their faces bright and warm as a midsummer breeze brightened the gloomiest of days.

Amilee adored her girls and felt blessed as no other to have them and her good life in the village. But as the years passed she realized that the fighting had taken her beloved Nicolas and darkness descended upon her heart. Nicolas would never return. Belaine and Begata would never know a father's love and protection. She herself would never have a companion in her older years. She would never have the opportunity to bear a son to help her and her family to work their small farm. Gradually the poison of her discontent crept into her face and dug deep lines across her brow. Her melancholy grew large fed by her constant complaints and bent her back with its uncommon weight.

Amilee grew old before her time. Her dark thick hair became thin and gray. Her once fine mind sought bitterness and her thoughts soured, becoming dull and repetitive.

Villagers marveled at the change in Amilee. She appeared older than her kinswoman Jerusa.

One day an old warrior found his way to Rogan Kincardin and asked his way to the McIlry door. He pulled a dirty piece of fabric from his pouch and wordlessly held it out to Amilee. Beneath the grime she could see the red tartan with azure lines running throughout and the embroidered family shield, topped with a proud buck's head. The clan's motto rang in her head again and again. "Be mindful, be mindful," Amilee started to laugh then to cry. "Be mindful ye fools who march so proudly to attend yer own butchery!" Her voice rose to a scream. All of her kinsmen were lost in the barbaric battles until hardly a worthy man was left in the village. She screamed and cried until her poor mind and heart cracked like the egg of a goose.

On the anniversary of their twelfth year, the twins were left with a raving madwoman that was once their mother.

***

When Courtney looked more closely at the face of the ruined Amilee she was shocked to see that it was the face of Esther Camden. Her grandmother had been her mother in that ancient Scottish lifetime.

Suddenly Aeonkisha's cloak was pulled back and Courtney could see Angie reminding everyone that it was time for lunch. It seemed that no one was aware that anything unusual had occurred. Several of the patients looked curiously at the sisters but everyone was acting normally. Angie smiled and gestured toward the door where the others were leaving.

Courtney walked with her sister and the others to the patients' cafeteria. Her legs were shaking. She wondered how C.C. was feeling. At that moment the girl turned without missing a step or changing her expression. She spoke a single word, "Tired."

C.C. had read her mind. Courtney was stunned. They continued on slowly. C.C. had a limp. Her left leg or maybe it was her foot, did not seem strong and her left arm was bent at the elbow. Her fingers on that hand were drawn into a fist. Her thumb was the only digit that seemed to be able to move at all. Doctor Baylor had mentioned the problem during their conversation that morning. He thought that the lack of oxygen at birth and probably some small strokes at some point were the most likely cause of the lack of mobility on her left side.

Courtney bought her lunch in the cafeteria then walked to the patients eating area and sat beside C.C. It felt so right to be with her sister.

"C.C. you understand we are sisters, twins,"

"Sisters, twins," C.C. mumbled as she rocked gently and ate her lunch.

"Would you like to come home with me for a visit?"

"Home for a visit. Home for a visit," C.C. chanted as she rocked and bit into her sandwich.

"That must mean yes," Courtney chuckled.

"Must mean yes," C.C. echoed.

"Then I will make it happen," Courtney said firmly. She decided to try to speak with Dr. Baylor again and find out what arrangements were required. The smallest flutter wriggled in her stomach when she thought of him. It took her by surprise although she quickly dismissed it all together. She had no time or interest in anything or anyone except her family and her sister. She was determined that nothing would separate them again.

CHAPTER FIVE

Esther Camden lay helpless and immobile in her hospital bed. She was aware of the doctors and nurses entering, leaving, talking, poking and moving her around. She felt as though she was at the bottom of a well, seeing things from far away. She knew that no one could understand her mumbling gibberish. She was so frustrated, angry and more frightened than she had ever been in her life. She just wanted to scream and throw something, but her body would not cooperate.

"Mother, are you ok? I mean I know you aren't ok but I just don't know what to do for you. The physical therapist is coming soon to…oh Mama are you cryin'?" Clarisa reached for a tissue and gently dabbed at the tears that streamed from the corners of her mother's eyes. "Everything is going to be all right," she crooned as though she might have been speaking to a small child. "The doctor says you are making very good progress."

Esther gazed into her daughter's beautiful face. Her voice was soothing and her light floral scent was refreshing after so many antiseptics. She thought Clarisa's eyes looked tired and her skin was too pale. She wanted to reach up and touch her face and tell her not to worry so much.

"Mother, you touched my face," Clarisa whispered excitedly, "you *are* getting better. Your arm moved. See I told you, everything is going to be just fine."

Esther's arm dropped heavily back down to the bed. She was utterly shocked to see that her arm had moved! Her body felt like a foreign entity that belonged to someone else.

Piercing brown eyes materialized in front of Esther's face. She was unable to scream or show her fear. She could not pull back or call for help. Her mind was screaming in terror and indignation, demanding that the owner of those fierce eyes explain what was happening.

"I am the one who pulled you from the water," came the reply *"I have something to show you."*

The feathered cloak enfolded Esther. Clarisa saw only that her mother's eyes drooped and closed. "Mother you just go on to sleep now." Clarisa whispered. Esther however was traveling with Aeonkisha, the twins and Avery on a journey by invitation only.

***

Latoia sat at a small table in The Posh Bar on Sunset Boulevard in Beverly Hills. Her agent and friend, Stephanie Mills, was late as usual. It was a perfect place to be seen though, so waiting could be a good thing. She supposed that Stephanie chose to do business there as often as possible so that *she* would be noticed as well as her clientele.

The waitress brought her Appletini and a small tray of appetizers. Latoia sipped her drink and let the cold burn of the liquid slip down her throat. The Posh Bar was always kept very dark in an effort to preserve the privacy of any ultra-famous patrons who might want to enjoy a quiet drink or meal.

Latoia had visited The Posh Bar many times but had never seen any Hollywood stars. Either they had been in disguise or the rumor was started by the owner to make people *think* that the rich and famous were always there. She did recognize a model and her agent on this day but mostly she saw men in business suits, likely lawyers and executives in the entertainment business.

She finished her drink and two of the appetizers. Stephanie was really late this time. She ordered another drink then stood up to go to the powder room. Even though the restroom too was dimly lit, it was still much brighter than the interior of the bar. When she finished washing her hands and applying lip-gloss she opened the door to return to her table. The darkness was momentarily disorienting. It took her a few minutes to allow her eyes to adjust to the change before she cautiously began to weave her way through the small clusters of chatting customers. She emerged successfully into the dining area and began to navigate the obstacle course of small cloth covered tables. Suddenly large strong hands held her arms to her sides and a male voice whispered near her ear "I like the way you smell," then he was gone, melting into the heavy shadows. By the time she turned around he was only one indistinguishable shape among the many that filled the room.

In the time it takes an eyelash to flicker, Latoia thought that maybe Raeford had not left town yet. Just as quickly she dismissed that thought since she had driven him to the airport herself just last night. He had to fly to Europe. He was unable to disclose his location but she had guessed it might be England since he had joked about going to see an uncle named Big Ben.

Latoia shivered as cold chills raised goose flesh on her arms. She turned and tried to hurry through the dark maze of tables. She was trembling badly by the time she found her table and sat down. Images of her nearly fatal experience just a few months ago flashed through her mind; the faces of men, the models on the runway, the dead girl and her own dangerous escape.

"There you are Honey. I am so sorry to be this late. The phone has been ringing off the hook, of course that's good news, and of course its not *all* business," this last sentence was spoken with a lifted eyebrow and wink "But that's good news too!" Stephanie spoke fast hardly taking a breath and just loud enough for some of the other tables to hear. They all knew how to play the game. Some people turned their heads to look at the flashy blond older woman, but most of the customers continued their own conversations in hushed tones.

"Uh oh, what's wrong Sugar? You're shaking! Are you sick…it's just too chilly in this place, where is our waitress? You need some brandy or maybe an espresso. Here take my jacket and put it around your shoulders.

"Enough!" Latoia managed a weak smile and an unconvincing chuckle. "Thank you. I will borrow that jacket for a few minutes but I already have a drink and that is quite enough."

"Well okay fine but you can't fool me. Something is wrong and now give, give, give. What is it?"

"Nothing to worry about Steph. I just got spooked for a minute."

"Hmm. Ok. But if you're having a problem I want you to tell me. This is not the time to be going bonkers on me. There are some great things ahead for you Baby and that's why I asked you to meet me here today. I've got an audition for you with the biggest fragrance company in the world."

Latoia was speechless. The whispery man's voice echoing in her memory *I like the way you smell*, and suddenly a possible job with a fragrance company. She shivered again.

Stephanie was a tall large-boned woman. She was close to waving good-by to forty but she did not look her age at all. She enjoyed wearing her hair in a bleached pageboy bob and she favored bright colored clothing designed on the flamboyant side of style. At first glance she gave the impression of an aging showgirl still looking for a good time. That description would not be far from the truth. She had actually been a showgirl in Las Vegas for a few years. She had a pleasing singing voice and had enjoyed some notoriety in supporting roles in the Hollywood movie scene. She was "spicey" in a few bit parts on the big screen and critics were, *gasp*, complimentary of her acting skills. As time moved on so did Stephanie. She discovered that her real talent was matching models and actors to the right gig. She started in a tiny office in Studio City but was rocketed to the Mecca of the stars, Beverly Hills. Her office though still small had the most desirable of all qualifications, location, location, location.

"It doesn't seem like you are very excited with my big news!" Stephanie faked a pout that was so ridiculous that Latoia had to smile.

"When I am offered a contract for a million dollars, you better believe I'll be smilin'…and laughin'…and jumpin' up and down. In fact I'm gonna call you and scream for joy into the phone so loud you will be deaf!"

"That's my girl, there's a little voice in my head that says you are going to be exactly what they are looking for. This could be the biggest break of your life!"

"Now Steph, I don't want you to get mad at me but I have to ask. Are these people legitimate?"

"Oh God I deserved that. Are you ever going to forgive me for that awful mess? You know those people pulled a fast one on me, and a lot of other agents. It was just a horrible situation. Now, like I told you on the phone, you need to be ready to go back to work because Honey, this is the big one! I called in a favor and you are being considered even before the announcement is being made!" Her voice had dropped to an exaggerated whisper. She poked around in her over-sized bag and finally found a folded paper, which she handed across the table to Latoia.

"That is the address. It's just around the corner from here. You are to be there at three o'clock sharp tomorrow."

Latoia unfolded the paper and looked at the address. She knew she could find it easily.

"There is something written at the bottom. I can't read it." Latoia squinted as she tried to read the faint letters.

"I wrote the name of the new line in pencil. Hold it by the light so you can read it but don't say it out loud." Stephanie cautioned. "It is top secret and you don't even want to know how I got it! Nothing illegal," she said hurriedly when she saw her client's eyes open wide.

Latoia could just make out the words Butterfly Noir "Great name," Latoia told her.

"Yes it is Dear. Now take this marker and scratch through the words just in case someone sees that paper!"

"You are being just a little too dramatic don't you think?"

"I certainly am Honey. Drama is my middle name but 'Finished' will be my *first* name if this information gets out before the company releases it! Now what do you have to wear tomorrow. Oh and let's think about how you can incorporate all of that ballet training you've had."

The two women sipped their drinks and planned their strategy for the next day. Finally Stephanie looked at her watch and beckoned to their waitress.

"This is my treat today Latoia," she paid their tab and left a generous tip. No matter how many years passed Stephanie never forgot the times when she herself was forced to depend on an hourly wage and generous tips.

"Now you go home and get your beauty sleep so you will be fresh and ready to fly like a you-know-what!" Latoia giggled, "I will meet you in front of the building at two thirty. Don't be late Sugar Pie!" Stephanie winked at her number one protégé.

"Ha. Look who's talking! You better listen to your own advice Ms Fashionably Late Hollywood Agent!" The two women shared rollicking laughter and a warm hug before turning to go their separate ways.

Latoia felt great. This could be the right thing for her. She knew that most of the really coveted modeling jobs and agencies were in New York. She had wanted to finish school and stay close to her mother as long as possible. Her mother had suffered so much loss and grief. She knew that if it was her turn, her destiny, to be chosen for this job then she could help her mother like never before. The prospects were dizzying. She smiled to herself as she got into

Courtney's little VW Rabbit convertible. Courtney had asked her to drive it until she decided what she was going to do with her life.

The white VW pulled out into traffic and she turned toward the beach. Courtney had also given Latoia her little studio apartment to live in. The rent had been prepaid for a year, by Courtney's parents the Hammonds. Everyone had agreed that since Courtney was staying with her grandmother in Charleston, South Carolina, Latoia should stay in Courtney's apartment. Both girls could then recuperate from their respective life threatening experiences and decide what direction their lives should take.

Latoia was happy and grateful for everything as she expertly negotiated the heavy traffic. There were so many traffic lights and they all seemed to be red today. She was in no real hurry and spent her time daydreaming about her interview the next day. She mentally reviewed her wardrobe and thought about what sort of outfit to wear. Then her thoughts turned to Raeford and how it felt when he gently touched his lips to hers at the airport. Her heart sped up a little and her cheeks grew warm as her thoughts raced ahead to what it might be like to have his arms around her and his lips following the outline of her throat.

She found herself breathing a little harder as beads of sweat sparkled on her forehead. She glanced in the rear-view mirror to dab them away. "Whooo girl you have got to stop thinking that way or you are going to be in big trouble," she chuckled to herself. She patted her face with a tissue one last time and noticed a man in the car behind her. Her heart did a little jump when she realized that the same car had been behind her for quite awhile.

The Caucasian driver wore dark glasses. His shirt was open at the collar and his hair was cut short like someone in the military.

She had been studying the man behind her so intently that she missed the brake lights flashing on the car in front of her. She pounded her foot down on the brake pedal forgetting that she needed to push in the clutch at the same time. The VW screeched to a halt and the motor died with a disconcerting jerk. Drivers behind Latoia lurched right and left as they frantically spun steering wheels and stomped on brakes in an attempt to avoid plowing into her from behind. Thankfully there were no collisions. Red-faced commuters honked their horns in frustration. Curses were hurled through the chaotic moments as Latoia nervously tried to restart the car. At last the valiant little motor came to life and Latoia glanced into the rear view mirror. The man behind her lifted his hands off the steering wheel and made exasperated motions for her to hurry up and get moving.

"Oh boy, Stephanie isn't the only one who is being overly dramatic," she felt foolish…and relieved when the tan car turned down another street two blocks later.

By the time she pulled into the driveway and unlocked the door to her apartment, she had pulled herself together and dismissed her uneasiness. She threw down her purse and went into the little kitchen for a glass of iced

44

cranberry juice. She did not want her eyes to look puffy or red for her interview. She wanted to get the alcohol out of her system as quickly as possible. She hoped the cranberry juice would work.

The harsh jangle of the telephone startled her so severely that she nearly dropped her glass. She was happy to hear her mother's voice and was able to calm herself quickly.

"Hey Toia, how's my baby girl?"

"Ma it's so good to hear from you. I'm fine. In fact I'm great!"

"You been drinkin'."

How did she do that? "I'm drinking cranberry juice," Latoia responded with a slight edge to her voice.

"Which means you been drinkin' somethin' else!" Her mother was always worried. She did not want her daughter to end up like her twin brother. He had been the slave of more than one substance and it resulted in his death before his life had even had a chance to start.

"Mama, don't worry," her tone softened "even if I did take a drink I am not going to be like Lawrence. I have never tried drugs and I have no interest in them. Alcohol doesn't interest me either except on rare occasions. You need to trust me Ma."

"Baby I do trust you. It's that alcohol and drugs I don't trust."

Latoia had to smile. She felt such love for her mother and she understood the pain she must still feel about Lawrence. She felt it too.

"I've got a big interview tomorrow Mama. It is the biggest one I've ever had! If I get this job I will make so much money! Maybe I can buy us both a nice house and new cars. Wouldn't that be something?"

After a moment of silence her mother answered, "Baby you know I'm proud of you no matter what. If all of that happens then fine, yes it will be wonderful, but Baby you think too much about money. You are around all of those rich friends of yours and that's all *they* think about!"

"No Mama, now you stop right there. The Hammonds are good people and they never flaunt, talk down or make an issue of their wealth. They have lives with troubles just like we do."

"I know you're right. I just don't want you thinkin' that money is all there is. I would be happy if you decided to be a nurse and married a nice young man with a good job and then had me some nice little grandbabies that I could show off in church. Speaking of church, how long has it been since you attended one?"

"Well I've been a little busy," she mumbled defensively. No one could bring you to your knees like your Mama. "But you know Mama, I never forget my prayers."

"That's my girl."

"Thanks Mama. Thanks for everything. That's all I meant by talking about money and buying a lot of things. I just want to say thank you to you

45

for all of the sacrifices and hardships that you've gone through. I want to make your life easier and more comfortable."

"Thanks Baby." Her mother stifled a sob. "I have everything I need right now. Just talking to you has made it a better day."

"I love you too Mama."

Latoia sat quietly thinking about their conversation. Suddenly she remembered her big day coming up. She jumped up and ran to her tiny closet to see what she had to wear.

***

Courtney and her sister were finished with their lunch, so she decided to ask C.C. if she wanted to go for a walk on the grounds.

"Walk on the grounds." C.C. echoed as she pushed her chair back and stood up.

Courtney consulted Angie about taking C.C. outside. Angie thought it was a good idea but instructed her not to go too far. She pointed out that with C.C.'s weak left foot she might have to sit down on one of the benches for frequent rests.

The afternoon was typically hot and humid but there were lots of trees to provide shady respite from the sun. Just as Angie had predicted, it wasn't long before C.C. found a bench nestled between two huge Oaks. She plopped herself down without comment or question. Courtney was glad to sit down too. It was pleasant to be away from the strange noises of the other patients. She sensed that C.C. felt at ease as well. She watched her sister's eyes following a small brown wren as it hopped from one branch of the tree to another.

"Grandmother Camden has a big beautiful house; that's where I live at the moment. She's sick right now and she's in the hospital but I don't think she would mind if I brought you out for a visit."

C.C. lowered her eyes and began to rock gently. Nearby a cicada started up its high-pitched twang. Another was inspired to join in and yet another. They must have been close by because the sound was nearly deafening. Courtney wanted to take her sister to another shady bench but she found that she could not muster the will to move.

A cool breeze dried the sweat on her temples and once again she and C.C. felt themselves pulled up out of their bodies and transported through time to the ancient land where their history together first began.

***

Aeonkisha's feathered cloak appeared to work like the fabled magic carpet. The twins and Avery were held snug and secure with the power unleashed by

46

their guide. The outer edges of the cape fluttered as though propelled through time by enormous wings. Ages and places passed them in a blur. To most observers their journey would be imperceptible. They hovered over the sparsely populated ancient Scotland then settled as softly as a feather very near two girls who sat on a cluster of large boulders. They were the now twelve-year-old twins Belaine (Courtney) and Begata (C.C,).

The girls watched their goats grazing nearby. It was late spring and the air was still cool and crisp but the sun shone warmly between fat white clouds. A few birds followed the air currents and called out to one another.

The girls were silent for a time. They sat slumped forward each frowning and pale. Their hearts were troubled. Their beautiful mother, Amilee had nearly lost her senses and her lovely face was etched with worry lines, hard work, loss and anger.

"Do ye think our kinswoman Jerusa, will come soon Begata?"

"I din'na care if she does the old hag."

"Begata! Din'na speak ill of Jerusa. You know how much she has helped us from the time we were in swaddlins."

"She is forever tellin' us what to do, and those foul potions she wants us to drink. Ugh!" She wrinkled her nose and stuck out her tongue.

"Those foul potions got rid of the fever I had and those terrible red itching spots on my skin!" Belaine argued heatedly.

"Well I din'na have them. For all I know her potions caused your illness and our mother's too I'll wager!" Begata jumped down from her perch and ran toward the goats causing them to prance and shy away. The bells that each wore around their neck tinkled prettily with every move they made.

"Stop your foolishness! I din'na want to chase these stubborn goats today!" Belaine jumped down and grabbed her sister's arm.

Begata's temper snapped and she shook herself free from her sister's grasp. She whirled and struck Belaine on the side of her face with her fist. The girl staggered backward and fell. Her head struck the unforgiving stone with a sickening dull thud.

Small eyes well hidden, peered at the girls as they fought. A tiny form as weathered and gnarled as the tree he hid behind, clapped his small hands in fiendish glee as he planned a terrible trick to play on the humans. He considered them ugly barbaric creatures that fought incessantly over land that had never belonged to them in the first place. In fact the silly creatures could not seem to understand that earth could not really ever be owned by anyone. How could it? It was supposed to be free to all.

Though he, Yreva and his clansmen, the Wee People had great powers and could sustain life for hundreds of years, they were not immortal. His wife and children had perished at the hands of the violent human meat eaters. Their deaths occurred at a time when many of the Wee People died while trying to help or communicate with primitive superstitious homosapiens. Soon after that they began to fade into the shadows and use their powers to separate their world from the human world.

Yreva knew it was too dangerous to cohabitate with the earth's people and when he lost his family, his mind was lost too. His loss was so great that it robbed him of his power of reason and the compassion for all that lives. The loss of respect for other life forms was a foreign event for those of his kind. He was instantly overcome with a black depression that lasted for two hundred years. When he finally emerged, his eyes had grown dark and wild and he was taken with fits of maniacal laughter that chilled the marrow of anyone unfortunate enough to hear it. As the crazed wee creature witnessed the fighting twins he leaped to the top of the boulder where they had been sitting and allowed his physical form to appear to the girls and projected his laughter in a surge of hysterical glee.

The girls turned and abruptly stopped pulling each other's hair.

"Ye foolish females! What could be so wrong that yer fightin' and clawin' at each other like she devils?"

The twins were struck dumb. They had only heard tales of creatures such as this but they did not believe in their true existence.

"Ye were talkin' and screechin' just fine before I came along. T'wasn't me that struck ye speechless."

"Who are you?" Begata managed to gulp.

"Yreva is my name." He took off his hat and made a little bow.

"It seems ye lasses are in need of some fun! I know of a place where there is always a festival with pipes and dancing and more food than you've ever seen in one place."

Begata clapped her hands. Her anger instantly dissolved. "Where can it be? I've never heard of such a place."

"There is no such place Begata. He is spinning a tale! Don't ye listen to him." Belaine pleaded. "We have to lead the goats back soon."

Begata grabbed Belaine's arm and brought her head close to whisper in her ear. "I've heard it said that the Wee ones have hordes of wealth hidden everywhere. Let's follow him and see if we can find it!"

"No! I'm bleedin' and torn from your ill temper Begata McIlry. I'm takin' home our goats and I'll see to our mother. If ye know what's good for ya ye'll do the same!" She turned and stomped toward the little herd of goats.

Yreva sniffed the wind. A storm would be coming soon. That would be all the better. A distant rumble that only he could hear alerted him to an even greater danger. He was not surprised that the girls were unable to sense it since he had the gift of sight. Like all of his people he knew of the great unrest within and beyond the borders of Scotland.

Begata had been born with her own gift. She too sensed a disturbance, accompanied by brief scenes of death and destruction. The McIlrys were a lesser clan that was protected by the larger and more powerful clan Macgillivray. In the snippets of vision that hovered ominously in her third eye, she could see the warriors that wore their familiar red and blue tartans, but they were covered with blood. Even her selfish heart was chilled to the core as she saw marauders hunting down her clansmen. Horses fell, villages burned and still the aggressors rode forward. Most horrifying of all, she glimpsed what she knew to be her village and her own home being destroyed.

Powerful horses trampled everything in their way and the strange men that rode them swung swords with one hand and looted with the other. She saw herself in their midst, trampled, mangled like a doll of straw.

Her decision was made. She would go with the Wee man to find the wondrous place he foretold. To hell and be damned those lunatic kinsmen and women who toiled from dawn to dark for a mud hut, a peat fire and never enough to eat. Her own mother's senses were lost and probably would never notice whether she had one twin or two if she even lived through the destruction to come.

"I've a mind to have some fun for a change. I'll follow ye to that place of color and light," the haughty lass tossed her curls and held her chin high.

"Ah and fun ye shall have fair Begata," Yreva had worried for a moment. He saw in her eyes the gift of vision but he was not gifted with the ability to intrude. Whatever the girl saw, it must not have warned her of his intent.

Belaine's gift was to call. She reached out her thoughts to the herd and they obediently bunched together and ambled toward home.

"Go you foolish girl," Begata called when she saw her sister moving the goats. "You'll wish ye had followed me!"

"No! I din'na like your selfish ways, t'is you who'll be sorry!" Belaine glanced over her shoulder briefly and continued toward the village. She was worried about her headstrong sister but her head throbbed painfully and she knew she must get back home to tend to Amilee. Hot salty tears left streaks in the dirt on her cheeks. She did not want Begata to see her cry so she kept going and did not look back again.

Moments passed. Begata fought back her sudden fear and listened to the Wee man's ramblings about the marvelous sights and sounds that awaited her. He cast a spell of glamour around himself and Begata could not look away. She ignored the feeble flutterings of the warning in her heart and turned away from all she had known.

CHAPTER SIX

Jerusa looked into the pot of boiling stew and stirred it round and round with her carved wooden paddle. It seemed a vision would make its appearance. She dreaded these moments because one this urgent was bad-tidings absolutely. She had just helped a wee bairn into the world. His lusty cry was a good sign. His family needed a strong son. She knew this child would be a blessing to the clan Chattan and would live well under the protection of clan MacKintosh.

The vision would not be stopped and soon she saw so many dangers, she had no idea what to do. The young woman who had given birth was strong and already sitting up looking rosy and satisfied. She had a kinswoman to help her for a few more days. She knew she must leave at once. She bid her farewells and accepted a horse in payment for her many services to their village. She packed her provisions for the long journey back to Rogan Kincardin.

It was a poor time to travel. The storms could come at any time. Her own horse, McMorgan, was sure-footed and steady. The new horse was smaller but seemed gentle enough so Jerusa settled herself on the wooden seat and gave the reins a flick. McMorgan pulled the small cart and Totter plodded behind, secured by his lead rope.

The storms did come and blew their cold breath across the travelers. Jerusa and her horses bravely bent their heads into the wind. A cold fierce rain that stung their skin and blinded their eyes mercilessly pelted the courageous little band. For a week, the woman and her horses fought muddy trails and mind numbing cold. It had taken her three days longer due to the weather.

Jersua slowly climbed down from her cart and let the horses graze while she built a fire near some large rocks. She warmed some salted meat over the fire and took off her wet clothes. She spread them out on the rocks and rummaged through her belongings for something dry to wear.

It was somewhat comfortable there. The heavy clouds parted and the sun shone at last. The sun and the warmed meat revived her body and spirit. It was very few women who would travel alone with no kinsman to defend her. Jerusa was well protected by her visions though, and she knew when danger was about. She wished she could protect all those she loved. There were times like now when she cursed her visions because she was unable to change the events that she witnessed. She often longed for a normal life like the young mothers she helped. As the visions opened to her again she wished more fervently than ever that she could not see such terrible things. She prayed that she would never have to make such a choice again. She did not know then, that her wish would be granted a few hundred years in the future when she would be reborn as Clarisa Camden Hammond.

Jerusa knew it was time to make a decision. If she followed Begata first, she might save her and capture the treacherous creature that had led her astray. If she took the path to the village, she might help many of those who would be wounded. Belaine might even be alive and poor daft Amilee.

The vision had shown her the mauraders that raided the villiage but she was unprepared for the level of devastation they left behind. She was sickened when the cold wind carried the smell of carnage, smoke and death into her nostrils. Her stomach churned at the horror she beheld, while McMorgan pulled the cart into to a very different Rogan Kincardin.

Spirals of smoke rose in silent testimony to the vicious assault wrought upon the little village. Blackened timbers jutted in every direction like agonized skeletons of their former cozy homes. Many of the mud huts with thatched roofs had been trampled and torn apart. Animals lay dead, senselessly killed; others ran wildly in the surrounding countryside. Villagers lay where they had fallen while fighting for their families and their homes. Young girls had been snatched from the arms of their families and would never be seen again.

Jerusa drove her cart to Amilee's house. The thatch had been burned and the living space was open to the sky. Everything of value had been taken and a cold dark silence lay like a shroud at a funeral pyre. She knew Amilee was dead. She sensed that her spirit had entered the passageway of light. She sent a prayer and a blessing with hope that the poor woman had found some peace.

A pull in her heart let her know that Belaine still lived and was calling to her. She secured her horses and went to ask someone about Belaine. She was taken to the girl straightaway. She lay in one of the damaged homes near other injured people. She opened her eyes and that was the only way Jerusa knew her. Her face was swollen and cut. Her hair was matted with mud until there was no telling whether it be true red or black. But it was the girl's body, twisted and broken on her left side that brought the stoic Jerusa to her knees.

Belaine sighed and closed her eyes. She was filled with relief to see her kinswoman. Even through the darkness of shock and wrenching pain she knew that Jerusa could help her and she would not be alone.

Jerusa pulled herself together and began to give orders to the tattered survivors. They searched the village for the wounded and separated them from the dead. Those who were able worked to create secure and warm temporary sleeping spaces. Others found utensils, built cooking fires and prepared food. They were able to save some animals and their hopes of being able to start again were lifted as each task was accomplished.

From dawn to dark, Jerusa worked without rest. She tended the wounded and held the hands of the dying. She cleaned wounds, mixed herbs, prepared food and used all of her considerable skills to help ease the damaged spirits of those frightened souls.

On the fifth day, the weather warmed. More homes were repaired. The water supply was renewed and meat turned on spits. Cooking pots bubbled with vegetables and wild roots. Belaine opened her eyes again. She spoke slowly and told Jerusa what had happened. She had just arrived at the village with her goats. Her mother had run out of their house and was in a fit, ranting in craziness. Belaine could see that a storm was gathering so she hurried to secure the goats in their shelter. The sky turned as dark as night and the rain hit as hard as the thunderclap that brought it. Belaine's memory was unclear but she thought the rain had pounded them for two days. One night the horsemen came. People were screaming and there was fire even in the rain. The goats were crying and she ran outside. Her mother ran out behind her. The horses pounded the ground like the thunder above. Amilee's mind jerked back into balance for the time it took to throw her own body in front of the stampeding animals and push Belaine aside.

"She saved my life," Belaine whispered to Jerusa "but the horses hurt me too and there is somethin' bad wrong on the inside of me. I know I'll not live long."

"Shush shush. No ye din'na talk so child, ye have many years to dance in the sunshine." Jerusa crooned in her most soothing voice.

"Begata is in danger too. She followed the Wee man and I could feel his lies. Can ye see her Jerusa?"

"Aye Lass. I will do what I can for her but now ye must rest."

Belaine began to cry silently. Her hair had been cleaned and her red curls gleamed in the firelight. She had the look of an angel even with her poor banged up face.

Amilee's house had been repaired enough so that Belaine and Jerusa were quartered there. It would be a very long time before the village was restored fully but on this night there was a peace born of the knowledge that they were rebuilding, they had survived and with hard work they would once again thrive. Fires died down and those who were not standing watch had fallen into an exhausted sleep.

Jerusa was feeling fatigue in every part of her body as she stirred the boiling water and summoned the vision. She had searched her soul to find forgiveness for the wayward girl. She was young after all and with a mother who had no grasp on sanity it was no wonder the poor girl had made wretched decisions.

The vision formed and Jerusa could see Begata where she lay without warmth or food in a muddy bog. An ugly small creature danced and laughed with dreadful menace under ancient gnarled trees. Eyes stared from the tree roots and small faces scowled from knots and twisted limbs.

Begata was weak. Her skin bore a gray pallor but she lived. Tears rolled from her eyes just as they had from Belaine's.

Jerusa jumped up with sudden inspiration. She knew that bog! It was near her hidden retreat!

"Belaine, Lass, ye must try to tell me the name of the creature who has taken Begata. I must have his name so that I can set her free."

"Yreva." Belaine whispered without opening her eyes.

" Lass, now you must begin the call to your sister and then you can sleep." Belaine reached out and at last felt the weak signs of life in Begata.

Jerusa left immediately with her cart and horse. She followed the heart pull between the two sisters and after only two hours, found where the girl had stepped unwittingly into the black sucking mud and languished in its cold trap near death.

Jerusa took the precious goose egg that she had miraculously found near a small pond at the edge of the forest. It was perfect and not even a hairline fracture marred its pristine surface. She held it carefully and whispered her intent to the egg. Yreva danced madly into the little clearing his strange voice rising loudly in the language of his kind. Begata lay quietly crying while her life force seeped away as she sunk deeper into a muddy grave. Jerusa gathered all of the energy and power she could muster. She held steady until the moonlight moved through the trees into the clearing. She was sweating and trembling with the exertion but she would not allow herself to fail. No matter what mistakes Begata had made Jerusa was determined to hold onto the girl with her power. The child must not drown! She refused to give in to her tired body. She would wait for the right moment and... at last it came. The moonlight touched the girl and bathed her in its glow. At that very instant Jerusa hurled the egg with all of her strength. Before the little man knew what was happening it hit him in the face.

"Yreva be gone! I bind ye from ever doing further harm to another!" If anyone had observed Jerusa at that moment, they would not have seen a tired old woman but a powerful and statuesque being who could strike fear into the heart of any who would oppose her.

It is generally known that the Wee people are momentarily incapacitated when touched by moonlight. This is especially true when one of them has lost his reason and tries to harm a human or one of his own kind. Yreva had cast a glamour spell so that he appeared to be more appealing to Begata. But the spell was broken when the egg hit him. He fell backward screaming and clawing at his face. Jerusa ran to the girl and lifted her out of the sucking mud. An odd blue shimmer lay on the surface of the mud where the girl had cried for days. Jerusa thought it looked like a blue stone. She did not have the time or strength to try to pick it up or go back to see what it was. She wanted to get the girl back home as quickly as possible.

Jerusa tucked warm skins around Begata and then turned McMorgan and the cart toward the village. As soon as they left the bog, forty pairs of eyes became a small clan of Wee People. They were mightily angered with their crazed clansman. They understood his madness. They knew he was driven to his actions by the evil of some long dead humans. They decided that he must be dealt with so that there would be no further wrong doing between their two worlds. The Wee People wanted to fade gently away from the humans so that they could live in peace.

The elders contemplated long and hard over Yreva's fate. The final decision was made when all were in agreement. Yreva should be relieved of his powers and longevity. He was to be banished to the fate of humans by riding the wheel of reincarnation. When his soul finally absolved itself for all of his wrongdoing he could move on in the cycle of evolution. The face of Yreva was Avery. It seems that Yreva/Avery had taken on the task of befriending Begata/C.C. the very human he had tried to kill in the bog.

The elders approached Yreva in the binding circle where Jerusa had sent him. The Old One told him of his fate and he accepted the judgment without a murmur. Begata's tears had mingled with the magic in the clearing and had hardened into a blue jewel. The Old One gave Yreva the glittering stone and told him he must carry her tears until his debt was paid. He was given enough power and responsibility to make sure that at the appropriate time the stone would be returned to her. Their work was concluded and the small ones faded into the shadows. Yreva began his journey and the bog was silent.

Jerusa arrived at the village just as the first streaks of light shot through the darkness of the eastern horizon. She carried Begata inside and laid her on a pallet near her sister. She built up the fire and quickly prepared herbs and broth.

The sun was warm and bright at midday. Both girls were feverish and weak. At nearly the same moment they both opened their eyes and saw each other. Begata's tears flowed again but this time with relief to see her sister. Belaine too cried and she brushed at them with her good hand. She knew she was slipping away and reached out to Begata in a gesture of love. Their tears came together as their hands touched. In the next moment Belaine's spirit lifted from her fractured body and sought out her mother in the Hall of Light.

Begata watched her sister's spirit leave and again she cried with terrible wrenching sobs until she was empty of everything except a sad and broken heart. She wiped her face and felt something hard against the youthful skin of her cheek. She gasped when her eyes beheld a small glittering blue stone that had formed from the blending of their tears. She closed her fingers around the stone and pressed her hand to her heart. The jewel was all she had left of her beloved sister.

That afternoon four aged men arrived to assist in yet another tragic burial. Begata watched as they solemnly lifted Belaine's small inert body and gently placed it on the cart. Jerusa straightened the girl's clothing and lovingly smoothed her tartan. The narrow blue stripes running through the red plaid seemed to gleam brightly in the new spring sun. All too soon it was time to go.

Jerusa and a village woman helped Begata to get up so she could attend the funeral. Some who survived the assault clung to life even with serious injuries but others succumbed, dying from their wounds one after another causing the villagers to attend burials nearly every day. Now among the dead, her sister and her mother.

Though the day was bright and warm, Begata's body trembled beneath her layers of ragged clothing. She clutched the blue stone of tears to her heart. The little cart bumped over the rough ground as McMorgan's hooves clopped sedately behind the mourners. The little group stopped at the burial site and someone began the prayers as they placed Belaine's body in the earth.

Begata too felt dead. At only twelve winters she should have been a tender blossom, full of color, life and promise. Instead she was weaker than the village elder woman. When the service was over they started back. Begata was so exhausted she could hardly sit up as the cart bounced over small rocks and ruts.

She knew her visions could have saved the village, her mother, and her sister. All of this damage and grief could have been avoided had she not been selfish and foolish. The people could have been warned and fled with their children and animals. It had been a place of comfort and joy and now no one could even smile. Many of the children had been killed. There would be few left to laugh and play.

Begata had not spoken a word since Jerusa had rescued her from the bog. The older woman watched as the girl retreated deeper inside herself. She had stopped crying and showed no emotion of any sort during the service for her sister. Jerusa feared the girl would never recover.

Begata was obsessed with the stone of tears that had come from her pain and grief. She stared at it and poured her gift of sight into the stone day after day. She refused to put it down even when she slept, which was not often. The sun rose and set for many months but she was unaware of the passage of time. She sipped broth when the bowl was held to her lips but she made no effort to eat or otherwise care for herself and still she made no sound.

Jerusa noticed one day how bright the stone had become as the girl held it against her forehead. She gasped as a brilliant light shot out of it no different than the lightening strikes from violent storms. In stark contrast Begata had lost her life light. Her skin took on a sickly pallor. It was as though she poured her very life into the stone made of the sisters' tears.

A year passed and Begata was hardly aware. She had traveled far within and closed her inner door on the outside world. She no longer sipped her broth or herb potions. She grew weaker and yet she fiercely clutched the stone.

It was dawn on the first day of early spring. Jerusa had just come from milking the goats. Her heart was lighter today after the long winter. The village was greatly restored and many new bairns would be born within the next two moon cycles. She built up the fire and turned to look at Begata. At that moment her blue eyes opened. She smiled and reached out her hand.

Jerusa heard her whisper "Belaine". Her other hand opened and the now brilliant stone fell to the floor. She was gone.

Jerusa picked up the stone and was instantly thrown back with a terrible force. Visions flashed and pounded through her mind with ferocious clarity. Her mind could not bear it. She dropped the stone and fell to her knees, her breath coming in short gasps. When she had recovered to some extent, she took a small square of cloth and carefully covered the stone before she picked it up again. That prevented the visions from striking her when she touched it.

Begata was laid to rest near her mother and sister. This branch of the family had come to a tragic end. Jerusa knew it was time for her to go back to her own secluded dwelling for some much needed renewal of her own. Within the next week she took care of trading most of the goats to villagers in exchange for getting her cart fixed and extra feed for her horses. She closed up the house knowing that she would return to help out with the coming births. She wore a pouch on a long thong tied about her neck. This time it was not filled with herbs. It held the blue stone. It must never fall into the wrong hands since such power could be used for evil just as well as good.

It was good to be going back to the little home she loved. Her heart was heavy with the burden of all she had witnessed in the year just passed. She looked deep into her own being to search for answers to the troubling questions that had left her sleepless. She was tired when she reached her cozy home but she cleaned and set things to rights after her long absence. Her mind was busy with the making of a serious decision. When she finished her tasks her mind was firm. She was grateful for all she had learned in her life and she was grateful for the chance to see beyond the veil, but she knew with great certainty that she did not want to possess that gift and the responsibility that went with it ever again.

She slept very little that night as she prayed fervent prayers for the souls who had passed from the earth. Just before dawn, the universal breath was drawn in, and the sacred silence waited to birth a new day. Jerusa awakened as the blue light of the third eye opened and she was given a glimpse of the distant future. A voice spoke revealing that she would be the guardian of the stone through future generations until the rightful soul matured with earthly experiences and achieved enough wisdom and strength to accept the enormous responsibility that its wisdom would carry. When that soul should become ready hundreds of years in the future, she promised to relinquish it to its rightful owner.

The out breath came. The dawn was born. The promise was kept. Jerusa/Clarisa no longer experienced the visions, but she did become the guardian of the stone through each lifetime until the time was right for it to be used for the good of mankind. Then, according to her ancient promise she presented it to Belaine/Courtney, as a gift from her contrite sister Begata/C.C.

.

56

Courtney found herself pulling into the gravel drive at Willows. She had no idea how she got there. She parked near the kitchen entrance and got out of the car on shaking legs. Hattie appeared at the screen door almost immediately. As soon as she saw Courtney's face, she rushed to her side and enfolded her in a huge embrace.

"You awright baby? No you are not! Come inside. I'll help you."

Courtney felt cold despite the heat. She was nearly overcome with nausea and dizziness.

"Mmm. Mmmm. Honey you had one big dose today. Let's sit you down here at the island. Now here, I've just made some strawberry shortcake. Take a bite right now and then sip on this sweet sun tea. I promise you will feel better in about five minutes."

Courtney did not think she could hold anything in her stomach, but she trusted Hattie and did as she was told. The strawberries and cake stayed down and so did the sweet tea. Just as Hattie promised, she felt better within a few minutes.

"Thanks Hattie. You saved my life with strawberry shortcake," Courtney joked weakly.

"Well everybody knows about that remedy don't they?" Hattie laughed. "All you needed after an over-extended time out of your body is a nice helping of sugar and caffeine to get you right again. So did you get the whole story about you and your sister?" Hattie had not been privy to the vision but she felt it happening.

"I did Hattie. It's just so much to take in. I don't think I even remember driving home."

"You will Sugar. Just give it a little time. You will remember it all. Your momma called from the hospital. Seems Miz Camden moved her arm today." Courtney gasped and smiled at the good news. "Also seems Miz Camden was talking in her sleep. That means she will be making some big improvements in the next few weeks. Miz Clarisa is going to supper with some people she met at the hospital. She said she would check on your grandmother after that. So it may be awhile before she will get home. That means you have some time to get yourself together before she gets back Sugar." Hattie had been watching Courtney closely. She smiled when she saw a little color begin to ease back into her pale cheeks. "Now Baby, tell me all about it."

Courtney continued to eat shortcake and sip her tea as she related the events of the twins' ancient life in Scotland and a blue stone made of tears and filled with visions.

"Whoooeee child. That's one amazing story. Well it sure do explain a lot don't it?"

A noise at the screen door startled them both.

"Storm Cat! You nearly scared the life out of us. C'mon in here you ol' cat. I have somethin' to put in your bowl."

Storm Cat walked in with a dignified pace, tail held high. He went straight to Courtney first and rubbed against her leg. Then he turned and walked sedately to his bowl. He sat down and politely waited until Hattie had prepared his treat.

"Hattie I want to bring Caitlin here for a weekend visit. What do you think Grandmother would say?"

"Well I don't rightly know Sugar. But your grandmother is not in any position to make judgments right now. I think you are capable of making that decision. It would only be for one night so how bad can it be? I can make up the yellow room for her so she'll be sleepin' next to yours. It was a nursery a long time ago so it's a little smaller than some of the other rooms, but it's cozy and bright with those big windows and yellow flowers on the wallpaper."

"You're right Hattie. That sounds perfect. I don't know why I'm having this anxiety about everything." Courtney put her elbows on the hard wood of the butcher-block island and rested her head in her hands. A throbbing ache began beating a painful tattoo behind her eyes.

"Now listen child, you need to remember a little bit more of that vision. Your sister was not very nice to you back in Scotland. I wouldn't be a bit surprised if maybe you're havin' a past life anxiety hangover! Hee Hee. I think I just discovered a new dis-order! Lord have mercy! I don't mean to make light of your discomfort, but, hee heee sometimes you just got to have a good sense of humor about it all!" Hattie wiped her eyes with a kitchen towel. Courtney was smiling and nodding but she still rubbed her temples.

"Uh oh. Looks like a nasty headache has got hold of you. Here rub a little of this oil on your temples and between your eyes. I think you got a third eye headache. They can be brutal. Now you go on upstairs and take a relaxing bath. Then have a little nap. If you're hungry when you wake up I'll fix us a nice salad"

When Courtney got to her room, Storm Cat was already waiting for her. He sat in the middle of her bed looking at her expectantly.

"Well, it looks like you want a nap too," she told him, "I'll just take a quick shower and then you'd better move over."

She did feel refreshed and totally spent after the shower. Her hair was still wet but she was too tired to bother drying it. She pulled a dry towel from the linen closet and draped it over her pillow to soak up the dampness then literally collapsed on the bed. Storm Cat had to move quickly to avoid being bumped. He stayed on his side of the bed and proceeded to take his own careful bath. Before long both were sound asleep.

"Hello," came the soft voice nearby. Courtney turned her head with great difficulty. "Thank you for coming to see me." Courtney was incapable of forming any words in response.

C.C.'s image gazed at her through eyes filled with love. "Please don't try to talk. This is the only way I'll ever be able to talk to you in this life, so just listen now." Courtney nodded. "I now know why I have to be crippled and mostly mute. I caused you and many other people so much harm back then. I'll never do it again. I've grown to understand that the gift of sight with the assistance of my art must be used to help as many people as possible until I leave my body for my home in the Light. My paintings will display my visions and you dear sister will speak for both of us. That is of course, if you can forgive me for what I did. I am only now learning to forgive myself." Tears glistened on the cheeks of the apparition and she faded just a little. "Go on and sleep now. I'll be waiting to see you again." The vision moved away until the blue light around her was only a pinpoint in the darkness of her slumber and then it was gone.

Something rough and warm rubbed against Courtney's cheek. She turned her head to get away from it. Then something soft hit her nose and she awoke with a start. Storm Cat began licking her cheek with his rough feline tongue. She giggled at his antics and scratched behind his whiskers and the top of his head. She was promptly rewarded with a contented purring near her ear. He closed his eyes and nuzzled against the side of her head.

The sun was sitting low in the sky and that meant that her nap had been a little longer than she intended.

By the time she put on a pair of white shorts and a pale green cotton shirt, Storm Cat had left. She moved with a dancer's grace her feet barely making a sound on the stairs. She loved looking at the polished floors and lovely antiques in the old plantation home. Her eyes strayed to the crystal chandelier in the parlor and the heavy cherry wood desk where her grandfather had spent so many happy hours working and reading in the library. It felt like home.

"Now don't you look fresh," Hattie smiled warmly. "C'mon sit yourself down here and sip on this lemonade. Our salads are already made. I just found some dinner rolls that I had in the freezer. Soon as they are all warmed up, we'll have us some supper. Did you sleep well? Is your headache gone?"

Courtney smiled through Hattie's energetic conversation. "Warm rolls and salad sound perfect. I slept great and my headache is completely gone, thank goodness."

"Hmm well you do look a lot better but maybe still a little too pale for my liking."

"Thanks for caring about me so much." Courtney walked around the island to give Hattie a hug.

"Can't help it Baby. We just got a soul connection and it makes me care."

"I had an interesting dream." Courtney told her about the vision of Caitlin and her plea for forgiveness.

"Well I just knew that there was some big time karma goin' on in this here situation. I'm so lookin' forward to meetin' your sister. I think you are both in for an extraordinary relationship for the rest of your lives." Hattie nodded sagely and took a step back. A loud squawk and hiss startled them both. "Storm Cat, now you know I didn't mean to step on you, but you got to watch out for your own self when I'm workin' in this here kitchen."

Storm Cat glared at Hattie and Courtney when they laughed at his indignant reaction then sprinted to the screen door and stood there twitching his tail while he waited for someone to let him out. "Now Storm you know I love you and I would never want to do anything to hurt you." Hattie picked up the indignant cat and stroked his fur. He immediately began to purr signaling his forgivness. He snuggled up to Hattie's cheek and she gave him a smacking kiss on his soft furry neck.

The two women had just finished their salads when Clarisa's car pulled up near the kitchen door.

Courtney embraced her mother and they all exchanged greetings.

"Mom I heard about Grandmother today! She moved her arm and she was talking in her sleep?"

"I know Darlin' I am so encouraged by her progress." Courtney noted that her mother's distinctive Charleston accent had deepened due to her extended stay in her home state. It made her smile and her heart filled with love for this woman who had consented to be her mother.

Clarisa sat on one of the stools and gratefully accepted a glass of cold lemonade from Hattie. She closed her eyes and sighed after a long thirsty drink. Then she told Hattie and her daughter about her day at the hospital. When she finished she sighed again and sipped from her glass.

"You know, I think I might not go in tomorrow until after lunch. I need a break from that place. Darlin' what is your schedule like? Maybe we could go shopping in the morning and then have some lunch together."

"I'd love it Mom. It's been awhile since we have done anything like that." Courtney responded enthusiastically.

They chatted happily for a time while Hattie cleared away their dishes and then set out a plate of her home-baked pecan and chocolate chip cookies.

The sky was dark now and the inhabitants of the night took up their songs. Tree frogs, cicadas and crickets sang to the night. Tiny sparks of light from lightening bugs added to the magic as they decorated bushes and trees with their mystical twinklings. Hattie turned on a soft light in the corner of the kitchen. Then she lit several candles and set one of them on the island and the others on the surrounding counter tops.

"I like a little candlelight every so often," Hattie smiled and settled on her own stool.

Courtney took a deep breath and began a discussion with her mother. "As you know I went to The Oaks today. I had a long talk with Dr. Baylor. He really is a nice person and he gave me as much information about C.C. uh Caitlin, as he could. He said that no one seemed to notice her abilities until he started his art therapy sessions just a few months ago."

Hattie raised her eyebrow and stared at Courtney. There was something brighter and more animated about her suddenly. *What is this*, she wondered to her self, *that girl's heart has been touched.* Aloud she only said "Mmm hmmm."

"So anyway we must have talked for at least an hour. Then I went to see my sister. I was there most of the day. We uh…had a vision together Mom. It was about a past life. You were there and Grandmother Camden. *She* was our Mother then. She lost her mother and father very young. She got married and pregnant and her husband had to go fight in some battles where he was killed." Courtney paused to take a sip of lemonade. Clarisa felt little chills run up and down her spine.

"She gave birth to twins with your help, Mom. You were this village wise woman healer in Scotland."

Clarisa gave a little start at those words and her heartbeat quickened.

"Grandmother, our mother then, eventually lost her mind and wasn't able to take care of us. We were sort of good twin bad twin. I could make animals come to me and Caitlin had visions. She had a vision that the village was going to be attacked. But she didn't tell anyone and she ran away looking for fun. The village was almost wiped out. I died and Caitlin nearly died in a bog. You found her though, Mom and brought her back. She was sorry for what she had done and finally she died too. You were very sad and decided that you didn't want to have visions ever again. Her tears created the blue topaz. She poured all of her visions into it. You vowed that you would guard that stone and someday give it to me when our souls were developed enough to handle everything."

Clarisa was crying and Courtney reached for her hand. It was ice cold. She shivered and wiped at her eyes. "I don't have the gift you have Honey but I can feel the truth as wild and imaginative as that story seems, I still want to believe it."

"The rest of it is Mom, that I believe that Caitlin and I are going to be working together. Our job in this life is to help people with our abilities. I don't know exactly how all of that is going to happen but I want to start a relationship with her as soon as possible. I want her to come here for the weekend." Courtney took another breath; "I don't want to do anything to upset Grandmother, after all this is her house…"

"I happen to know that Mother wants to leave this house to you if you want it. I had a meeting with her lawyer today. I am the executor of her estate if she dies or becomes incapacitated. So yes bring your sister here for the weekend and let's get acquainted." Courtney sighed with relief.

Hattie stifled a yawn. At that moment they all felt exhausted. Storm Cat begged to be let in with a plaintive little poor kitty meow. The candles were extinguished and the kitchen was thrown into darkness save the glow from the night light. They bid each other "good night" and made their way through the large house to their various bedrooms. It seemed that once again their lives would be changed and a new course would be set for an unknown destination.

CHAPTER SEVEN

Clarisa sighed deeply as she finally lay down on the cool white sheets of her bed. She was truly exhausted. She had been at the hospital for so many days with her mother, she could hardly remember doing anything else. She wanted to see Esther recover but she also wanted to go home. She longed to be with her husband and have a swim in their pool with the sound of the waterfall lulling her into peacefulness.

She turned on her side with another long sigh. Hopefully Esther could be moved to the convalescent center very soon, maybe another week. Then Clarisa could fly home and come back in a few weeks, depending on her mother's pace of recovery.

Reincarnation, just imagine the implications of such a possibility; she kept going over and over in her mind, the story that Courtney had told her. She guessed it could be possible and she had certainly felt some strange sensations as the story unfolded. She began thinking of her life and wondering what sort of actions might have precipitated her being born into a life of privilege and wealth. An ugly flash in her mind startled her into a sitting position. For some reason she was thinking of the debutante ball again. But the flash was not of the ball, her beautiful gown or the music and dancing. She thought of red veined eyes and the smell of liquor soured breath. It was Charles, her late brother. "No, no, no," she whispered to herself as she fell back on the pillows, "I won't think of that. I won't," she whispered vehemently into the dark. She used all of her will power and forced the memories away and instead, began to plan where she and Courtney would shop the next day. Pleasant expectations of their morning together helped her to relax and then slip into the relief of sleep.

***

"Bloody hell!" Abigail Whiting cursed as her eyes scanned the article in the newspaper. He was alive when I left his flat! Mutilated body?" She was aghast at the description of horrors that were done to the man in the article. "Well somebody must not have taken kindly to your romantic notions you bloody fool," she raged at the newspaper. "What? Blond woman sought for questioning!" She read aloud to herself. "But I didn't do any of that. Of course if he had the chance he would 'a killed me and I guess I would'a killed him if I'da had to, but I didn't. I swear I didn't."

Abigail's hands shook as she finished reading the article. Then she crumpled the paper and threw it across the room. "Who ever did that must've wanted what I took." She started pacing and kicking at anything she passed regardless of whether it was her slipper or even the chair. She aimed a vicious kick at a small end table and sent it toppling to the floor.

Her small but beautifully appointed flat was on the opposite side of London from where her mark was found dead. She tried to think of who could have seen her coming or going from 'ol Kenton Barsop's flat that night. She had not seen a soul in that building. "Probably some nosey ol' biddy peerin' through a bloody peep hole. I'd like to wring her scrawny neck or poke 'er rheumy eyes out!" She fumed and paced.

"It said the place was ransacked, so for bloody sure they was lookin' for what I got. Somebody thought that bastard was holdin' out on 'em."

Abigail stopped dead still and all of the color drained from her face. "That means I got two kinds a' wankers looking for me. Scotland Yard for one and some kind of criminal butcher for the second." She felt weak and sick as she absorbed the enormity of the situation.

"I wasn't planning to leave London quite so soon was I," she mumbled to herself as she paced over to an ornate wall mirror. "Looks like I'm going to need a make-over right away." She fluffed her curly bleached blond hair and studied her reflection. "Hmmn it was a stroke of luck that I was actually born with sort of almond shaped eyes. I could use my Asian look again. Nobody would think of looking for an Asian. I think I make an adorable China doll." She spent a few minutes fantasizing about what she should wear and how she could change her makeup. It would work she decided with a satisfied smile.

Now it was time to work out the details of what she should do next. She did not mind these sudden twists and turns in her life. In fact she felt really alive right now. Planning a con was great fun and there was an ecstatic adrenaline rush when it went well. But by God's honest truth there was nothing quite like the rush she felt when things didn't go so well. The element of danger and the race to, not only survive, but to win, to be better than her pursuers! Ah, now that was the ultimate turn on. That is what she lived for. It was the only time she could really feel *enough* to know that she was alive.

The familiar buzz hummed through her body as her mind focused to a razor sharp edge. First she concluded that she needed to unload a bushel of her treasures. She would need to liquidate as many of her assets as possible in order to start her new life, and it needed to happen now! She had plenty of contacts from years of *collecting* treasures. She possessed a large number of jewels that she could turn into thousands of pounds sterling almost immediately. "Yes, yes that will work. Too bad it all has to be done so fast!" She would not be able to get as much for everything by rushing the sales. It wouldn't matter though she comforted herself, there would always be a way to *find* more wherever she decided to go.

Then of course there were her new prizes, she remembered. The packets of money and the plates were the cause of her current danger, and she was sure that they were for counterfeiting American dollars. "Ah well I suppose I've been wantin' a bit more excitement," she shrugged and sighed as she stopped her frantic pacing to think. At first she had thought it strange that a Brit would have plates for making counterfeit American money. But she reasoned that the U.S. dollars might not be so easy to detect in another country. Well it didn't matter to her. She was not going to get her knickers in a twist about that. Abigail intended to make a huge profit from *their* loss. Oh she was clever wasn't she now. Laughter spilled into the quiet room.

The image of Sara Whiting flashed into her mind and her laughter stopped abruptly. Both of her parents had died when she was in her twenties. They were hard-working middle-class people with no aspirations beyond their comfortable daily routine. They had provided a stable home environment and had attended church every Sunday. Abigail had hated their mind-numbing dull daily routine and of course, Abigail had made it her mission to give things a good shake now and again. Her Mum often shook her head and complained about all of the gray hair that Abbie was giving her. The truth was that Sara, her mother, had been completely gray for as long as she could remember.

Reginald Whiting was a short round balding man with a ready wit and hearty laugh. When his daughter was young his laughter was truly merry. During her teenage years his laughter was seldom heard. In some ways she regretted causing so much trouble for them. Who knew that they had saved all that money? They left her a bloody fortune. Well that's the way it had seemed at the time. The money had only lasted a few years and then she had to think of some other way to get money, and she did.

Abigail had a natural gift for stealing and had carefully honed her skills since she was very small. It was easy to take a shilling or two from Sara's handbag. Taking money from her schoolmates was easy too. Her looks had always been an advantage as well, since everyone told her she looked like a cherub with her reddish-brown curls and amazing blue eyes. She had always been petite and even now at forty-three she was a slim five foot two inches tall and still not a line on her face. What a great joke it was to fool people into thinking she was still twenty-five. This thought brought on more peals of laughter and another trip to the mirror.

Sara Whiting's round face appeared in her mind again. "Don't get your knickers in a twist wee girl. Tend to your business and don't dilly dally," her Mum always told her. She turned from the mirror and went to the small antique roll top desk in the corner. She opened drawers, pulled out papers, looked up phone numbers and tapped steadily on her small calculator.

Hours passed. Abigail lined up her current stash of stolen jewelry on a small cherry wood table. Diamond rings, gold watches encrusted with precious stones, earrings and bracelets glittered under the lamplight. She had closed the drapes to hide her cache from prying eyes. She loved her sparkling jewels. She could never get enough of them. She loved to look at them and run her fingers over the smooth surfaces of the stones. Then there was the *listening.* They spoke to her in their own special language. She could feel their humming vibration and she loved the way it always pulled at her. How could she part with any of them?

She had no compassion for the people she took from. They were the very rich after all and these little baubles were meaningless in their lives. Abbie always fancied that the stones called to her because she loved them so much more than their owners. When she was attending a party or visiting the home of one of her wealthy acquaintances, a piece of jewelry would catch her eye. It would almost light up. Her heart would quicken and she was nearly sure she heard it calling to her. At times she would close her eyes and feel the cool weight of it in her hand.

"Well, now," she sighed, "I think I'm ready." She looked at the lists she had made and determined which accent and disguise she would use for each one. In more than one instance she planned to use the protective presence of some hefty strong-arm blokes. It was going to be the most complicated and difficult thing she had ever tried to do. Never had she attempted to fence so many items in such a short period of time. She was taking a huge risk. But, she always had a good sense of her surroundings and she had an uncanny knack for knowing when serious danger threatened near by. If that warning came in the pit of her stomach, she would immediately abort any operation she was working on. She picked up her telephone and made the first call. Most of the contacts she spoke to were relatively easy to do business with and the risks were minimal. The only time her heartbeat madly accelerated was the call she made to a contact that dealt with someone involved in organized crime. She knew that selling one of the plates to those blokes would be the most dangerous thing she had ever done. When the last series of calls was completed sweat beaded up on her forehead. She dropped her head into her hands and prayed she had made the right decision to do business with them. She took a shakey breath and went over her plan again for the twentieth time. Another terrifying thought struck her in that moment. What if the people who had killed ol' Barsop were part of the organized crime group she was planning to do business with? And even more terrifying what if Barsop was part of that group and what if the plates belonged to them in the first place? No she wouldn't, couldn't think of things like that! She had to follow through with her plans and get out of London!

Ok, she would think of her antiques. Antiques were another passion for her, especially cherry wood. She was sad to part with her carefully chosen pieces but she knew she would have a jolly good time picking out a whole new collection when she arrived at her new location.

Her flat was nearly empty when the movers left. The dealer who had agreed to purchase her antiques was grinning madly when he bowed his way out of the door. She smiled to herself as she watched him. He had gotten a good deal and he knew it. There would be some nice fat profits for him when they were resold. She didn't mind so much. It was more important for her to travel lightly, except for her bundles of money of course, and even a lot of that had to be disbursed into different accounts, under different names. No problem! She felt she was in complete control.

The metropolitan police were extra busy for a Monday late afternoon. Abigail peered nervously from behind her heavy curtains. Some rowdy had caused a ruckus on the opposite side of the street. He had been routed and escorted to the official van. A short time later the medical rescue team had arrived to take some poor soul to hospital. She hated unexpected interruptions and ground her teeth together as she fought the urge to simply charge into the implementation of her plan. At last the street was quiet and it was time to go.

The hallway in her west side building was clean, well lighted and empty. It was always empty this time of day. Most of the other residents were quiet elderly people who either napped or were out walking. She stepped into the hall closing and locking the door behind her. She shifted the strap of her handbag to her shoulder and walked nonchalantly toward the lift. She pushed the button to summon it and listened to the grinding clank of motor and metal.

Unexpectedly her stomach clenched. This was a warning that she never doubted. Something was wrong. She turned abruptly and ran for the back stairs. As she descended, she could hear men talking and knocking on doors. She had no idea who they were and she was not going to wait around to find out.

She slipped quietly out of the back entrance and walked calmly across two streets. Then she caught a Double Decker and climbed to the top to sit in the waning sunlight. She was not too worried. After all no one was looking for an Asian girl.

She rode for a while and then changed to another bus traveling in a different direction. From there she found a cabby and gave him the address she needed. She had decided on a small but nice hotel for her Asian persona to stay in. Her bags had already been delivered and all she had to do was check in. The lobby was not too busy and the check-in went smoothly.

Her room was pleasant and clean. She ordered dinner from room service and then lay down on the bed to wait and run through the sequence of events again.

One thing she had not counted on was a problem with her passport. When she had presented it to the Travel Bureau the clerk told her it had expired. She should have been more careful. The only snag that had come up was when she searched for her official birth record. It had gone missing. Well that would not happen again for two reasons. The first was because she had paid a visit to the adoption agency where Sara and Reginald had found her. The administrator was only too delighted to earn a fistful of pounds stering in exchange for her entire file. Now that was an eye opener. The second security measure involved a very talented forger who was discreet and expensive. The rest of her plans had come together nicely. The next phase would involve exchanging a lot of jewels for a lot of money.

Her friend with the muscle arrived at their designated meeting place astride his powerful motorbike at precisely half past ten.

"Oh baby, you otta dress like that all the time!" Ace let out a low whistle when she stepped out of the shadows dressed entirely in black leather. She had taken a cab back to the street where her old flat was. She didn't want to reveal her plans and new location to Ace in the event that he got too greedy. She climbed on the bike behind him and slid her arms around his hard lean body as they roared off into the night. After a thirty-minute ride through the darkened London streets they stopped at the prearranged meeting place.

The contact was late. Ace lit a cigarette and dragged in the smoke with a look of deep contentment on his face. Abigail was antsy but she willed herself to lean casually against the bike. The plan was for her to look like the go-between. When an appropriate offer was made, she was to turn and look at Ace as if he were giving the okay to complete the transaction.

At last a dark sedan rounded the corner and rolled slowly to a stop. The passenger door opened and a tall man got out. He walked slowly toward them until he stood only a few yards away. Ace pushed Abbie forward according to plan. She feigned reluctance but she didn't have to try too hard. It was over quickly. Someone inside the car inspected and verified the value of the purchase. Then jewels and money changed hands. Abbie's heart pounded with excitement and nerves as she positioned herself behind Ace. A dependable London fog was creeping through the dark streets as the bike rumbled to life and carried them into its' nearly opaque shield. She wanted to laugh hysterically. It had been so easy.

Ace pulled up in front of the flat Abbie had recently vacated. She jumped off the bike and hurriedly began to count out his payment. When she held it out to him he grabbed her arm. "C'mon what say we 'av a bit o' fun," his voice was deep and husky. She had enjoyed a *little fun* with Ace on many occasions, but not tonight.

"No not tonight," she murmured as he pulled her close. "Let's plan to spend time together tomorrow night." She pressed herself against him hoping he would not guess how agitated she felt.

"I say we make it tonight!" His tone was rough and insistant. Abbie was prepared for something like that from him and yet she was unprepared for the turmoil of her own feelings. She suddenly wanted to be with him more than ever and for the first time since she had decided to leave London she was close to changing her mind. Practicality won out and she stepped back.

Ace sensed there was something under the surface of her words and tightened his grip nearly bruising her small wrist. She kicked out with her high-heeled boot and knocked him back against his bike. Before he could recover she shoved him with all of her strength knocking him and his bike over, then she turned and ran as hard as she could toward her building. She raced easily through the familiar building and out on to the next street. She could hear Ace cursing followed by the distinctive roar of his bike.

She was grateful that she had kept her muscles lean and fit as she raced through yards and into the mews. She was quite out of breath by the time she found a small pub and ducked inside. She noticed a young barmaid serving drinks to the noisy crowd. She judged the girl to be close enough to her own size and made her an offer.

When Abbie emerged from the loo she was dressed as casually as any other patron minus the black wig and boots. "Bugger," she swore under her breath, she hated to give up that outfit.

Ace roared down the street and screeched to a halt in front of the little pub. Soo Ling had not answered when he pounded on her door and he was sure she had ducked through the building. He was going to have a nasty bruise on his rib cage from those wicked boots. His bike was scratched from falling to the pavement and his dignity was bent at a painful angle. He was mad as hell at the little twit and yet there was something illusive and intriguing about her that made him want to keep her in his life. He stomped into the crowded pub and looked around. He was certain that this was the most logical place for her to duck into on this street. She just couldn't have gone too far unless she had jumped into a car or on a bus. The pub was dimly lit and nearly impossible to single out any familiar face. Several patrons glanced warily at the large man with a murderous look in his eyes but no one chose to confront him.

A loud group of people was heading for the door and Ace had to step aside so they could make their exit. Abbie was on the far side of the group and he never noticed her as she left with them.

Abbie took a bus to her hotel. No one gave her a second look as she walked purposefully through the lobby and took the lift to the fourth floor. Once inside her room she stripped off the borrowed clothes and got into a hot shower. She was drained of energy and flopped down on the bed. "Well, there goes Soo Ling," she sighed. "Too bad, I rather liked her." Ace only knew her, as Soo Ling and that brainless hunk of muscle would never think to look for anyone else. She was exhausted and fell asleep instantly.

Abbie rose early the next morning and checked out of the hotel disguised as Soo Ling's somewhat beefy older assistant. The doorman flagged down a cab and she was off to a new location.

Selling the gold and silver settings was a much less dramatic procedure. It was more to her liking to do business during the middle of the afternoon. She knew of a small jewelry shop just two blocks from the bustling city center of London. She had donned a mousey brown wig and wore no cosmetics. She used brown contact lenses and large glasses. She was dressed in a non-descript beige pantsuit and no jewelry. She knew this disguise would help her fade quickly into the masses. She trusted the owner of the small establishment as much as she was capable of trusting anyone and had been to the shop on many occasions. The one thing she had *never* done was use the same disguise more than once, well except for her Soo Ling disguise, which she used whenever she got together with Ace. She would miss Ace. She carried a tattered brown leather briefcase and wore low-heeled pumps. As she had hoped, no one gave her a second look. The shop owner looked the part of a kindly grandfather and conducted himself with quiet dignity during their transaction. When their business was concluded she left the shop breathing a sigh of relief. One more step had been completed. Just a few more details and she could be on her way.

There were two more stops to make in small shops at other locations in the city. She altered her appearance just slightly after ducking into a public loo the first time. After that she purchased her new look from a high-end shop. The owner was delighted that her new customer insisted on wearing her new clothes out of the store to "surprise her husband".

When it was time for the last jewelry shop she decided on a grieving widow story. She tearfully explained to the clerk that she had to sell her enormous diamond ring, earrings and bracelet after falling on hard times due to her husband's untimely death. These pieces though nice, were not custom made and would not be terribly easy to trace. She had taken those pieces on her last trip to Scotland. It was there that she had found the one jewel that she knew she would never sell. The large blue stone had called to her like no other as she climbed the staircase to the attic in the grand old home in Inverness. They were a great old clan, the McGillvrays. She had so enjoyed listening to the stories of their ancient ancestors.

Abbie did not personally know the family but by chance she had been in a very upscale dress shop in London and overheard a young woman discussing her wedding plans with her mother. They were obviously wealthy. It was a simple matter to ingratiate herself to mother and daughter. By the time they left the shop they were old friends. She was an expert at convincing people that she was a wealthy sad heiress. It was her favorite scam. Naturally after only a few weeks she was invited to the wedding in the northwest highlands and once there, made friends with a whole new circle of wealthy people.

Abbie was careful to maintain her friendships from a distance by writing amusing friendly letters, describing lavish vacations that she had heard *other* people talk about. Some of the adventures were hers, but mostly she just made them up. *Her* families never suspected her of being a jewel thief. She had always been very careful not to take the largest flashiest jewels. She hungered for them but kept her hunger satiated by taking smaller pieces that could easily have been *misplaced.*

Once she obtained most items, she immediately removed the stones from their settings. After an appropriate amount of time had passed she would take a few small stones to one or two of her contacts and it was done. The gold and silver was always sold to a separate dealer and thus far she had encountered no problems and had never been detected as even a person of interest in a single robbery. Her wealthy friends would never suspect *their* wealthy friend of anything of the sort.

She always followed newspaper reports carefully to see if a robbery had been reported. The only time it had ever happened, Abbie had not been the thief! Some fool had taken a valuable family heirloom along with a magnificent emerald and diamond necklace and several rings, one being a huge two-carat blue diamond. Abbie knew her jewels. She remembered seeing those items in their velvet-lined drawers, but the only thing she took was the lovely diamond bracelet that she was selling today. She wondered if maybe the family had faked the robbery in order to collect insurance money.

Once her transactions were completed she was feeling easier about everything as she tucked away the money in her Gucci bag and left the shop. She strolled toward the main boulevard at a leisurely pace never changing her demeanor even though she heard the distinctive whine of a familiar motorbike. Ace shot by her with only a cursory glance her way. The grieving widow persona was not his type.

Abigail decided right then and there that she would give up the tough and seedy types such as Ace and poor ol' Kenton Barsop. Of course, Barsop she had targeted as having more than most and he, like she, had a penchant for living on the wild side. She realized now that this bit of perversity in her nature had nearly cost her life. It had taken a long time for all those bruises and scrapes to heal. She had no idea why she dallied with low life losers like that. Maybe low self esteem. Now Ace she could understand. He was ruggedly good looking with all that long black hair and the scar running through his right eyebrow. Not too shiny in the brain category but oh the bloke was a righteous stud.

Abigail turned abruptly and walked into a large store as Ace roared by once again. Maybe he did like tight-assed grieving widows. She quickly bought a modest tan and brown pair of pants and a matching turtle neck and a cardigan. The size was a bit large just as she planned. She stuffed her widow's black in the front of her pants until it bulged in a nice paunch. The cardigan hid the harshness of the improvised disguise and mellowed the whole look. She asked one of the sales women for a shopping bag and in a moment of inspiration she bought an umbrella. When she left the store she was a heavier, older woman using an umbrella as a cane. Her hair was covered with a scarf and no one looked at her twice.

Rather sad, she thought as she limped along the street, how one's appearance can make you invisible. She sighed then looked up as she heard Big Ben chiming in the distance. "Ahh tea time," she smiled, "that is just the thing, a nice cup of tea."

Ace roared by once again. She held her breath but she really had no reason to worry. His interest was directed toward a group of long-legged girls gathered near the double decker stop.

Abigail felt just the smallest twinge of jealously jab at her heart while she watched him work his charm with them. She stood just inside of the Tea Room waiting for an empty seat at one of the small round tables. She unconsciously put her hand over her heart as she thought of Ace.

"Madam are you ill?" A kindly older gentleman stood up and gestured toward his vacated chair. "I was just leaving. Sit yourself down. Can't be having you faint now can we," he smiled, "A nice cup of tea for the lady," he gestured toward the waitress.

Abigail gratefully accepted the chair and eased herself down as one who was older and walked with a limp. Soon she was sipping her tea with milk and gazing out of the tearoom windows at Ace. One of the girls climbed on the back of his bike and he roared away.

The hot tea revived her and she began to feel better after a few sips. Somehow she would have to remove Ace from her mind, but she kept thinking about the bulge of muscle in his arms when he pulled her into an embrace, and how she looked up into his eyes as he bent his head low bringing his face close to hers.

Abigail sighed as she remembered a particular night when his lips had felt agonizingly soft at first then became more demanding. His large hands had tenderly removed one strap from her shoulder then the other. She thought of the delightful feeling of her exposed warm skin touched by the cool night air. She shivered with the memory of his sensual kisses as he firmly held her slender arms over her head as their passion….

"Is everything all right here? Should I call someone?" The waitress leaned forward anxiously.

Abigail was mortified to discover that she was breathing hard and sweating. God, she had to stop this mooning and get to work. There was one last sale she needed to make and it was going to be the most dangerous situation. She could feel it in the pit of her stomach. There could be no more thinking about Ace and a blanket on the grass in an open field under the stars.

The new hotel room was slightly more up-scale than the last one. When Soo Ling had checked out of the previous one she made sure that the front desk attendant knew she was returning to Taiwan and was not coming back to London for a very long time.

Her new story was to be that she worked as a writer for a documentary that was being filmed in London. This would explain her comings and goings at odd hours. There was also access to a lovely safe for her increasing wealth. It would not do for some shifty housemaid or bellman to stumble upon her stash and steal it.

She slept well once again and proceeded with her plans. She had set up new international accounts under various aliases in different banks. One

72

account was even for her executive employer. That was the one she would keep for a really enormous emergency should it arise. At this rate she might even open a Swiss account, but she decided that might be jumping ahead of things. Stay with the plan for today. Her spirited nature could be impetuous at times so she wisely decided to keep a tight reign on her impulses.

Everything was ready for the last phase. Her travel arrangements were complete and the luggage she would actually take with her was packed and stored. Her cash was now deposited and ready to transfer wherever and whenever she needed it. She had her disguises ready and now it was time to wait for the proper final hour. The countdown had begun for the domino reaction of events that would take her out of her country and hopefully into safety and a new life.

***

Raeford stood a full head and shoulders above his British counter parts. Birdwell was closer to his height but even then he had to lift his chin slightly upward to look directly into the Texan's steel blue eyes. The British were all very polite and welcoming in their manner but he was still very uncomfortable. Every few moments he would catch one of the men surreptitiously stealing a glance in his direction. As soon as he caught someone doing so the man would quickly look away. He simply couldn't figure out what they were staring at. He wondered if maybe they had never seen a Stetson hat before.

They walked as a group down a long narrow hall past doorways, some open revealing desks piled with papers and files and busy people talking on the telephone or bent over a document. The hallway ended and the group made a hard right and headed toward a door at the end, which opened into the conference room. They took their seats at a large oval table and continued their low conversations until the leader of the operation stood up to speak.

"On behalf of all of us at Scotland Yard, I would like to welcome agent Raeford from the United States," he stated in his flat voice and precise British accent.

Raeford touched the brim of his Stetson with his index finger in a typical Texas salute. There were murmurs all around as the men nodded and acknowledged his presence. They all continued to stare at him so he decided that they wanted him to say something. He pushed back his chair, took off his hat and stood up.

"I thank ya'll for the warm welcome and the invite to join yer posse. I'll be glad to help you in anyway I can. I was rodeo trained to ride any bronc you throw at me and if you loan me a lasso I'll show you some interestin' rope tricks that'll tame the orneriest bull doggie in the herd," Raeford sat down with only a slight smile pulling at the corner of his mouth. He normally would never have addressed any group of people by throwing around his Texas drawl and local slang, but he recognized that the Brits were taken aback by his

Western style suit, Bola tie and cowboy boots and yep, of course the Stetson hat. He knew he must look as though he had just stepped out of an old cowboy movie to them.

The room was silent for a moment as the men looked at him and one another. Raeford's smile finally widened, "What's the matter, ain't ya never met a cowboy before?" Birdwell was the first one to chuckle. Raeford joined him and soon the room was filled with polite muted laughter. The ice was broken and they could work together more comfortably now.

The leader gestured to a middle-aged man on his right. "Toddey, will you bring us up to date on the latest developments? Introduce yourself for the benefit of our visitors.

"Brandt Toddey! At your service." He clicked his heels together and executed a smart little bow, his contribution to the previous round of humor. No one laughed. He cleared his throat and began.

Brandt launched into a detailed account of what the Metropolitan Police had found at the Kenton Barsop murder scene. They discovered a stash of counterfeit money that the murderer had missed. No one had known the money wasn't real at first. That fact was not discovered until later. There was evidence that Barsop had been with a woman who had bleached blond hair. They had not been able to track her down yet. There were several sets of fingerprints found and one set matched up with a guy named Mangeone who was connected to organized crime.

Raeford's attention got a little sharper as he thought of the incident with Antonio Scolari in California just last spring. He had been tracking the counterfeit money since Scolari's violent demise. His hunches were rarely wrong and his laser sharp senses were thrumming with anticipation. He knew he was getting close to some answers and possibly the source of the operation.

Toddey droned on going over monotonous details in his methodical style.

"Toddey," the leader prodded, "we have a busy day ahead and we are a bit short on time lad. Can you just shorten it up a bit? All of that information is in their files."

Toddey nodded and continued, "It seems a fellow by the name of Dorian Rutherford deposited quite a lot of American money in his bank account. Come to find out it was counterfeit. The best we've ever seen but bogus none-the-less. Him coming from a fine up-standing old family we didn't think he really knew what he had. We brought 'im in for questioning. Seems he's a bit of a wild hare. Dresses in black, rides a motorbike and generally hob knobs with the wild bunch. Never been in trouble with the law though and most of the time he helps run Rutherford and Sons Inc. . Claims he got the money from his Asian girl friend. She believed he was down on his luck and gave him the money. Wouldn't take no for an answer. He didn't want her or anyone in his rough and tumble crowd to know his real identity."

Rough and tumble, Raeford thought to himself. Next we'll be playing cricket and saying 'God save the queen'. *I love these Brits* he thought with a smile.

Toddey continued, "Seems that Mister Dorian Cambrey Rutherford IV, leads a double life. When he rides his motorbike he goes by the name Ace."

"We've looked for the Asian woman but the trail ended when her assistant checked her out of a hotel. There was no forwarding address but the fellow at the front desk remembered the assistant saying they were going back to Taiwan."

"Thank you." The leader stood up, "We never found a record of a Miss Soo Ling on any flights leaving Heathrow. Either she didn't leave or she changed her name."

"Now this is what has happened during the past fortnight. One of our informants told us that a French woman is trying to sell some plates used in making money. American twenties and hundreds to be exact." He stopped for a moment and looked around the table. All eyes were on him, including the American's.

"We are planning a sting. Could get a bit dodgey though, so everyone look sharp. Agent Raeford we would like your input as well since you have had experience with a group in the United States which we believe is connected to this one and possibly one in Hong Kong and yet a third in Munich."

"Be glad to," Raeford began and continued on for the next hour.

By the end of the second day a plan was in place. They hoped to be able to find the originators of the counterfeiting enterprise and it was their hope that this operation would reveal much needed information that would help them penetrate the dense wall of silence and false leads that had led them on a not so merry chase for far too long.

CHAPTER EIGHT

Dorian strode into his office at seven on Thursday morning. He was tired and shaken after his encounter with Scotland Yard. He was also furious with Soo Ling for what she had done. He had begun to care about her and that made it worse.

Today he was dressed in a gray custom-tailored suit, white shirt and pale blue silk tie. His long black hair was pulled severely back in a low ponytail. His father hated his long hair but because his son dressed in conservative business attire every day, worked a longer day than anyone else and continually helped to bring the company to higher profits every year, he made a concession about the hair.

Dorian made phone calls, set up appointments and generally sent his employees scurrying in every direction. His mother had black Irish blood in her family and it was that dark temper that the normally mild Mr. Rutherford showed to his startled employees that day.

His secretary announced that a man was calling on his private line and wouldn't give his name. He had hired a retired ex-policeman turned private investigator to follow Soo Ling. He listened to the caller for a while and then burst out laughing. "Cheeky bird that," he muttered as the laughter stopped abruptly. Suddenly his face drained of color and his jaw muscles bulged as he clenched his teeth. Dorian hung up and sat quietly for a few minutes as he wrestled with the decision about what action should be taken. He stood up and strode briskly through the office barking out orders to secretaries and assistants. All appointments were to be cancelled for the day and he would look at the reports he had previously demanded, tomorrow or the next day. Then he was gone. For a time after his abrupt departure everyone sat or stood silently staring at the door he had just slammed shut.

"I believe I'll 'ave some tea" a woman with wisps of gray hair falling over one eyebrow whispered to herself.

"Just 'oo does 'ee think 'ee is?" said another as she removed her glasses and rubbed her eyes.

" 'ee thinks 'ee owns the comp'ny that's 'oo," spoke a third with sarcasm dripping from every syllable like the thick honey she used in her tea.

Abigail awoke with a start. She had been dreaming and it was not pleasant. There were guns firing, an explosion, screams. She tried to shake it off, but her heart just would not calm down. "Well it will be over soon," she told herself, "Tonight I will be on a plane. I will be rich. The day after that I will start my new life." The adrenaline was already starting to rush through her system.

A quick hot shower helped her to calm down and get focused. Her stomach was in turmoil so food was out of the question. It would just have to be tea until all of this was behind her.

When she had come home after that fateful night with Kenton Barsop and discovered what was in those wrapped packages, she had hidden the plates behind some loose bricks in the old boiler room beneath her building. Her father had been handy with all sorts of repairs and had taught her the fine art of repairing loose bricks among many other things.

It was an easy matter for Abigail to become an elderly repairman visiting the building with his toolbox. The repairman stayed a short time just long enough to remove the twenty-dollar plate from its hiding place. The other one would be her insurance, if anyone got testy.

Nicole was a French woman working as a part time stripper and a pub singer. Soo Ling had met her while wandering in the poorer section of London with Ace. Abbie knew the woman could use the extra income while she was trying to raise her daughter alone. Nicole was well paid for the part she would play today. Abbie felt that no harm would come to her no matter what course all of the events took.

Dressed as a nurse, Nicole rode the cranky old lift to the third floor and found the door she was looking for. As she put the key in the lock, an elderly couple stepped into the hallway and eyed her questioningly.

"Oh Deary, you know she's moved out, or are you going to be movin' in?"

"Ah yes, I am conseedering a move. She gave me the key so that I can see for myself what eet is like," she smiled at the couple.

"You French?" The man asked.

"Oui, I am. Bye Bye," she winked at him and his wife yanked his arm so hard that he was forced to turn his back and shuffle toward the lift.

Nicole entered the vacant flat and took her place by the window. She made herself as comfortable as possible in the one chair that had been left for that purpose and waited for Soo Ling to call. A chair and a telephone were all that remained in Abigail's flat. She took out a pair of binoculars and peered through them scanning the street and buildings. Everything looked quiet. She was concentrating so intensely in the quiet of the empty room that the ringing phone caused her heart to leap into her throat.

Abigail was dressed as a delivery boy. She had bribed a little bakeshop to let her use their small delivery truck for a few hours. She made a few deliveries for them and was now at a restaurant using their telephone. She gave Nicole explicit instructions and a number to call. It would be over soon now she thought with marginal relief as sweat dripped down her back. She fought the desire to scratch her head under the itchy wig and cap.

Finally a heavy-set man appeared in front of the small fish and chips eatery. He was dressed casually in cap, slacks and jacket. The only item of note was the big pale yellow square of cloth that he coughed into and blew his nose on. He also carried a briefcase.

Nicole made the call to Soo Ling and then the proprietor of the eatery. Within seconds the large man with the briefcase was called to the phone. Nicole gave him instructions. A few moments later a bakery truck pulled up in front of the eatery and the young driver emerged carrying an order of baked goods for the restaurant. Geoffry, the owner of the eatery walked out of the front door, his arms laden with a carefully wrapped take out order.

Every second seemed to march by in leaded boots. Traffic passed, shoppers strolled; a dog pulled on its owner's lead and lifted his leg on the base of a street sign.

The briefcase was handed over to the delivery driver after a brief exchange of words. Then the large man turned to Geoffry and snatched the covered take out containers. He partially removed the cover of one of the containers and nodded his head in approval. The delivery driver took the briefcase and quickly shoved it into an empty bread bin aboard the truck and took his place at the wheel. Geoffry grinned broadly as he walked back into his eatery with a wad of money bulging in his pocket.

The bakery truck shot forward just as the large man took off his cap and fanned his face with it. A signal. Two men appeared running fast and tried to jump onto the back of the truck but just missed it. A Cooper pulled out with screeching tires and gave chase. The street was suddenly alive with angry shouts and people running.

Nicole spotted a man creeping stealthily across the top of a neighboring building. This was not good. The large man was still carrying the wrapped take out as he began to run across the street. His cap fell off in his haste, but he paid it no mind. He raced to a small sedan and jerked open the door and pushed himself behind the wheel. Within a few seconds he had pulled out into the light traffic, made a u-turn and sped off in the opposite direction of the delivery truck.

Her binoculars turned toward the delivery truck as it neared the end of the block. "Oh la la that one can drive," Nicole smiled as she watched the truck speed up and weave through traffic.

Suddenly loud pops startled her. "Merde!" Nicole swore as she realized it was gunfire. An ear-splitting whine announced the arrival of a powerful motorbike that was moving fast down the busy street. The bike jumped the curb and screamed up the walkway. Women screamed and ducked into doorways. A window in the bakery truck was shot out as it careened around the corner and disappeared from view. The bike steered crazily through traffic causing cars to smash into each other and create a monstrous barricade of twisted metal and angry shouting drivers.

78

Sirens blared and Metropolitan police cars surrounded the large man who was escaping with his *take out*. This man was the informant that Scotland Yard had employed. The plan was that he should be arrested so that the dangerous people he was informing on would not suspect him. He got out of the car with his hands in the air. Sweat ran into his eyes nearly blinding him. Four guns were pointed at him but they knew not to fire and therefore gasped in collective shock when their man crumpled slowly to the street, dead as blood seeped from his head. During the following chaos, a man dressed as an officer reached into the car, grabbed the take out package and covertly removed what was inside. He hid the counterfeit plate under his jacket and disappeared in the crowd.

Nicole saw none of that. She ran to the kitchen and opened the designated cupboard door and pushed on a panel in the back. It opened easily and she pulled out a package, which contained the disguise of an elderly woman complete with cane, hat, wig and a handbag. She opened the bag and found that Soo Ling had followed through on her promise to pay her very well for the part she agreed to play. She immediately pulled off her breakaway nurse's uniform and donned her new disguise.

Nicole was ecstatic to find that Soo Ling had paid her more than the agreed price. She blew kisses into the air and said a prayer for her generous friend. She quickly donned the new clothes and within a few moments her new disguise was complete. She stuffed the nurse's uniform into the hidden panel then hurried to the front door and checked the hall. Two residents were peering out of the window at the end of the hall both with their backs to her. She slipped out quietly and went down the back stairs. She crossed two streets and took a double decker just as she had been instructed. She blended perfectly with other passengers with one exception. She wore a smile that was positively beatific.

Raeford had also noticed the same man on the roof that Nicole had spotted. He immediately began working his way to that building. He was dressed like any casual Englishman walking his dog. The dog however was uncooperative and jerked and strained against the lead determined to go his own way. That maniac biker had caused a terrible ruckus but it turned out to be a mighty good thing because the dog finally jerked loose and chased the biker leaving Raeford free to run to the opposite side of the street and duck into the building as if he were escaping the pandemonium that was occurring near Geoffrey's eatery.

Once Raeford had entered the building he darted through the hall until he found the staircase and pounded up the eight flights as fast as he could. The roof access was closed, and locked from the outside. It only took one shot to break the lock but the door remained closed. He aimed a powerful kick at the door but it moved only slightly. When he rammed it with his shoulder whatever was blocking the door fell away and he pushed through from the dim stairwell to the bright sunlight of the open rooftop. He arrived just in time to hear the shot that fatally wounded the informant. He knew he was too late to save the targeted victim on the street below but he hoped to at least apprehend the shooter.

Raeford burst through the door just as the man's head vanished below the roofline. He was climbing down a metal maintenance ladder that was attached to the side of the building. He descended fast and at the sixth floor he climbed out on a ledge and sidestepped to an open window. Raeford heard a woman scream as the stranger climbed through the window into her flat.

Rafford was not far behind and followed the same route down the ladder, onto the ledge. The tall Texan focused all of his attention on careful side steps as he inched toward the open window never once looking down. As his long strong fingers felt along the cold concrete wall he took a long slow breath and reached a little further to the side. He felt the window frame and gripped it with nervous fingers then scrambled through the opening with a sigh of relief.

The woman was screaming again. Raeford ran through the flat glancing hurriedly into the rooms as he passed by open doors. A man screamed followed by a string of curses. Raeford ran toward the commotion and pushed through the kitchen door. He dropped to a crouch with his gun drawn, "Hold it, Police! Drop that…pot?" The screaming woman was spraying the killer's face with an aerosol can in one hand and she was hitting him with a cooking pot with the other. A large black cat with long fur clung to his leg scratching and biting. The criminal was trying to dodge the spray and the painful blows from the heavy pot while at the same time shake off the biting cat. "Well don't that beat everything I've ever seen!"

Raeford quickly took charge and handcuffed his suspect. He calmed the brave little woman then prepared to march his man downstairs and into custody. He was going to enjoy telling this story for many years to come.

Birdwell along with a dozen or so trained agents from Scotland Yard knew that they were facing a dangerous situation. The agents had spotted known mob members and those that they simply suspected of being mob members. What the agents had not expected was the large numbers of them. Mob activity is not unheard of in England but witnessing the gathering of so many was astounding. They knew that the informant would be closely watched during the sting operation and they were acutely aware of the danger he would face but the assassin on the roof was a surprise. Birdwell was angry and sick that the poor man was dead. Someone dressed as a Metropolitan Policeman had stolen the counterfeit money plate right out of the informant's hands and the pay off money disappeared with the bakery delivery boy. He groaned inwardly as he realized it would seem that an internal investigation would soon follow this terrible fiasco. He couldn't bear to think about a leak amongst his trusted men.

Birdwell felt his blood pressure hit the sky-high mark as he thought about that bloody mad biker. It certainly put a new spin on things but in the end it worked in their favor. When the kid in the delivery truck drove off, some of the mob members gave chase and started firing at him even with all of those innocent people around in broad daylight. The undercover cars also gave chase but the mad biker changed all of that. Due to his interference the cars had all collided so the rest of the chase occurred on foot.

Birdwell was winded and sweating from climbing over twisted broken cars but at the same time he was exhilarated. Some of the bad guys had been chased down or had been so banged up in the collisions that they couldn't move fast enough to get away. One of his men had sustained a shoulder wound, and another a severely bruised ankle, but other than their informant that was the worst of it. He was disappointed that the delivery truck got away and if it turned out to be that bugger Ace on the motorbike, he wanted to have a serious talk with him.

* * *

Abigail, dressed as the delivery boy, maintained her cool nonchalance as she drove calmly to Geoffry's Fish Market. She trusted Nicole to follow her instructions. She just had a good feeling about her.

Thomas Twining was standing in front of the market with his yellow kerchief as planned. Abigail did *not* have a good feeling about *him*. In fact she felt as if the whole street had eyes and ears watching her. Thomas showed her the money inside the briefcase. It looked like the million pounds she asked for. There was no time to stop and count it.

Her uniform cap was pulled down and her eyes were covered with dark glasses. She had padded the shoulders of her jacket and she wore a short brown wig that easily resembled the shaggy cut of a young man. As long as no one looked too close or heard her speak she looked, for all the world, like a young deliveryman.

As soon as Twining showed her the money she pulled out a realistic looking toy gun and pointed it at him. She held up a white card printed with black letters that read 'HAND IT TO ME'. The moment the trade was completed she stowed the heavy briefcase, jumped behind the wheel and stomped the accelerator to the floor.

"Shit fire and bloody hell," she cursed as she saw cars pulling into the traffic behind her. Then one of the windows to her right exploded. "What the hell are ya bloody bastards trying to do, kill somebody?" She had not expected all of this commotion. She heard more loud pops and glass flew around her head as the rest of the windows were shot out. She was nearly to the corner. Several streets came together there making it a bad place for a lot of cars to try to turn quickly. She held her breath hoping she could make it to the turn and keep her little truck from turning over.

"What the bloody hell is going on now? Ace? Christ what are ya doing?" She was yelling at the rearview mirror as she watched the familiar motorbike weaving through the traffic and bump up onto the sidewalk behind her. As she approached the corner she saw Ace pulling in front of cars and then of course came the crunch of metal. She yanked on the wheel and screeched around the corner. She drove madly for two blocks and turned again. At last she was headed straight for the outskirts of the city.

She located the abandoned building where she had hidden her rental car. A slow London drizzle morphed into a full out downpour and the dirt turn out was suddenly a mud hole. The little truck skidded but didn't flip. She corrected toward the slide and straightened it out. Her heart had already been racing with adrenaline but this near miss was almost too much. She was shaking badly when she finally pulled in behind the building out of sight of the main road. She leaped out of the truck and shoved the large metal doors open then drove the truck inside and slammed on the brakes near the rental car she had hidden there.

Rain was coming down in torrents as Ace slowed to make the turn to the old storage building. The motorbike began a slow slide much as Abbie's little truck had done just a short time before. No matter how he tried to right it the bike was out of control. He hit a rock and the bike skidded sideways out from under him and crashed against another vacant building. He landed on something hard and a bone snapped in his left arm.

Abigail scooped her money out of the briefcase and stuffed it into the hidden panels of two suitcases she had prepared for the occasion. She cringed at the sound of the crashing motorbike but she didn't dare stop or slow down. Time was slipping away and she was not sure if that biker was Ace or someone else. She had to be in her new disguise and ready to talk her way out of whatever or whoever had followed her. She slipped out of her delivery boy clothes and began putting on the business suit. She would be a serene professional woman returning from a business conference. Abigail was not sure she could ever feel serene again though and something hurt. She really did not feel good at all.

"Well, well," the deep male voice came from the doorway startling her severely "What have you done with the lovely Soo Ling?"

"I don't know what you're talking about I don't."

"Don't even think about it," his voice snapped out like a whiplash. "My mood isn't exactly *sunny* at the moment," the word sunny was gritted out through clenched teeth.

"I've just ridden through a massive wreck of cars, been shot at, chased by the armed police, rained on, crashed my bike and my arm is broken!" His voice rose with each word and now dropped down to an ominous whisper, "Don't even try to bloody lie to me right now or I'll wring that slender little...." he stopped whispering and put his good hand up to her throat then trailed a finger down the front of her unbuttoned blouse.

"Bloody hell!" His eyes opened wide "Yer bleedin everywhere."

"I think a bullet caught me," she whispered as her eyes rolled up in her head.

"What happened?" Abigail opened her eyes. Her shoulder burned. The small cuts from the flying glass had been cleaned and bandaged. Her gray jacket and white blouse were gone. A soft white blanket covered her and the lights were turned low.

"Well, back from the dark are ya," the voice came from a round-faced man with thick white hair. "You'll be fine dearie. Bullet just grazed your shoulder. You lost a good bit of blood though so don't try to sit up too fast. You'll be a might dizzy I'm thinkin'."

She sat up slowly and he propped pillows behind her back. He turned and reached for a glass of water. She drank it greedily as she suddenly realized her mouth was so dry she could hardly swallow. "Thank you. What is that smell?"

"Oh," he chuckled, "that's the little woman's chicken soup. Here you should try to eat a little."

Abigail was not sure her stomach could hold anything, but after the first sip she knew she was ravenous and she ate until the bowl was empty.

"That was a rare treat. Thank you. Now please tell me where in the bloody hell am I?"

"This is my house, Doc Kelly at your service. I am a horse doctor to be exact, mostly retired but still enough juice to fix up a fine filly such as yourself." His eyes crinkled with a smile that lit up his entire face.

Then it all came back to her in a rush. "Oh no! My car, my my clothes..."

"Everything is fine. Including yer friend. He got you here driving with a broken arm. Said you'd both been in some kind of freaky accident."

"Uh yes that's right. Where is he?" she asked tentatively.

"Oh he's asleep in the next room. Gave him a sedative so's I could set the bones. He'll be up and about soon too."

Doctor Kelly's wife brought in her clothes. "Oh that is so kind of you," Abbie smiled. The blood was gone and they had been washed and pressed. After a brief exchange Mrs Kelly left the room. Abigail began pulling on her clothes grimacing in pain with every move. She noticed that darkness had fallen but she had no idea of the time. The cozy home was softly glowing with light from several unique lamps placed at tasteful intervals around the room. If circumstances had been different she would have enjoyed spending an evening with the owners of this comfortable home. She was worried about being able to make her flight. She noticed a clock on the mantle and sighed with relief. If she had no more incidents then she might still be able to catch her plane.

Dr. Kelly and his wife were watching a noisy game show on the telly so Abigail slipped out of the first door she found and looked for her rental car. She spied it parked in the driveway to the left of the house. Someone had found Ace's motorbike! It was parked on the other side of her car. She walked quietly around the bike then looked through the windows of her car. The keys were in it! She grabbed the keys and opened the boot. Her suitcases were still locked in it! She slid behind the wheel, started the motor and eased the car forward without turning on the headlights. It was only a short distance to the main road and once there, she got her bearings and turned toward London. When she arrived at her hotel she tipped the bellman generously for carrying the heavy bags to her room but she made sure they were never out of her sight.

The luggage she planned to take with her was already packed with the new clothes she bought for the trip. She had hidden stacks of American money in the lining and had wrapped some of them as if they were gifts complete with nametags and ribbons.

The front desk was very accommodating when she asked them to mail several packages to her *sister* staying at the Woodward hotel in New York. She also wired a rather large sum of money to the same address…for her *sister* of course, her non-existant sister. Everyone was given nice tips and gracious smiles as they again carried her luggage out to the waiting shuttle. She had thrown her gray suit in the trash bin and was in a comfortable black skirt and jacket.

The airport was still bustling when she arrived despite the late hour. She paid an attendant to check her bags and another to give her a ride to her gate. The last of the passengers were disappearing into the plane just as the cart pulled up.

She didn't want to bring too much attention to herself but she had chosen to fly first class. Now she was supremely happy that she had made that choice as she settled into her large comfortable seat with a sigh of absolute relief. The stewardess appeared immediately asking what she would like to drink.

"The strongest thing you have please." The attractive woman smiled and returned with an acceptable Scotch. "Thanks. No water or ice." She drank the golden liquid in two gulps. "One more please." After the fiery descent of the second drink she began to really relax.

The airplane taxied into position and sat poised for flight. Within moments the engines revved and her body was forced back against the seat as the powerful jet lifted off and the landing gear lurched into place. The lights of London faded into the cloud cover as they climbed. She wrapped the airline blanket around her body and leaned her head against the small pillow so she could watch the night as they flew. She was wearing heavy makeup to cover the many small cuts she had sustained during that afternoon and she was careful not to rub her face. Those would heal in time.

She was saying good-by to the land of her birth, maybe forever. Her eyes filled with tears for the first time since…well she couldn't remember the last time she allowed herself to cry. It felt rather good in a way so she just let it happen. She would miss some of her favorite places like the Fitzroy Tavern, Covent Garden, shopping at Camden Market, tea at the Ritz and the Piccadilly Circus she had enjoyed as a child. Just before she drifted off to sleep she wondered what Doc Kelly would think about the wad of bills she had stuffed between the screen door and entry door. She hoped that the money she put under the seat of Ace's bike would be enough to fix it or maybe help him buy a new one. Doc Kelly must have driven back to the storage buildings and hauled the bike in his old truck. At the thought of Ace she felt her stomach clench. He had saved her life. God he was hot. She was going to miss him.

CHAPTER NINE

Courtney and her mother were up early but when they entered the kitchen, Hattie was already dressed and busy. The coffee was ready and there were delicate glass bowls filled with fresh fruit, a plate of warm buttered toast and a dish filled with Hattie's homemade strawberry preserves. She sang as she served their breakfast. Her choir was going to be performing at the revival and choir competition in Myrtle Beach in August so she was using every spare minute to practice much to the delight of all who were in the vicinity of her amazing voice.

Clarisa drove and Courtney directed her to the studio where she had been teaching classes. There were no workshops being conducted at that time leaving the dance studio eerily dark and still. Courtney conducted her mother on a guided tour through the classrooms and office area. She became quite animated while explaining some of the plans they had for future performances and fund raising projects. Clarisa felt her daughter's excitement and noticed the sparkle in her eyes as she spoke with pride about her work with the company.

"Darlin' do you think you're going to stay here indefinitely?" Her tone was wistful and somewhat sad. She pretty much knew the answer without asking.

"You know Mom I haven't thought about my long term goals yet. I do know that after all of... after Antonio, I'm just not ready to go back to California yet. I'm finding myself here. Things don't remind me of *him* here. I want to get to know my sister. Those are the things I know. I'm just trying to live each day and find happiness in it." She stopped abruptly as her throat tightened with unexpressed sobs.

"I understand honey. I only want you to be happy and safe. I just...I will miss you so much!" Clarisa too shed tears a she embraced her daughter. "Now come along and let's shop!"

They climbed back into the car and headed to the nearest dress shop.

By noon Clarisa had purchased two evening gowns for herself and a beautiful black cocktail dress for Courtney. She insisted on buying earrings, shoes and evening bags for them both.

They drove to Market Street for lunch and tall refreshing glasses of sweet tea. They joked and talked, reminiscing about past shopping trips. Each felt closer to the other and once again reestablished the mother-daughter bond that had always been there.

Courtney suggested that they drive to the waterfront park and have some ice cream. The breezes from the water were pleasant and almost cool as they sat in the shade licking their ice cream cones.

Clarisa remembered the little girl that Courtney once was but she saw her now as the young woman she had become. The experience with Antonio and her subsequent move to Charleston, South Carolina had changed her deeply. Her young carefree daughter was no more. In her place a beautiful, mature young woman had sprung up before her eyes.

"Well my dear we haven't bought out all of the stores yet. We have a large task to perform. Now I can see you starting to object..." Courtney had in fact frowned and was going to admonish her mother for spending so much on the glittering cocktail dress and matching accessories. "Spending money on you is such a joy darlin' please don't deprive me of my fun. Besides I am going to find things for myself as well," Clarisa grinned with mischief. "Your father needs to see me in some new lingerie. I don't want him to think he should trade me in for a newer model."

"Mom, I think that is more than I need to know right now, but if you're interested in lingerie I think I know the perfect place to go."

Clarisa found some beautiful black and pink lace lingerie that she knew would put a smile on her husband's face. They moved on then to silk knit pullovers with pearls and delicately embroidered trim. They each found a three-piece summer suit and strappy little high heels that matched everything.

When they passed an art supply store mother and daughter looked at each other and nodded in silent agreement. They entered and spoke with the young man behind the counter. After they explained their special needs he guided them through their purchases. He kindly assured them that if anything wasn't right they could bring it back for a full refund or exchange. They bought brushes and paints both water color and acrylic. They found a sturdy easel worthy of any great artist. They also bought an adjustable drawing table, pens, charcoal and colored pencils. There were containers for cleaning brushes, canvases, a drawing tablet and a pallet for mixing colors. They even found a smock, which would protect the artist's clothing from stray splatters.

"I want to buy C.C. some clothes and shoes too," Clarisa stated authoritatively. "She seems to be your size. I would like to buy her a few things for the weekend, maybe a little robe, nightie and some shorts and tops to start with. Then I think we should take her shoppin' for the rest. What do you think Honey?"

"That sounds wonderful, Mom...but..."

"No buts now. What's wrong with taking her shoppin'?"

"Nothing is wrong with it Mom, it's just that she hasn't been out much that I know of. Dr. Baylor told me that she has had some screaming fits from time to time. I just don't know how she'll handle everything yet."

"Oh yes of course Darlin'. I'm sorry I forgot. I just got a little carried away with my shoppin' madness. I don't know though, she is a girl. Surely there is a place somewhere inside of her that would love some new clothes." Clarisa raised her eyebrow and winked. Courtney had to laugh at that.

Clarisa's rental car was loaded with bags and boxes, art supplies, clothes, cosmetics, kitchen gadgets for Hattie and an array of delicate satin bed jackets in soft cream, peach and pinks for the ailing matriarch, Esther Camden. She pulled into the parking lot of the medical facility late in the afternoon. They found Esther's gifts amongst all of their packages and carried them up to her room. Esther was not there when they arrived.

"Oh my God, I wonder what has happened," Clarisa breathed as fear clutched at her heart.

"Let's go ask at the nurse's station, Mom," Courtney spoke in sure firm tones, calming her mother's initial panic.

They put their bags down and hurried into the hall to find someone to ask. There was no one at the desk when they arrived so they waited in fidgety silence until a nurse came out of a nearby room. Both of them started talking at once until the poor woman held up her hands in self-defense. "Wait, wait you are the family of Miz Camden?" Both Clarisa and Courtney did not like the way that sounded and it must have shone on their faces. "No, everything is fine," the nurse assured them. Clarisa let out a breath and put her hand on her chest in relief. "She got up today and went to the solarium," the nurse continued.

Clarisa was thunderstruck. Her mother was basically paralyzed. How could she get up?

"Oh here she comes." The nurse spoke cheerily and pointed behind Clarisa and Courtney. They turned, not knowing what they would see.

Esther sat straight-backed in a wheelchair. She was frowning and gesturing with a clawed hand toward her family. She mumbled gibberish and drool dripped from one side of her mouth. The orderly that pushed her chair laughed and seemed to understand exactly what she wanted. He pushed her right up to where Courtney stood with her mother.

"Miz Camden and I have had a nice little stroll. Hi, my name is Howard. You her family?" Howard was five feet ten inches tall with a powerful stocky body. He looked enormous beside the tiny frail woman in the chair.

"Yes, I'm her daughter Clarisa and this is her granddaughter Courtney."

"Glad to meet you both. She is a little tired now so I'm going to get her back to bed and ready for supper. I'll let you know when she's ready for company."

Esther was leaning back against a mound of white pillows when Clarisa and Courtney entered her room. Her cheeks had a pink tinge and her eyes were bright. Courtney hurried to one side of the bed and pecked her cheek with a light kiss. Clarisa did the same on the other side.

"Mother you look wonderful today!" Esther responded with a very slurred and sputtering, but unmistakable, "Thank you."

"We've been shopping, Mother and bought you some presents," Clarisa sing songed lightly. There was no mistaking the delight in Esther's eyes. For a few seconds there was an exchange of love between the three women without a word being spoken.

Clarisa got out the bed jackets and Esther indicated which one she wanted to try first by moving one hand to touch it. They gently worked to get Esther's arms through the sleeves then settled her back against the pillows.

Delicious smells began to permeate the air. Soon an aide brought in a tray and set it up over the bed.

Clarisa and Courtney kept up their pleasant banter throughout Esther's effort to eat. It was painful to see the elegant little woman struggling with food. Clarisa fed her but also encouraged her to try to hold the spoon herself. She was unable to work her hands yet so the nurse had strapped on a fabric device held together with Velcro. The spoon handle fit in a small narrow pouch. This enabled her to raise and lower the spoon while she relearned how to feed herself. She even succeeded in taking a few bites of applesauce. She choked repeatedly and food often dripped from the side of her mouth. Finally she could eat no more and held her mouth tightly shut when Clarisa held the spoon near her lips.

Courtney felt strange washing her grandmother's mouth and hands with a warm cloth. When it was finished, she scooted a chair near the hospital bed and took her grandmother's rigid cool hand and held it between her strong, warm young ones.

"Courtney I'm goin' to the powder room. You and your grandmother might like some time alone." Courtney nodded and smiled.

Esther's eyes followed her daughter as she walked around the bed and out of the door. Then her eyes locked onto Courtney. For a moment they just looked at each other in silence. Then Courtney spoke. "Grandmother I want you to feel something." She then closed her eyes and called upon the healing energies that she used on herself after being badly injured by Antonio.

Though her eyes were closed, she could see a beautiful brightness coming from above her head. The energy flowed down like a gentle waterfall and poured through her body, through her arms and hands and into Esther. After a few minutes Courtney's vision opened and she could see where great damage had been done to muscle, nerves, organs and the brain. She made no judgments but simply allowed the energy to flow where it wanted to go.

Courtney had no idea how much time had passed since she had first let the energy flow into her grandmother. She felt a subtle change in the tension of the contracted muscles of the ailing woman's hand. It seemed to relax and two of the fingers twitched. When Courtney opened her eyes, the first thing she saw were the fingers of Esther's hand relaxing and straightening out. She looked up to her grandmother's face. She was smiling with one side of her mouth.

"Grandmother, I am so happy to see you smile. I know you felt the energy. This is something I can do. It's a gift. I want to use this gift to help people. This healing energy and my gift of visions helped me to find my sister. She has gifts too. I am going to bring her to your house this weekend because I want to get acquainted with her. I believe that she and I will work together to help others." Courtney spoke in short direct sentences, hoping that Esther could clearly understand what she was trying to convey.

"I know that you were given the past life vision where all of this started. We all need to heal our souls from those mistakes so that we can continue on in good works, happiness and harmony. I love you and I want you to heal up quickly so that we can get to really know each other. It's time for us to get busy with the work we were meant to do." Tears welled in Esther's eyes and spilled down the pale thin skin of her cheeks. "I'll be back soon to see you."

Clarisa was just coming back to the room as Courtney was leaving. "It took me longer than I thought. I ran into Mavis an old friend from high school. She was always a talker and bless her heart, she just hasn't changed much. She looks wonderful and it sounds like she is doing *so* well. She's here with her father. He just had a heart attack but he's out of danger now and recovering nicely. How is Mother?"

"Mavis isn't the only one that can talk when she wants to," Courtney smiled "Grandmother is doing just fine, she was dozing off when I left."

"Okay dear, why don't I just grab my pocket book and we can go home and stash our loot!" Clarisa's eyes were brighter than Courtney had seen them in a long while.

Hattie appeared at the kitchen door as soon as they pulled up. She saw their bright smiles and sensed the closeness that they had reestablished. Then she spotted the bags in the back seat of the car and her eyes widened. When Clarisa pushed the trunk release it slowly opened to reveal even more purchases.

"Lord have mercy! Have you all brought home the whole town of Charleston? I don't believe there will be a single thing left for anyone else to buy! Here now let me help with all that." Hattie scooped up as many bags as possible and headed for the door. "We should take everything to the living room near the front stairway," she called back over her shoulder.

The women were tired and perspiring when they were finally finished carrying everything inside. They gazed with satisfied smiles at the bags and boxes stacked on the beautiful wood floor along with the new easel and drawing table.

"Now Hattie these bags are for you," Clarisa noisily rattled bags as she dug through a few of them until she found what she was looking for.

"Well my goodness, for me?" Hattie was utterly astonished that she was receiving gifts too. Her eyes grew large as she discovered three beautiful scented candles, incense and a colorful woven mat, scented soap and body lotion. She made clucking sounds as she pulled out a new garlic press, an apple slicer and a strawberry stem picker. There were colorful new potholders and a beautiful apron with ruffles around the bottom. Hattie grinned from ear to ear.

"Here is another one Hattie," Clarisa beamed. She had chosen three pastel nightgowns and a matching bathrobe and slippers. She then presented Hattie with a gift certificate for the lingerie store just in case she needed some new dainties. The last box was a small one containing a silver charm bracelet. Small hearts, stars and angels dangled from the wide looped chain.

""Miz Clarisa, this is too much. There was no need for you to go and do all this," Hattie's eyes were big and she kept shaking her head in disbelief.

"There was a need Hattie. You have worked here since I was a young girl. You have been a loyal and loving family member for me, my mother, my daughter," her voice broke "I don't really know what any of us would have done without you during the good times and bad. I wanted...needed...to say thank you in this small way. You have been our Angel."

Clarisa went into Hattie's open arms. They both sobbed for a moment. When they pulled back, both started laughing. Courtney's heart was deeply touched and she spontaneously joined the giggles with tears in her own eyes. She didn't know exactly what had transpired on a very deep level, she only knew that it felt right.

Storm Cat purred near her ear as she lay in the darkness that night. She thought of the day she had spent with her mother. She was so happy to have those warm close feelings with her. She thought about their spending spree. Her mother and father had always been generous with her but it was different today. Some sort of wall had crumbled inside of her mother. Warmth and joy had just spilled out everywhere. She puzzled over it for a few minutes and then her thoughts turned to her new clothes and the shimmering black dress. Well she had no idea where she would wear it, but it was fun to look at it.

Courtney awoke to the phone ringing downstairs. She could hear female voices then she drifted off to sleep again. She could hear the telephone ringing again, more voices. It must have been very early because the sun was just pushing its light through her window. The ringing started again. She decided to get up and see what all of the commotion was about. Within fifteen minutes she had showered, brushed her teeth and pulled on a pair of white shorts and a top decorated with embroidered flowers in a rainbow of colors. She slipped into a pair of tan sandals and started downstairs.

"Oh darlin' I hope we didn't disturb you," Clarisa was dressed in a pale yellow skirt and white blouse. She looked and sounded lively and happy.

"No problem, Mom. I heard the telephone ringing and I wondered if everything was all right."

Hattie motioned for Courtney to sit down at the island. She poured coffee and then pranced back to the counter for a plate of cinnamon buns and sliced melon. She did a little twirl before she set the plates down. Then she put a hand on her hip and another to the back of her head in a sassy pose.

"Wow. Your robe and nightie look great on you Hattie!" Courtney smiled.

"Why thank you ma'am. I do feel like Miz Gotrocks today." Hattie grinned and sashayed to her own stool and cup of coffee.

"The hospital called to say that your grandmother is much better today. She is miraculously able to move the fingers on her right hand. But that's not all," she held up her finger as Courtney started to comment, "the next phone call was from mother herself. I don't know if she could possibly have dialed the number herself or if someone helped her, but even more than that she spoke clearly enough for me to understand her." Clarisa's smile was radiant, though her eyes filled with tears.

"What did she say, Mom?"

"She said she wanted her gardening gloves." There was a moment of silence then the three of them burst out laughing. They were laughing in relief and joy not to mention Esther's little joke. They all understood what she meant. Many cut flowers as well as potted plants adorned Esther's hospital room. Whenever she received potted plants as a gift or purchased some from a nursery she always had the right place to plant them in her vast and beautiful gardens at Willows. She wore out her gardening gloves constantly and just as often misplaced them. So her comment about them was a message to everyone that she felt good and was ready to come home and put her plants in the ground.

Esther lay back against her pillows with a long sigh. Something remarkable had been happening to her. She remembered her fall into the river; the strong arms that pulled her out, then things got fuzzy. There had been terrible pain somewhere, maybe in her head and chest, then darkness.

It was the strangest experience of her life. Her brain worked...sort of. She knew people and the sounds they made. She knew she could make those sounds too but try as she would she simply could not control her mouth or her thoughts. It was so frustrating and so frightening. She felt as though aliens surrounded her; or maybe she was the alien. She had never felt so alone in all of her life.

The passage of time had no meaning to her. People came and went. Delivery people brought flowers. Sometimes she wondered if she had died. It certainly did not seem like heaven. She was not sure she deserved heaven but then this place didn't look like any hell that she knew about either.

Eventually her mind had cleared and she saw Clarisa's face leaning close with tears seeping constantly from her eyes. Beautiful Clarisa, she wanted to tell her things. She wanted to brush away those tears. Why hadn't she been kinder to her daughter she wondered. Clarisa loved her. Here she was leaning close and she could actually feel the love pouring off of her daughter in such a tangible force, she could almost reach up and touch it. But her body would not let her do that. It felt like a heavy marshmallow.

Then that woman with the outlandish cape came to visit. Esther wondered where she did her shopping. The poor woman was a little too pushy and that scanty clothing was a bit over the top for Charleston society. That movie she brought or was it a dream, she just could not decide. No matter, she told herself, she understood the message that she was given. She must not give up. Esther knew that she was going to work hard to get well. She wanted to walk through her gardens and visit with her friends. She wanted to speak with her granddaughter. That child must be an angel incarnate. Never had she felt anything so wonderful as the power that came through her delicate hands.

Esther closed her eyes and remembered the sensations as her mind actually cleared. She could feel the thick webs of confusion falling away. It was like the sun peeking through the haze of a cloudy day. Then the miracle happened. Her hand rose easily the air and she had watched with wonder as her fingers moved independently. Tears spilled once again.

A nurse walked in as Esther was looking at her fingers. "Well just look at you! You are doing so well. I think we are going to be able to move you to a nice convalescent hospital very soon."

Within the next two days it was decided and arranged that Esther would be moved to a private facility with an excellent reputation for having the best therapy for stroke and cardiac victims.

Clarisa, Courtney and Hattie were impressed with the outside of the building. It looked more like a private residence than a medical facility. The ambulance carrying Esther arrived just before noon. The medical technicians were young and strong. They handled the gurney with expert ease. One of the men continually looked at Courtney and did everything he could think of to strike up a conversation with her.

Courtney was flustered by the young man's attention. She spoke politely to him and answered his questions. Oddly though she found herself comparing him to Dr. Baylor. She decided she would much prefer some attention from *him*. This thought too surprised her. Since her terrible experience with Antonio she had no desire or thought of having a relationship with any man. Until now she had thought there would be nothing like that in her future. She still wasn't thinking of a man in her future, just some nice conversations with the interesting doctor.

CHAPTER TEN

Latoia fretted over what to wear for her interview the next day. Finally she abandoned her everyday wardrobe and pulled out a box marked DANCE, printed with a thick black felt marker. She opened the box and began to search through the contents holding up one thing and then another, considering it for a moment then tossing it aside.

She knew that an opportunity like this was a once-in-your-life opportunity. After all most of the hottest models and agencies were in New York. She supposed she would move to New York anyway before long. Just imagine if they liked her, she grinned as the thought lit up her imagination. What if she actually got the job! She just *had* to get this job. Her heart began to race at the thought of changing her life so drastically.

She jabbed her hand down into the mound of leotards, tights, chiffon and sequins. Her fingers found something soft and she brought up a bit of black velvet. It was a scanty little off-the shoulder top bordered with gaudy gold sequins that had seen better days. It was then that the ideas began to flood in.

In a matter of minutes the shabby sequin trim lay in sparkling disarray on the floor. She found some matching French cut briefs. They hid her navel but were cut high on the thigh making her already long legs look even longer, hmm not bad. Her chest size had increased since she had last worn that costume but come to think of it, the snug fit didn't hurt the look at all.

She went through another frenzy of throwing bright costumes from the box into a colorful pile on the floor until she found a piece of shimmery sheer black Georgette. Perfect. Originally it had been a handkerchief skirt. She put it over her head and let the skirt waist drape gracefully around her shoulders. She found her sewing kit and went to work. She created a plunging neckline and the rest floated over her arms like wings. She found her three inch black stilettos and slipped them on. Then she rose and stood in front of the mirror. She turned to the side and looked at her profile. Not bad.

She had a good feeling about this job. If she was ever going to get the *big break* it had to be now or at least very soon. She was already twenty-one. The clock was ticking. She tried some sultry expressions in the mirror. No, no good. She flung her arms around causing the fabric to float out from her body. Getting better. Still not right. She spun into a soutenou turn finishing in a contraction with bent knees, pulling in her abdominal muscles and slightly rounding her back. Then slowly she straightened her legs, pushed her hips forward and arched her back. Both of her arms were extended in back allowing the fabric to flow out simulating wings. She arched her flexible back even more and brought her left arm in front and kept the right arm in back. Then she turned her head toward the mirror with her chin tilted up and a dreamy expression on her face.

She was almost startled to see her reflection. This could be it. Her heart pounded. This could really be it. She lifted her right leg to the back in an arabesque. She had always been complimented on the lines of her arabesque. Very slowly and carefully she bent her torso forward as her leg rose higher in back. She studied her reflection in the mirror and decided that indeed her penche' arabesque looked as good as ever. Yes, this could be it!

The next morning Latoia's stomach was tied in knots. She forced down some yogurt and a granola bar and went to work on her makeup and hair. She decided on a clean sleek look with maybe a little tendril of black hair twisting into a soft curl on either side of her face.

She applied a thin coating of base makeup and accented her high cheekbones with a light bronze. False eyelashes would dramatize her large dark eyes and would look good if they were not too long.

Hours slipped away. She was finally dressed, coifed and made up. She went to the full-length mirror to peruse the finished product. She practiced her pose and expression. It was good. Well anyway it was as good as she knew how to create it. "Wow, you know God, if you gave me this body and these looks I can't go wrong. Thank you. Please help me to do my best and accept their decision with grace, amen." She never forgot to begin any job with a little prayer of thanks. She had suffered poverty, life without a father and the death of her twin brother and a close call with those wretched people in Vegas. Latoia was sure it was time for some good things to happen. She was pretty sure that living through all of that meant there was some real purpose for her life.

The Beverly Hills address was easy to find and she arrived with ten minutes to spare. She managed to find a parking place on the street, which was nothing short of a miracle. She had an aversion to parking decks ever since her narrow escape in Las Vegas. Thank goodness for Courtney's little white VW Rabbit convertible. It was so easy to maneuver.

Five minutes later she was on the seventh floor facing the closed door of Suite seven-o-nine. She had her resume and headshots in a small zippered briefcase. Her hands were shaking. Time to breathe deeply and calm down.

The woman sitting behind the reception desk barely looked up as Latoia entered.

"Please be seated. He will see you in a moment." The woman spoke sternly as she briefly glanced over the top of her glasses and frowned.

Latoia's spirits plummeted. She probably looked ridiculous wearing a cover up over the costume she had thrown together. She took a deep breath and sat down. *She felt like a giraffe. Her neck was too long and so were her legs. Why did she think she could ever get a job of this magnitude.*

"He will see you now," the woman got up and opened the door to *his* office.

Latoia stood up and walked to the door. She towered over the small receptionist as she walked past her into the office.

She licked her lips and gulped. "Good afternoon sir. Thank you for seeing me." Latoia held out her hand. It seemed to startle the short balding gentleman that sat behind the enormous mahogany desk. He did take her hand though. She was almost sorry that he did. His hand was fleshy and damp. Latoia had to fight back the urge to wipe her hand on the black and white cotton dress that she was wearing over her makeshift costume.

"Resume? Headshots?" He was a man of few words.

He gestured toward a chair and she sat down while he studied the portfolio she handed him. There was no sound in the room except the rustling of paper as he shuffled them and then a small squeak in his chair as he leaned back. Latoia couldn't help thinking about how small he looked behind that huge desk.

Finally he looked up and said, "Hmmm," with his chin propped on a stubby fingered fist.

"I uh took the liberty of creating a possible look, if you would like to see it," Latoia prayed her voice didn't shake too much. She was sure that it sounded high and nasal in the tense silence. *Good thing she wasn't trying to get a speaking part.* His only answer was a silent nod.

She stood up and with shaking hands fumbled with the clasp on her cover up until she finally managed to unfasten it. She awkwardly shrugged out of it and let the fabric slide to the floor. She tried to step out of the discarded fabric and caught her spiked heel in one of the mounds of soft cloth. Finally she managed to free her shoe and backed away from the desk. She took a deep steadying breath and began the turn she had practiced, ending in a contraction. Then in a long sensous move she straightened and arched back thrusting her arms behind her and tilted her head up. Then she brought one arm forward and smoothly turned her head toward him, lifted her eyelids and chin just as she had in front of the mirror at home. She continued the fluid motion into an arabesque tilting her body and head back until she appeared to be folded in half.

His sharp intake of breath was quiet, but she heard it. She knew or at least thought she knew, that the man was impressed.

"Uh huh," was all he said. He cleared his throat and looked at the head shots once more. "You will leave these with me," it was a statement rather than a question. "Thank you. I'll be in touch." He gave a little nod and gestured toward the door.

Latoia shrugged into her cover-up, picked up her briefcase and shoulder bag. "Thank you sir."

She was so happy to be back in her little car. She just sat for a moment gathering her wits together as she tried to stop shaking. She was not sure she was cut out to go through these nerve-wracking auditions and interviews.

Stephanie had asked her to come by her office after the appointment so she pulled out in traffic and headed toward her agent's office. A car pulled out just as Latoia neared the building and one more time she had a parking place on the street, this had to be her lucky day and maybe a good omen, she hoped.

The office was located in a monstrous concrete structure that took up an entire block. Three buildings were connected by an imposing marble and glass entry with a security guard stationed at each of the three sets of elevators. Security could often be an issue here due to the high profile clients that sought out the services of the theatrical agents, law firms, publicists and even some studio executives.

Latoia pushed open the heavy glass door and went straight to the security desk of building A. She barely glanced at the guard who was intently watching his monitors.

"Afternoon," the guard glanced in her direction briefly before returning his watchful gaze to the black and white screens.

"Good afternoon," Latoia answered with a cheerful lilt to her voice, "Have you seen Stephanie Mills today?"

"Yes, Ma'am. Last I saw her she went into her office at about thirteen hundred hours. Sign in here if you're goin' up."

Latoia signed her name and smiled at the well-built man.

"How'd your interview go?" The guard asked.

"Interview? How'd you know I went to an interview?" Latoia was startled by his question. Did Stephanie know him well enough to talk about her clients?

"It's my job to be observant. You are most likely not going to a costume party. Normally when you come to see Ms. Mills you're dressed and made up in a more conservative manner." His tone was on the formal side. Latoia was reminded of someone with a military background.

"Of course, I had almost forgotten how I must look. I can't imagine how you are able to remember me or anyone else with so many people coming and going all day."

"It's my job and by the way I think you look just fine." He gave her a thin professional smile. His hazel eyes carried no warmth as they studied her without a blink as many silent seconds passed.

"Thank you…"

"Darmon." He pointed to his identification badge.

Latoia glanced at his badge and noted the company name as ProGuard Security with E. Darmon printed in plain block text underneath.

"Thank you uh, security officer Darmon. I appreciate the fact that you take your work seriously and that you are here to keep a watchful eye on everyone."

The stoic man's answer was a silent nod before he turned his attention once again to the monitors.

Latoia felt good. She really thought the interview had gone well. Her life was moving in a prosperous direction. The nightmarish Las Vegas experience was beginning to fade into the past and the sharp edged memories were blurring just a little. It was good to be alive.

She got off of the elevator on the fifth floor and turned to go down the hall toward Stephanie's door. A movement just above her head was startling. She saw a security camera slowly panning the hallway and another in a fixed position to monitor those using the elevator. She smiled thinking of the stiff officer Darmon. She gave a playful little wave to the camera before continuing to her destination.

When Latoia pushed open the door to her agent's tiny but elegant office, she saw Stephanie talking on the telephone. The woman smiled and beckoned her in, then put a finger to her lips in a shushing signal. Latoia folded her five feet ten inch body into a chair and crossed her legs while Stephanie quietly listened to someone on the other end of the telephone.

"Yes sir, you will not regret your decision. Thank you." Stephanie's face was set in a grave expression. She hung up the receiver and leaned back in her chair with a long sigh.

Latoia spoke first. "Well it's over. I lived through it. I don't know if I overdid it or not. I think the guy might have liked me at least a little bit, but I'm not absolutely sure. He is a man of few words." Latoia nibbled on her lower lip as she replayed the whole interview in her mind once again.

Stephanie marveled at the intense beauty of the young woman who sat so casually in her office. This girl had no idea what sort of impact she made on people. "What 're you wearing?" Stephanie frowned at the black and white cotton cover-up dress that Latoia wore. "Show and tell, now! What did you do and say during your interview?"

"Well it wasn't much of an interview, but this is what I did." Latoia unfastened the dress and it slid to the floor. She repeated the moves she had made earlier.

"Holy hot tamale, girl," Stephanie put her hand over her mouth.

"Oh no, not good hunh. Damn. I'm sorry. I just didn't know what to wear and I got this idea from some old dance costumes that I had...."

"Will you shut up!" Stephanie cut her off. "You just don't even know do you?"

The agent shook her blond curls. "You are the most devastatingly beautiful young woman I have ever seen. Your skin looks like chocolate satin. I love what you've done with your makeup and hair and the way you move... Oh and by the way he liked it too. In fact he wants you on a plane to New York by Thursday. He is going to have our tickets on my desk by tomorrow. You are to do the same thing you did today at their office and they will make the final decision next week." Stephanie's mouth twitched at the corners then spread across her face in a huge grin.

Latoia's jaw dropped as her agent spoke. Her legs felt shakey so she dropped into the nearest chair and tried to take in what her friend was saying. Her heart was racing but her mind had gone numb.

The former showgirl rose from her chair and danced around the desk until she stood directly in front of her young client. "Honey," she said in a whisper as she bent down to look into the dark pools of Latoia's eyes. "Let's go to The Posh Bar and order some champagne. You...are...on...your...way baby!" Her voice got louder with every word. She grabbed Latoia's hands and pulled her up for a hug. Latoia began to come out of her shocked silence and a giggle rippled out into the room. Then both of them started laughing and jumping and crying.

The Posh Bar wasn't crowded. Stephanie and Latoia shared a bottle of the house champagne and they ordered grilled salmon dinners. Then feeling very daring they ordered a rich slice of cheesecake drizzled with a chocolate liquor Grenache and two spoons.

"Now listen young lady, you had better not be eating like this every day. I don't want you to ruin that magnificent body with love handles and a belly pooch." Stephanie winked as she slid a piece of cheesecake into her mouth and closed her eyes in purest delight. She savored the flavor as long as she could and then swallowed. "On second thought, maybe I should just eat the whole thing so you won't have to even worry about gaining any weight."

"I don't think so. Don't even think about coming any closer to my share of this little slice of heaven. Anyway I have always had this huge appetite and I never seem to gain any weight." Latoia licked a drop of Grenache from her spoon and moaned with pleasure.

Stephanie glared at her, "I hate you."

"My mother too. She's tall and skinny just like me."

"I hate *her* too," Stephanie took another bite.

"Oh God, I can not eat another bite. Latoia leaned back in her chair and licked her lips. Her eyelids drooped shut as she tilted her head up. Suddenly she had a prickly feeling on the back of her neck. She glanced at the mirror tiles on the wall and noticed a lone figure at a table to her far left. The room was exceptionally dark as always so she only saw the glow of his cigarette and the outline of the man's head and shoulders.

"I think someone is staring at me Steph," Latoia leaned toward her friend and lowered her voice.

"Ha I'll bet they are. I think every man in this place has been staring at you ever since we came in here!" Stephanie laughed, "I guess you'd better get used to it. The *world* is going to be staring at you before long."

By the time Stephanie dropped Latoia off at her car, it was ten o'clock. The evening had flown by. She was feeling the effects of the let down as her adrenaline rush faded. She was exhausted as she turned toward Santa Monica. That little studio apartment was going to be a welcome sight.

Her eyes were drooping as she stopped at a red traffic light. "I need some caffeine!" she told herself. As soon as she saw a gas station she whipped her wheel to the right and pulled in without signaling. The driver of a red Porsche behind her honked angrily and screeched his wheels as he accelerated very fast. A trio of cars drove sedately past and continued on down the street.

"Probably shouldn't have had that champagne. My judgment is a little off," she muttered to herself. There was a soft drink machine in front of the Mini Mart. She deposited some coins, and selected a can of Pepsi. The cold bite of the bubbles helped to make her feel more alert. She got back in her car and pulled out into the line of traffic.

She had driven only a few blocks when she glanced into the rear view mirror and tried to keep a tally of the cars pulling into the lane behind her. She had that little prickly feeling on the back of her neck again. She decided that it was really time to get home but she couldn't shake the feeling that someone was watching her.

When she arrived at the city limits of Santa Monica, she turned toward the business center just in case her phobia of being followed was not imaginary. Several cars turned onto side streets but one car followed her. She knew that one car following her didn't mean there was anything to be afraid of but her heart pounded harder just the same. She drove three more blocks fighting off her growing terror and finally turned left toward the beach. The car was still behind her. Though lights from the businesses were bright she was unable to see neither the shadowed face of the driver nor the color of the car. She turned left again without using her turn signal and sped up as fast as traffic would allow.

Frantically she changed lanes weaving in and out in an effort to get away. She looked up just in time to see a traffic light turn red. She slammed on her brakes and at the same time accidentally killed the engine. She jammed her foot onto the clutch as her shaking hand fumbled with the ignition switch.

The front end of a dark car eased up on her left. She was near complete panic now as she tried and failed to start the motor over and over.

A tap on the window caused her to shriek.

"Whoa. Don' hurt me," the young man joked as he backed up with both hands in the air. "Joo having car trouble? I teenk joo jus' flood it. Whait jus' a minute an' hit will drain out. Then joo try to start it again. My brother and I will whait until joo start it hokay?"

Latoia nodded mutely. Tears were pooled in her eyes and she was panting. She could see that although the boys drove a dark colored sedan, it was far from being the sinister looking car that she thought was following her. Profound relief flooded through her as the young man climbed back in his car and cranked up the Mariachi music they had been listening to. She calmed herself by taking a few deep breaths then she tried the key again and the little VW purred to life.

The boys worked the hydraulics so that their car bounced a few times. They smiled and waved as they pulled away.

She looked around and still there was no sign of anyone following her. She drove straight home and even with a close watch on side streets and the traffic behind her there was no further visible threat real or imagined.

When she pulled into the driveway she locked the car and hurried to get inside locking the door behind her. She felt so grateful to be safe. She leaned against the closed door for a moment and then she felt a little sheepish after her bout of fear and over reacting to something that wasn't even there. She decided that her fear most likely stemmed from the terrible Vegas trip. She still had nightmares sometimes.

Then the realization hit her that she had heard some wonderful news just that afternoon and she was instantly filled with hope and joy once again. "Oh God I can't wait to tell Courtney," she said aloud. She decided that with the three-hour time difference she couldn't make the call tonight. It would have to wait until morning. It was just as well. The last bit of adrenaline was gone. She was limp with fatigue.

Latoia removed her makeup and stepped into the shower. The steamy hot water loosened the tight muscles in her neck and shoulders. That bed was going to feel good. She dried herself and brushed her teeth. Then she shook out an oversized cotton T-Shirt and pulled it over her head. She pulled back the covers and lay down. Lights out and she was nearly asleep before her head hit the pillow.

It was a cool night and a wind off of the ocean rustled the palm trees making a papery fluttering sound as a black four door sedan with tinted windows slipped noiselessly down the street. It pulled to a stop momentarily blocking the driveway where a white VW Rabbit convertible was parked. The glow of a cigarette was the only discernible shape within. The driver's window opened a crack and the cigarette was flipped out onto the street. Then the car moved forward smoothly accelerating until it reached the end of the block. Red brake lights glowed like the eyes of a night predator then disappeared as the car turned the corner.

It was a small house dwarfed by modern two story townhouse complexes on either side. The sturdy structure was built in the quaint style of the late nineteen fifties. Concrete steps led up to an expansive covered porch. The owner had refused multiple offers from developers claiming that the land was too valuable to remain undeveloped. Ezeikiel's father had built the house when he married his mother. His parents had never lived anywhere else since that time and Ezeikiel had grown up there and attended school in North Hollywood until he graduated from high school and joined the military.

He unlocked the front door and walked into the dark house. The sound of his hard-soled shoes striking the wood floors with the weight of his muscular one hundred ninety pound body echoed eerily. He flicked on a light in the sparsely furnished living room. Everything was still the same. The old sofa was faded and the cushions were sunken and thread bare. The television no longer worked but he had a new one in his bedroom upstairs.

The kitchen and small dining room were the same. He remembered his mother's excitement when the delivery truck brought the new table. It was scarred now. His father had pounded the knife into it over and over. He swallowed and walked quickly past the table where the imagined image of his father continued to drive the knife into the wood. He knew the image was only an imprint from the past but it never failed to unnerve him when he saw it. He just needed to get a glass of water to take upstairs with him. He was tired but he knew it was imperative for him to carry out his daily ritual.

There was no carpet on the wooden stairs, just like it was during his childhood. His father's steps had been loud and heavy as he brought his son a glass of water. He would send fear into the heart of his father now. He stomped hard up the steps relishing the thought that the old man would be the one shaking and crying just like he did as a child and his mother too!

When he got to the top of the stairs he stopped in front of the first closed door and banged it open. He strode into the room and then pounded his feet on the floor as he approached the bed he had once occupied as a child. He yanked back the bed covers and threw the icy water into the face of his father. Now it was time to light a cigarette and then he would be ready to begin the lecture.

The still figure in the bed never flinched as the cold water was thrown into his face night after night. When the cigarettes burned round black scars into his skin he never struggled or screamed as his son had. No, in fact he had not moved or breathed for twenty years. The man was dead.

Ezekiel felt some relief now as he walked down the hall to his parents bedroom. It was *his* room now. He reached to turn on a lamp and the room was bathed in a soft light. Everything was the same except the pictures on the wall and the clothes in the closet all of which now belonged to him.

There were pictures of his father in his uniform and another picture beside that one of his parents smiling happily at each other on their wedding day. His mother had been so beautiful then and he needed that picture to remind him of her beautiful smile. The only picture of her in his mind was the last time he saw her, as she lay on the stairs dead. Her beautiful face was battered and bloody after his father had beaten her and pushed her down the steps. He had wanted to keep her and take care of her but *they* insisted that she had to be taken from him and put into the hearse. He had no memory of the funeral or the graveside service; his mind had been too traumatized to accept her death. His father claimed an intruder killed her and the police couldn't prove otherwise so he was never arrested. Ezekiel couldn't prove it either since he didn't see it happen; but he knew in the deepest reaches of his heart that the old man was guilty.

He pulled open a drawer and slowly, reverently brought out the picture he cherished the most. It had been taken at the pier in Redondo Beach. Martita was always smiling. Her jet-black hair was pulled tightly back from her face showing off her exquisite cheekbones and dark features. She had inherited the best of her mixed Latin and African ancestors.

They met while he was on leave in San Diego where he was stationed. In a wild flurry of Tequila soaked days and nights filled with making love, they had impulsively slipped into Tijuana and got married.

They had been so happy for the first three months. She was pregnant with his child and she wanted to meet his father.

His head started to pound so hard he felt sick as the memories flooded back. He held the old picture of Martita up near his new pictures. Yes he was sure she was the one. Martita had come back. The pictures were so alike and she had the same smile. She even waved at him today. He was sure she was starting to remember who she was and that she belonged only to him. He was certain this girl was finally going to be his beautiful Martita.

Latoia awoke with a smile on her face. She just felt good. It took her a few moments to remember what had happened as she opened her eyes and cleared the sleepy haze from her mind. Then it hit her again. She was very likely going to be the representative for Butterfly Noir! She buried her face in the pillow and squealed. It was time to call Courtney. It would be eleven thirty in the morning eastern time.

"Latoia! I was just thinking of you. In fact while Mom and I were out shopping yesterday I found the most beautiful pin in the shape of a butterfly. I had the store ship it to you right then and there. I hope you're going to like it," Courtney stopped suddenly annoyed with herself for spoiling the surprise of the gift.

"Well girl, you never cease to amaze me. In fact you just take my breath away. Wait until I tell you why that thoughtful gift is going to be so unbelievable." Latoia told her friend about the interview and the subsequent trip to New York.

"That is so wonderful! Well you deserve every bit of good luck and fame and fortune that you get. I have a feeling that you are going to be very successful. Now are you going to get so famous that you can't talk to us *little people* anymore?"

"Not to worry I'll send you an autographed picture and you can talk to that." They both laughed as the friendly banter continued.

"Well I met with my sister for the first time on Monday. It was really interesting. I've decided to bring her here for the weekend, so we can get to know each other better."

"How does your mom feel about that?"

"The first time I brought it up, she was a little hesitant but she has come around since then. Actually when we went shopping Tuesday she bought some clothes for her and some art supplies."

"Well that's good. Hmm that shopping trip sounds like it was a big one."

"You wouldn't believe the things we bought. I don't know what happened but once we got started we just couldn't stop. Of course, it was mostly Mom insisting that she should buy everything. I think she's been cooped up too long taking care of grandmother."

"Speaking of Mrs. Camden, how is she doing?"

"She's doing so well that she was moved to a convalescent hospital."

"Sounds like we both have some great things going on in our lives."

"We do Latoia and I can't wait to hear about what happens for you in New York!"

"Don't worry, I'll call you second. My mother would kill me if I didn't call her first!" They laughed and chatted on then promised to stay in touch with frequent updates. When they hung up each was smiling broadly filled with thoughts of happy future events.

Latoia pulled out her suitcase and began trying to decide what she should wear for her New York trip.

Courtney climbed the stairs with an armload of the new clothes that she and her mother had bought for C.C. and carried them in to the yellow room where Hattie was putting fresh linens on the bed. Courtney happily shared Latoia's good news with Hattie.

"That girl is a real beauty. I don't doubt but what she is goin' to be somebody famous all right. Hmm."

"Okay Hattie now what does that little *hmm* mean?" Courtney chuckled.

"It means little Miss Curiosity, that you might be famous too."

"Ha. Well you know I have decided not to do any more performing so that can't be it. Maybe I'll choreograph something really good or teach a student who might become a famous dancer."

"We'll just see now won't we? Now fold that sheet on the corner like I taught you young lady. Then we can hang up those clothes you got for your sister."

"Yes ma'am. I am so looking forward to this weekend. I'm a little nervous too though."

"I understand sugar, but everything is gonna be just fine. You girls was meant to be together. Just be yourself, be patient and have faith." Hattie smiled and came around the bed to give her a hug.

They worked together and within the hour the room was freshened and the clothes put away.

At one o'clock they sat down in the kitchen to eat a green salad and sip some iced tea; the telephone rang just as they were finishing.

"It's for you Courtney, says his name is Doctor Baylor." Hattie gave her a little wink.

104

CHAPTER ELEVEN

"Miss Hammond, this is Doctor Baylor. Uh how are you?"

"I'm fine. Is everything all right with my sister?"

"Oh yes it is. In fact things are great with her. She learned a new word and she says it over and over. Sister. I really think that now, since the two of you have found each other, we are going to see a few changes in her behavior…for the better I mean, of course." Stephen was happy that Courtney was unable to see the flush on his face. He just could not seem to get himself under control when he was talking to her.

Courtney was so moved by what he said she had to swallow hard before she could continue.

"Miss Hammond?"

"I'm here, I am just so touched. I am really looking forward to having her here for the weekend. So, may I pick her up at about three o'clock on Friday?"

Stephen heard the slight quaver in her voice. He knew this was an emotional time for her and an important development in his patient's life. He had to ask the question. The idea had thrust itself into his mind until he could think of nothing else. He took a deep breath and plunged ahead, "Miss Hammond, the reason I called is that I have been thinking about an idea that came to me recently regarding you and your sister. Your circumstances are highly unusual. I was wondering if you and your family would object if I could observe and perhaps document her uh, your interactions, responses to the stimuli of your home and uh…I know it sounds clinical, of course that's what I do…but in the interest of helping future autistic patients…it might…"

"Of course," Courtney cut in. She sensed his discomfort and that fact let her know that his humanity was intact. She had also thought about doing something like that. She had never heard of a situation like this and she doubted that anyone else had heard of it either.

"Oh good, thank you. I'm hoping that maybe I will learn something that could help other people."

"It sounds like a good idea. I actually was thinking of something along those lines myself. I got my BA degree in psychology and I started the masters program last year but, uh I was interrupted."

"That is very interesting. I hope you will consider going back into the masters program. There is a great need for exceptional people in this field."

"Thank you," it was Courtney's turn to feel happy that he couldn't see *her* flushed cheeks. "Would you like to come to the house on Saturday then?"

"Yes that would be perfect. I am not on duty that day or Sunday either, unless of course, I'm called in for some reason, emergency or something," he had begun to sweat much to his own annoyance.

"Good then. I'll give you directions when I pick up C.C. Shall I come to your office?"

"Yes that will be good, fine uh thank you. I'll see you then."

When Courtney hung up the phone she turned to find Hattie watching her with an amused smile playing around her mouth.

"So that Doctor Baylor has an interest in you," it was voiced as a statement rather than a question.

"He just wants to observe C.C. and me as we get acquainted on Saturday. He says our situation is so unusual that if he documents it there might be something to be learned and maybe it could help other people."

"Ahh I see," Hattie nodded and decided not to pursue the subject at the moment. "I'll make sure to fix a nice lunch then. Why don't you ask him to stay for supper. I'm certain your mother would enjoy meeting him too."

"Thank you Hattie," Courtney gave her a hug. "I've got some work shop classes to teach this afternoon so I'll see you about eight o'clock!"

Stephanie leaned back in her first class seat with a sigh. She sipped her bourbon and seven. Life was good. She had always thought she might hit it big some day. The beautiful young woman next to her was very likely the one who would create the success she dreamed of. Heads turned whenever Latoia walked by and the amazing thing about it was she was never even aware of the stir she caused.

"How are you feeling?" Stephanie glanced at Latoia.

"Nervous. I want it to be over. I want it to be tomorrow so I'll know what they think and whether I got the job." Latoia had her hands clasped tightly together and her back was rigidly straight.

"Honey, I know exactly what you mean. I remember when I first started auditioning for shows myself. I would be *so* nervous." She put her hand against her chest. She wore rings on every finger and her nails were long and red. "I would feel sick to my stomach and my knees would be so shaky I could hardly walk. Those were the jobs I didn't get. The jobs that I *was* chosen for just seemed to fall in my lap. It was so ironic that when I thought I wouldn't even come close to getting a certain job I would just prance into the audition very calm like I didn't give a...you know what... and b-i-n-g-o I got a call-back or got the job." Stephanie was prone to swearing when she started drinking bourbon but since she knew Latoia's objections to her use of swear words she did her best to curtail the impulse.

"You know sometimes I think there's a great big plan out there," she waved a bejeweled hand expansively, "we need to try to do the best we can, but I think there are opportunities that come along that just belong to you if you're willing to be there and just try." She sipped her drink again. "When I realized that, I stopped being so nervous and I started getting more jobs.

Latoia nodded silently. That was as close to a philosophical statement as she had ever heard from Steph. She was probably right about all of that but she still wished it was tomorrow and she already had the answers. She did feel a little better though and she turned to tell Sephanie, but the blond head was leaning against the window and her eyes were closed. A small snore confirmed that her friend was asleep.

It was early evening when their plane landed. They retrieved their suitcases from baggage claim and boarded the hotel shuttle. Latoia could not keep herself from gawking at the tall buildings and the bustling crowds that crossed the street in large groups regardless of what the traffic signals were doing.

By the time they were checked in and settled into their room, they were both hungry. Stephanie knew her way around and decided that they should have dinner at a restaurant that she liked located on Fifth Avenue. They took a cab ride that made Latoia squeeze her eyes shut and hold onto her seat with both hands. "Just pretend you're at an amusement park and have some fun," Stephanie smiled.

When they finally entered the restaurant, heads turned as Latoia and Stephanie followed the maitre'd to their table. Latoia was somewhat uncomfortable, wondering if Stephanie's choice for her dress was a little too much. Had she been able to read the minds of those that observed her, she would have known that yes it was a bit much but only in the way that it made the men want to drift into slacious fantasies and their wives or girlfriends glared with venomous expressions of envy as Latoia moved gracefully by their tables.

The sharp-eyed agent saw it all. She walked with her head up and a knowing smile. Yes, this was going to be the big one.

"Now you order whatever you like. It's my treat tonight. After all it is a business trip," Stephanie winked.

Latoia was horrified when she saw the prices on the menu. She tried to find something that wouldn't be so expensive.

"Tell you what," Stephanie said after a time, "How about if I order for you. You like steak don't you?"

Their meal was the best Latoia had ever eaten and she began to relax and enjoy herself. Stephanie kept up a constant stream of chatter and the waiter kept bringing one course after another. People dressed in evening clothes came and went. She heard a variety of accents and languages all around her. She loved it. Latoia noticed a slender brunette woman sitting alone at a table nearby. She wore a blue dress with a plunging neckline. It was the flash of the blue jewel that she wore on a silver chain that caused Latoia to frown. There was something so unusual and even familiar about that stone. Just then the woman looked up and her blue eyes very nearly matched the color of the large stone. The effect was riveting. In fact many patrons appeared to agree as they repeatedly glanced in her direction. A waiter appeared at her table she ordered her meal in a beautiful British accent. Latoia felt envious for a few moments. The woman looked and sounded like royalty from England, obviously she had never had to fight her way up from poverty.

***

Abigail loved New York and her new freedom. Just imagine, dual citizenship and she never even knew it. She had only just arrived and in a matter of days she had purchased a terrific old warehouse that would be made into a beautiful place to live. She had ideas for a new business, some amazing contacts, and money in the bank…well in lots of banks actually. She smiled to herself. Now she was in the most exciting city in the world surrounded by beautiful people like that gorgeous young model at the next table. At the moment their eyes met, Abigail smiled at Latoia, thinking that she had most likely never had a frightening miserable day in her life. She looked rich, privileged and poised. She was probably a model for a fashion magazine or even a runway model. Some people have it bloody damned easy she told herself.

Stephanie was talking about what Latoia should wear the following morning when they met with the people from the fragrance company. Latoia made a valiant effort to absorb what her agent was saying but she was getting so tired. The large meal had made her feel drowsy on top of the fact that she had been too excited to sleep very much the night before. She ordered a cup of tea, not wanting too much caffeine; she would need to be able to sleep well tonight. She absolutely must be well rested in order to look and feel her best for the interview on the following day.

Latoia felt the presence of someone who had walked up to the table. When she turned she looked up into the brown eyes of a tall handsome man with a shock of thick white hair impeccably groomed.

"Please excuse me," He said as he bowed in a courtly old-fashioned manner, "My name is Quinten Rossgoode. I am trying to put together a very important project. It will require someone with modeling experience. I assume you have done some work already have you not?"

"Well yes some," Latoia responded almost shyly.

"I am her agent and I can tell you for a fact that she has experience and she is fantastic," Stephanie spoke up enthusiastically.

"I am sure she is. In fact I have been unable to take my eyes off of her ever since I walked in. Oh no don't worry this is strictly business. I am with my wife over there," he noticed the wary look on Latoia's face and the beginnings of a frown creasing the smooth mocha skin of her forehead. When he gestured to a nearby table Latoia saw a beautiful woman smartly dressed and coifed who appeared to be about the same age as her husband. She nodded and smiled cordially.

"Here is my business card. I would like both of you to come to my office tomorrow morning at eleven thirty. I am seeing another girl at eleven o'clock, but I've never met her and I am only seeing her as a courtesy to an old friend. I really believe that if you are interested, you might be the perfect one for this job. You would have to be approved by my colleagues as well, but I have a good eye for choosing the right person so I am confident that they will agree with me."

Quinten Rossgoode made another little bow and returned to his table and his smiling wife.

"Wow," Latoia's eyes were huge as she turned to Steph.

"Hmmm, this address looks familiar. I think it's on the same street as your appointment tomorrow," Stephanie frowned. "I don't have it with me so I'll check it when we get back to the hotel."

"Well it does sound interesting so it would be fun to go to both if they're logistically workable," Latoia felt little quivers of excitement at the possibilities that could open up for her.

When they arrived at their hotel Stephanie searched through her papers for the address while Latoia took a shower. She was surprised and pleased to find that both addresses were in the same building on different floors. They could go to both appointments with relative ease.

They were awake early and both women were filled with nervous anticipation and excitement. Stephanie wanted a full breakfast but Latoia could only manage a few bites of toast and coffee.

The building was not far from their hotel and they had plenty of time so they did what so many New Yorkers do and walked to the appointment.

They found the address and took the elevator to the twelfth floor. Business people hurried through the halls and the elevator stopped frequently to let people off and new people on. Latoia's heart was pounding. At last they entered the offices of Frazier Inc. Fragrances.

Latoia's hand shook as she reached for the door handle. She had an electric sensation shooting through her body as a premonition of imminent success flashed through her mind. This meeting could be the biggest moment of her career! She opened the door and as she did a little thought flitted in and made her smile, *I am opening the door to my future.*

The interview went well as Stephanie would tell her later. Everything was a blur of meeting people, shaking hands and touring the offices. At five minutes before eleven Bryson Marsh announced that he wanted to take them downstairs to meet with Martin Frazier and Quin, his Vice President.

Latoia and Stephanie looked at each other silently. Bryson led them to the elevator and they silently dropped to the eleventh floor. The doors opened revealing another elegantly appointed space divided into offices and cubicles. Well-dressed men and women answered phones, perused drawings and photographs as others bustled from one office to another with an energy that nearly crackled in the wake of their movement. Every office was provided with a spectacular view of the New York skyline. Bryson and Martin walked briskly to the reception desk situated near a set of arched double doors. Latoia tried to appear nonchalant but her eyes were wide with wonder and her heart was racing.

An attractive middle-aged woman sat behind the desk. As they approached she looked up and flashed her beautiful smile. "Go right in" she said gesturing toward the doors, "They're waiting for you!"

Bryson smiled and nodded to the woman then strode ahead of Stephanie and Latoia to open the doors revealing an enormous office with floor to ceiling windows that covered the entire length of the outer wall. The unexpected brightness was temporarily blinding.

When Latoia and Stephanie were able to focus after the initial shock of the brilliant glare, they were in for another shock as they found themselves looking at the tall handsome figure of Quinten Rossgoode. The two women looked at each other. Bryson was trying to make introductions when he noticed the silent looks of surprise exchanged by Stephanie, Latoia and Mr. Rossgoode. Then Quinten laughed and strode purposefully toward them with his hand outstretched. The two women laughed with him while Bryson and Martin looked on in puzzled silence.

When the situation was finally explained there was amazed laughter all around. Martin Frazier spoke in a deep baritone voice, "Gentlemen, I think we are all in agreement," the other men looked at each other and solemnly nodded, "Latoia, how would you feel about being our Butterfly Noir?"

***

Courtney's heart was so filled with joyous expectation that she fairly danced up the steps to The Oaks. It was two thirty. She had arrived early in order to have a few minutes to speak with Dr. Baylor and give him directions to Willows. Her stomach gave a little jump at the thought.

She remembered where his office was and quickly arrived at his open door. He was seated at his desk with his head bent forward intently studying an open file. He jotted something down with a gold pen. Rays of sunlight streamed through the high window and as he wrote, the gold pen flashed bright reflections as it moved across the paper.

"Oh hello Miss Hammond. Good to see you," he stood abruptly and once again his foot caught on the wheel of his chair. Fortunately his coffee mug was empty this time and though he knocked it over the only thing that spilled was a file that sat on the corner of his desk.

Courtney observed the Dr.'s clumsy moves and marveled at the difference she saw between he and the polished but cruel Antonio. When Dr. Baylor shook her hand she was infused with the realization that this man was good, through and through. She looked directly into his eyes and knew that at that moment they both felt something. There was almost a sense of recognition as

110

though they might have known each other in the distant past. There was comfort and safety in the emotion that passed between them. Most unusual of all she felt a heaviness leave her as though she had been tense or stressed for her entire life until that moment, and suddenly it lifted from her soul.

"I brought the directions for you." The moment passed and Courtney could think of nothing else to say. She looked down and fumbled in her pocketbook for the directions she had written out. A blush started at her neck and worked its way to her cheeks as she handed him the paper.

"Thank you. Yes this looks good. I'm sure I can easily find this. Uh I appreciate you allowing me to observe you and your sister like this. I will be sure to stay out of the way so that the two of you have a chance to begin establishing a relationship."

"Actually it will be nice to have you there just in case I need advice or if she has an episode...uh behavioral episode."

"Everything should be fine. I have the feeling you will be able to handle whatever comes along."

Courtney signed the release papers and they went to find C.C.. She was in her room waiting with a ragged brown Teddy bear clutched against her chest. Avery stood nearby. He babbled sounds that were almost incoherent to anyone else, but C.C. echoed some of the sounds back to him as though they were conversing in their own language.

"Avery, for goodness sakes, what are you doing in here? You are supposed to be watching cartoons in the Day Room," an attendant unfamiliar to Courtney bustled in. "Uh oh. Did you give Brown to C.C.?" Avery said nothing but just pointed to the stuffed animal in the girl's arms. She said nothing but continued to rock back and forth.

"I never would have believed it," the woman shook her head, "he won't let anyone touch that bear. It's his most cherished possession."

Avery was led away and Courtney took a deep breath, "Well C.C. are you ready to go?"

"Ready to go," she echoed as she stood up and reached for a small backpack that looked as though it was stuffed to bursting.

"I have some new clothes for you so you don't have to bring anything with you." Courtney spoke gently.

"New clothes for you," C.C. echoed but she held the backpack even tighter.

"Okay. It's okay you can bring your backpack," Courtney chuckled.

"Bring your backpack okay," C.C. swayed with her constant inner rhythm.

"She doesn't like to be touched," Dr. Baylor cautioned as Courtney held out her hand to C.C..

"Oh. Well she held my hand when I was here before. See?" C.C. shifted the Teddy bear and the backpack so she could reach out with her good right hand.

111

"I see what you mean," his eyes opened wide in surprise but he accepted the new development with a smile and raised eyebrows. He walked with them out to Courtney's car.

"Now Dr. Baylor I want you to plan to stay for supper with us tomorrow. My mother wants to meet you and Hattie is planning one of her fried chicken dinners."

"I haven't had a home cooked meal in so long I've forgotten what it's like. Now who is Hattie?"

"She's…well I guess technically she is my grandmother's housekeeper, but that does not come close to describing who she is and what she means to me. On top of all that she's an extraordinary cook."

"I wouldn't want to impose but my mouth is watering already."

Stephen watched as the car pulled out of the parking lot and turned down the narrow exit road and finally disappeared over a small rise. He had the strangest empty feeing as if he should be going with them. Must be the heat. Definitely time to go back inside.

As Courtney drove back to Charleston she talked to her sister. C.C. merely looked out of the window without expression or comment. Courtney talked about their grandmother, Hattie, Willows, Clarisa and the new painting materials. There was no way to know for sure if her sister understood anything she told her, but in her heart she knew that Caitlin was listening and understanding.

Hattie hurried out of the kitchen door wiping her hands on her apron, as soon as the car pulled up. She was grinning at the same time tears ran down her cheeks.

"Lord have mercy child. I thought this day would never come. Praises be, you are finally here." Hattie walked up to C.C. as she got out of the car and without a moment of hesitation, wrapped the girl in her arms in a welcoming embrace. C.C. didn't respond but she didn't pull away either.

The three of them trooped into the kitchen and filled their noses with the mouthwatering smell of freshly baked oatmeal raisin cookies. Courtney helped her sister onto a stool and they sat at the kitchen island nibbling on cookies and sipping iced sun tea.

A noise at the door alerted them that Storm Cat wanted to be included in their conversation. Hattie let him in. He rubbed against her legs first with his tail straight up. C.C. had dropped her backpack on the floor and Storm cat made a beeline for it. He rubbed his head against it several times and purred noisily. C.C. watched him then gently dropped Brown to the floor. Storm Cat sniffed the stuffed animal then made three little circles and lay down with his head on the soft tummy of the love-worn bear.

C.C. made a purring sound with her mouth then took another bite of cookie.

"His name is Storm Cat. He does a lot of purring when he's happy," Hattie explained.

112

"Purring happy," echoed C.C., to the delight of Hattie and Courtney.

After their snack, Courtney took C.C. upstairs and showed her the yellow room. She opened the closet and pointed to her new clothes. C.C. immediately began taking her own clothes off and stepped out of them leaving a small wrinkled heap.

"Well okay," Courtney laughed, "if you want to wear some of your new things, whoops okay I bought you new underwear too. I hope it fits." Courtney laughed as her sister removed her bra and panties too. Courtney was appalled to see scars on her body and the shrunken state of her left arm and leg.

"Do you need help? Well I guess not." C.C. was already pulling on the new underwear that Courtney had placed on the bed. The bra fastened in front so she seemed to be able to do it herself.

"Guess not," C.C. echoed.

Courtney held up a pair of pink shorts and matching sleeveless top. Then she held up a white duo with green trim. C.C. reached for the pink one. When it was on she continually rubbed her right hand over the soft fabric.

"My, my, now don't you look purty," Hattie walked in.

"Look purty," C.C. clearly liked her new clothes though she still showed no expression on her face.

"Where are her art supplies?" Courtney wondered.

"Your mama suggested that we clear out a space in the sun room. That ol' Magnolia tree has got so big that it keeps the room cooler but it still has plenty of light comin' through all those windows. Miz Camden don't keep many of her plants in there any more either. Come on downstairs and I'll show you what it looks like now."

C.C. grabbed Brown and reached for Courtney's hand. Courtney was filled with warmth for her. She knew instinctively that C.C. understood everything that was going on. She was unable to react or respond as most people could, but who knows, maybe even that would change.

Hattie led them to a door located just off of the kitchen. Courtney couldn't remember if she had ever even been in the sunroom before. Hattie told her that the door had been locked after Esther's husband had died in there and had been virtually unused for years.

As they stepped in C.C. pulled away from her sister and went straight to the artist's easel. She ran her hand all over the wood. When she saw the drawing table she did the same thing. Brown was forgotten and discarded in a furry heap on the floor as she moved to the paints and charcoal then on to the paper.

"Do you want to paint?" Courtney asked.

"Want to paint," she was already looking at the brushes and the artist tablet.

"Okay. When you paint, you wear this to keep your clothes clean," Courtney helped her put her arms through the new painting smock she and her mother had found during their shopping spree.

Hattie left the room when the telephone rang. She came back in wearing a big smile. "Latoia's on the phone, she sounds very happy."

Courtney smiled as she listened to Latoia's narration of the New York interview. She squeezed her eyes shut as she heard about the *coincidence* of meeting the Vice President of the fragrance company when he walked up to their dinner table the night before the interview!

Courtney was properly impressed and made little noises of approval with a final joyous shriek at the good news. She even performed the mandatory jumping around happy dance.

"Oh...my...God. I am so happy for you. No one deserves this success more than you do!"

"Thank you. I don't know if that's true or not but oh, thank the Lord, it does feel good!" Latoia let out a long exhausted breath. "I feel like a huge weight has been lifted right off me. I haven't slept well with all of these nerves either."

"You should be able to sleep now except when they start working you to death."

"Honey this is one kind of job I am going to be happy to work at and I can't wait to get started."

"When *will* you start?"

"They said about three or four weeks. I'm going to Paris!"

Both girls squealed again but their happy dance was cut short when Stephanie told Latoia that they had to catch their plane. They ended the call with promises to talk again within a few days.

Courtney replaced the receiver and just stood hugging herself for a few minutes. She sensed someone watching her and turned to find C.C. holding Brown and rocking from side to side. She almost looked frightened.

"C'mon C.C. let's go tell Hattie the good news about Latoia and then we can take a walk in the garden, okay?"

"Don't touch the flowers," C.C. intoned several times as she reached for Courtney's hand.

"I am so happy for Latoia. That is one beautiful girl," Hattie clapped her hands and laughed. "Uh oh, C.C. baby what is the matter?" Hattie noticed a change in the girl's usually bland expression.

"I know, she looked sort of scared when I finished talking to Latoia too. Maybe we've been making too much noise. I told her we would take a walk in the garden."

"Don't touch the flowers," C.C. said immediately.

Courtney and Hattie laughed delightedly as C.C. spoke and started pulling Courtney's hand as she leaned toward the kitchen door.

"You girls go on outside. Miz Clarisa will be home in a little while and I gotta fix us some supper."

It had been a long time since Courtney had walked in the gardens. There were two men from the Garden Care Company edging the flowerbeds. C.C. pulled back when she saw them and would not take another step.

"No. No. Don't touch the flowers." C.C. became very agitated, "Hurt, hurt!" Tears rolled suddenly from her eyes and she held Brown up to her face after she jerked away from Courtney's grasp.

"What's wrong C.C.? Everything's okay. Those men are not hurting the flowers...wait a minute, did someone hurt you? Someone who works in the gardens at The Oaks?"

C.C. was crouched down with the stuffed bear over her face. The men were packing up their equipment and finally disappeared down the driveway.

"They're gone now. See you're just fine. No one is going to hurt you. In fact I'm going to try to make sure that no one ever hurts you again. I'm terribly sorry that your life has been so hard. I want to help make it better." She continued to speak in soothing tones until at last the girl quieted. Courtney pulled her up and C.C. put Brown under her left arm then reached for Courtney's hand. She seldom made eye contact and kept her gaze down or turned away. Despite her outward display of disinterest Courtney *felt* her listening intently to everything she said.

Courtney didn't know how far C.C. could walk due to her profound limp. She coaxed her to a bench so they could both sit down and rest a few minutes before they started back to the house.

Clarisa drove up just as the girls returned from their walk. She waved and called out "I bought some ice cream for dessert."

Hattie set the dining room table for their evening meal. When everything was ready they sat down to eat a small salad followed by green beans and broiled pork chops seasoned as only Hattie could.

Clarisa was at first visibly nervous and ill at ease. But as the meal continued and the conversation flowed, she relaxed. C.C. had her own brand of charm as she held Brown and sometimes offered him food. C.C. rarely spoke but she echoed selected phrases from the ongoing conversation at times thereby in her own way contributing to the family chatter.

Once the table was cleared, C.C. went back into the sunroom to inspect her painting materials and Clarisa went in to Esther's office to pay some bills. When the telephone rang. Clarisa spoke to the caller for a few minutes, then summoned Courtney to speak to her father. Courtney thought he sounded forlorn. She knew her parents missed each other since their normally quiet lives had been so disrupted earlier in the year. She wished for a moment that their lives could settle down and go back to the way things used to be. She knew though that their lives were forever on a different course. She felt a moment of grief for the life she would never have again, but it was replaced by a sense of anticipation for a new future. She knew that her own strength and maturity had been challenged causing her to grow as a person. She understood that challenges were a necessary part of life for everyone.

"Courtney! I think you should come and see this!" Hattie called from the kitchen door.

Something in her tone struck a chord of fear in her heart. She hurried to the kitchen and then followed Hattie into the sunroom.

C.C. sat on the artist bench. She was wearing her cover up and had obviously been painting. Courtney followed Hattie around to a position where they could see her work.

The painting was a magnificent butterfly with large black wings swept back and the head was human. It was Latoia! A dark menacing figure hovered in the background. The facial features were indistinct, but the eyes glowed red and were clearly full of malice.

Courtney was chilled to the bone. She exchanged a glance with Hattie. They knew without speaking that their friend was in trouble.

CHAPTER TWELVE

Courtney helped her sister find her new nightclothes. She was able to take her own shower and get ready for bed. Clarisa peeked in to say goodnight. She hugged Courtney and went to C.C..

"I am happy you're here," she said softly. "I'm sorry you were lost for so long." C.C. covered her face with Brown then slowly peeked over him like a baby might do when playing peek-a-boo. "Oh, I think you know what I'm saying don't you?" Clarisa exclaimed enthusiastically.

C.C. turned and jumped onto the bed, bouncing several times before pulling back the covers and climbing under. As she lay on the pillows she rolled her head back and forth. They started to leave and Clarisa turned off the light when she got to the door. C.C. let out a piercing scream. As soon as the light was turned on she stopped screaming.

"Guess we know she wants the light on," Clarisa said.

"Light on, light on," C.C. chanted.

"The light will stay on, don't worry," Courtney soothed.

"What in the name of goodness is all this noise," Hattie had come up the stairs to say goodnight. Storm Cat trotted in behind her with his tail held straight up.

"Just a little misunderstanding about the light," Clarisa assured her.

"Well now that it is understood I think we all need to take a moment to say thank you and ask a blessin'." Hattie said a short simple prayer of thanks and then she sang, Bless This House. Her voice filled the room and their hearts. When the last note faded, Storm Cat was on the bed with C.C.. He was curled up and already closing his eyes. C.C. had stopped rocking and her eyes were closing. The women left her room and soon the house was settled for a restful night.

That night as Clarisa lay in bed trying to fall asleep she restlessly stared up into the darkness. Her mind was reeling with the information she had found in her mother's financial papers. She had no idea that her estate was worth so much. An enormous trust was set up for Courtney as well as ownership of Willows and its vast properties. There was a trust for Caitlin and for Hattie. She had found an inheritance for her son Shane that he would receive on his thirtieth birthday. As near as she could surmise her mother was worth somewhere in the neighborhood of thirty million dollars give or take. Clarisa and Clyde were comfortably wealthy and enjoyed a privileged lifestyle in

Palos Verdes, California. Clyde was a senior partner in a prestigious law firm and they never had to worry about finances, but thirty million dollars was just mind-boggling.

Clarisa was emotionally and mentally exhausted. First her mother had fallen and was injured. She had flown to Charleston immediately. Then Courtney had gone through that dreadful ordeal with the Scolari boy, then Esther's stroke, the discovery of Caitlin… Tears fell onto her pillow. She just wanted to go home, rest and see her husband. She missed his humor, their long talks, sleeping next to him every night. Yes, it was time to go home; maybe she would stay for another week or so. She could go home for a while and then come back after she was rested.

***

Courtney missed Storm Cat's purring beside her, but she was grateful that he offered his comforting presence to her vulnerable sister. She thought of C.C. as her little sister even though they were only minutes apart. She was so innocent and child-like it was hard to imagine that they were the same age. She felt a protective instinct toward her and she was sickened at the thought of the things that must have happened to her. She had to work on getting her moved in to Willows as soon as possible. How could grandmother have let this situation occur?

"It was meant to be," the softly glowing image of her sister hovered nearby, "Remember where it began. Our lives have purpose. Our souls are learning. Please don't be so angry with Amilee. She became Esther in this life to learn what is right and to provide a place for important work to be done. Because of her, countless numbers of children will be helped in the future. You will see in time."

"C.C. you sound so wise. I am so fortunate to have you as my sister." Courtney and her sister spoke only with their minds but to them their voices were clear and audible.

"My feelings echo yours. I would like you to call me Caitlin now. It will help my body consciousness respond to the call of the work I must do and the work we will do together"

"I love your name Caitlin and I will call you by that name from now on. I want you to be here with me every day and we can get to know each other…"

"That will happen but not for awhile. I need to go back. There is work I must do there for a time."

"What? No. I don't want you to go back. I want you here. We are part of each other." Courtney felt some panic rise up inexplicably.

"Shhh, it will be fine," it was Caitlin's turn to be the big sister. "I understand why my body and mind need to be this way. I chose this form as the best vehicle to learn from because I did not use my gifts wisely when I lived as Begata, your sister from long ago. I am so happy to perform this role

118

and accomplish the work that will best serve those that I hurt in that unfortunate past life."

A new presence entered Courtney's bedroom. "Talk about a hurt, I'm gonna put a hurt on y'all if you don't be quiet and let everybody get some sleep. All this chatter goin' on in this here house is enough to wake the dead!" Hattie's strong etheric voice was unmistakable.

Courtney started to giggle. She heard Caitlin's giggle as her wavering image vanished. Then she giggled harder at the pure unbelievable absurdity of it all. Who would ever imagine such a strange thing could happen.

"No giggling," came Hattie's more distant but still distinct voice.

That of course, caused a nearly uncontrollable burst of mirth that had to be buried deep in her pillow.

A familiar bump on the end of her bed caused Hattie to lift her head. "Too much noise in this house for you too?" She could just see the outline of Storm Cat in the darkness as he stretched and curled up by her feet. After a few moments of purring and grooming he closed his eyes with an audible sigh. "I know what you mean," she muttered laying her head back down with her own sigh. "Lord have mercy," she sat up again and punched her pillow into submission. "Mmm mmm. This is one interestin' household, I do declare." Satisfied with her pillow she put her head back on it with yet another long-suffering sigh followed by a brief chuckle and then a soft snore.

Saturday morning Courtney awoke with a smile on her face. She just felt happy and lighter than she had in a long while. She ran through the list of things in her head. Caitlin was here and then Doctor Baylor would be coming by today. There was a little jump in her stomach as she thought about him. It was time to get up. She could smell coffee brewing and she thought she heard her mother's light quick steps going down the stairs.

The shower felt great but the anticipation of the coming day drove her to hurry more than normal. She towel-dried her hair and decided to just let the curls do as they wished in the summer humidity. It was going to be a hot day so she chose a cool green tank top to wear with her favorite white shorts. She dabbed a small amount of mascara on the ends of her lashes and a little clear lipgloss. She looked into the mirror and blushed as she realized she wanted to look attractive for Doctor Baylor. Well he probably wasn't interested anyway. She slipped on some sandals and hurried out.

Caitlin was not in her room. Her nightclothes were neatly folded on top of her smoothly made up bed. Brown was nowhere to be seen, and the backpack was gone.

A shock of fear struck her heart. Caitlin was gone. Courtney raced downstairs and into the kitchen. Hattie and Clarisa were sitting at the island sipping coffee.

"Honey what's wrong?" Clarisa became alarmed when she saw her daughter's frightened expression.

"Caitlin's gone," Courtney whispered.

119

"Caitlin's gone," her sister echoed as she came in from the sunroom. Courtney let out a breath. "You must have been in there painting."

"In there painting," came the echo.

"I was so worried," Courtney said holding her hand on her chest.

Clarisa stood to give her daughter a warm understanding hug.

"In there painting, in there painting," Caitlin repeated over and over even as she turned to limp back to her project. Her flat voice grew louder as she moved away from the kitchen.

"I think she wants us to go see what she was working on," Courtney raised her eyebrows and gestured toward the doorway.

"Oh dear God, I have to call Latoia today. There is no question about it she is going to have some trouble. Let's see, she should have gotten back home last night but it's still too early to call out there."

Caitlin had used her new acrylics on some pictures and charcoal on others. Latoia was depicted as a butterfly in most of the pictures. Always a looming presence hovered over her. In some pictures the being with red eyes hovered over a prone skeletal form. The three women were aghast at the frightening display. They all felt the chill of what those pictures could possibly mean.

"Hello?" They were all momentarily startled. Someone was knocking and calling out from the kitchen door.

"Doctor Baylor. Good morning," Courtney hurried to the screen door, "Please come in."

He was clean-shaven and he was not wearing his glasses. He wore a white short-sleeved Izod shirt and khaki pants. The whole appearance caused him to look much younger than his thirty something years. He was tan from riding his bicycle and the weight-lifting sessions with his friend Kevin had developed his biceps so that there were well-defined muscles filling up the short sleeves of his shirt.

"I hope I'm not too early. I left early so I would have plenty of time to figure out how to get here. I forgot that there is not very much traffic on Saturday morning so I really got here sooner than I expected."

"Not at all, I mean I'm glad you were able to find us so easily, oops..." Courtney was struck by his appearance and the fresh clean smell of his aftershave as he stepped into the kitchen. He seemed so much taller than she remembered and without the glasses his long dark lashes framed hazel eyes that were absolutely compelling. She felt his masculine energy pressing toward her. She took a few steps back and bumped into one of the kitchen stools, banging the back of her heel so hard that she knocked the stool off balance. Clarisa had come in behind her and caught the stool before it fell.

"Well I guess it was your turn today," his eyes sparkled with mischief as he referred to his own problems with the wheels of his desk chair.

"Doctor Baylor, I'm Clarisa Hammond, Courtney's mother, and this is Hattie Degrassenrad. She pretty much runs things around here," Clarisa smiled and offered her hand then gestured to the housekeeper who had also entered the kitchen.

Clarisa noted Courtney's reaction and flushed face. Volumes were silently spoken about her daughter's obvious attraction to this fresh-looking young Doctor. She could do worse she thought with a smile.

"Don't you know I do run things around here and I'm gonna run you all right out of my kitchen and into the dining room for a proper breakfast, starting with some fresh coffee," Hattie bustled them out and immediately prepared a tray with coffee and the usual assortment of sweetners and cream.

Caitlin followed along behind them with Brown tucked under her left arm.

"This is a real pleasure, Mrs. Hammond. Cafeteria food is great when you're hungry but there is nothing better than a home cooked meal." He pulled out a chair for Clarisa to sit down.

"Please call me Clarisa. There is no need for us to be so formal," she smiled and raised her eyebrows as she caught her daughter's eye.

Courtney was helping Caitlin pull out the heavy chair when she looked up and saw her mother's expression. She groaned inwardly as she recognized Clarisa's matchmaking antenna begin to go up and switch on the radar.

"Well thank you Clarisa, I would not want to put anyone to too much trouble. I am happy that C.C. has found her family. I want to help everyone adjust."

"Doctor Baylor," Courtney cleared her throat.

"Please call me Stephen."

Courtney blushed in spite of herself, "Um okay, actually speaking of names, I think C.C. would like us to call her Caitlin."

"Call her Caitlin," it was the first time Caitlin had spoken. It was her usual monotone but there was a firm decisiveness to it that Stephen had not heard before.

"What a beautiful name. Of course I will call you Caitlin if you like."

"Caitlin if you like," she echoed as she rocked front and back.

"In fact both names are beautiful, Courtney and Caitlin sounds like a team," he spoke brightly as he watched his patient for any reaction.

"Sounds like a team," she used the same tone as before but she spoke more softly. Her facial expression never changed and there was no hesitation in her rocking motion.

"How did you discover that she wanted to be called Caitlin?" Stephen looked at Courtney with a quizzical frown.

"Courtney and Caitlin," she was speaking softly and repeating the names over and over. Everyone looked at her for a moment and then back to Courtney.

"Hmmm. Well uh Stephen, that may take some explaining," she took a deep breath, "we appear to have some unique communication skills."

"Ah yes I have heard of that happening with twins but I have never had the opportunity to observe it."

"I think you will find a great many unique qualities with Courtney and Caitlin. You might want to finish your coffee and eat Hattie's nourishing breakfast before you tackle that information Stephen," Clarisa said with a knowing smile.

Courtney noticed that her mother's native Charleston accent had returned full force. She decided that once a Southern Belle, always a Southern Belle.

Hattie announced that breakfast was ready and Courtney rose to go to the kitchen and help her serve it. She was surprised to see that Hattie had not prepared a plate for herself.

"I'm goin' to eat in my rooms. I want to call my daughter this morning. You go on now. I'll be back out in about twenty minutes."

It was odd not to have Hattie at the table. She considered her to be a part of the family and a meal just did not feel complete without Hattie's presence.

Caitlin had stopped mumbling and rocking. She ate her meal and then left the table. Everyone watched her limp to the sunroom door and disappear inside.

"Mother bought her some art supplies and we set up an area in there for her to paint."

"Oh good. Has she painted anything yet?"

"She certainly has," Courtney nodded. After the light conversation her mother had inspired she wondered if Doctor Baylor would be ready for what she had to say.

"So does that mean she has been prolific?"

"Yes. She used her new acrylics and some charcoal. She must have gotten up early because there are six pictures in there."

"I know what you mean. When she painted at the hospital, she seemed to produce a lot of pictures in a short time. It was amazing. I have dabbled with watercolors myself so I know how long it takes to put a picture together, but apparently not C.C. or I mean Caitlin."

"Courtney why don't you two go on in and see about your sister. I'll help Hattie clear the table."

Courtney led him into the sunroom and sure enough she was engrossed in another painting. They looked at the charcoals she had completed and the acrylic painting.

"This is chilling," Stephen frowned.

"Even more so when you know who this is," Courtney could feel the fear for her friend twist in her stomach. She explained that Latoia was her best friend and that she had just been hired as a model for a company that will use a butterfly motif for advertising their product.

"How could she know Latoia," he asked shaking his head.

"She doesn't," Courtney stated simply. She let him think about that for a moment, and then she added, "My sister and I have visions…psychic gifts. Caitlin is painting what she sees in her visions. This painting and these drawings tell me that my friend Latoia is in trouble or will be in trouble. I don't know if this being with the red eyes is an actual person or if it's symbolic of a situation."

In the silence that followed, Courtney watched Stephen's expression. He frowned and studied the drawings in silence. She was relieved that he made no effort to refute what she said. He simply listened, nodded and contemplated.

"Well I have never come across anything like this," he murmured at last. "I would like to photograph these and see if we can document the paintings and what events may or may not occur as a result. Have you spoken with your friend about this?"

"No, not yet. She's in California so I'm planning to call her this morning. She just got back from New York and there's a three-hour time difference. I wanted her to get some rest before I wake her up from a sound sleep."

"You know I had a great grandmother that was part Lakota-Sioux. There are a lot of stories in our family about how she always knew what the weather was going to be and if a woman was pregnant, she knew whether the child would be a boy or a girl. Of course that is pretty small acorns compared to this," he smiled at her warmly.

Caitlin put down her brush suddenly and stood up.

"Oh you need the bathroom don't you. Let me show you where it is down here," Courtney walked from the room with Caitlin following behind.

Stephen let out a breath. This was going to be an amazing and interesting time. He felt an excitement start to build as he thought about what he had just heard. Then he looked up at the painting Caitlin had just been working on. It was unfinished but there was no question about who it was. He was looking at a portrait of himself. His new look, with no beard and contacts instead of glasses. There was no menacing figure on the page yet so maybe she just liked his clean-shaven face. A memory of Doctor Mann flashed into his mind. For a moment he felt a little guilty about not shaving after Doctor Mann had ordered him to follow the rules. Doctor Mann had died in an explosive car crash months before. He hoped that if Doctor Mann were watching him from some *other* place that he would understand his reasoning at the time. When one is faced with a beautiful girl, one must present oneself in the best possible way. He hoped Doctor Mann would understand that reasoning as well.

***

Latoia and Stephanie were exhausted by the time they landed at the Santa Monica airport. Stephanie had talked nonstop about the exciting future that was just around the corner and she had consumed several bourbons. She held her liquor better than anyone Latoia had ever seen, but she was still a little worried about her friend's ability to drive.

"Stephanie, I don't think you're in any shape to drive. I have my car here and I want you to come home with me. I only live a few minutes from the airport. Tomorrow is Saturday. You don't have to work do you?"

"Un. Unh."

"Well then it's settled. C'mon." Latoia took her firmly by the elbow and led her through the airport to the parking deck and finally to the white convertible. It was a beautiful night, so while Stephanie settled herself in the car she put the top down. She also thought if Stephanie got sick…well she just did not want Courtney's beautiful little car to get dirty.

She pulled out of the airport and shortly she was on Ocean Park Boulevard. Stephanie's head was bobbing around as she wavered between enjoying the night air and passing out. Just two more turns and she was in her driveway.

The neighborhood was dark and quiet as she got out of the car and hurried to her front door. It would be dawn in only two or three hours she thought as she finally got her key into the lock. She reached in and flipped on the porch light and one interior light before she hurried back to the car to help Stephanie in and carry their bags.

Stephanie had opened the car door and swung her feet out. She sat slumped forward holding on to the door handle.

"I could swear the ground was down there someplace," her speech was slow and slurred as she squinted her eyes in an effort to focus. "Whoa, I found it," before Latoia could get to her, Stephanie had tried to stand up but her knees buckled and she gently just melted onto the driveway.

"Oh Steph are you okay? Here let me help you up."

"Of course I'm Hokay. I was jus' resting I think. The ground was farther down than I remembered Miss Buffterly. Miss Neroir or whatever the hell it's called. Yer jus beeyutiful. Uh oh I hope yer shtrong too because my feet ain't workin' too well."

Latoia laughed as she helped her up. Her friend was as tall as she and outweighed her by nearly one hundred pounds. Latoia was strong though and the balancing techniques that she had learned in her many years of dance training served her well as Stephanie's bulk staggered and swayed against her.

"One of these days…" Stephanie held up her finger as though she were going to make a profound statement, "I'm goin' to stop drinkin' bourbon."

"Sounds good," Latoia groaned as she struggled up the steps to the front door.

"I think I should swish to vodka. Bourbon makes me drunk."

"Logical thinking," Latoia assured her. "Now grab that door handle and push the door open."

"Oooooh! This is sooo cute!" Stephanie's voice rose to a little squeal as she looked around at the tiny studio apartment. "Where is the bed. I'm going black…no offense,".

"None taken. It's a trundle pullout," Stephanie held on to the wing chair while Latoia pulled out the bed and grabbed sheets and a blanket from the closet.

"Jus' give me a pillow and I will be fine!" She was already crawling onto the bed.

Latoia returned to her car and hoisted both shoulder bags into position and then lifted the small suitcases out of the back seat. She was feeling tired and antsy to get inside and out of the eerie early morning darkness. When she got everything inside she locked her door and turned to see Stephanie sitting up looking at something.

"What is that stuff on your drawers," Stephanie pointed at the small chest of drawers where she kept her underclothes. "Why does it smell like cigarettes in here? I've never seen you smoke."

Latoia had noticed the smell when she came in but with her efforts to get Stephanie inside she had discounted it. "I have never smoked!" The mirror above the bureau was covered with red marks. She saw now that the marks were letters. It was a message. 'You are mine' it read. She drew her breath in sharply.

Her legs had turned to jelly but she forced herself to walk closer. The words were written in lipstick. She found the tube that had been used lying open on top of the chest. She noticed that the drawers were not closed tight. She pulled one open and it was empty with the exception of the cigarette butt that had been left behind. There were small burn marks all over the bottom of the drawer.

She pulled open the next drawer and the next. They were all empty except for another cigarette butt in each one. Each drawer was similarly burned with small round marks as though the person touched the end of the burning cigarette to many different locations inside the drawer.

Latoia put her hands over her mouth and stumbled back in horror. Her mind was numb. None of it made any sense. Bile rose up in her stomach and she staggered toward the bathroom and flicked on the light. She lunged for the toilette and began heaving violently.

When the sickness passed she looked up and found messages written all over the bathroom walls. Then she saw a pair of her panties on the floor and a matching black bra lying nearby. They were both wet with something...Latoia started screaming then everything went dark.

When she opened her eyes someone was putting something cold on her head. She looked around and discovered that she was laying on the trundle bed. People, men were milling about in her apartment.

"Hey baby, take it easy. Just lay still and keep this ice pack on your head." Stephanie was sitting on the side of the bed. Her breath still reeked of bourbon, and her eyes were blood shot but her speech was perfectly clear.

"I called the police and an ambulance came too. I didn't know if you were hurt or what. You fell and bumped your head so they carried you out of the bathroom and got you on the bed."

"Oh. Thanks Steph. I just don't understand what is going on."

"Honey don't try to work it out yet. Just lay here and get yourself back together. We'll talk in just a minute."

It was more than just a few minutes. By the time the ambulance personnel were convinced that Latoia was not seriously injured the Eastern sky was bright with the fiery colors of dawn. Then the policemen questioned her. A plain- clothes detective arrived and she was questioned again. Her head was throbbing painfully.

It seems that whoever broke in must have still been nearby. After she had gone inside, someone had tied one of her bikinis to the steering wheel of her car....Courtney's car.

Stephanie had made one pot of coffee after another. She passed around mugs of it to everyone and drank several herself. So much so that her normally quick way of speaking became faster and her eyes were open so wide that quite often the whites were visible over the tops of her pupils.

Latoia was shaking on the inside. Sometimes she wanted to laugh hysterically and in the next moment she wanted to cry and scream at everyone to get out and leave her alone.

The sun was well up over the horizon when a news crew showed up. People in the neighborhood were up and the news people were interviewing them, trying to piece together enough events for a story.

It was finally decided that the police would take the white VW in and try to determine whether or not they could find any fingerprints or other evidence. One of the detectives told Latoia that she would need to stay somewhere else for a few days and that she should call a friend to come and get her. Stephanie immediately put a protective arm around her friend and declared that her Beverly Hills condo would be the best place and that she could move in immediately.

Stephanie was publicity savy so she made sure that the young reporter got a brief but clear picture of Latoia's sad beautiful face. She impressed upon the media that she was a model who was just offered a big contract and that she was Latoia's agent. She knew that this news story would run over and over for days maybe even a week or two. If that didn't get her phone ringing then nothing would. She would never want anything bad to happen to her client and especially Latoia since she was such a good friend, but publicity is publicity and as long as it was available she intended to use it.

Detective Denton stood with his back to the media conferring with two local police officers when the telephone rang. Everyone was startled. Latoia was standing in the driveway with Stephanie but she heard it plainly through the open door.

The detective beckoned to her. "Are you expecting a call at this hour?" His forehead wrinkled with deeply etched frown lines.

"No. Most of my friends know not to call me so early." She glanced at her watch and was surprised to find that it was only eight thirty in the morning. It seemed as though it should be late afternoon.

"Any hang ups recently or maybe obscene phone calls?" Detective Denton had his notebook out and his pencil poised to take notes.

"No," Latoia shook her head.

"Okay come on in and answer the phone. I'll listen with you in case he is trying to see how you feel after coming home."

Her hands were shaking and she felt queasy again as she hurried to the telephone with the detective right behind her.

"Hello," her voice was quivery and quiet compared to her usual robust exuberance.

"Latoia, I know I woke you up and I'm so sorry but I have a good reason, I promise," Courtney gushed.

"Courtney," Latoia swayed against the kitchen counter with a long breath of relief.

The detective stepped away a few steps when Latoia signaled that it was her friend. Then she turned back to the telephone and listened intently.

"Oh my God," Latoia's eyes grew large when she heard what Courtney described in the painting, "You would not believe what has just happened to me," suddenly Denton's meaty hand shot out and covered the receiver.

"Don't tell anyone anything about this. We don't want a lot of details going public. I'm having a devil of a time keeping too much information from getting to the publicity mongers out front as it is," he growled.

"Latoia are you all right? Is there someone with you? Do you need help?" Courtney was starting to feel panicked. She could not make out what the rough male voice was saying, but she was getting some very bad feelings in the pit of her stomach.

"No, no, I'm fine but just hang on a second. Okay take this number down. It's Stephanie's house. I am going over there for a few days. Now listen," she continued after she had given Courtney the telephone number, "Detective Denton is here with me and I think you should describe each of those pictures to him. I haven't had any sleep so I'll call you probably tomorrow when my brain isn't so fried, now hang on a sec."

Latoia turned to the frowning middle aged man, "Now listen," she said, some of the strength returning to her voice, "I want you to open your mind and just listen to what my friend has to say. I have witnessed her ability and I know it's real. She is psychic. She lives in Charleston, South Carolina so there is no way she could know what happened here. Take notes." Latoia shoved the receiver at him. He slowly lifted it to his ear, his expression clearly displaying his skeptical attitude.

CHAPTER THIRTEEN

Latoia watched as the detective listened and occasionally scribbled something on his note pad. After a few minutes he asked for her full name and a number where he could contact her. He gave her his own contact information and hung up.

"Well?" Latoia said raising one eyebrow.

"Very interesting," was the noncommittal reply.

A small stir of excitement from outside caught their attention. The impound truck had arrived and the VW was loaded onto the open flat bed. Latoia wanted to cry. She felt dizzy, sick and hyper awake all at the same time. Her brief bravado had dissipated as quickly as it had come.

Just as the impound truck pulled out, a black limousine glided slowly through the gathering crowd honking to get people to move and finally blocked by a patrol car with flashing lights it came to a full stop.

"C'mon girl our ride is here!" Stephanie hurried to Latoia's side. " The driver will grab our suitcases. Don't bother trying to get any more clothes. We'll just take our New York bags with us and figure out the rest later.

"You ordered a limo?"

"Of course Honey. Might as well go out in style for the cameras doncha think? Anyway he is just going to take us to the airport to get my car. The press doesn't need to know that though. But that way it shouldn't cost much and I'll just write it off on my income tax." Stephanie smiled covertly, but when she faced the reporters her expression was serious and urgent.

"You are something else Stephanie Mills." Latoia shook her head.

The driver took their bags and held the door open for them even acting as a shield against the prying red eye of the press cameras. He stowed the suitcases and drove off as rapidly as possible considering the now crowded street.

Within a few minutes they were at the airport and loading their bags into Stephanie's car. They were both feeling the strain of nerves and lack of sleep.

"I have some wonderful sleeping pills and muscle relaxers at home. We can get something to eat and then shut down the telephones. We can sleep for hours undisturbed. I have a beautiful guest room that absolutely no one has ever used . I think you'll be very comfortable there." Stephanie kept up a steady stream of chatter during the drive to her house.

Latoia's mind barely registered anything she said. She was so numb and disoriented. It was just too much. Her mind jumped from one scenario to another. She flashed back to the death of her brother; the runway in Las Vegas, being drugged in the hotel room, the poor girl beside her dead. Now some deranged pervert had broken into her home, took her underwear and wrote strange messages all over everything.

"Here we are," Stephanie chirped, as she slowed down to wave to the guard at the entrance to her luxury condominium complex. "Just hang on for a few more minutes and you can have a bath, some food and a long nap. Oh God my head hurts. I think I need about half a bottle of aspirin," Stephanie moaned pathetically.

They took the elevator to the second floor and dragged themselves to Stephanie's door. It was a hot day and both women were grateful for the air-conditioned interior.

The rooms were spacious with high ceilings and tall windows. Thick white throw rugs dotted the shiny hardwood floors. End tables made of glass were topped with crystal-based lamps and a beveled glass coffee table added to the airy feeling. Crystal vases filled with pastel flowers matched the mounds of soft pillows that lay like pastel clouds on the cushy cream sofa and loveseat. The room exuded an aura of ultra femininity. Latoia loved it. She wanted to just lie amongst all of those pillows and melt into them. She decided that it suited Stephanie perfectly.

"You like it?" Stephanie asked from the kitchen.

"I do. It's beautiful. It really looks just like you."

"Leave your bag there and c'mon in here." Stephanie had already broken several eggs in the frying pan and buttered two bagel halves. She shoved the bagels under the broiler, poured orange juice and set out two white plates with dainty pink flowers around the edge. "They were my grandmother's. These are the only heirlooms I own except for my ring. Hope you like cream cheese and strawberry preserves. I seem to be out of everything else."

"My goodness this is perfect. I've never seen anyone put together a meal as quickly as you do Steph." Latoia watched in amazement as the large beautiful woman moved efficiently around her kitchen.

"Don't' tell anyone but in my younger days I worked as a cook in a little diner. Now sit down here and eat and don't tell me no, you will hurt my feelings."

Latoia found that the food did taste good and she felt almost normal.

"Now," Stephanie watched her friend relax and when she had eaten her fill she stood up speaking briskly, "you come with me upstairs and I'll show you to your room."

Latoia could feel the fatigue tugging at her limbs as she lugged her bag up the staircase.

"Here we are. Bathroom is in there," she pointed to the left with long laquered nails catching Latoia's attention. "Get in the shower and I am going to bring you a nightgown and robe. I am also going to put a sleeping pill and a glass of water here beside the bed. I want you to take it and go to sleep. We'll talk about everything when we wake up even if it's tomorrow!" Stephanie laughed and hurried from the room.

Latoia showered standing under the hot spray for a long time. When she finished, she wrapped herself in an enormous bath towel and walked into the bedroom. Stephanie had left a soft silky beige gown and matching robe folded neatly on the bed. A small white pill lay on a little plate next to a glass of water. She slipped into the gown and sat on the side of the bed. She swallowed the pill with several gulps of water and then eased herself under the covers. The bed and pillows were ultra soft and sweet smelling. It took only a few minutes to feel the heaviness of sleep pushing down on her eyelids. She gave herself completely to her fatigue and soon floated into a restful deep sleep.

***

Courtney was shaken when she hung up the telephone. Not again. How could this terrible thing be happening to Latoia? It was simply too bizarre to have someone breaking into what used to be her studio apartment. For a few seconds she flashed back to her own frightening experience with Antonio. Could it be coincidence or were the break-ins connected.

"What happened?" Stephen had come into the library with Caitlin following behind.

"I just spoke with my friend Latoia. It seems that ol' red eyes has already struck. He got into her apartment, which used to be my apartment. He did obscene things. She wasn't able to give me details. The police were there, but I could sense how awful and violated she must feel."

"Unbelievable! Well does she have family or at least a safe place to go?" Stephen frowned with concern.

"Yes, she is going to stay with Stephanie, who is her friend and also her agent, so I think she'll be okay there."

"I'm glad. Having your home invaded and the belief in your own safe haven disrupted is one of the most disturbing upsets of the psyche."

Courtney was touched as she felt his genuine compassion and concern wash over her.

"Hattie told us to go for a walk in the garden or out on the pier before it gets too hot. She is preparing lunch and says it will be ready by the time we get back. Do you feel like joining us?"

"Of course. I know Latoia is safe for the moment."

"Safe for the moment," Caitlin murmured.

The three of them followed the path down to the river and walked up onto the pier. It was cooler there and they all fell silent, captivated by the sound of the water and the beauty of the willow trees lining the banks. The willow branches swayed along with the tall grass growing along the river. It seemed that they performed a graceful dance in the breeze.

Caitlin limped forward to the end of the pier. Courtney stiffened as her sister neared the edge. But she dropped Brown on the wooden planks and then lay on her stomach. She stuck her head out over the water and reached her good hand down to trail her fingers in the water.

Stephen and Courtney following her example, sat down on the wooden bench nearby.

Courtney breathed deeply and relaxed. The three of them together just felt right. They remained in a comfortable silence. It was enough to simply listen to the conversation of nature. Latoia's plight replayed in her mind. She visualized her sister's paintings and pondered their prophetic nature. She wondered if, together, they would be able to help the police find the man that was terrorizing Latoia. She prayed that her friend would be safe.

Stephen noted the frown on Courtney's brow. He had the sudden desire to erase all of the worry from her life. He knew that logically it would not be possible, but his heart would not listen to logic. He breathed in the summer air and smiled. Here he was with two of the most extraordinary women he had ever met in his life, on a dock over-looking the Ashley River. He had eaten the best breakfast he could remember in an aging plantation home descended from the Civil war. He had witnessed an autistic girl paint an event that she saw only through her psyche. If that wasn't magic then nothing was.

A clanging bell jarred all of them from their reverie.

"That's Hattie telling us that lunch is ready," Courtney smiled. Even Caitlin responded to the bell and had begun to scramble to her feet. She picked up Brown and lurched forward as she turned to go back to Willows with Brown under her arm.

Courtney watched as her sister walked, and thought maybe she would try to use the energy on her sometime soon. She also wondered if exercises would help her strengthen her weak leg. There would be a lot of time in the future for things like that to be worked out.

During lunch, Clarisa announced that she would be going back home on Tuesday but that she would return in a few weeks. She needed to see her husband and see to her home and her son Shane, who would be home for a long weekend before his classes began again at the end of August.

The tug in her heart was unmistakable. She was her own person but she would miss her mother. She knew from within the deepest region of her inner self that this would be their life now. Courtney knew she belonged at Willows and her mother belonged with her own life in California. She had always known this day would come but now it had. Something had changed in their relationship. Courtney knew that she had matured and become more sure of herself and her mother was recognizing her on another level as a young woman, independent and capable.

"I have gone through mother's accounts and I think everything is in order. I've spoken with her attorneys and it looks like they have everything under control," Clarisa smiled, "Courtney I think you are going to be doin' a wonderful job with your sister. I am so happy that you have found each other. But I'm going to miss you so much. Your father has had to spend a lot of time by himself this year. I need to keep him company."

"Of course, Mom. I'll miss you too but I do need to stay here now," Courtney and Clarisa gazed at each other sharing a mutual understanding.

"Stephen I certainly hope you will be a regular visitor here. It would make me feel better to know that Courtney has a friend like you."

"I would be very happy to accept every invitation that is extended to me. Thank you Clarisa."

"Thank you Clarisa," Caitlin echoed.

When the lunch dishes were cleared, Courtney suggested they go into the library. She wanted to talk to Caitlin and show her some picture albums. She did not know how much her sister would understand with her physical consciousness but she felt that on some level Caitlin knew everything that was going on around her.

Stephen went out to his well-worn van to retrieve his notebook. There were so many things happening, he had to start taking notes so as not to lose any part of it. He nearly sprinted back in so that he could observe everything.

Courtney chose the album with the most recent pictures. She sat down on the large brown leather sofa and called out to Caitlin using only her thoughts. At first there was no response. Caitlin merely held Brown up to her face covering her mouth and nose so that only her eyes were visible. She rocked gently back and forth as her eyes roamed the bookshelves restlessly from top to bottom.

Courtney focused and tried again, calling her name silently and then asking her to sit down on the sofa so that she could show her the family pictures.

"I heard you the first time," came the silent response, "This is the first time I have ever been in a library."

Courtney was stunned and pleased. It was the first time she had actually tried to reach out to her sister with thoughts and then illicited a response. Their previous communication had been almost accidental or spontaneous. Tears welled up in her eyes as she realized the possibilities that were now open to them.

Caitlin turned and walked over to the sofa and sat down near her sister.

Courtney's heart swelled with joy and she had to hastily wipe away escaping tears. She opened the album and pointed at each snap shot. "This is me when my parents adopted me. This is my…our grandmother, Esther Camden. She had a stroke and is in the hospital right now. That's why my mom, Clarisa Hammond, is here," and so it went. They spoke in the silent

132

whispers that only they could hear and understand. To them it would become as natural as any two people having an ordinary conversation. To the world it would be a phenomenon difficult to believe, impossible for most to accept and something the average person would never understand.

Stephen entered the library unnoticed. He stood in the doorway holding his notebook watching the sisters as they sat quietly looking at the album. He watched Courtney pointing to images and Caitlin as her head bobbed around and her eyes continually looked around the room then darted back to the open page. Suddenly Courtney giggled and Caitlin imitated it. It was eerie the way they seemed to communicate without using words. A chill of realization rippled through him as he dared to think that they might be doing just that. Extraordinary, was all his mind could register. He made his way quietly to the desk and sat down so that he could observe them without disturbing them. He opened the notebook and began documenting everything since his arrival early that morning. This would be one for the record books. Speaking of books maybe he would write a book about all of this someday and that thought brought a smile to his face. There would be only one problem; no one would believe the part about the prophetic paintings. For that matter the scientific community much less the general population probably would not believe the telepathic communication either. Well he would think about all of that at another time. Right now he was just going to observe and make notes.

***

Zeke Darmon sat on the little chair that had belonged to his mother's vanity table. Instead of cologne and dainty jars of cream, he had covered the table with all types of lacy underwear. The new collection made him happy. It had been a long time since his last one. Recalling the memories of that shattering experience made him shudder. He would never look for his Martita on the street again. He was choosing very carefully this time.

Zeke shook his head as he remembered thinking that Martita was walking down the street in a bad part of town at midnight. She was a good person and she would never do something like that. The Martita he had found wasn't even a woman, at least not where it counted anyway. What a foul mouth that person had. He could not abide filthy language. Bad words could not be spoken with no tongue; simple. Just like Vietnam. He hated all of that nasty babble no one could understand. With no tongue they said nothing.

He thought fondly of his snug little cave in the Topanga Canyon hills. Hippies had lived there for a time in the sixties. He had literally stumbled into it after he got back from Vietnam. He had just lost Martita. It was his father's fault and they had fought visciously until the older man succcumed under Zeke's superior strength. He had put the body in the trunk and drove to the hills to think. He always did that. This time when he took his usual path it was nearly dark and he slipped on some loose rock and fell a few feet through dry brush and landed at the entrance to the cave. No one could see it from the trail because the trail was on top of the cave. He had walked over it hundreds of times. It was fate. He knew it was meant to be his.

He had put his father in the cave for a while. The smell of decomposing bodies was repugnant to most people but it was not so bad in the cave. There was some sort of seepage about fifty yards in. The body had served as snack food for various rodents but ultimately it had become mummified. That's when he took it home. He wanted to show his father how it felt to be abused and maligned as he had been as a child.

He had also put his latest find in the cave. But that was not his beloved Martitia. Once he had removed the tongue that spoke such vile words he had planned to enjoy his honeymoon. The whole thing was spoiled when he tried to put some pretty underwear on her and discovered it was not a 'her' at all. He had removed the offensive appendage, but it just wasn't the same. He kept all of his Martitas in there except that one. He had buried pieces and parts in various places. It is so much easier to do a little at a time. His mother had taught him that. If you cannot get the whole task done at once, then just do a little at a time. Before you know it you're finished.

He held up a pair of satin panties with lace around the waistband. He loved the feel of the soft fabric. He put it up to his nose and drew in the womanly scent tinged with a light trace of cologne. Then his eyes moved up to Latoia's picture pinned firmly to the wall near Martita. All of the other pictures had once held that position of honor but they had fallen from favor so he moved them to the outer perimeter.

The candles flickered around the room helping him to relax. He had not slept for two nights. The first night was because the excitement stirred up his anticipation to the point that his mind simply would not allow him to rest. The second night was because he had been there, near her. He could smell her and it was intoxicating, so much so that he had almost stayed too long getting out just minutes before she got home. It was to have been so perfect. But the one with the filthy mouth had come with her. If that had not happened they would be together right now. At first he had been so angry he had wanted to kill them both. But then he calmed down when he realized that it was meant to be. It would have been a hurried encounter. What he really wanted was to take his time with her. He wanted to take her to the cave and then when she was ready, bring her home.

Choosing carefully he picked up his favored articles and lay down on the bed. He rubbed his face with each article of clothing. It was soothing to know that his Martita would be coming home soon. Now he would sleep at last.

***

Latoia's eyes fluttered open. She sat up with a start not knowing where she was. Sun streamed through small spaces in the blinds and curtains that covered the windows. She felt a little fuzzy but she knew that would be from the sleeping pill. Well no matter, it was good that she had been able to sleep all day. She felt somewhat rested. Then she remembered that she had come home with Stephanie. Latoia stretched her arms up over her head and felt the stiffness in her back and shoulders. A long low rumble came from her stomach. That was the only wake up call she needed. She showered and dressed in the over-sized pink drawstring exercise pants and matching shirt that she found folded on the cream chaise. She didn't see her travel bag anywhere. Stephanie must have moved it.

The smell of fresh coffee greeted her as she got to the staircase. Her stomach was now on continuous growl mode so she quickened her descent. There was a pronounced weakness in her body. The stress from the trip and the break-in had taken its toll.

Stephanie sat in a little breakfast nook just off of the kitchen. Her face was hidden behind a newspaper. Someone was in the kitchen cooking. Latoia was startled to see an attractive gray-haired woman bustling to and fro, opening the refrigerator, slicing fruit, checking the oven…what was that wonderful smell?

"Good morning sleeping butterfly beauty. I was almost beginning to worry," Stephanie smiled as she put down her paper.

"Morning?" Latoia was completely confused. "What do you mean morning?"

"Honey, I mean morning because it *is* morning, Sunday morning to be exact. You've been asleep since yesterday. Come and eat. Margaret is a great cook," Stephanie beckoned to Latoia to join her on the other side of the small table. The woman in the kitchen looked up and smiled. Little lines around her eyes gave the impression that her eyes were sparkling.

"Oh my God! I slept like twenty-four hours!" Latoia's eyes were huge with disbelief.

"Yes you did baby." Stephanie grinned and arched one eyebrow.

As Latoia sat down on the cushioned bench, Margaret placed a steaming cup of coffee in front of her. Another mournful growl came from her stomach.

"Margaret you need to feed this girl. Her growling stomach is giving me a headache." Stephanie laughed.

"Look here, you've made the headlines," Stephanie held up a section of the paper; 'MODEL SHAKEN AFTER BREAK IN' the headlines announced on the front page of section B. There was a small picture of her face streaked with tears. There was a larger one that she instantly recognized as a headshot from her portfolio.

"Oh my God, I hope my mom hasn't seen this yet. She is gonna kill me for not calling her. She's probably at church but maybe Aunt Pearl is home." It took Latoia twenty minutes to persuade her aunt to calm down while Latoia convinced her that she was in a safe place. It seems that Auntie not only read the morning paper but she watched the news right before her church program came on. She liked the television minister better than the one at the local church. Pearl was ten years older than her sister, Latioa's mother, and complained of arthritis in her knees. It was easier for her to stay home and watch Sunday services than trying to cope with the pain of getting in and out of the car. Besides, though she loved her sister and loved sharing the house with her, it was very nice to have some time to herself on Sunday mornings.

"Steph, Aunt Pearl says the story is on television too," Latoia said with a touch of misery in her voice.

"Yes!" Stephanie punched the remote and searched the channels for a local news program. She did not have to search very long. "Oh girl you need to cheer up. This is great publicity. You are famous before you're famous!" She was chuckling and commenting about everything as the somber news anchor narrated what they knew of the story.

Latoia felt better after she finished her eggs benedict and a small dish of fresh fruit. Margret cleared away the breakfast dishes and straightened the kitchen. At some point she disappeared.

"Margret has been with me for about five years. She doesn't seem to have any family except a son who lives in Seattle, Washington. She is semi-retired but mostly not. She always does more than I ask her to and she makes it seem so easy. I'm happy to have her. I don't really have much family either. I think she is taking care of your clothes. Don't even try to protest. It won't do any good. She'll just do what she wants anyway." Stephanie smiled.

"Now we have to talk, or I should say, I have to talk and you have to listen."

"Steph I've never known it to be any other way," Latoia sighed with mock irritation and an exaggerated eye roll.

"You'd better believe it, Honey. Now this is the plan. You are moving in with me and don't even think about saying no. You've got some creep stalking you and it's not safe for you in that cracker box place. You have a contract pending that will make you rich and famous and that's only the beginning. I don't want some idiot pervert hurting you or preventing you from a life that a thousand other models would kill to have," she stopped to take a breath and gave a little nod of her head as if to signify that everything was final.

"Okay," Latoia said quietly.

"Okay? You're not even going to give me a decent argument?"

"Would it do any good?"

"No," Steph's blond hair bounced and swayed as she vigorously shook her head.

"Well okay then and thank you. I love that little place and Courtney was so good to let me use it, but I don't think I could go back there anyway. This makes the second time someone has broken in there." Latoia's hands twisted nervously.

"Bad vibes," Stephanie nodded sagely pursing her lips. "As soon as the police are finished there I'm going to hire someone to clean out that place and bring everything here."

Latoia's eyes filled with tears as she reached across the table to grasp her friend's hand in gratitude.

***

Stephen was astounded at the amount of food that covered the oval dining room table. Fried chicken, macaroni and cheese, vegetable salad, baked beans and freshly made hot biscuits. He had already eaten more than normal that day, but in spite of the previous meals his mouth still watered and his stomach growled as though he had not eaten a good meal in days.

They had all become comfortable with each other and enjoyed light conversation with their meal. Hattie kept jumping up to answer the telephone. She was planning to stay after church the next day for a potluck lunch and then a big choir rehearsal.

"I want to thank all of you for your hospitality. I hope you might indulge me one more day. I'd like to come back tomorrow if you don't mind. I have seen some incredible things since I've been here. In fact I could take C.C. back, I mean Caitlin."

"I mean Caitlin," came the echo.

"That would save you the drive Courtney."

"I certainly don't mind driving her back but if you want to do it then that's fine. And yes you are welcome to come back," Courtney smiled.

"Do you live here in Charleston?" Clarisa asked.

"No. I have one of the old staff cottages on the grounds at The Oaks. It's nice since I'm the only one out there, except for the ghosts," he joked. "They are probably going to tear them all down one of these days."

"Oh dear. Well there is no reason for you to make that long drive all the way out there and turn right around and come back again in the morning. I won't hear of it." Clarisa used her southern belle tone with him. "There is so much room here you can have the room at the end of the hall. We have all of the toiletries you might need and I'm sure we have a nice shirt you can borrow for tomorrow. Now it's all settled."

"Yes ma'am. Thank you." He did feel a little odd at having received such a generous offer from people he had just met, but it was nice to know that he would not have to drive the hot old VW van the next day.

Sunday morning Courtney woke early. She heard someone walking past her door. She knew from the uneven steps that her sister was already going downstairs, probably to paint.

"Yes I am." The voice was very clear in her head. This new communication was disconcerting but already she had grown more accustomed to it.

137

She showered quickly and within a short time she was in the kitchen starting the coffee. Hattie had already left for church but there was a series of little notes and covered dishes on the counter and in the refrigerator. Courtney smiled. Hattie was making sure that everyone was well fed in her absence.

"Good mornin' darlin'," Clarisa was up early too.

"Hi Mom. You going to see Grandmother today?"

"Yes. I'm only going for a short time this morning. She seems to be more alert at the start of the day. She gets tired and forgetful toward afternoon. Besides I want to spend a little more time with you before I leave."

They sat at the island sipping their coffee and talking until a crash bruised the silence of the house. They looked at each other with widened eyes then pushed their stools away from the island and hurried toward the sunroom with hearts racing in alarm.

Storm Cat raced past them on his way to the screen door in the kitchen. Courtney noticed that something was off but she would attend to him later. Her concern at that moment was her sister.

Caitlin stood holding Brown under her left arm and a paintbrush clutched in her right hand. White pages from a drawing tablet were strewn over the floor. Some of them had paw prints on them. Storm Cat had become a little too curious and stepped in wet acrylic. It obviously startled him into a flying leap knocking over bottles, charcoal pencils and drawing tablets.

Courtney and her mother laughed as they straightened the disarray after learning that Caitlin was unharmed. She ignored them and went back to work on the picture she was just finishing.

When Courtney focused on the painted image the smile left her face. It was Latoia again, her eyes wide with fear as a man's hand stabbed downward holding a knife.

CHAPTER FOURTEEN

"Captain Martin here. Listen, I'm running a fever and I've been pukin' my guts out all night. There's no way I can cover my shift today. I tried to get hold of Darmon but there's no answer." His usually deep booming voice was low and husky as he spoke to his superiors at the ProGuard main office in downtown Hollywood on Sunset Boulevard. A sheen of sweat covered the dark skin of his face and his dark brown eyes were dull with fatigue.

"Well, hunh. There must be some kind of bug goin' around. I got three men out sick today with the same symptoms. Two guys on vacation…had to pull in an extra guy for that charity function and Ross has already pulled a double."

Both parties were silent for a moment.

"So you tryin' to tell me you don't have anyone to cover my shift?"

"That about sums it up," came the reply.

"I repeat. I have a fever. My head is pounding. I'm weak from puking and you want me to protect a ten story building with half a brain and a sick stomach?" His voice rose to nearly full volume.

"That's the spirit. You just needed to get the ol' adrenaline pumping. Tell you what. I'll get Branley to stay until noon. That'll give you a little extra time to sleep in. All *you* gotta do is work five hours. It's Saturday, not too many people in the building today. Then you can have Sunday off. Give you time to get better. How's that."

Martin wanted to blast the smug young man and get rid of the cocky grin that he knew the kid was wearing. But the sad fact is he just didn't have the strength at that moment.

Wearily he swung his long legs over the side of the bed. His head throbbed with unrelenting ferocity. For a moment the room tilted then spun. He grabbed hold of the edge of the mattress until everything righted once again.

Gingerly he put some weight on his feet and slowly stood up. The empty nausea rolled through his stomach again causing him to fold his six foot five inch bulk forward and lurch toward the bathroom.

After a long shower, a cup of chicken bullion and several doses of over-the-counter cold and flu medications he felt close to human. In fact if he hadn't felt so weak he would like to go find that son of a bitch Darmon and drag him into work by the scruff of his neck. Just thinking about it made him feel better.

Finally he climbed into his Chevy pick-up and started the tedious journey from Burbank to Beverly Hills. Maybe one day he would sell the little house he and his wife had shared happily for so many years. He could probably make a tidy profit on it now. He just had not wanted to change anything since her death two years ago. They never had children and that was a disappointment to them both but they had a good fulfilling life together. He could move back to New York, he still had family there....naw, he liked California.

His musings came to an end as he parked and made his way to the guard's station. He thanked Branley, the guard who had worked an extended shift, then settled in for a quiet day.

The monitors showed no activity on any of the floors, so he decided to get some coffee from the first floor break room vending machine. The coffee was bad but the caffeine might help him get through the next few hours.

Two men entered through the glass doors and walked to his station. They were casually dressed and spoke to each other about a brainstorming session with someone else. They each signed in and asked directions to a third floor office. Captain Martin watched them take the elevator up. The light indicated that they had stopped on the third floor. He idly glanced at the monitor screen but for some reason the camera did not record their departure from the elevator or their presence in the hallway. He snapped to attention, forgetting about his bodily discomforts.

Captain Martin loved order, rules, discipline and routine. Those qualities were instilled in him by his father and were later reaffirmed in his military career. When something was out of order he was like a bloodhound sniffing around until he found the source of the problem. He immediately reported in to the main office, filled out his log and unlocked the safe box where the master keys were kept. Everything appeared to be in order. He checked the day's codes and found the appropriate master for the security camera and film room.

The large man walked with authoritative purpose as he strode to the elevator. His mind was running at full speed. What could possibly be on the third floor that someone would want to steal if that was even the reason for the camera glitch...maybe some movie star... No, no, no he told himself, head office would have notified me and the other guards, in fact they would have wanted even more security for something like that. No he was sure that it did not feel right. Illegal intent was behind this and the perpetrators did not want anyone to see them doing it....whatever *it* was.

He checked his garrison once more and found his mace, flashlight, keys and radio securely attached with strong leather straps at his waist. Then he stepped out of the elevator onto the second floor just as if he were making his normal rounds. He walked briskly along the carpeted corridor checking office doors and the janitor's closet. He made a cursory inspection of the breaker box and one unoccupied office space. Everything was quiet on the second floor.

Instead of returning to the elevator he walked to the stairwell and quietly opened the door. For such a large man he moved with smooth agility taking the stairs two at a time. When he reached the third floor landing he eased open the door and held his breath, listening. Silence. Then he heard a muffled sound like a door closing inside the office to his left.

He blew out his breath silently and waited while his heart resumed a regular cadence as he mentally ran through the list of third floor tenants that were not scheduled to be in the building over the weekend. Taylor and Sweeny Law Offices were on that list and were located in the space where he now heard other sounds. It was a small; mostly family run firm and they had specifically mentioned that they would be closed due to the wedding of one of the partners.

Wouldn't hurt to check.

The big man took out a large white handkerchief and wiped the beads of sweat from his face. He stepped into the corridor and tried to walk with a casual air as he approached the windowed door to the law offices. He tried the door and found it locked. Not good. In the past, anyone working here on a weekend did not lock the front door.

Using his third floor master key he unlocked the door and walked in.

"Paul?" He called, knowing full well that Paul Taylor was at his own wedding.

"Paul is not coming in until a little later," a young man stepped into view carrying a handful of files.

"Zat so?" Captain Martin responded. He noted the man's eyes darting around. "Well tell him I came by on my rounds," he continued nonchalantly.

"Will do, I spoke to him earlier and he is anxious to get this, uh, case off his desk. See ya, bye."

It was obvious to Martin that the man did not belong here. He turned to leave and heard another noise coming from the back. A file drawer was firmly snapped shut. He walked briskly to the next office and again used his master to open the door. Once he was inside, he radioed the head office and called the local police. Once all of the calls had been made he left that office and strode to a small janitor's closet and opened the door, thinking he could watch the door of the law offices in the event the intruders tried to leave.

He was startled to find that some new shelves had been built and a locked metal cabinet now stood against the north wall. Wire cables were fastened to the wall and disappeared down behind the cabinet. A quiet hum came from behind the locked doors.

"Hoboy. This isn't supposed to be here," he muttered. "What the hell is goin' on in this place!"

Within minutes the police arrived. The whole operation was quiet and efficient. The two men were still in the law offices and were completely surprised by the arrival of law enforcement. They were badly shaken and easily convinced to explain their unauthorized presence there. It was learned that the two men were trying to steal information and pictures of indiscretions of wealthy clients for future blackmail schemes. Not smart. The captain and the other guards would have a good laugh about the wannabe blackmailers. They had made a practice of breaking into Private Investigators offices for the same reasons and got the lunatic idea that lawyers would have even more information and pictures to sell.

Captain Martin was happy that this situation was easily resolved except for the lengthy reports that would need to be written. In his opinion the big discovery was in the metal cabinet. A representative from the building's management company, the owner's representative together with ProGuard Security and the maintenance company were called and Martin showed them what he had found. There was a series of cables and switches that led to the security cameras on every floor. Someone could control what the security cameras saw whenever they wanted to.

The owner of ProGuard Security took out all of the old film and installed new film. The idea being to study what someone was watching for and why. It was decided that buildings two and three should be inspected as well.

The hours since his shift had started had passed quickly with all of the excitement of the intruders and the discovery of the camera problems. Everything was once again quiet and the captain sat peacefully writing up his reports. He had been so stimulated that he had actually forgotten how sick he had been that morning. He was just finishing his report when the next guard reported for his shift. The captain was grateful to relinquish his duties. He briefed the guard on the events of the day and reported to head office. Just as he was ready to hang up, another voice interrupted his conversation with the dispatcher.

"Say, Martin….what do you know about security officer Darmon?"

"Darmon! I know I wanted to beat his ass for not being available this morning. He's quiet, grim…actually I don't think he ever said more than two words at any one time. Don't know much more than that. Why?"

"Don't know exactly. But he shows up on some of these tapes as going into several offices on a regular basis especially on the third floor. Of course I've only just started going through the tapes that we pulled today, so I guess I'll let you know if I find anything else. You go on home and rest. You got the day off tomorrow so talk to you Monday."

As Captain Martin turned his beloved Chevy pickup toward home his mind ground out the details of the tapes, cameras and Darmon. Something was up. He could feel it but he couldn't quite figure it out. His head throbbed as his mind tore into the puzzle of the mysterious cameras and tapes. When he finally pulled into his driveway, dinner, shower, aspirin and bed were the only things he wanted to think about. The one exception would be a large dose of nighttime flu medication…ahh yes now that was something to look forward to.

Clarisa was exhausted and keyed up at the same time. She felt so torn. She wanted to go home and fill the void that she felt by not having her husband with her. She missed him every time they had to be separated for more than a few days. The pain of missing him had become a physical ache. On the other side of it there was so much going on in Charleston with her mother and her daughter that she felt the need to be here for them as well. Then of course there is the whole issue with Caitlin and her well-being. She turned off the reading lamp by her bed and lay back on the pillow with a long tired breath.

There was something good and right about that young doctor. She thought about how the two of them looked as they sat on the dock by the river on Saturday. She had watched them from the house. Then on Sunday she observed their interaction and she sensed his sincerity and basic goodness. She was sure that something was happening between them. The thought of a relationship blossoming was actually comforting. That is when she knew it would be all right for her to go home.

Courtney had been through a terrible ordeal with Antonio, but she could see that her daughter had grown from the experience. She was handling a job, the discovery of her twin sister and her grandmother's illness. Clarisa smiled into the night as her heart filled with pride and love for this mature and wonderful young woman. "Just imagine something so wonderful coming from...my brother and that poor little Tessa." Clarisa's stomach clenched as she thought of the long dead Charles and she struggled to cleanse him from her thoughts.

Minutes ticked away and after an hour of restless tossing and turning, Clarisa began to relax. She thought of Courtney and her sister and the unbelievable events of the past two days. She knew that their coming together must have been ordained by a higher power. Their relationship was nothing short of a miracle. She was inexplicably comforted by that thought. Observing how everything had unfolded was proof to her that there truly was a higher power at work in all of their lives whether they believed in it or not.

Clarisa drifted to sleep with the image of her handsome smiling husband meeting her at the airport and for a time she slept peacefully and deeply. Her dreams took her back to her college days in England where she and Clyde had first met. The first time they danced together she knew he was the right one for her. She wanted his arms holding her close forever.

The beautiful dream began to turn dark and the loving arms grew tighter until she could hardly breathe. She struggled against the terrible embrace pushing with all of her strength. Clyde's loving expression was gone, replaced by the alcohol-crazed look of her brother Charles, as she had seen him after the debutante ball so long ago. The memory stabbed through the dream world and into her consciousness, penetrating the thick protective covering that had formed like calcium on a broken bone. Her psyche had not been able to cope with the horrors of that night and had firmly shut the door to her memories.

Clarisa fought with all of her strength to keep the terror of that night from intruding on the good life she had created for herself. It was too late though. The wall was breached. Clarisa's scream filled the night with agony, horror and helplessness.

"Mom! Mom?" Courtney knocked on Clarisa's door then opened it without waiting for an answer. "Mom, I heard you screaming. What is it? Are you all right?" Courtney had switched on the lights and was looking wildly around the room for a possible intruder.

Clarisa was standing against the wall with her arms wrapped around her self. She was sobbing uncontrollably and occasionally swatting at the air in front of her.

Courtney ran to her, "Mom! It's okay. I think you were just having a nightmare. I've got you now. Everything's okay. It's okay, shhhhh," Courtney gently touched the shaking, whimpering woman and slowly enfolded her in her arms.

Clarisa's legs buckled and both women slid down the wall to a sitting position on the floor.

"Lord have mercy and bring on the angels. We need help in here!" Hattie had grabbed a heavy flashlight and was holding it like a club. She was awakened by the screams and had hurried up the stairs a fast as she was able. She turned on lights and panted out prayers every step of the way.

Storm Cat dashed in and out of Clarisa's room, frantically adding his meow as if to hurry everyone along so that Clarisa could get the help she needed.

"Dear Lord Jesus what has happened here?" Hattie's eyes were huge and her breath came in short gasps.

"It looks like Mom had a nightmare, Hattie. I don't think there was an intruder."

"Oh my," Hattie shook her head as she looked down at Courtney's pale face. The irony of the daughter comforting her mother, a woman who had also been a daughter comforting and caring for *her* mother, was not lost with Hattie.

"Awright, now awright," Hattie put the big flashlight down and hurried into Clarisa's bathroom to find a washcloth. "Here you go child let your momma wipe her face with this cool cloth. I'm goin' to make all of us some tea. You just sit right there and I'll send it up on the dumb waiter."

Clarisa's sobs grew quieter within a few moments. Courtney stood up and found a box of tissues. She pulled some out and handed them to her mother and then sat down on the floor, cross-legged beside her.

"Mom. That must have been the mother of all nightmares," Courtney tried to smile though her own mouth was quavering badly. She hoped to lighten the mood and help her mother recover from the gripping terror that the dream had evoked.

Clarisa sputtered through a cough and sob combination as she fought to gain composure. She was shaking uncontrollably and her hands were cold and colorless. She was so happy to have her daughter's strong young arm around her shoulders, but a part of her was utterly mortified to have created such an hysterical scene. Courtney had been through so much of her own trauma in recent months, she needed her mother to be strong and stable.

"C'mon Mom, let me help you up. I'm sure you would be more comfortable sitting on the bed." Courtney helped her to stand and then guided her forward a few steps until she reached the bed. Clarisa was dizzy and disoriented. Courtney supported her with one arm and with her free hand she moved the tangled bed linens so that Clarisa could sit on the edge without tripping over the sheet and coverlet.

"Oh, I I'm sso sorry to have disturbed you," Clarisa finally managed to blurt out. She blew her nose with more tissues and dabbed at her eyes.

Courtney heard the mechanism for the silent waiter and hurried to help Hattie with the tray. Soon they were all seated on the large bed surrounded by magnificent cherry wood antiques as they sipped tea from English china.

Clarisa was calmer and the tremors had abated. "You are both so wonderful to be sitting here at..." she glanced at the beautiful German clock on the dressing table, "Two-thirty in the morning! Oh no I can't believe this. Hattie you had such a long day with your choir and Courtney you with your sister and then the worry about Latoia!" Clarisa's eyes were starting to fill again.

"Miz Clarisa you can just stop that right now. We want to be here for you and besides that we can all sleep late in the morning so don't you worry for one minute about it. Now drink your tea," Hattie spoke with gentle firmness. She wanted to reassure this woman that she had grown to love through the years, but something was bothering her about the nightmare. She felt something disturbing but she was not able to pinpoint it. She did know one thing for sure, this was no ordinary bad dream.

The three women spent the next thirty minutes sipping tea and talking. Clarisa declared that she was not able to remember anything about the dream or getting out of bed. "I think my hormones might be a little out of balance and then there has been a lot of stress with mother being ill," her voice trailed off and she brought the cup to her lips and drained it of the remainder of her tea.

"Mom, I'm glad you decided to go back home. You must be exhausted from spending so much time at the hospital with grandmother. I'm going to miss you but I think you need some time for yourself," like Hattie, Courtney had the sense that there was more going on with her mother than she would admit.

By three-thirty they were all back in their own beds and each had opted to leave a small night light on to chase away the menacing shadows real or imagined.

145

Rain pattered lightly on the roof and windows as Courtney lay wide-eyed and tense. She thought about the hours she had spent with her sister. She marveled at the amazing artistic talent that she displayed on a daily basis. But even more than that the incredible gift that they had both been given; the telepathic conversations that would enhance their relationship as well as helping others in some way. Then her thoughts drifted to Doctor Baylor, Stephen. She felt a kind of warmth toward him. He was kind and good with Caitlin. She found herself smiling as memories of the weekend replayed in her mind.

A soft knock on her door came as no surprise, "Are you still awake?" Clarisa whispered, "Would you mind keepin' me company tonight darlin'? That big ol' bed seems too lonely tonight."

"Sure Mom. You can sleep in here if you like."

"No, I mean…my bed is bigger. Why don't you come in here with me."

Courtney noticed the intensity of her mother's refusal to sleep in the bed that she had occupied as a child. That was something she would think about at another time.

As soon as Courtney climbed into the big bed with her mother she felt a tingle from the blue topaz that hung on a gold chain around her neck. How odd that it seemed to react at this moment. What could that possibly mean?

Clarisa sighed deeply and within moments her breathing was deep and regular. Courtney knew that she was falling asleep. Hattie's tea was obviously helping her to relax along with the sound of the rain. Her eyes closed and for just a split-second Courtney thought she heard a familiar whisper, "Thank you sister."

The rain was gone in the morning but it left a muggy dampness in the air. A ground mist hovered over the gardens of Willows, giving the flowers and giant topiaries the appearance of floating in an enchanted fairy world as the sun rose on Monday morning. None of the women were awake to enjoy the ethereal beauty. The mists were long gone and the sun was already heating up the Southern earth creating the steamy heat typical of August by the time any of them were awake.

At nine-thirty the fragrance of coffee brewing blended nicely with the feminine voices that chirped along with the birds greeting the day.

Clarisa smiled brightly as she joined her daughter and Hattie in the kitchen. Dark smudges were visible under her eyes despite her attempts to cover them with make-up.

"How are you feeling this morning Mom?" Courtney rose from her seat at the island and gave her mother a warm hug.

"Oh I'm just fine. I don't know what got into me last night. I am so sorry that I caused so much trouble." Clarisa flashed a genuine smile that fooled no one.

"Miss Clarisa, there is no reason to apologize for havin' a nightmare. We have all had them at sometime or other. How 'bout some coffee and croissants.

146

I have fruit too, unless you want some eggs. Now I could cook you up a mess a' eggs and grits and sausage if you want. I'd even bake some biscuits and gravy if it would make you feel better," Hattie grinned.

"No, no I can feel my thighs expanding just thinking about all of that delicious no no food!" Clarisa laughed. "I'll just have coffee, fruit and good company."

They talked and joked while they sipped coffee and nibbled on the colorful fruit that Hattie had artistically arranged in clear glass breakfast bowls. Storm Cat finished his breakfast and began a lengthy careful bath as he listened to his ladies talking.

"This has been wonderful as always," Clarisa stood up slowly. She discovered that her legs were a little shaky. "I need to pack and get ready to leave tomorrow. I want to go say good-bye to Mother this afternoon. Would either of you like to go with me?"

"That's a good idea, Mom. I'll be making visits out there too after you leave."

"I'd like to go too, Miz Camden is very special to me. I'll be glad to see her come home," Hattie chimed in.

Storm Cat decided that he had other business to attend to and stood at the door demanding to be let out. Hattie's hands were wet and soapy from cleaning up the breakfast dishes so Courtney did the honors of letting him outside.

Clouds hung low in the sky though the sun burned through revealing occasional patches of blue. Courtney stepped into the humid air and watched Storm Cat pick his way carefully across the gravel drive and disappear into the kitchen garden. She knew that what her mother had experienced the night before was more than just your average nightmare, but she had not been able to discern exactly what it was all about. Her inner knowing however, told her it was something she would be helping her mother cope with eventually.

She began to feel uneasy as though she were being watched. Her eyes darted back to the kitchen garden but whatever she noticed in her peripheral vision was not to be seen when she looked for it. Impulsively she sprinted across the drive and found the bush where Storm Cat had disappeared. She saw him crouched over something that wiggled and thrashed.

"Ugh, Storm Cat what are you doing to that poor creature?" She called. Storm Cat loosened his grip for an instant and she saw a flurry of activity in the tomato vines as the little being ran for its very life. Storm Cat backed out of the vines and she could see that he had something in his mouth.

"Come here you crazy cat and let me see what you have," Courtney spoke sweetly hoping to coax him closer. He came willingly and quickly, and immediately dropped the brown bundle he had held clenched in his teeth. Gingerly she bent to pick up what he dropped, expecting it to be a little brown bird or some other small animal.

"What in the world?" Courtney was speechless when she saw that it was nothing more than brown cloth. One edge was jagged telling her that Storm had ripped it off of his victim. "An animal wearing clothes?" She wondered what had just happened.

For the next twenty minutes Courtney looked under bushes, behind plants and up in trees. Storm Cat walked calmly beside her observing the search as if he knew that the creature she searched for was nowhere to be found.

"Courtney, child what're you doin' out there? You awright?"

"I'm here Hattie. I've got something to show you."

Hattie examined the small piece of cloth intently. Frown wrinkles creased her smooth dark skin and she muttered to herself for a few seconds.

"Well, well, well if I didn't know better I might say we had a visit from…something I've only seen once in a vision. You saw it too." Hattie looked up and directly into Courtney's eyes.

"Which vision? We've seen some truly unbelievable things Hattie," Courtney smiled.

"Do you remember the one with your sister in ancient Scotland?"

Courtney thought for a minute before the realization hit her. "What? Do you really think that's possible?" Courtney was incredulous.

"You askin' me about possibilities after all we've seen and experienced this past year? What's it gonna take to get the point across to you that there are no limits to possibilities. What we got here is a piece of homespun cloth from the Wee people of another time."

The two women did not speak as their minds worked to make sense of what they were seeing.

'Let's go help your momma pack. I'm puttin' this somewhere safe. We'll talk about it later."

Courtney nodded mutely and followed Hattie into the house.

CHAPTER FIFTEEN

Abigail had established herself very quickly in New York. She possessed an uncanny knack for ingratiating her way into whatever level of society she chose. For the first time in her life she was feeling excited and hopeful for the future. She had done a lot of thinking since she arrived in the Big Apple and was surprised to find that she had learned a few things about herself.

The first realization was that she liked the idea that the new people she was meeting, thought of her as a legitimate entrepreneur. She was almost ashamed that she had taken money and jewels without asking. One could not really call it stealing, after all, those former *clients* were born wealthy and there was no end in sight for their lavish lifestyles. She told herself that no one had come to harm or was reduced to a disgusting state of poverty because of anything she had done. Of course there was that unfortunate business with Kenton Barsop. It couldn't be said that it was all her fault. Well maybe it was, but the man was a criminal after all. His own greed, stupidity and lacivious appetites had led him to be murdered.

A nagging little voice inside her head reminded her that by taking that money and the plates used to make the counterfeit US dollars it was indeed, herself who unwittingly orchestrated his violent death.

"Ugh." She grimaced at the thought and shook her head vigorously trying to rid herself of the dark thoughts. "No he was not a good person and would have met a vile fate sooner or later!" Having spoken aloud in her hotel room made her feel better. This was the first real encounter with guilt she could ever remember. It was terribly uncomfortable and she did not like it at all. It might even make her give up her former profession entirely. Well that was a bit extreme. Maybe she needed to give it a little more thought before reaching any final conclusions.

Abigail finished dressing and applied a small amount of makeup. She wanted to look professional but not over-done. She had a meeting with two potential investors, a lawyer and an investment banker.

Financing her own business would not have been a problem. She had more than enough money to do nearly anything she wanted to do. She knew though that it woud be important to secure business contacts who would be her allies in the future should she need them. In any case she liked Alyson Stanwik, and Babette Dade, two wealthy women living in the mysterious netherland of fifty looking forty wishing thirty. Both women had already begun to travel the secret path to the land of eternally youthful appearance guided by the claims of a well-known plastic surgeon.

Abigail had no need for surgical intervention to date, but she was not averse to making that choice should it become necessary.

The meeting went well and everyone seemed to be happy with all of the proposals. There were only a few minor changes in the agreements and when all of the new papers were drawn up they would sign them probably on Friday.

"Shall we have lunch at the Russian Tea Room?" Abigail smiled at her new friends and soon to be business associates.

"Absolutely," Alyson nodded.

"You know I won't turn down an opportunity for a wonderful meal," Babette batted her expensive fake eyelashes.

As they chatted between bites of salad and tiny sandwichs cut in small triangles, Alyson finally brought up the subject she had been thinking about for several days. "Abigail, I know you have probably already engaged a decorator to help you put together your new home, but since I won't have anything to do on…"

"As far as I know you don't have anything to do anytime," Babette teased her friend with a sly look. They had known each other long enough that comments such as this were acceptable without any offense taken no matter how acerbic the remarks.

"Quiet please, my brain is about to have an idea," Alyson retorted mildly.

"Now that's something to listen to," Babette smirked.

"I would love to help you with your new home. I just love the idea of making that old warehouse into an exquisite living space!"

"I would love your input. As a point in fact I have as yet to engage a decorator. Perhaps we could put our heads together and toss about some ideas," Abigail felt a genuine excitement at the prospect of all of the plans she had made to settle herself into her new legitimate future…well almost legitimate.

"Just don't lose sight of our business interests ladies," Babette reminded them. "I don't deny that I'm looking forward to our Antiques and Sweets shop but I want a return on my investment too."

"Don't we all darling," Abigail lifted her teacup.

"Here, Here," Alyson lifted hers and the three women touched their cups together daintily.

"Too bad this isn't a Cosmo," Babette sighed mournfully.

They sat in silence for only a few seconds "I say we go in search of Cosmos and then we'll make this alliance official. All in favor say Martini!" Abigail spoke with appropriate solemnity for such a serious occasion.

"Martini," they chorused as the vote was finalized.

The laughter was immediate and uproarious and continued through the afternoon. It was a time of fun, bonding and business, followed by early evening headaches and hung-over remorse the next morning. Each woman suffered the consequences of the over-indulgence but it mattered very little to them. Each was thrilled to find new purpose and self worth in their venture together and each had found new friends to share it with.

Abigail had never really had any girl friends, at least none that lasted for more than a short time, even in school. Having feminine business partners who were also friends was an utterly new experience. She approached this as she did everything, relying completely on her gut instinct. It had never failed to warn her if she was making a mistake so there was no reason to think that this situation was any different. If she had even the slightest inkling that there could be trouble she would easily be able to let it all go and disappear. At least that was what she told herself.

The next morning she lay in her bed hanging on to her mattress for dear life as the room spun madly out of control. Her stomach made ominous gurgles and she declared to the spinning room that she had never felt better in all of her life. Then she hurtled toward the loo in hopes she would not heave on the carpet.

Cold tap water on her face and a hot shower swept away some of the cobwebs in her head. The raging headache behind her eyes was undaunted. She hoped the aspirin would take care of that in about twenty minutes. The trouble is she would not be able to tolerate the pain for that long without clawing her eyes out. She stumbled her way to the well-stocked mini bar and groped through the small bottles squinting at the labels. "Oh bloody hell, I don't care what it tastes like or what it is as long as it stops this pain!" She tore off the protective seal and removed the top as quickly as her shaking fingers could manage it. She tipped the bottle to her lips and guzzled the contents.

The molten liquid choked her and she coughed violently. The telephone rang at that moment. Her throat felt scalded but she reached to answer it regardless.

"What!?" She sputtered into the receiver.

"What? I'll tell you what. I hate you!" It was Babette's husky voice made deeper with the morning hour and liquor consumption of the previous night."

"Yeah, me too," Abigail groaned.

"Listen, I just wanted to say that I am looking forward to our mutual venture," Babette paused and Abigail heard a sound like ice cubes hitting the side of a glass.

"It's a bit early for the cocktail hour isn't it?" Abigail smirked as she studied the label of her mini bottle.

"Not early enough to get ahead of this miserable headache."

"I am in complete accord," Abigail sighed as she took another gulp. "I am in high anticipation myself, but surely that is not the real reason why you defied the monster hangover just to call and tell me that," the pounding in her head eased just slightly and Abigail's senses were on high alert.

"How can you be so, so British even with a hangover," Babette sounded edgy.

"I am British so it's easy. Now tell me what's going on."

"I am not the sentimental type."

"Yes, all right. I don't think I've ever been accused of that either," Abigail felt impatience tugging at her ragged mind as the room took another spin.

"It's just this, I've known Alyson for a long time. She has her troubles like we all do, but she is more fragile than most of us. I don't want to see her hurt."

Abigail was momentarily taken aback. "Ah, you mean you don't want her overtures of friendship rebuffed is that it?"

"You're not as hungover as I first thought," Babette's tone had become lighter.

"I've no intention of doing anything to hurt either one of you. I don't know too much about maintaining friendships but I know how not to. I suppose if I just do the opposite of that we should get along just fine."

Babette laughed. "I think you know a lot about how to get along in the world and get what you want. I can do that as well. Alyson is different than you and me. Somehow she has been able to keep a measure of innocence and excitement about life. It gives me hope when I see her enthusiasm. I just don't want her to lose that."

"Far be it from me to take that from anyone. And in fact I like her and you too even though we have only known each other for a short time. I would like to see us all become good friends as well as business partners."

"Hmm, that sounds good." More clinking sounds as ice cubes were shaken vigorously. "Okay then I will see you Monday morning when we meet at the location with the carpenters."

"I'll look forward to it," but Babette had already hung up.

Abigail sat unmoving for a few minutes, then slowly replaced the receiver. She respected Babette's directness and her abrupt manner. She knew that they were cut from the same cloth. It was going to be very interesting to see how their friendships and business interests would mix… or not mix.

***

Clarisa checked her luggage and received her boarding pass. She felt out of sync and nervous. She would be so glad to get back home. Her son Shane would add his humor and energy to the house when he came home from college and her beloved Clyde would lend his strength and support to whatever she needed in her life. Her mouth nearly watered at the thought of Maria's cooking though she loved Hattie's as well. Oh her own bed. How she wanted her own bed. She felt certain that if she could just sleep in her own bed the nightmares would stop and she would regain her peace.

"You should tell Dad that you need to be pampered and spoiled, Mom."

"I don't imagine I'll have to tell him. He has already decided to take a few days off so we can lounge around together and get caught up on everything." Clarisa already looked brighter at the prospect of going home.

"Don't forget to check with the Santa Monica police about my car."

"I won't forget dear. I told your father about everything. He said he would look into it."

"Mom I think my old apartment must be cursed or something. I just don't think Latoia or anyone else needs to live there. Anyway she said Stephanie has asked her to move in until the contracts are completed for the fragrance line."

"I agree honey. This has been a terrible ordeal for her. Do you think this incident is related to her other one or to what happened to you?"

"No this feels like something else, Mom. I'm going to do some thinking about all of this and see if I come up with anything."

Clarisa was quiet for a time as she gazed first at her daughter and then out of the large windows where planes taxied to and from passenger loading areas.

"Courtney, you have been through so much already. Please don't overly tax yourself further."

"I know Mom, but as you have told me so many times, things happen for a reason. I am stronger and hopefully wiser now. I'll be fine."

"Yes. I believe you will be fine."

Clarisa's flight was announced and the boarding process began. Mother and daughter looked at each other with tear filled eyes. They hugged tightly then turned to go their separate ways.

***

"Raeford? Oh. He ain't here Luv," the gravely voice hesitated and coughed deep wracking sounds and then wheezed noisily for a few seconds before continuing. "He'll ring you when 'e gets back."

"Okay, ask him to…"

Latoia found herself talking to a dial tone. She sighed and hung up just as Stephanie walked in.

"I am so happy that you have agreed to move in with me for awhile Miss Butterfly! You are going to be off and running before long and all of this will just seem like a bad dream. You'll be whisked away on the big silver bird to be photographed in France and your face will be seen around the world. Baby you'll be rich and famous and don't you dare forget us little people who helped get you there!" Stephanie was gesturing dramatically during her speech then suddenly turned with her hand on her hip and pointed a finger in Latoia's face.

"Don't worry, I'll never forget what you've done for me." Latoia smiled weakly. She was still jumpy and had almost no appetite.

"Have you been eating young lady? Stephanie was very aware of the weight that Latoia had been losing. "It's okay to be a little on the thin side for

153

the modeling gigs baby, but don't you let it go too far and make yourself sick. Now do you hear me?"

"Yes ma'am. You're actin' like my mother now. I might as well be livin' at home gettin' this ration of grief every day," Latoia playfully shot back.

"Don't mess with me now girl. I'm just getting started! Besides you are gonna think I'm a saint compared to those people who are directing you and telling you what to do every minute. Then of course there will be the promotional tour and you are going to be pushed and pulled in every direction for awhile," Stephanie stopped to take a breath and examine a long red nail that had a tiny chip in the polish.

"I already do think you're a saint," Latoia said softly.

"Right. I'll be a saint when pigs fly or hell becomes the Artic North," Stephanie laughed trying to keep the conversation light. But she was deeply touched by Latoia's heartfelt sentiments.

"Now are you ready to go into the office with me? I've made that appointment for you to speak with Doctor Krantzman on the eighth floor. I think it will help you cope with everything."

"I'm ready but the only thing that's going to help me cope is if they catch the freak that caused all this in the first place," Latoia rolled her eyes then grabbed her shoulder bag and followed her friend out to her car.

It was Wednesday morning and the first time Latioa had left Stephanie's apartment since she had arrived on Saturday. A wave of nausea hit her as she put her hand on the car door handle. That night flashed back through her mind. She saw the messages on the wall and her clothes on the floor. The shock of the memory made her knees weak.

"C'mon Latoia you can get through this," Stephanie's voice was strong and firm as she spoke from inside the car.

Latoia swallowed and opened the door. Her heart hammered against her chest and her mouth was dry.

"I'll walk you up to meet the doctor. He is the nicest man and in fact he even made me feel better after just a short conversation," her head bobbed back and forth as she talked while backing out of her parking place. She chattered on about a meeting with another client, where they would go for lunch and a shop that was having a sale on shoes.

By the time they reached the parking garage Latoia was feeling a little better. It was a beautiful day with very little smog. The temprature would climb no highter than eighty degrees and as usual there was very little humidity. The two women walked to the glass entry doors and Stehpanie pulled one open allowing Latoia to walk through first.

Two security guards stood at the sign-in desk. Stephanie knew both guards and she started to call out a greeting, but she stopped as she noticed that they seemed to be arguing. The shorter one was the first to turn in their direction as they walked to the desk preparing to sign in. His eyes lingered for a moment on Stephanie and without changing his stony expression he nodded a silent greeting to her then his eyes shifted to Latoia. There was no visable change in his demeaner, but Latoia felt chilled to the bone.

"Good day ladies," Captain Martin's voice boomed through the granite and marble reception area. He made an effort to be cordial but both women sensed his strained effort.

"Are you both guarding these hallowed doors today?" Stephanie smiled making an effort to lighten the moment.

"No ma'am. Just me. Security officer Darmon is just leaving on his way to another site," Captain Martin's smile was forced.

"Well then let's hope we all have a good day," Stephanie gushed as she and Latoia turned toward the elevators.

"Well just a little tension at the guards desk wouldn't you say," Stephanie's voice was lowered as she pushed the up arrow for the elevator. "Uh oh what's the matter sugar?"

Latoia had wrapped her arms tightly across her chest and squeezed her eyes shut. "That one guy gives me the creeps," she nearly stuttered as her lower jaw quivered like someone who was very cold.

"I know what you mean but I'm sure he's harmless. Anyway Captain Martin said he's moving to another site. He's a security guard so he must be ok, I mean they do background investigations on their people from what I understand. I think ProGuard is one of the best security companies," Stephanie continued to chatter as was her habit until she unlocked the door to her office.

"You sit down and make yourself comfortable while I heat up some water for tea. You have just enough time to collect your thoughts and sip some tea before your appointment!"

Latioa watched her friend's movements but she was unable to focus on anything she said. Terrifying pictures of her narrow escape months ago appeared unbidden, flashing through her mind. Then those pictures slithered into the ugly scene in her Santa Monica studio. Suddenly she couldn't breathe. Her lungs felt as though they were shut down completely and she knew she must be dying as Stephanie's office tilted and grew dim.

"Stop it," Stephanie commanded sharply. She could see that Latoia was held immobile in the steely grip of her painc. She ran to the tiny sink and hurriedly filled a small paper cup with cold water and tossed the water in the face of the terrified girl.

The shock of the cold water caused her to inhale sharply. Immediately she was breathing great gulps of air followed shortly by a storm of sobs.

"I'm sssorry. I just don't know what is wrong...with me," Latoia was crying hard and giant tears fell in a glistening waterfall down her brown satin cheekbones.

"I do Miss Superwoman. You have had some very bad things happen to you recently and you are not going to just get over it in one or two days. That is exactly the reason you are going upstairs to talk to the doctor!" Stephanie put her arm around Latoia's shoulders and held her until the sobs became sniffles and finally stopped altogether.

When it was time for her appointment she was calm and able to smile at one of Stephanie's wisecracks. She insisted that she was fine and to prove it she scooped up her shoulder bag and strode confidently out into the hall. Stephanie snatched up the telephone and called the doctor to give him a brief description of what had just happened. She was not at all sure that Latoia was fine.

***

Captain Martin reported in to the main office as soon as Darmon left. He was hoping that the man would drive directly to his assigned site and not cause any trouble. There was the other school of thought that if he chose not to follow orders then he could be fired. That thought brought a smile to the captain's face. Then he remembered that the company was short-handed and there were shifts that needed to be covered. A fierce scowl replaced his smile. He glared at the monitors while he nearly held his breath until his telephone rang thirty minutes later. Darmon had showed up at the new site and relieved the other guard.

Martin sighed as he hung up the receiver and though he wasn't smiling; his face took on a more peaceful expression as he turned back to his work.

***

Latoia deliberately fixed a smile on her face as she walked back into Stephanie's office. She really did feel better and the darkness of her earlier panic had lightened to a mere gray mist.

"Well now don't you have a pretty smile on your face," Stephanie spoke brightly, but she was not fooled by Latoia's smile. "How 'bout if you sit down for a few minutes while I make another call and then we'll go to lunch."

Stephanie's few minutes turned into another hour by the time she finally finished talking to a potential new client. She had been taking notes on a yellow legal pad. She dropped her pen and vigorously massaged her hand.

"Well I am famished how about you?" She leaned back in her chair and stretched. "Can't have all work and no play can we?" She raised her eyebrow and grinned with a glint of mischief in her eyes.

"The question is, do you ever work?" Latoia baited her with a little of the old self-confidence returning to her voice.

"I don't know what you're talking about. I work my dainty fingers to the bone in this sweatshop every day just trying to do the right thing for all of my clients. I'll have you know Miss Know It All. That means I get to take a nice long lunch and you and I get to have facials! Now don't argue with me," she put her hand up to stop Latoia's protest. "I have already made an appointment

156

for us after lunch so we'd better get moving. Celeste gets touchy if her clients show up late."

They decided on salads and iced raspberry tea for lunch followed by a scoop of vanilla ice cream drizzled with strawberry sauce, topped with a dollup of whipped cream and sliced fresh strawberries. A beautifully presented dish of crisp sugar wafers sat between them as they savored the end of their meal.

"Oh dear. I am so full but I simply can not leave one red berry in my bowl to be thrown out," Stephanie speared the last slice and popped it into her mouth. She shut her eyes and moaned with pleasure. Latoia laughed.

"Well imagine meeting you here," the deep masculine voice startled them both.

The tall slim man was wearing tailored beige pants and a matching short sleeve golf shirt. His smile was charming and flirtatious as his eyes raked over Stephanie's voluptuous form. He was probably a few years older than the agent according to the gray streaks in his dark hair. His even white teeth fairly glowed in contrast with the deeply tanned skin of his face and nicely toned arms.

"Daniel Taylor, I haven't seen you in months."

Latoia could see something pass between them. She pushed back from the table and excused herself. She took her time in the ladies room, washing her hands carefully, patting them dry and using some of the floral scented lotion on her skin. When she returned to the table, Daniel was seated in the extra chair and was leaning toward Stephanie.

"I need to be going," Daniel stood up as she arrived at the table. "Steph told me that good things are going to be happening for you," he grinned at Latoia but his attention was clearly directed at Stephanie.

"So I'll pick you up at your office about seven?"

"I am counting on it," Stephanie was beaming and her face was flushed.

"All right lady give it up, just who is that hunk?" Latoia demanded.

"It's a long story and we have a very important appointment. I'll tell you on the way."

Stephanie quickly outlined the relationship she had formed with Daniel. They had known each other for eleven years. He was a restless talented man that could never seem to settle into one career. He had produced two motion pictures and tried directing. He owned a small production company and produced documentaries. He invested in land and the stock market all of which made him very rich. Then he sold everything and moved to Europe. This was the first time she had seen him since he left.

The facial was relaxing and Latoia felt close to being her normal self. She was happy to follow along when Stephanie announced that she *needed* something new to wear on her date with Daniel that evening.

They visited several shops carefully selecting a tasteful dress and accessories that could be utilized on many different occasions.

157

It was nearly five o'clock by the time they arrived back at the office building. Captain Martin was gone and a new guard signed them in.

Stephanie took her purchases out of their bags and soon they were scattered across her desk and small sofa. "I'll just have time to bathe and get ready," she nearly giggled.

"You don't have time to go home and come back do you?"

"No dear. You are going to take my car home. I'm going to shower in the work out room down stairs. I have makeup and a hair dryer in my locker. I'll just have Daniel drop me off after dinner. Oh by the way, don't wait up. It could be a long dinner," Stephanie winked at Latoia as she rummaged in her purse for her car keys.

Latoia carefully pulled out into traffic and turned left. The car seats were leather and she felt a little thrill as thoughts of success and the possibility that she could own a beautiful car like this one filled her imagination. The traffic was heavy as she crawled along during the peak rush hour, but she was enjoying every moment.

Finally she turned off of the busy boulevard onto a quiet residential street and drove four blocks to the gated entrance of Stephanie's condominium complex. She had forgotten to ask Stephanie for the entry code. She could see two guards in the guard shack so she pulled close to the open door and stopped. A young security guard saluted and asked if he could help her.

"Yes I'm staying with my friend Stephanie Mills. She is at a dinner meeting and I forgot to get the security code.

The other guard turned as she began speaking. His face was partially shadowed. The young guard spoke to him respectfully explaining the situation. The older man mumbled something, flipped through some papers then walked toward Latoia.

"You're on the guest list," His stern blue eyes bored into hers and she felt the chill in her her body. "Enjoy your visit," his thin lips stretched into a smile but his eyes showed no expression at all.

Latoia's hands shook so badly she could hardly fit the key into the front door and punching in the security code nearly required a Divine miracle. She stumbled inside and went straight to the kitchen for a glass of water. When the phone rang a few ninutes later she jumped and dropped the glass onto the counter.

"Hello," Latoia's voice was breathless.

"Hi, are you okay?" Raeford's deep voice was exactly what she needed at that moment.

"I am so glad to hear your voice," she tried to choke back the tears of relief that threatened to flood down her cheeks. She just wanted to be in his arms right now. "Are you in town?" She asked hopefully.

'No, but I wish I could be."

Latoia wished he could be too, but even talking to him made her feel as though she were safer.

CHAPTER SIXTEEN

Courtney could smell the coffee brewing as she got out of bed. It seemed to her that no matter what was going on in her life during the past few months, when she woke up in her grandmother's plantation house to the pungent aroma of Hattie's coffee, she had the pleasant sensation that everything was okay. She felt safe.

The shower was hot and invigorating as she scrubbed her skin with fragrant soap and then shampooed her hair. Stephen's dark blue eyes and handsome face materialized in her thoughts. She smiled into the hot spray as mounds of bubbles slid down her hair and face carried by the rush of water. She remembered his voice, their long talks and the stirrings that she felt when he was near.

She wrapped a large white towel around her wet body then began to brush her teeth. She wondered what it would be like to be with a nice man like Stephen. She glanced into the mirror wondering if he would find her attractive like this. She ran her fingers through her long wet hair, which was already starting to form wispy curls around her face. Her skin appeared smooth and clear and even without mascara her eyelashes formed a dramatic dark frame around her Camden blue eyes.

She thought about him coming up behind her and lowering his lips to her bare shoulder. She imagined his warm breath on her skin and his lips softly kissing her and moving toward her neck and hairline. Her breathing quickened as she imagined his hands gently removing her towel and his hands sliding along her curves and…….

Suddenly she jolted out of her musings to find herself alone and her bath towel in a fluffy white mound around her feet. She actually blushed at her reflection and grabbed up her towel giggling like an embarrassed schoolgirl.

Later a flushed and smiling Courtney walked into the kitchen just as Hattie finished slicing a ripe honeydew melon.

"My oh my. Don't we look happy this mornin'. Does that glowin' smile have anything to do with a certain person comin' to call?" Hattie teased gleefully.

"Now Hattie you know I'm looking forward to seeing my long-lost sister again this evening," Courtney retorted with a small hint of defensiveness.

"Ummhmm, I think that's true all right but I happen to know that the young doctor bringing your dear sister here is what brings that blush to your cheeks,"

Hattie wagged a finger at Courtney after she poured steaming hot coffee into a flowered mug.

Courtney giggled in spite of herself. "Hattie how do you do that?"

"Child, did you forget who you was talkin' to?" Hattie stood with both hands on her hips and one eyebrow raised.

"No ma'am. I could never forget that. You won't let me!"

"You got that right young lady and I don't need no smart mouth back talk from the likes of you," Hattie grinned and opened her arms for a friendly hug.

Courtney speared a chunk of melon and chewed it slowly savoring the cold sweetness. "Seriously what do you think of Stephen? Is he for real? Is anyone...any man really that nice and dedicated to helping people?" She swallowed her melon and took a small sip of her coffee.

"Of course there are nice men, Baby, look at your own father." Hattie spoke softly knowing that Courtney spoke from the trauma she had suffered at the hands of Antoinio.

"I know but Dad is from a different era," she paused for a moment and then her face paled. "Oh my God! I just realized something. My real father was just like Antonio," her eyes filled with tears.

"Now you listen to me," Hattie spoke firmly,"Clyde Hammond is your real father. He is the one who worried over you and taught you to skate. Charles Camden was a spoiled boy with good genes who wanted his own way. He sweet-talked little Tessa and donated his sperm to create the two beautiful twins that will dedicate their lives to helping troubled people and lost souls." Her voice voice had risen and taken on the deeper tones of Aeonkisha.

Courtney shivered as she watched the image of the spirit woman form in a transparency over Hattie. Her spirit lion ran in mid-air over their heads and around the perimeter of the kitchen. She could feel the breeze ruffle her hair as he passed. After three rounds his powerful muscles bunched and he gathered his energy leaping toward the door. His growl reverberated and echoed for several seconds even after he disappeared into a ball of light.

"Now I hope you haven't forgotten all of the lessons you have been taught recently," Hattie's brow was deeply furrowed and her voice was stern. "You have been shown the circumstances and misdeeds of some of your past lives on earth. You are an evolving soul just like everyone else here on earth. You made bad choices in other times and places. You have the Divine Right to choose which path you want to follow at every fork in the road. Each path and every choice brings challenges and rewards according to the Divine Plan of your evolution. Karma teaches, rewards and guides every soul to the same ultimate destination, which is the highest possible consciousness."

The old kitchen was completely silent as Hattie stopped speaking. There was no sound from the refrigerator or the dripping faucet. Faraway voices sang in heavenly unison momentarily parting the veil of blind silence between heaven and earth.

Strobing flash points of clarity popped in Courtney's mind as the golden thread of her life path connected random circumstances, people and events bringing her to this place in time. She knew that everything and everyone had been training her for a future filled with service to others and rewards of wealth and joy for herself.

She saw also that the core of every person truly was good. The Creator's creation was a beautiful and pure energy. When the gift of free will was bestowed upon the pure forms, they were eager to sample everything and in those experiments they became obsessed with density and fascinated with bodies that drew them away from their home of brilliant light and perfection. Some began to try to find their way back after millenniums of satisfying blind appetites. Any Soul who searches for their way home begins to *see*, *know* and live in a more conscious way. Souls who are ready to advance are led to search for a way to create a magnificent paradise on earth filled with gardens, pure water, good health, joy and peace for all who choose to live there.

Courtney blinked as the visions and voices faded.

"So...I guess the answer to my question is yes, there are nice men," Courtney was dazed from all that she had seen and felt, but her ever-present sense of humor had not abandonded her.

"Child, hee hee hee you just never know what you're gonna get when you ask a question, do you?" Hattie's laughter bubbled into the room. All of the normal sounds returned including the insistant shriek of a blue Jay perched on the Azaelia bush just outside of the screen door.

Both women were surprised to find that their coffee was cool and that the sun had risen high in the sky. The morning had passed with surprising swiftness while they dallied beyond the earth's veil.

A plaintive meow signaled Storm Cat's desire to escape the noon heat. He climbed up on the screen using his claws to hang there before Hattie could get to the door.

A large van drove up and parked near the kitchen door. The weekly cleaning crew unloaded their equipment and trooped into the house. Two women were dispatched to the second floor while two other women and an older man began work on the first floor.

Courtney gathered up her own soiled linens and headed for the laundry room. She sorted out colors, whites and dance clothes and began the first load with a scoop of detergent.

The old plantation house was filled with the sounds and smells associated with industrious people doing their work freshening, scrubbing, polishing, vacuuming and above it all Hattie's booming voice sang joyous praises and blessings straight from her heart.

By four o'clock the cleaning crew was efficiently packing away their equipment and getting ready to leave. The newly polished furniture gleamed and the entire house seemed to stand taller as though it had taken on new life while being scrubbed. The clothes were washed and Courtney folded the last stack of towels before putting them away. She loved the smell and feel of clean clothes and she found the task of folding to be calming and normal. It settled her spirit while performing every day tasks.

She thought of her grandmother and her struggle to recover from her stroke. She had been to see Esther every morning during the past week. The recovery process was painfully slow but Courtney could see steady progress. She thought for a moment how grateful she was to have all of her faculties and to be living such a blessed life.

Voices on the first floor drew Courtney's attention. She left her room and stood at the top of the staircase listening. The unmistakeable sound of Caitlin's halting walk reached her before she caught sight of the girl's slim figure advancing through the wide open doors of the hall.

"Uh hello," Stephen's voice called from behind her sister, "I'm a little early I hope it's okay."

Courtney's heart gave a little lurch. It was more than okay.

"I thought it might be fun for us to all go out to eat, maybe just something casual. Caitlin loves hot dogs so I thought we could go to that little place on the Battery and get some seafood while she has her hot dog?" Stephen asked hopefully.

"She has her hot dogs. Caitlin loves hot dogs, hot dogs, hot dogs, she has her hot dogs," Caitin echoed in her flat sing song.

Courtney's breath was gone for a moment as she was struck by the rightness of the moment. It was as though some giant puzzle piece was put into place. Caitlin labored up the stairs dragging her ragged blue backpack with one hand and she clutched the worn brown Teddy bear with the other. Courtney decided she should try to teach her sister how to use her grandmother's lift. It was just so right. Stephen grinned at her from the floor below and Hattie bustled in from the kitchen wiping her hands on a dishtowel. She knew that no matter what had happened before in her life, it had brought her to this place at this moment and it was good.

Caitlin went straight to her room. She dropped her backpack on the floor with a muffled thump. She came back out immediately and started down the stairs still clutching Brown and mumbling about hot dogs.

Stephen turned to Hattie and did his best to convince her that she should go with them.

"Well thank you for inviting me but I already have plans to go to my daughter's house for dinner tonight. You all go on now and have a good time. There are plenty of things to eat in the refrigerator if you get hungry and decide to stay here."

Courtney grabbed her small shoulder bag and nearly skipped down the stairs.

The Battery was busy with tourists and those who simply wanted a stroll and a delicious snack. There was a breeze but the heat caused many faces to sparkle with perspiration. Courtney and Stephen ate their fill of shrimp and fried clams while Caitlin munched contentedly on a hot dog and French fries. Courtney noticed that people turned to stare on occasion. They would look at her sister noting her disabilities and then openly stare at her. It was disconcerting at first but she supposed that the three of them were a somewhat unusual sight.

Stephen appeared completely at ease and with his gentle lead they both kept up a steady stream of conversation. Time slipped away as they walked and talked. They found a shady bench with a view of the water. It was cooler there and they bought ice cream cones to eat in the shade.

Courtney felt a peace stealing over her. It was combined with a sense of well being and feeling safe in a way she had not experienced in a long time.

The sun began to slide noticeably toward the shimmering Atlantic. Caitlin sat transfixed with the sights and smells. Sometimes she rocked gently other times she closed her eyes with her head tilted back, nostrils flaring as if she were savoring some delicious fragrance. Then she would suddenly start kicking her legs and scuffing her shoes against the dirt just as though she was a small child.

Stephen and Courtney watched her as they talked, laughed and settled into a companionable silence.

"This has been one of the most remarkable experiences of my life," Stephen shook his head as if in mild disbelief.

"Well I can certainly relate to that," Courtney chuckled.

"Oh yes, I don't mean to diminish your experience at all. What you have been through…well no one can imagine how you are able to cope with it all. I have seen people emotionally disintegrate when they go through dramatic changes. But you seem very strong and centered."

"Thank you," she suddenly felt a little shy as he leaned closer and looked into her eyes. "I have been through even more but I'm not ready to talk about it yet. I know that I've been processing everything in small increments so my strong facade could crack at some point." She smiled trying to lighten the suddenly serious mood.

"I must say though, that I am truly fortunate, maybe blessed is what I am. I have…certain gifts and beliefs that have helped me make sense of my life. Otherwise I am absolutely certain that I would have come apart a few months ago." When she stopped speaking she noticed that Stephen had leaned even closer to her and his brow was furrowed with concern and concentration.

Her throat was suddenly dry and she desparately wanted to swallow but it was impossible. Her breathing quickened and the heat of the ignited chemistry between them was nearly unbearable. He leaned closer still and she lifted her face for the soft gentle press of his lips against hers.

Both of them were startled from their magnetic pull by strange sounds coming from Caitlin. She held Brown's face up to hers and was pressing the stuffed animal to her lips making loud smacking noises.

Courtney's face flushed red as she pulled away from Stephen. They both laughed trying to cover their nervous embarrassment.

"I'm sorry. I hope I didn't upset you," Stephen frowned with concern as he noted Courtney's retreat.

"I'm not upset. I mean I enjoyed the kiss. I just had a bad experience awhile back so I'm a little hesitant not because of you but because of that situation."

"Ah, yes," he nodded. "Well I just want you to know that I think you are beautiful, talented and remarkable in every way. I would not knowingly do anything to hurt you or your sister. I would really like us to be friends and maybe one of these weekends you will allow me to take you to dinner," Stephen spoke softly looking directly into her eyes. "Just the two of us."

Courtney watched his face as he spoke, but more than anything she felt what he was saying. Exploratory tendrils stretched from her heart to his. She felt his sincerity and tenderness. He was a good man. She wanted time with him, to create a friendship and possibly more. She was certain he was kind, genuine and honorable.

"You know Stephen," he nearly shivered with pleasure as she quietly spoke his name, "I am looking forward to every step of that journey."

He swallowed audibly and little beads of sweat popped up on his upper lip. "So am I Courtney," his voice was husky with emotion.

"So am I Courtney," Caitln echoed several times while intermittently smacking her lips on Brown's scuffed black plastic nose.

"Well I always wanted a little sister," Courtney chuckled.

"Be careful what you ask for," Stephen smiled.

Reluctant to leave they strolled slowly toward Stephen's old van. The air was oppressive as ominous dark clouds suddenly blockd the August sun. Thunder rolled from the watery horizon to the tourist filled streets of Charleston. When a flash of lightening streaked across the sky they began to hurry hoping to get to the car before the rain came. Caitlin's limp prevented them from moving as fast as they might have liked.

Large fat drops hit the sidewalk first, then within seconds the downpour was blinding. They were instantly drenched to the skin. Stephen ran ahead to the van and found an ancient umbrella with two loose spokes. Gallantly he tried to hold it over the two sisters, but the wind was hurtling powerful gusts through the crowds and successfully turned the umbrella inside out, rendering it useless.

Rainwater ran from their hair and their clothes were plastered to their skin when they finally clamored into the protection of the van. Stephen rummaged through the back and managed to produce four small towels that he kept for wiping his face when bicycling.

Courtney laughed with complete abandon as she wiped water from her eyes and attempted to dry the dripping hair around her face. She felt an inner freedom and joy in that moment that she had never before experienced.

Stephen handed a towel to Caitlin who sat in the back seat. She snatched the towel from him but instead of drying herself she rubbed Brown's face vigorously. He tapped Courtney on the shoulder and gestured for her to turn and look at Caitlin. She laughed again at the sight of her sister and the teddy bear. Her heart filled with emotion. It was a love so strong that she didn't know how there could be enough room in her heart to hold any more. She wanted to laugh and cry and run around in the rain. She had an adorable wonderful sister. She was blessed.

They waited in the van until the rain subsided. When they finally pulled onto the gravel drive of Willows it had grown dark. The house was dark and silent. Hattie was still with her family. It was strange for Courtney to feel like the hostess of the house. She was so accustomed to having someone else there to turn on the lights and welcome visitors. She had the odd sensation that a change had just taken place. It was she who would be taking on the role of the lady of the house.

Caitlin had fallen asleep immediately after her shower. Courtney gently disengaged the soaked Brown from her fingers and took him downstairs for a whirling ride in the dryer.

Stephen sat in the library writing in his notebook.

"Would you like a glass of wine?" Courtney spoke softly not wanting to startle him from his deep concentration.

"Sounds great. How is Caitlin?"

"She is sound asleep. I'm going to put this bedraggled animal in the dryer and then I'll get the wine. I wish we could go outside to drink it but after a rain like that the mosquitos will be buzzing around in a thick black ravenous cloud."

"Ugh. Sounds like the perfect set up for a horror movie. I have a fondness for wine in the safety of the library or the kitchen or anyplace that the little beasties can't get in." Courtney laughed at his comments and quickly took care of Brown then found a bottle of red wine. Just as she removed the cork she heard an urgent meow.

"Storm Cat. I guess you must be hungry." He answered her with a series of sounds while he rubbed against her legs and walked in figure eights through and around every step she took. She filled his dish with kitty crunchies and poured fresh water in his bowl. He purred loudly then got down to the business of eating. He made little crunching noises as he carefully chewed his dinner then sipped from his water bowl before delicately dipping his paws into the fresh water.

She leaned down to pat the damp fur between his ears. He didn't seem to mind being touched while he was bathing so she continued for a few more strokes until he turned once again to crunching on his dry food.

A blinding flash streaked by the window followed by an ear splitting clap of thunder. Storm Cat dropped his jaw mid-crunch allowing partially chewed pieces of his dry food to fall back onto his dish with small clattering sounds.

In the next second he was air-born with his front and back legs stretched to the maximum length as he leaped forward to disappear into Hattie's rooms off of the kitchen. Storm Cat did not like storms.

Courtney nearly doubled over laughing at his frantic escape. Then she felt guilty for laughing knowing that he was frightened. Laughing at the fear of another being was probably not a nice thing to do, but it was a funny sight. She hoped he would forgive her.

Stephen appeared in the doorway, "Everything all right?"

"Yes...Oh dear. I can't stop laughing. It was just so funny," Courtney had to wipe her eyes. "Storm Cat got scared of the thunder and virtually flew into Hattie's room. He joined her in laughter as she described the scene.

The wine was poured but before they could decide where they wanted to sit down and drink it, another lightening strike took out the electricity. They stood in shocked silence until the roaring thunder quieted.

"How about if we stay in the kitchen. I just happen to know where the candles are. You stay where you are and I'll get the matches and candles since I know my way around," Courtney chuckled. Her hands easily found the drawer where the matches and candles were kept. She lit the first candle and Stephen helped her light several more.

The old kitchen took on a soft inviting glow in the candlelight. They sat down at the island and sipped their wine while the storm battered the windows and whipped the branches of the trees just outside.

They commented on the wine and the storm, chatting then falling into silence. They felt comfortable with each other. Courtney was feeling the warmth of the wine. She remembered the vision of the lion that galloped around the top of the high ceiling. How odd that it had happened just that morning. It seemed as though it must have happened at least two days ago.

"Time is such an oddity," she spoke softly now that the wind had abated. The rain continued in a steady pleasant patter on the roof and windows.

"I agree, but in what way do you mean?" Stephen asked as he refilled their glasses.

"Well this morning seems like two days ago, but three months ago seems like this morning. I don't really have that many flash backs any more, but when I do it's as if everything just happened."

"When you have suffered a severe trauma then it isn't uncommon to revisit the event in the form of flashbacks. Have you had treatment or counseling to help you through it?"

Courtney heard the concern in his voice. She felt the warm person coming through the professional training. She sensed the urgings of unseen beings who help guide mortals along the treacherous earth paths. This was the time to reveal what had transpired with Antonio.

"Yes I have had some, but it may be time for some additional therapy."

"Tomorrow when the light is back I'll write down some names for you if you like. I've met some really fine doctors here in Charleston."

"Thank you. I do appreciate it." Courtney smiled, "Actually I would like to tell you what happened, so that you will understand some of the difficulties I have when considering a relationship with someone. I have watched you with my sister and the other patients. I know you are good. Your heart is good. Behind your gentle ways I sense strength and strong character. I have never told anyone outside of my family what happened until now."

Stephen let out a breath. He simply could not imagine anyone abusing this beautiful, intelligent young woman. He knew though, through his years of education and his work in the profession of psychology, that abuse of every type is all too common and that there is no discrimination. It happens to anyone regardless of gender, race or social status.

Courtney began her story. She started with the day on the beach when she saved Bernie from drowning. She explained how her mother gave her the blue topaz for her birthday and the visions that came afterward. She left nothing out including her fears about being crazy.

Stephen made no comments while she talked. He listened with an occasional shake of his head, a sound of surprise and interjections of encouragement.

She described the astral visits to the Oaks and thinking at the time she might be seeing her future self. When she told him about Aeonkisha and the lion, his eyebrows shot up and his face registered surprise but not disbelief.

It was more difficult to talk about the Scolari family wedding and Antonio's descent into madness. She felt so foolish at having been deceived by him and then was nearly killed.

Stephen took a large gulp of wine when she described the miraculous events leading to her rescue. She saw his jaw muscles working as he clenched and unclenched his teeth while she detailed the extent of her injuries and her subsequent hospitalization.

Courtney sipped her wine and wiped away the tears that had pooled in her eyes, before continuing.

"You know, while I was in that hospital bed I was in and out of consciousness but I was able to think clearly in an altered state. I discovered more about who I am and I learned more about my gifts than I had ever *consciously* known before. It was during that time that I fully accepted all of my eccentricities without making any negative judgments about myself for the first time. I used my abilities to help heal my injuries. I used my visions to tell the authorities what happeed to Antonio. It was then that I knew I had to come here and live with my grandmother and work with the ballet company.

"By moving here, you found your sister," Stephen murmured.

"I did, yes. I think there was a destiny at work here. I can't really hate Antonio, though what he did was despicable, but it did force me to accept myself and it led me to Caitlin. Those two events almost make me feel grateful to him."

"That is an amazing attitude. I think you have reached a degree of understanding in just a few short months, that most people spend many years searching for." They sat in silence for a few moments. " I can see why you might be reluctant to talk to a therapist about all of this," he grinned, "but I think you could speak with someone about the trauma of it all…Maybe leave out the part about the lion."

Courtney laughed and he joined her. They touched their wine glasses making a little clinking sound. They noticed that the rain had tapered off. The thunder was only a distant rumble. The night was quieting.

"So, does the lion come around very often?" He was joking but his eyes *did* dart to the shadowed corners of the kitchen.

Before she could respond, another bolt of lightening pierced the darkness followed by an earsplitting thunderclap that erupted over their heads. During the peak of the ominous explosion the unmistakable primal roar of a lion could be heard. The lights flickered back on.

"Holy….I think I might need to go hide under my covers now," Stephen's eyes were wide and his face had paled.

Courtney nodded and began blowing out candes and rinsing their glasses. They walked upstairs together holding hands. They stopped in front of Courtney's bedroom door. He bent to kiss her lightly and wish her good night. Then he continued down the hall to the room he had used during his last visit to Willows.

Exhaustion and at the same time relief over-took Courtney as she slipped out of her clothes and into a pale green cotton nightshirt. She let herself sink into the safe softness of her bed with a huge sigh. Her eyes drooped even as she reached over to turn off the lamp throwing the room into darkness. There was one small glow that would not dim.

"What?" Courtney whispered.

Caitlin's face appeared at the center with her stuffed bear. There was a glint of mischief in her eyes as she planted several loud smacking kisses on the bear's face.

"Lord have mercy everyone's got to get into the act," Courtney grumbled as she turned over and shut her eyes. Girlish giggles came from the vision before it faded, leaving only the pattering rain to play a soothing rhythm.

CHAPTER SEVENTEEN

When Courtney opened her eyes, she knew she had over-slept even though the sky was obviously still cloudy. The light coming through the lace curtains told her that the sun was well on the way toward mid-morning.

She stretched luxuriously and when she sat up she was surprised to find Storm Cat sitting at the end of her bed. He stared in unblinking silence for several seconds not uttering a purr or his usual greeting sounds.

"Uh, oh. Are you mad at me for laughing at you during the storm last night?" Storm Cat looked away.

"I am very sorry I hurt your feelings. I promise I won't do that again. Come here and I'll just scratch your chin." Storm Cat turned and looked at her but stayed where he was.

"Please forgive me. C'mon Storm Cat," she wheedled softly and held out her hand. He stood slowly and picked his way across the covers and sniffed at her fingers. Then he climbed up on to her leg and walked into her arms where he snuggled in for a hug and a moment of purring.

Courtney showered and dressed in cool turquoise as she thought about the muggy hot day ahead. She was surprised to smell coffee brewing and she wonderd if Hattie had already come back from her daughter's house.

When she walked into the kitchen it was Stephen who greeted her. He had made the coffee and had found some fruit and Hattie's cinnamon raisin muffins. He looked crisp and freshly shaved in his white Izod shirt and Khaki shorts.

"Good morning," he greeted her brightly, "I am not as good as Hattie but I did find enough for breakfast."

"Well thank you. I didn't mean to sleep so late. Have you seen Caitlin or Hattie?"

"Caitlin was up before me. She's in the sunroom painting and I haven't seen Hattie. Her car isn't here."

Courtney had just taken a sip of coffee when the telephone rang. Hattie was calling from her daughter's house. She wouldn't be back until late afternoon. Some trees had fallen during the storm and several roads were blocked. She wanted to wait until the roads were cleared before she tried to drive back.

"Guess it's just us until later today. Hattie has crammed the fridge with food so we'll have plenty to eat for lunch and snacks," Courtney smiled.

"There is probably enough in there for two more families to join us," Stephen laughed.

"Hattie has this *thing* about always having enough to eat. She was born on Daufauskie Island and all of the families there were poor. She was sent to live with relatives on the mainland so she could attend school. I think her life was always hard and getting enough to eat was a huge issue."

"She is amazing. I would love to just sit and listen to her talk about her life some day," Stephen commented thoughtfully. He had his notebook open and was busy making notes.

"So, how is the coffee?" Stephen frowned as he watched Courtney take another cautious sip.

"Good. Hot. Whew, a little on the strong side but I like it," she managed to keep from grimacing as she swallowed.

"Uh oh. I thought I was doing a good job of cutting back on my usual measurements," he laughed. "I've been drinking hospital cafeteria coffee for so long I guess I've forgotten how to make it for normal people."

"No, it really is fine. I think I'll just put a little cream in it," Courtney surreptitiously emptied some of the black brew in the sink and then poured in as much half and half as the cup could hold. She sipped daintily and turned toward Stephen, "See this is great. It just needed a little cream. I'm going in to say hello to Caitlin."

Stephen nodded and continued to write in his notebook.

Caitlin was completely engaged in her work. The well-worn brown bear's head peeked over the top of Caitlin's somewhat atrophied left arm. She held a paintbrush in her right hand and was expertly stroking across the white canvas, leaving bits of color wherever the bristles touched.

Courtney spoke her name softly but there was no response. Then she tried reaching out to her through her mind. Still there was no response. She tried again but found only silence. Worry frowns creased her forehead and her heartbeat quickened. This new communication with her sister was something she treasured and she did not want to lose it.

Quietly, Courtney took a few steps closer. She was sure that distance was not an issue in telepathic communication, but it was all so new and she just wasn't sure...

"Please step back and allow me to work in silence," the voice was distinct and clear in her thoughts.

"Ok, I just wanted to speak to you," Courtney put her hands up and backed up a few steps.

"Wanted to speak to you," Caitlin's body began the habitual rocking as she echoed aloud the words that Courtney sent silently.

"I am bringing in an important message. Let me work alone," the voice was again in Courtney's head.

"Okay, if you need anything just let me know," this time Courtney spoke aloud. She sighed then turned abruptly and nearly bumped into Stephen.

"You two are almost spooky," he mumbled as his eyes darted from one sister to the other.

"Is that a medical term, Doctor?" Courtney raised one eyebrow.

The telephone rang again as Courtney returned to the kitchen. One of Esther's garden club friends was visiting her at the convalescent home and had made the call for Esther.

"Grandmother, is everything all right?"

"Yes. I…am…fine. I want you to….mee wih my….lawya is week," Esther spoke slowly, hesitating often and slurring some words, but her mind was obviously very clear. "I wan …you…oo know abou my affiai. You wee….ow…Widdows…one day," Courtney could hear her ragged breath as she struggled to speak. "Numer…call….Lawya."

"Yes ma'am I will," but someone else was on the line again.

"Esther looks a little tired. Were you able to understand her?" the woman asked.

"Yes, perfectly. Thank you," Courtney closed her eyes and wondered how she was going to cope with everything as she hung up the phone. She had known it was coming after the long discussion she had with her mother. Somehow she had hoped that the inevitable meeting with the lawyers could be delayed. She did understand that it was important to begin meeting with them under the circumstances.

"Stephen, I am supposed to meet with grandmother's lawyers next week. After the meeting I want to take steps to become Caitlin's legal guardian."

Stephen nodded "I'll be glad to do whatever I can to help you with the process. I'd also like to discuss the possibility of conducting some tests with the two of you." He was excited about his ideas but he tried to present them with a calm enthusiasm that would in no way diminish the serious nature of his intentions. He had been interested in the subject of autism since he had witnessed the condition as an intern. He hoped to be able to write a book about the twins and while doing so, learn what could be done to understand and perhaps treat the condition more successfully. He had a fleeting glimpse of treatments that could possibly be groundbreaking and lead science closer to a cure than ever before.

The morning passed and the temperature climbed higher as did the humidity in the afternoon. Courtney tried to coax Caitlin away from her painting but she was met with stubborn refusal. She filled a plate with fruit and a sandwich cut in small pieces then placed it on a small table near her sister. She left a plastic cup of sun tea nearby and then stepped back. Caitlin did not look up from her work and when Courtney tried to look at the picture Caitlin started making a flat moaning noise everytime she got close. After two trys she left the room.

Hattie drove in at four o'clock. "My oldest grandson, Tyree, is got himself engaged. Can you believe it? Some one of these days I'll even be a great grandmother. I really do think I'm too young to be a great grandmother.

That's a job for old ladies not someone as young as I am!" Hattie huffed in carrying a large suitcase.

"Here let me get that for you Hattie," Stephen hurried to her side and reached for the suitcase.

"No, no it's not heavy. It's empty. I am still strong enough to carry an empty suitcase!"

"Yes ma'am."

"Now you can go on out to my car and bring in those bags of zuccini and tomatoes that my daughter gave me from her garden."

Hattie disappeared into her rooms and Stephen hurried out to the car to do her bidding.

Courtney suppressed the urge to smile until they had both left the room. Hattie could be a powerful force when she set her mind to it. When the little woman was gone the house felt so empty it almost caved in on itself, but when she returned everything took on a new life.

Hattie and Stephen returned to the kitchen at about the same time. The three of them worked to put away the vegetables and set the kitchen to rights. Then Hattie directed them to sit down while she prepared three tall glasses of iced sun tea.

Hattie sat down with them and fanned her perspiring face. They discussed the storm and fallen trees. Courtney told her about the power outage and spending the evening in candle lit discussion.

"Well, I will say one thing, I have never in my life heard anything like the thunder we heard over this house last night," Stephen interjected with a shake of his head. "I don't think I'll ever forget that sound. I could swear it sounded like some sort of big roaring cat."

"Well, well," Hattie murmured as she glanced at Courtney.

"I have seen and heard things in the last few weeks that I am, well let's put it this way, if someone were to tell me about these experiences I would just shake my head and ask them how much moonshine they had to drink. If I wasn't living these experiences I would think they were fabricated." When he finished speaking he briskly rubbed his tanned forearms where goose flesh had raised the fine sun-bleached hairs that grew there.

"You're a good man doctor Baylor. Good things comin' for you." Hattie nodded with a faraway look. "You know, it's not what happens in life, so much as how you handle what happens."

"I see a strength in you beyond most men. Women was made strong to bear pain. They was made sensitive so their bodies could carry another soul. Men were given detachment so they could perform brave deeds, hunt for food and protect their own. Now to find a man who has all those qualities as well as the gift of listening, openness, faith and understanding, is rare indeed."

Stephen's face had flushed red under his tan. "Thanks. My parents are responsible for anything good that I've become," he mumbled modestly.

"Now where is that Caitlin?" Hattie asked.

"Well she's painting in the sunroom and I haven't been able to get her to come out. I've been taking food in and she eats it. She comes out to use the bathroom and that is the only time she leaves her work." Courtey shrugged.

"Hm. Well somethin's in the air," Hattie leaned back and closed her eyes. "There are powerful forces at work here," she spoke with her eyes closed. " Your destiny calls you in the voice of the thunder. When the painting is finished your work will begin and you will understand your purpose."

Courtney's eyes felt heavy and she was compelled to close them. The blue topaz grew warm against her skin as Hattie's deep voice filled the kitchen. She saw flashes of light piercing the darkness behind her eyelids. A blue light formed and images came into focus as though on a movie screen. There were women's faces with heavy makeup. They were strangers to her. Each was different but all had dark brown hair and brown eyes. She felt danger prickling at the back of her neck. Fear knotted up in her solar plexis. Then one by one the faces took on expressions of fear. Their eyes wide with terror, their mouths open as if screaming, and then when the garish red lipstick that they wore turned to blood it dripped with ghoulish abandon down their tortured faces. In moments expressions froze and each young visage deteriorated as flesh does once the spirit has left the body.

Familiar eyes blinked at her from the darkness. She knew those eyes but she could not grasp where she had seen them or to whom they belonged. Courtney felt herself straining to see who it was that was in trouble.

"Courtney, are you all right," Stephen had touched her hand causing her to jump.

When she opened her eyes both Hattie and Stephen were watching her closely.

"What did you see, Baby?" Hattie asked softly.

"I saw a lot of faces. Women. Blood was around their lips. Faces that died and deteriorated. There was one set of eyes that I should know but I can't quite figure it out."

"Your hands are freezing," Stephen frowned as he rubbed her hands vigorously. "Are you sure you want to dabble in all of this? Do you think it's safe?"

"I don't know if I really want to or not but I know that I have a job to do in this life and I know that my psychic gifts are to be used in some way to help others. I know that these same gifts helped to heal my injuries and save my life. I believe I am perfectly safe. I react to what I see but I'm not in any danger." Courtney spoke quietly but her voice was firm.

"Emotionally you will have to be strong child, but your physical self is not in danger. People are often dangerous, but visions, spirits or ghosts will not cause you any harm." Hattie looked from one to the other. Stephen leaned protectively toward Courtney and his dark blue eyes were filled with concern. Inwardly she smiled a secret knowing smile.

The shrill ringing of the telephone made all of them jump.

"Doctor Baylor, the hospital is calling for you," Hattie held out the receiver for him.

Hattie returned to her seat and questioned Courtney about how she was feeling. Once she was reassured that Courtney was fine she went on to remind her that this was the week that she was going to be out of town with her choir. They were going to leave Wednesday morning and would not be back until Labor Day weekend.

"Well I hope you have a wonderful time on your trip. This old house is going to feel very empty without you," Courtney lamented.

"It's awful nice to be missed before I even leave," Hattie chuckled. "Don't you worry now, I am going to leave plenty of food cooked up and some things is in the freezer. Now don't you frown at me young lady. I know you are perfectly capable of taking care of yourself and anything else that comes up, but I like to make sure that my people are taken care of."

They made plans to visit Esther at the convalescent home on Tuesday and they discussed the various gardeners and housekeeping employees that were scheduled for their routine visits.

Finally Stephen hung up the telephone with a sigh. He would need to leave for the hospital sooner than expected due to a problem that had come up.

"I'll go get C.C. and we'll start back. We'll just grab something to eat on the way back. I'm sorry we can't stay for dinner this time." Stephen disappeared into the sunroom.

Courtney was surprised at the depth of her disappointment. She hadn't realized just how much she was looking forward to visiting with him and her sister during the evening meal.

Hattie and Courtney both were startled to hear the unmistakable flat wailing of an agitated Caitlin. It grew louder and both women moved quickly to investigate. Stephen appeared at the door before either of them could move more than a few steps.

"She refuses to move. I think you should see what she's been doing." He turned without another word. Courtney and Hattie hurried along behind him.

Caitlin had propped up several paintings around the room and was deeply involved in yet another one. The subject of each painting was a girl. A different girl in each one but with a common denominator, dark hair, dark eyes and light brown skin tone and lips painted red. The paintings all had a black or dark brown background and just the faces were visible in one corner. Then there was a set of lips turning to blood. Yet another face was horribly decomposed.

Courtney was stricken with the realization that these were the faces she had just seen moments before in her vision.

The three of them stood in silent shock as they alternately watched the girl working and gazed at the frightening completed drawings and paintings.

"These women were killed," Courtney whispered shakily. Somewhere in her mind she could hear their cries. She moved slowly forward and dropped to her knees near one picture that leaned against a wicker chair. She held her hands out over the picture and felt the years flying by. "This happened a long time ago." She scooted to the next one and held out her hands. She knew this one was more recent.

"So do you think she is picking up on the...what...spirits of dead girls?" Stephen asked without taking his eyes off of the spectacle.

"Lord, Lord, Lord have mercy. That is exactly what has happened." Hattie shook her head, her eyes bulging in disbelief.

"This has been happening for years. I think it could still be happening. I don't understand why she is seeing these things and painting them. She has been at this for hours now," Courtney continued to stare at each picture.

"Well I guess there could be other explanations, but knowing the two of you and the other paintings that she did, I would be willing to bet that you know more about it than I do," Stephen finally dragged his eyes away from the pictures and looked directly at Courtney.

"I don't know if I know anything," Courtney blinked and shook her head. "Caitlin looks awfully pale to me. I can't seem to reach her with my thoughts."

"Uh oh," Hattie lurched forward and caught Caitlin just as she toppled backward off the stool where she had been perched.

Stephen and Courtney rushed to help. Together they lowered her to the floor. Stephen checked her pulse. Hattie dashed into the kitchen and came back with a cold wet cloth and a glass of water.

Courtney sat on the tile floor beside her and held her hand while frantically searching with her mind.

"No need to worry," Caitlin's voice came as the silent whisper into Courtney's mind.

"Thank God," Courtney replied in their silent language.

"My body has low blood pressure and low blood sugar. It appears that it won't be able to work in the other world for such long periods of time. I am going back in to help my body become conscious again. Get something sweet and a little caffeine for me. Thanks."

No sooner had the voice faded than Caitlin's eyes fluttered open. She moaned in a flat monotone and started to fling her head from side to side. She jerked her hand away from Courtney and her arms flailed wildly causing all of them to dodge out of the way to avoid being hit.

Stephen took the glass of water from Hattie and held it in front of the struggling girl. She suddenly stopped thrashing and reached for the glass.

"She needs some sweet tea," Courtney said as she got up and went to the kitchen. When she returned with the tea, Hattie was gently wiping Caitlins face with the cool cloth.

"Here is the sweet tea Caitlin," Courtney held out the glass of tea. Stephen took the empty water glass and they all sat quietly while she gulped noisily at the tea. Her face was terribly pale and her hands had been cold and clammy, but they could see she was doing better.

"She spoke to me," Courtney explained. "She said she is not going to be able to paint for such long hours any more. Her body has low blood sugar and low blood pressure. She needs something sweet and with caffeine to keep this from happening.

"Well she's lookin' better now. There's a little pink comin' back into her cheeks now," Hattie smiled.

"I think she's going to be fine," Stephen was smiling with relief. "I hate to rush off but I need to get back to the hospital. Would you just go up and get her things?" He turned to Courtney.

"She doesn't want to go back to the hospital today. She says her body needs to rest and then she has a message that needs to be delivered. It must be the paintings she's been working on."

"The paintings she's been working on, working on," Caitlin murmured in a singsong whispery voice.

"This is just extraordinary," Stephen breathed as if all of the unusual behaviors had just impacted his consciousness. "I …almost can't take it all in. Well okay, she can stay here this week and I'll take care of getting a temporary visiting release for her and then when you speak with the lawyers Courtney we'll proceed with the custody arrangements."

"Thank you Stephen. I know all of this is…strange…to say the least. I have my own troubles with it too…"

"Now you all just listen to me for a minute," Hattie broke in "this isn't nothin' different than what's been happening through all of recorded history. If you have read the Bible it's plumb full of prophets, visions and miracles. Some of our most revered genius minds claimed to have visions of their inventions or messages in dreams about what they was supposed to create next. This ain't no different," she harrumphed and marched out to the kitchen.

Stephen let out a long breath and the pallor of his skin was slowly replaced by a rosey flush. He stared at the two sisters and a grin lit up his face. In this moment they looked so much alike that if you didn't know of Caitlin's disability it wouldn't be immediately evident.

Strong emotions rose in the young doctor as he grappled with his scientific training and the many events he had witnessed, which brought scores of questions and very few answers.

Caitlin finished her tea and set the glass on the floor. She leaned forward and reached for Brown, who lay near Stephen's knee. He picked up the worn bear and handed it to Caitlin. She tucked the bear's head under her chin and started her familiar rocking motion. Her eyes closed and she started humming in a tuneless flat sound that nearly mimicked the squeak of a wooden rocking chair.

"I think she needs to take a nap," Courtney gently urged her sister to stand up. It was one of the rare moments when Caitlin allowed anyone to touch her without having a tantrum.

"Do you think you can manage her by yourself this week?" Stephen's forehead was furrowed with worry lines.

"Yes. I think we will be just fine," Courtney nodded as she began walking Caitlin through the sunroom to the door that exited near the stairway.

"I do have to leave now since the hospital needs me, but I want you to call me if you need anything. Agreed?"

"Yes. I will and thanks again," Courtney and her sister disappeared through the door.

Stephen went into the kitchen and picked up his notebook and his small overnight bag. Hattie turned from the kitchen counter where she had been working. She held out a large paper bag filled with neatly wrapped parcels.

"Just a little snack so you can keep up your energy," Hattie smiled, her stern demeanor had vanished and her eyes had softened. "Everything's gonna be just fine for you too Doctor Baylor."

Courtney watched as her sister climbed into bed and rolled onto her side still clutching Brown. She rocked her body back and forth but she no longer hummed.

In the distance an airplane droned and she heard Stephen's van start up. She went to the window and watched as he disappeared down the long drive. She could feel his absence and it made her feel almost lonely.

Courtney sat in the soft comfortable chair near Caitlin's bed. The rocking had subsided and there was only a hint of movement now as she relaxed into a peaceful sleep. She marveled at the serenity of Caitlin's face as she slept. She thought of her own strange journey and how she came to be here sitting beside a twin sister that she had not known of until a short time ago. Past lives, karma, the vast intricate design of it all was staggering. Her eyes closed and like her sister she slipped effortlessly into a restful sleep.

Someone called her name. Courtney's eyes fluttered open. She was surprised to find that she had fallen asleep in a field. She sat up and looked around. There were wild flowers everywhere. The sky was a lazy summer blue and white wispy clouds rode the wind currents.

"C'mon!," came the urgent shout. Courtney could hardly believe her eyes. Caitlin was dancing through the flowers. "C'mon. Get up and dance with me," she called. "As soon as you dance the music will start!"

Courtney stood up and moved her arms up by her ears in the rounded ballet position of en haut. Sure enough the music began. She opened her arms in second position and began a series of chaine' turns then, by pulling up one foot, she changed to pique turns.

Caitlin joined her and the music swelled as they moved in perfect unison. They gathered power and rose into the air. Their bare legs were outstretched in the astounding airborn splits of the grand jete'. When they finally landed from the slow motion leap, they rose again in the tour jete'. The turning jump sent them high enough to disturb the shape of low hanging clouds. They floated down and landed on one foot in the classic arabesque position with one leg held high behind them. Little cloud wisps floated around them creating a glowing halo. Above them a rainbow arched across the sky.

Courtney opened her eyes. The room was nearly dark. Someone had draped a light cover over her. Caitlin still slept quietly. Her regular breathing was the only sound in the room. Cooking smells came from the floor below. Her stomach growled.

"Your sister still sleepin'?" Hattie smiled as she looked up from the pan of pork tenderloins that she had just pulled out of the oven.

"Yes. Oh that smells yummy."

"I thought you might be hungry when you woke up. There's enough here for Caitlin too if she wakes up. I have a feelin' she just might sleep through the night."

"I know. Thank you for covering us up. The air-conditioning can get chilly." Hattie just smiled. "We dreamed together. It was wonderful."

Hattie prepared their plates while Courtney described the dream.

"Umm hmmm. Yes I think that must be where she goes to feel joy. I bet she watched you dance from that place in her mind and she goes there to practice. She invited you there to show you her real self. She is only wearing her disguise as someone who has limitations so that her soul can advance to a highter level of wisdom and experience."

They sat at the kitchen island eating their meal and discussing the weekend. It was times like these she loved the most. Somewhere deep in her mind she knew that one day she would look back at the mundane every day moments that carried no adrenaline or miracles and without a doubt they would be the most important and comforting that life can offer.

"Well Hattie thank you for supper and for everything," Courtney gave Hattie a hug. "I need to go call Mom and Latoia. I've been worried about both of them. Mom seems to be going through something and of course Latoia with that break-in. I have this nagging feeling that she may have to be careful for a while."

"Whooee, when you talk about her like that it makes me get chill bumps. Now you know those are...the glory bumps of truth," Courtney chimed in on the phrase she had heard so often.

"I'm goin' in to start packing for my trip and watch a little television. I'll see you in the morning," Hattie disappeared into her rooms and Courtney heard the television click on.

It was eleven thirty when Courtney stretched out on her bed. She had checked on her sister and found her sleeping peacefully. She thought back over the conversations she had with her mother and Latoia. They had both sounded strong and upbeat, each in her own way but Courtney was convinced that they were both hiding their fears and problems from her. She was very worried about both of them.

178

It took a long time for Courtney to fall asleep. When she finally did sleep, her dreams were restless and disturbing, far from the field of flowers and music where she had danced with her sister.

CHAPTER EIGHTEEN

Caitlin was already in the sunroom painting when Courtney entered the kitchen the next morning.

"Good morning. Did Caitlin eat something this morning Hattie?"

"She sure did sugar. She ate eggs, baon, biscuits and grits," Hattie smiled triumphantly. "She cleaned her plate and headed straight for the sunroom. I checked on her and she is sittin' up on that stool as big as you please. Workin' on her next picture."

Courtney went to the entrance of the sunroom and peeked in. Her sister sat on the stool with Brown tucked under her left arm. She held her paintbrush in her right hand and dabbed at the canvas. She had the curious habit of making daubs and splotches of color amidst swirling lines and nebulous shapes. None of it made any sense until the last phase of color was filled in. Mysteriously an astonishing picture would then emerge. Courtney watched for a few minutes then returned to the kitchen shaking her head.

"I just don't understand how she does it. Her gift is the most miraculous thing I have ever seen."

"You both miraculous if you ask me," Hattie chuckled, "Now you just sit yourself down here an have some breakfast too so you can have all of the energy that you need to get your day off to a good start."

***

"Latoia," Stephanie called out as she entered through the front door. The rooms felt empty and quiet. Her pulse quickened as she walked briskly from one empty room to another. Light from the setting sun slipped through the partially open blinds on the west windows. She hurried up the stairs and searched the bedrooms. Her heart began pounding as frightening thoughts created unthinkable scenarios in her mind.

She nearly ran downstairs slightly twisting her ankle on the last step. She swore loudly but after a moment she realized that the sprain was minor and she hobbled to the security system by the front door. Nothing looked out of place. She reasoned that if someone had tried to break into the apartment the alarm would have gone off and the security company would have responded.

She limped to the telephone in the kitchen and called the guard station at the entrance to her private community.

She spoke briefly with the guard on duty and learned that no one had seen her leave. She decided that every shift should have a description of Latoia and maybe an extra patrol on her condominium.

Stephanie breathed deeply and tried to calm her nerves. Nothing looked out of place. No one had left ugly messages on the walls. She decided that she might be over-reacting. Latoia could be in the exercise room or even at the pool! She scooped up her keys and reset the alarm system as she hurried out through the front door.

The clubhouse was not far away but Stephanie was still wearing her high-heeled pumps and her ankle was still tender from the twist on the stairs, so she climbed into her car and drove to the south side of the building where the pool and workout room were located. She ran first to the large windows and peeked in. No one was using the equipement at this hour. She hurried around the corner to the pool.

The familiar smell of chlorine and suntan lotion filled the air. Several small children splashed noisily in the shallow end of the pool and two women sat on the edge dangling their feet in the water as they chatted while keeping a watchful eye on their offspring.

Stephanie squinted her eyes against the glare of the sun on the water. She searched the lounge chairs around the pool and the small round tables shaded by bright blue and white umbrellas.

"Steph, you're home a little early today. I was going to have dinner ready..." Latoia's voice trailed off when she saw the pallor of her friend's face.

Stephanie had jumped and whirled around at the sound of Latoia's voice. "Oh my God, I am so glad to see you," she breathed, "For a minute there I thought the boogeyman got you!"

"Oh, no, I'm just fine. I'm sorry I scared you, but I didn't think about leaving a note. I thought you wouldn't be home for at least another hour."

The two women hugged and got into Stephanie's car. Stephanie started the motor and turned up the air-conditioner. She let out a long sigh of relief. "Well, the reason I came home early is that I have a dinner meeting with a new client and I wanted to change. That's not the only reason though. I got a call from Paris. They want you in New York to sign the contract in two weeks. They want you to be ready to leave from there to fly to France to begin shooting the promos."

Latoia's large brown eyes opened wide as she tried to take in everything Stephanie was saying. Goosebumps rose on her arms and tears welled up blurring her vision as she absorbed the news and how it would change her life. Memories of her childhood poverty and the sacrifices her mother had made flashed through her mind. If only her brother had lived, she could have put him in a nice recovery program. She could at least give her mother and aunt a better life now. Finally she dropped her head into her hands and sobbed.

Stephanie backed the car out of the parking space and headed home. Latoia was still sobbing a few minutes later when they walked into the condo.

"C'mere honey," Stephanie enfolded the slender girl in her arms and patted her gently on the back. "Now listen babe, you need to dry those tears and let's open a bottle of champagne!"

Latoia marveled at Stephanie's seemingly endless supply of celebratory bubbly. They touched glasses and sipped, savoring the flavor and the moment.

"Stephanie how can I ever thank you for everything?" Latoia nearly choked on the words as the tears flowed again.

"Don't worry darling, my ten percent will do very nicely," that made them both laugh.

"Now, down to business," Stephanie turned serious, "I know that basically, you are safe here. I have an alarm system and I have called the guard station and instructed them to have each shift be aware of who you are. They have also agreed to drive by here once a day and knock on the door unless otherwise instructed. They are going to report to me each day after they check on you."

Latoia shook her head and rolled her eyes as her friend continued to outline the safety precautions that she wanted Latoia to observe.

"Now listen, Latoia, I can see by your face you think this is not necessary. I was with you when we walked into your apartment, and I saw what that lunatic did. I think he is capable of anything. When I walked in today and couldn't find you I was afraid he'd found you again. You are gorgeous, talented and you have a beautiful life ahead of you," Stephanie paused to sip more champagne. "Besides I want to redecorate this place in the spring and I want to take a trip to Hawaii next summer and I need my ten percent from you to help pay for it all." Stephanie's mouth twitched at the corners and a hint of mischief sparkled in her eyes.

"Right," Latoia grinned "It's always and only about the money."

"Bet your sweet bippy it is," Stephanie winked then drained her glass. "Well I need to get ready for my meeting. I have a whole case of videos if you get bored with television."

Latoia *was* getting bored with television and having to stay cooped up and not having a car. She sighed as Stephanie went upstairs to change. She thought of the extra efforts being made on her behalf. She was grateful for everything but her strong free spirit still felt imprisoned and momentarily stifled. She sighed again and decided to busy herself making lists of things to do and clothes to pack for her upcoming adventure. As soon as she thought about that her face brightened and she started to feel the excitement building. "Yes! I'm going to Paris!" She did a little happy dance as she opened the refrigertor door to look for a snack.

***

Clarisa opened her eyes and stretched. It felt so good to be in her own bed with her husband. She felt as though her well-ordered life had been turned upside down for the past few months. Nothing had felt right for absolutely ages.

Clyde was so understanding, kind and loving, she just could not imagine what her life would have been like if she had not met him. She turned on her side and stared at the back of his head while he slept.

It was early morning. There was a time when she could sleep in on a weekend. The doctor had told her that she was experiencing the early stages of menopause and that was the reason for the nightmares, nightsweats and nervousness. She was unable to sleep through the night any more even with the medication. She hoped that all of those disruptive symptoms would fade as promised in the brochure she had picked up in the doctor's office.

Clyde's breathing changed and he rolled onto his back with a yawn. "Are you just laying there in the dark staring at me?" his salt and pepper hair was rumpled from sleep and his eyes were droopy as he attempted to wake up.

"Unh huh," Clarisa grinned.

"Umkay Luv," he mumbled as he drifted back to sleep.

Well she needed to get up and move around. Maybe she could make some tea and toast or better yet some coffee and a cinnamon roll. Her mouth watered at the thought. She slipped into a light robe and soft slippers, then made her way through the semi-darkness to the kitchen.

She decided that one soft light would be enough to accomplish her tasks and switched on the light above the stove. It took only a few minutes to start the coffee and warm the cinnamon rolls in the microwave. While she waited for the coffee, she stepped outside to pick up the morning paper that lay near the front door.

Their home was one of the older ones in that area and sat on a large lot far back from the main road. She was grateful that the beautiful trees and shrubs that kept the elegant structure completely hidden from passersby, muffled the street noises.

Clarisa carried her coffee and rolls to the cushioned breakfast nook and settled herself comfortably. From this vantage point she could look into her lovely back yard and watch the sunrise.

She sipped gingerly at the hot coffee then bit into the warm sweet pastry. She chewed the soft texture and sugared frosting allowing her senses to take in every nuance of the flavor. Small birds flitted and chirped as they busily searched for tasty bugs in the lush green grass. Still others visited the bird feeder selecting exactly the right seeds for their morning repast.

A movement near her feet caught her attention. She had not noticed the silent approach of Pavlova, the elderly family cat. She sat perfectly still looking out the window closely studying the darting movements of the birds. Her long white fur was thick and lustrous despite her encroaching age.

Memories crowded into Clarisa's mind, pushing and shoving like a mob out of control. She thought of Courtney when she was a cherubic toddler, then her first day of school and all of the other firsts that created such joy and pride when they occurred. Now the absence of those events created loss and sorrow.

Shane, her precious surprise had been no less wonderful than her adopted daughter. She remembered when she first learned that she was pregnant. She and Clyde had been so surprised and happy, since both had believed that she could never conceive a child.

Clarisa shivered. A memory of pain and blood blocked out her happy meanderings. She had no idea what that was and she shook her head trying to blot out the sounds of screams and loud voices.

Pavlova jumped to her lap startling her and scattering the terrifying pictures into small fragments that were then easy to sweep away. The cat began to knead her lap and purr demanding all of her attention. She patted the white furry head with one hand and reached for her napkin with the other. She wiped the tears from her face then blew her nose. She was suddenly completely depressed. The tears continued to flow and she found herself sobbing into Pavlova's long soft fur. Her children were grown and she had nothing left to look forward to.

Sunlight finally managed to burn through the morning overcast. She felt the warmth coming through the expanse of windows. Pavlova was curled into a round furry ball on her lap. Clarisa felt the terrible darkness of her thoughts lift leaving her exhausted and bewildered. She had never experienced mood swings like that before. She had hoped that by coming home and getting some rest she would not keep seeing those strange flashes and hearing the shattering screams. She was so afraid that she might be losing her mind. Then another thought intruded that was potentially more frightening, brain tumor.

"You are the early bird this morning. Did you save any coffee for me?" Clyde shuffled over to the coffee maker and poured the remaining black brew into a mug that he retrieved from the cupboard.

Clarisa had been so lost in her thoughts, she was not aware of her husband's presence until he spoke. She lifted her coffee mug and held it tightly with both hands to disguise their trembling.

Once he had finished adding sugar and milk he turned to smile at his beautiful wife. He was still deeply in love with her after all these years and one of his favorite pastimes was to gaze upon her sleepy face and rumpled hair in the morning. He was startled to see dark smudges beneath her eyes and a pallor to her skin that he had not previously noticed.

"What's wrong Luv?" His forehead creased with concern as he hurried to her side. "Bloody hell, I have been working so much and being so self-absorbed I haven't been giving you enough attention, have I," he set his cup down on the table so forcefully that the light brown liquid splashed over the side and onto the table. Pavlova's head popped up from Clarisa's lap just in time to receive a drop of hot coffee on her little flat nose. She leaped onto the table with a squeak of surprised irritation. In her rush to get away her paws scrambled for purchase in the wet spill on the table. Her feet slid briefly to one side and her back end veered toward the full cup. Her tail was swinging madly in her haste and the cup was flung airborn, but before it could hit the floor, Pavlova too was airborn with loud yowling protests. The cat vanished and the cup hit the tile floor with a loud smash.

Clyde and Clarisa looked at each other, then down at their coffee stained robes and back at each other. They both started to laugh at the same time.

"Oh Lord, I don't think I have laughed so hard in a long time," Clarisa wiped her eyes. They were both reaching for paper towels and hurrying to clean up the shattered glass and spilled coffee.

"I didn't know that our bloody old cat could move that fast, " Clyde chuckled. "I hope she didn't hurt herself in the process. She'll probably remain in seclusion until the wound to her dignity has been eradicated," Clyde spoke with an exaggerated British accent.

They worked together making a new pot of coffee and heating muffins. Clarisa was full from the cinnamon rolls she had eaten earlier, so she opted for a slice of honeydew melon.

"Ya know Luv, I could do with a couple of days away from the office. What say we…get dressed and just get in the car and drive north…up the coast. We could see if that beautiful little place…what was it called, 'Whale Watch', we could spend the night…maybe take some good wine with us…" his voice trailed off as he traced her jawline with a soft touch, ending at her mouth where he touched her parted lips with his thumb.

Heat shot from her center and caused her heartbeat to quicken. Her mouth nearly watered at the thought of the warmth of their naked bodies lying together on a bed that faced large windows. She knew from experience that the little cabins atop the jagged cliffs offered a spectacular view over-looking the blue Pacific Ocean and an endless watery horizon.

Clyde lowered his face to hers and brushed her lips softly with his own.

"You still turn me on," he whispered against her lips.

"Me too," she whispered back.

His lips parted just enough to nibble softly on her lower lip. He moved his head down and placed a series of soft kisses down her neck. Careful not to touch any other part of her body he eased her robe open. Her womanly curves were barely concealed by the soft delicate fabric of her nightgown. Then ever so slowly he bent low for a kiss at the curve of her neck. Clarisa shuddered.

"I want you," he whispered.

Clarisa merely nodded as her body responded to the sensual need that her husband aroused in her.

"All right then," he lifted his head, but not his eyes. He pushed open her knees. Her robe fell to the side revealing the lacey edge of her silk gown. He loved the tiny sound she made as her desire was heightened and he loved watching her face as she experienced their intimacies.

"Now my dearest love. Remember these delicious moments, as you are getting ready for our little jaunt. There will be more…so much more of this for the next three days. Be ready to go in about two hours. Will that give you enough time?" Clyde kissed her one more time then stood up, turned his back and abruptly strode from the room.

He marched through the doorway with a self-satisfied smile and a little sweaty frustration mixed in, but it was worth it. He had been planning this little surprise even before Clarisa got home from South Carolina. From the moment she had arrived, he noticed how pale she was and out of sorts. It had been a difficult year for her starting with her mother's fall and hospitalization, then Courtney's crisis and abduction. Clyde clenched his teeth at the memory. The discovery of Courtney's twin sister was shocking but at least not traumatic. Esther's heart attack and stroke was probably the brick that toppled the heap. At any rate his wife had been through enough and he was determined to treat her to some personal pampering. He went to his study and made a phone call, then it was time for a hot…well make that a cold shower, at least for the moment.

An hour later Clarisa was putting the finishing touches on her makeup. Her mood had lifted and she was still tingling with the memories of her husband's surprising but welcome attention. She quickly packed a small bag with enough clothes for several days adding some new black lace undergarments as well as some casual shorts for walking on the beach. She would be ready in another thirty minutes. She spoke to the housekeeper but the woman said she had already received her instructions from Mr. Hammond. Clarisa smiled as she realized that Clyde was just a little too organized. She knew then that his little spontaneous trip had been preplanned.

She stood frowning and alone in the kitchen. Clyde had disappeared right after his shower, claiming to have things to do and wanting to check out the car. She could feel her moods swinging dangerously inside her. Anger welled in the face of the fact that he could not be completely spontaneous. Just as quickly it subsided as she reasoned that his sensible practicality was one of the things she so greatly admired about him.

Tears threatened again as she thought about their sensual encounter and how thoughtful he was to treat her with such love and plan a trip for just the two of them. She found a tissue and dabbed at her eyes. She was so happy that no one could see into her thoughts right now. She was acting positively 'round the bend' as Clyde might say.

"There you are madam," the slight glisten of tears in her eyes did not escape his sharp-eyed glance. He wisely chose not to mention it. He was very worried about her. She was so important to him. He had fallen in love with her the first time they had met. In the early years of their love, they had been hungry for each other. Both of them were survivors of old money and a certain detachment within their respective family environments.

The years passed and with the advent of marriage, children, career and the comfort of trusting each other and life's daily routine, they had drifted into a personal distance. The traumas of the past few months had brought the familiar need for refuge in each other's arms, but he missed their playful intimacy, the times when they came together just because they wanted to share themselves with each other not because they sought diversion or shelter from the harshness of the world.

Clyde was oddly nervous despite his earlier bravado. Clarisa had often teased him about his need to plan everything. He in turn had always reminded *her* that the ability to plan and organize had made him one of the best corporate lawyers in Southern California.

He opened the front door and motioned for the limo driver to come up the steps and get their bags.

"Clyde, you hired a limosine?"

"Right'o," Clyde smiled at her incredulous tone, "I thought we could ride more, comfortably in a limo." The driver held the door open and Clarisa stepped into the roomy interior. She was stunned to find the seats covered with white faux fur covers. The bar was set up and pink rose petals were strewn everywhere. It was not a full size limosine due to the fact that the road they would be traveling was the infamous Highway One. The road snaked along the coastline in perilous hairpin switchbacks that could not be negotiated by any extra lengthy vehicle. The luxourious car had a spacious interior though and could comfortably manage every curve with ease.

"Oh, I can't believe you've done this," Clarisa breathed with her eyes glistening yet again with tears. She slid into the softness of the fur and was immediately engulfed in the fragrance of the rose petals. She noticed a bouquet of red roses at the end of the bar and as her eyes took in everything she noticed that there were flowers, roses, everywhere. Small vases were secured by various means throughout their seating area. She felt as though she was traveling in a royal carriage from a fairy tale.

Clyde eased in beside her grining with satisfaction as he watched her expression of surprised delight. He had more surprises in store for her and he was looking forward to each moment with more anticipation than he'd felt even before their honeymoon.

Clarisa turned to look at him with those glorious blue eyes. He loved what he saw there. She was even more beautiful as a mature woman than she was as the stuning young college student that he had met at the University of London. He had loved her the moment he saw her, but that love could not compare with how he felt about her now.

Tears flowed freely down the soft smooth skin of her face. Slowly he reached up and caressed her face and gently wiped away some of the salty wet trails with his thumb. Clyde pulled her closer until their lips met in a long slow warm kiss.

"Now my darling, may I offer you a bit of libation," it was more of a statement than a question as he reached for the chilled glasses of Mimosa. They touched glasses and sipped the cold delicious liquid. "This little journey is from me to you. It says that I treasure you beyond all others. I have never spent an unhappy day since I met you. If I were a king I would give you my kingdom and share my treasure with you. Sadly I don't have a large kingdom or a large treasure, but I humbly share it with you." He pulled a velvet box out of a small compartment in the bar. He opened it and held it toward his dazzled wife.

"Ohh, it is so exquisite," she breathed as she reached for the diamond bracelet. "This is so much, I don't know what to say. Thank you. I love you," Clarisia's voice caught as she fought back tears once again.

Clyde fastened the clasp around her small wrist. Then he held her hand up so the precious gems would catch the sunlight coming through the tinted windows. It was only then that Clarisa became aware that the car was moving and they had already turned onto the interstate. She sank back against the cushions and white fur with a sigh and a heart so filled with love and joy, she could barely contain it all.

Music effectively blocked out any sound of traffic in the already nearly sound proof environment. The driver's compartment was sealed off from the passenger seating and the intercom was switched off. Clarisa had the impression that they were invisible as they moved swiftly along the busy roads. People often turned to stare at the impressive car, but the heavily tinted windows prevented unwanted eyes from spying on their intimate activities.

"I feel like a teenager only better," Clyde chuckled as he pulled his shirt back on and ran his fingers through his thick salt and pepper hair.

"Oh I know what you mean," Clarisa giggled girlishly. "Would you please fasten this for me?"

"Uh, no I don't think so," instead, he slipped the straps of her white satin bra off of her shoulders and kissed the back of her neck. Goose flesh rose up on her arms as he allowed his hands to travel down the front of her body lightly touching and exploring her soft curves.

When the limo turned onto Highway One the Hammonds were in the mood for something more substantial than the Brie, fruit and crackers that they had nibbled on earlier.

They stopped at a small restaurant known for its clam chowder and fresh shellfish. They sat outside watching the restless ocean's rising waves crashing against the rocks below. The driver sat inside to eat his lunch and no one else was around to disturb their solitude.

When they resumed their travels they sat snuggled together watching the breath taking views unfold at every bend in the road. They sipped wine and nibbled on nuts while they climbed ever higher on the coastal highway.

Clouds had rolled in by the time they pulled in to Whale Watch. The driver got the key and carried the luggage into their cabin. The air was misty and chilly. The ocean was fast disappearing in a gray shroud of fog. They could hear the high tide waves breaking on the rocks far below the cliffs. Clarisa shivered slightly as the mist closed around them.

A cheery fire snapped and glowed as they entered their small cozy room. The bed faced huge sliding glass doors that would allow them to awaken to an unsurpassed view in the morning.

Clyde had requested that the kitchen be stocked with thick steaks and all of the trimmings for their first night there. He immediately began making preparations for their dinner later on.

"Darlin', I believe I feel just a little tipsy, but I like it," Clarisa hugged him from behind.

"I concur Luv, now why don't you look through that extra suitcase I brought and find us something to put on after our bubble bath." Much later they contentedly lay wrapped in each other's arms listening to their own thoughts mingled with the crackling fire and the distant sounds of the ocean.

Clarisa touched the large heart-shaped diamond stud earrings that Clyde had put in her champagne glass during dinner. She never wanted anything to change. She felt safe and happy. It would be so wonderful to simply remain here just like this forever.

Clarisa was surprised that the sun was shining through the window in what seemed to be just a few minutes later. She didn't remember even going to sleep. She sat up and looked out upon blue sky and the ocean traveling in tandum to an infinite horizon. She remembered from previous years that the beauty of this view was beyond description. It was a sight that could only be understood and taken in with all of the senses.

Clyde was already up and pouring coffee for them both. Later they climbed down the long stairway leading to the private beach. They spent hours walking, talking and just sitting. They felt cocooned in a world where no one else existed.

That night Clyde presented Clarisa with a diamond solitaire necklace. The next night it was a magnificent diamond dinner ring and a sheer white neglige'.

Three days later as they prepared to go back home, they stood on the cliff watching the ocean with the wind whipping their clothes and hair. Neither wanted to leave. Clarisa felt a catch in her throat as she wondered when they would be able to return. An unexplainable sense of foreboding hovered around her sunny thoughts and though she fought to ignore it's chill she could not shake it off.

"My darling, thank you for this time together, for my gifts, for everything. I don't know if I deserve it or not but I am so grateful. Thank you. I love you," she looked up at him and giggled," you are one over-the-top Englishman and I love it!"

They both laughed and their laughter rode the wind out over the sea to faraway places. They held each other remembering their days together and held on tightly to the few moments that remained before they had to move forward again into the lifestream of work, routine and family. Each knew that moments like this did not happen too often and that it could be a long time before they could share such complete joy and privacy together and that the past few days would be an experience they would never forget.

CHAPTER NINETEEN

After many instructions and a flurry of last minute packing, the big church van drove up and carried a very excited Hattie off with the other choir members for their trip to Myrtle Beach.

Courtney had taken care of all of her sister's needs with great ease while Hattie was busy getting ready for her trip. She was sure that she could handle Caitlin just fine during the few days that Hattie was gone. Hattie had other ideas though and insisted that her granddaughter, Theresa should come to Willows and help out in her absence. Courtney liked Theresa and she decided that it would be nice to have her for company if nothing else.

Stephen had called only once to tell her that she had permission to keep Caitlin there for a few more days, but it would be necessary to speak with a lawyer to begin custody proceedings. He was friendly but she sensed a distance at the same time. She felt a little let down by that. She told herself that maybe he was just very busy. That thought rolled around in her head then plummeted to her stomach like a rock falling off of a cliff. She knew there was something else. There was a time when she pushed away those uncomfortable feelings in her gut, but that was in the past. It was time to wake up and pay attention. Ignoring those feelings a few months ago had nearly cost her everything.

"Hey Courtney, you have a frown bad enough to scare the devil himself," Theresa drawled, "Is everything all right? Grama Hattie will be back by next Monday."

"Oh I know, that's not it. Hattie is going to have a wonderful time and I'm so glad she has this chance to get away and have some fun."

"Well if I didn't know better I'd say that frown spelled m-a-n!" She laughed as she put one hand on her hip and rocked her head from side to side while she spelled out each letter.

"Uh oh, you must take after your grandmother. Have you got the *sight* like she does?"

Theresa's laugh was deep and throaty like her grandmother's. "It doesn't take the *sight* to see when someone has man problems. The answer to your question though is yes. I'm not as good as Grama is, but I can hold my own."

"Do other family members have it too?"

191

"Some do, some don't. Seems like everybody has some version of it, even my cousin Jody. If someone has a headache he just puts his hand up there and poof it's gone in just a few minutes."

"You know I just love talking to someone else who understands. It makes me feel less...freakish," Courtney shrugged her shoulders.

"You want to talk; now that's one thing I'm good at. I can talk a magpie off its perch. If there was a talkin' contest my momma says I should enter it because there is no one that could out talk me. I never run out of things to say and the more I talk the faster I go..."

Courtney held up her hands laughing, "I surrender. I believe you!" Both of them giggled.

The morning was filled with paperwork and phone calls to the lawyer's office. Courtney called her grandmother just before noon and was happy to hear her speech becoming clearer every day. She was sure Esther would be coming home soon.

Theresa walked into the study where Courtney was pouring over her papers. "Would you like me to bring you your lunch in here?"

"Oh, that's so nice of you, but I was planning to go into the kitchen and work on putting something together for all of us."

"No, no I have everything ready, all you have to do is decide where you would like to eat," Theresa smiled.

"Well, I choose the kitchen then or maybe the sunroom with my sister."

Courtney stood and followed Theresa into the kitchen. It felt good to stand up and stretch her legs after sitting still for so long.

Theresa had made a beautiful shrimp salad for each of them. Slices of cheese and several types of crackers were artfully arranged on a small floral platter. Tall glasses of iced tea atop green coasters and matching place mats gave the impression that the scene was clipped from a magazine.

"This looks wonderful Theresa," Courtney was pleased and surprised at how hungry she felt as soon as she saw the food.

"Thank you. I hope you enjoy it. I'm just going to take a plate in to your sister, but you just go ahead and start without me. I'll be right back." Theresa picked up a tray of food and disappeared through the door.

Courtney sat down and took a delicate nibble of shrimp, intending to wait for Theresa's return before seriously consuming the delicious food. She closed her eyes savoring the cold fresh flavor of the shrimp. A second later a sound nearby caused her to open her eyes.

"Uh Courtney, I think you better come in here and see this," Theresa's dark eyes were wide with worry and her hands were clasped tightly together in front of her chest.

Electric currents pulsed through Courtney's body and a queasy sickness hit her stomach. She had felt some vague unease about the message that Caitlin's spirit self had spoken of last weekend and she had tried not to think of it too much, in fact she had tried to convince herself that everything was going to be fine. She knew now that things were not fine. She could hardly breathe as she followed Theresa into the sunroom.

Caitlin had moved away from her paintings and drawings. She sat in the large wicker chair calmly eating her salad. The tray had been placed on a glass top coffee table within easy reach.

Courtney gasped and covered her mouth when she saw what Caitlin had done.

***

Latoia stepped out of the shower feeling refreshed and relaxed. Her thoughts were consumed with her upcoming trip to New York, the signing of the contract and then traveling to the most beautiful romantic city in the world.

Raeford had promised to meet her there since his work had taken him to London. She entertained fantasies of the two of them strolling through quaint street markets and sitting at sidewalk cafes. She had not admitted to anyone including herself, that there were strong feelings stirring deep inside for the tall Texan.

She slipped into a pair of pink shorts and matching pink and white striped top. She planned to spend the day going through her wardrobe to decide what she should take with her. She had her passport already. Next week would be here before you know it, she reasoned, no sense in waiting until the last minute.

The Hammonds had been so kind to her. They had arranged to have all of her belongings packed and delivered to Stephanie's home. She really didn't own very much, just some clothes and makeup. They told her that as soon as the VW was released from the impound lot she could continue to use it as long as she liked. Courtney no longer wanted it or needed it since she was planning to stay in South Carolina indefinitely.

Latoia had actually begun to feel safe again. She had been to several appointments with the psychologist and it did seem to help. Then of course, Stephanie's insistence at having security guards actually come to the door to check on her at least twice a day was maybe a little much, but truthfully it did make her feel better.

Yesterday, going with Stephanie to lunch and a little shopping, had really been fun. Strange faces seemed less threatening so she knew that her psyche was healing.

Detectives had called and she looked at hundreds of mug shots. She had not found any of them to be remotely familiar. That had to be good.

Stephanie had graciously invited her mother, Aunt Pearl and grandmother to come for dinner Saturday evening and then spend the night so they wouldn't need to drive back home in the dark. It might be the last time she would see them for a few weeks. She was uncertain how long she would be in Paris.

She took clothes out of the closet and began trying to choose the right things to wear. Stephanie had helped her find a beautiful beige suit to travel in and along with it accessories that would give it a different look. She loved the soft cream silk blouse that could be worn with it on a plane or out to dinner in the evening. The entire ensemble had been very expensive. Stephanie had charged it to her own account, while assuring Latoia that she could pay her back once the contract was signed and she was given an advance on her work. What an exciting thought.

The doorbell rang jolting her from her happy reverie. She hurried downstairs wondering who could be there. The first guard had already checked in.

The decorative beveled glass on either side of the door revealed a gray suited figure. She decided it was most likely another guard. The lightly frosted glass showed her only the familiar uniform outline and she had no reason to think it was anyone else. She squinted through the peephole and sure enough she saw a man wearing the distinctive Proguard uniform hat. It was only then that she let out a long sigh of relief. She punched in the alarm code and unlocked the front door.

The guard politely touched his hand to his hat and nodded. "Good morning," he said pleasantly, "Everything okay here?"

"Yes. I am just fine," Latoia responded confidently. "You are the second guard to check on me today," she smiled feeling grateful for her safety.

"Yes ma'am I know. We got a complaint from one of the tenants that someone was seen snooping around the north side of the property. I have orders to make sure your north windows and back exit are secure," he spoke in a firm authoritative manner.

"Oh, sure. Come on in," Latoia had seen this guard before. He was slightly taller than she with graying hair, a solemn expression, glasses and gray blue eyes. She had never seen him smile unlike the other guards who greeted everyone with a pleasant if not a smiling face. Today, the familiarity and the hint of a smile around his mouth gave her a sense of comfort. She stepped back from the door and gestured for him to follow her as she turned to lead him to the back of the spacious condo.

A blinding pain followed by a swirling darkness filled with white shooting stars confused her thoughts as she fell and crumpled onto the cool tile floor of the foyer. A pungent foul smell pierced her nostrils just before she lost consciousness.

At that moment nearly three thousand miles away in Charleston, South Carolina, Courtney dropped to her knees grabbing her head as though in excruciating pain.

Caitlin too, seemed to be literally thrown from her chair to the floor, scattering the remnants of her uneaten lunch and smashing the lovely floral china on the tile floor.

Theresa was momentarily stunned. One minute she was watching Courtney's reaction to Caitlin's painting, and the next minute both sisters were acting as though they had been struck violently. They both held their heads and moaned in pain.

"Sweet Jesus help us," Theresa knelt quickly beside Courtney. She searched for the pulse in Courtney's neck. Instinctively she knew that the sudden collapse was brought on by something other than a physical ailment.

Courtney's eyes opened. "Tell me what's happening," Theresa cried. "How can I help you?"

"I'm okay, I think. Yes I'm ... I'm Okay. The pain is leaving. It's not mine. Oh God! Latoia. It's hers! Oh my God," Courtney began to sob.

Theresa smoothed her hair and helped her sit up. Then she ran to Caitlin's prone body. "Courtney!" She spoke sharply, "Help me lift your sister. She's unconscious."

Theresa felt for her pulse and though it was faint, it was steady. After a careful examination Theresa determined that Caitlin was not injured other than a bump where her head hit the floor. They carefully lifted her to the sofa and covered her with the light cotton throw, which was draped over the back of the wicker rocking chair.

"You sit down here and stay with your sister," Theresa ordered firmly, "I am going to get you both some water and a couple of ice packs."

✳✳✳

The guard shack was getting hot and stuffy as the sun climbed higher and aimed its late summer heat at the tinted windows.

"Hit that AC unit will ya," the two guards had started their shift in the cool morning hours and were just now beginning to feel the heat of the day.

"I'm going to check over these log sheets and then report in," the senior guard settled himself at the small desk and began to flip through pages of hand written reports concerning each guard's comments for the previous twenty-four hours.

Outgoing traffic was often brisk in the morning hours as tenants left for work and children were taken to school. Incoming traffic was slow other than occasional cleaning crews and other service personnel. Then it began to equalize as the afternoon wore on. Often it required the vigilence of both guards as both incoming and outgoing traffic increased. During the slower times they would take turns making rounds in the little electric cart and the other guard would answer the phone and fill out reports as needed.

"Hey, did Darmon ever leave? I never did see his car come back through," the older guard asked the younger one who was just saluting to a pretty blond woman who drove out in her red convertible.

"Yeah, he drove out about twenty minutes ago while you were giving directions to that guy in the furniture delivery truck."

"Hmm, I don't see his last report."

"It's there somewhere. He handed it to me before he left. That guy is damn weird," the young man frowned, "Today is the first time I ever saw him smile. I kinda liked it better when he didn't. Gave me the creeps. He said he and his girl friend or maybe it was his wife. I don't know, but anyways they were gettin' back together."

"Hunh," the older man shuffled through more papers until he found what he was looking for. "If he just left I wonder what the hell took him so long. He should have already been off the property." Darmon's report did not reflect his true departure time. After a brief contemplation he made some notes in the logbook and decided he would not let Darmon make that last round by himself any more. He figured the guy was up to something and it just felt a tad sour.

**

Zeke Darmon had every reason to smile as he cruised smoothly through the Beverly Hills traffic. Everything had gone perfectly just as he had known it would. His Martita had received his message and the fates had brought them together. His heart was full. This time there would be no interference. This time he had the right one. This time he and his Martita would be together...always.

He flipped the turn signal on and prepared to change lanes. His driving record was impeccable. It was important to remain calm while driving, he told himself. He remembered how his father had taught him to be very cautious in the heavy traffic. He remembered the punishment if he forgot any of the rules. He would not forget the rules today.

He nosed the Buick into the left lane and continued on maneuvering carefully through the increasing traffic. He glanced into his rear view mirror and was surprised to see a gleaming red convertible threading purposefully through small openings in one lane or another. The blond driver wore dark glasses and a skimpy white tank top.

The day had heated up and beads of sweat popped out on his forehead. He rolled down the window to get some carbon monoxide flavored air. Suddenly the convertible was in the lane to his left. The girl's hair fanned out like a halo around her head. She honked impatiently at a gray-haired driver in front of her. She glanced at Zeke then coolly stomped her foot down on the accelerator and the car shot forward. She jerked her steering wheel hard to the right narrowly missing the front fender of Zeke's Buick. He punched the horn in a series of angry honks.

"Well move over you ass .....!" Her beautiful face twisted into an angry scowl as she screamed obcenities. She flipped up her middle finger and roared forward weaving in and out of the lanes ahead.

Zeke felt the blackness encroaching upon his thoughts. He heard his father's voice chanting biblical commandments. He could see the rules written in the air above the traffic. She was an evil woman speaking with the tongue of a viper; the Devil's tongue from the Garden of Eden.

"If thine eye offend thee, pluck it out," his father chanted in his mind.

Zeke was finding it hard to breathe. He wanted to get away from the awful threatening chant. He wanted to be alone and quiet with his Martita. His father couldn't know where they were though. His decision was made. Now he knew what to do.

***

Latoia was sick. Her stomach churned and she heaved repeatedly until there was nothing left in her system. Then cramps set in and she moaned in pain. It was too hot. Her lungs were starved for air. Hysteria snapped its jaws and rose in a fighting stance to clutch at her heart and mind. The tape on her mouth had loosened and flapped to one side but her throat was too dry and raw. She tried to scream but she couldn't make much noise. Her hands were tightly bound behind her back.

"Oh no, this can't be happening," her mind was screaming and she thrashed her body around in the suffocating darkness. It was a small space. She heard the roar of a motor and she was thrown from side to side. Then she realized she was in the trunk of a car. She had to get out! She thrashed and pounded as panic moved closer and began to consume her sanity and logical thought.

"Shhh," the gentle sound broke through the wild terror that was fast overtaking her. It was impossible for her to actually hear anything except the roar of the car engine and yet there it was. In fact the traffic sounds were fading along with the suffocating heat. Her body relaxed and she drifted into a dreamy suspended state. She knew her physical form was still being thrown from one side to the other with the movement of the car but at the same time she felt calm and sleepy. She wondered idly if she had died and if so would she see her brother. She lost consciousness before she could explore that thought any further.

***

Courtney accepted the cool water that Theresa brought. Her hands trembled violently as she brought the glass to her lips.

"Oh my God," she moaned, "I've got to do something. I should have been more forceful when I told Latoia about the danger before." Courtney was crying again.

"Now don't you go there," Theresa spoke with firm authority, "My grama says everything happens for a reason and only the good Lord knows what that is."

"Yes, I believe that," Courtney brushed away the streaming tears. "I also know that Caitlin and I were given this message for a reason."

"No doubt about that. I'm willin' to bet that if the two of you work together, you might be able to help the girl in that picture."

Caitlin flinched as Theresa adjusted the ice pack on her head. Her eyes opened but she remained very still and quiet.

Courtney closed her eyes and reached out to Caitlin with her mind.

"Is your body ok?" Courtney asked anxiously.

The response was immediately affirmative.

"Can we work together to save my friend Latoia?"

"Yesss," Caitlin's voice whispered softly in her head.

"Okay, Theresa," Courtney spoke aloud, "I need to go make some phone calls. Would you see if you can get Caitlin to eat a little more? Thank you so much for your help!"

First Courtney dialed Stephanie's home number. No answer. Then she called her office. When Stephanie answered she quickly explained that she thought Latoia might be in trouble and asked if Stephannie could go home and check on her just to be sure.

Stephanie was startled at first but then she tried to assure Courtney that she had taken every precaution and she was sure Latoia was safe. Moments later she called her home number. There was no answer just as Courtney had said. She was still certain that everything had to be fine. The morning guard had checked in with her and reported that Latoia was fine. She dialed the number for the guard shack. The guard that answered was very pleasant at first. His tone changed when she explained that someone needed to go check her condo again. He was indignant at the suggestion that he had not followed protocol. He did promise that he would be making rounds in ten minutes and would notify her if anything appeared suspicious.

Courtney hurried up to her room and rifled through the drawer of her nightstand. She was sure she had stuffed the paper with the detective's phone number in that drawer. She found it folded in the pages of her small personal phone book. She placed the call from her bedroom extention and waited impatiently for someone to answer. Detective Denton was not in but the man that answered promised to let him know that it was urgent that he call Courtney back as soon as possible.

The situation was so frustrating. She dropped her head into her hands and tried to get calm. She had used all of the conventional methods of communication. She was too far away to take action and go looking for Latoia herself. She had to figure out a coherent plan using the gifts that she and her sister were born with.

No matter what she tried she felt absolutely blank. She could not seem to get her thoughts together. Her stomach growled loudly and she realized how hungry she was. She went back down stairs and into the kitchen. Theresa and

Caitlin were sitting at the island. Caitlin was scooping up dripping bites of vanilla ice cream. Theresa was munching on her salad.

"I'm expecting some people to all me back. Hopefully very soon."

"You already look tired," Theresa observed, "I think you should try to eat something. You have done all you can for the moment. It's goin' to be very important that you keep up your strength."

Courtney nodded and sat down. The food was as good as it looked. She discovered that even with all of the worry she was able to eat enough to make her feel a little better.

When she had eaten all she could Courtney returned to the sunroom to study her sister's pictures. Caitlin followed silently and sat down in the rocking chair. Theresa busied herself with cleaning up the kitchen.

Courtney stared at the dark images of her friend. Red drops oozed down her forehead and her eyes were wide with terror and pain. Dripping red letters of the alphabet hovered over her head while a dark figure watched. The letters were written backwards. Maybe she could figure out what it meant.

After a few minutes it was very apparent that they were fragments of bible verses. Some were oddly phrased but unmistakably taken from the Ten Commandments. "Honor thy father" was run together several times around the edge of the picture and was also written backwards.

"Do not speak ill of the Lord" was the next phrase that she put together. The one that truly sickened her was the next one; "If thy tongue offends thee I will cut it out".

"Oh no, no, no. This just can't happen to Latoia. Where is that detective?" Courtney gritted her teeth and dropped her head forward to rest on clenched fists. Tears of fear and frustration flowed again.

"There is a reason," came the silent whisper into her mind. "I feel her life force," Caitlin's words continued. "Stop your worries and reach out. You will feel her too."

Courtney glanced over at her sister. She rocked the chair back and forth rhythmically while her eyes stared at the birds and butterflies visible through the many sunroom windows.

It would require tremendous effort to calm down, but she began with a series of deep breaths. She was surprised to find that she did feel better even though fear still clutched at her solar plexis and her hands were cold and clammy. Her heart calmed and she felt her essence reach out to her dear friend.

She traveled a long way, through hazy landscapes of the past. She was aware of oceans and continents, violent storms and warring conflicts amongst people of all cultures.

A glittering emerald drew her attention, but when she moved closer she saw that it was not a stone but a place. Dense jungles filled with colorful birds and frequent rain slicking the giant leaves until they sparkled in the rays of sun that occasionally penetrated the dense tangle of vegetation.

A village nestled beneignly under the protection of monstrous trees. A woman and man stood talking to a group of outsiders who had just climbed out of a few large boats that were anchored securely in the river that flowed by the village.

The village woman was dressed regally and wore Latoia's face. The man standing next to her also appeared to be a leader. Courtney knew what was happening. The strangers were barganing for the help of some of the villagers.

It was clear that in that life Latoia was not able to see the greed in the eyes of the foreigners. She readily agreed to allow them to take various people from the village to serve as cooks, guides and bearers in exchange for certain valuable trade items.

Latoia's male companion bore the face of Latoia's brother in their current life. He was sly and greedy and without her knowledge he also traded several young women to be used as the men saw fit.

Courtney understood that Latoia's soul had chosen to experience her first and now this second abduction so that she would understand what some of her people had gone through in that life. She was learning on the deepest level of consciousness what those souls had endured. She was also learning that positions of power hold great responsibility and that a leader must strive to know every aspect of the decsions that are made when the lives and well being of their people depend on them.

Courtney was saddened as she watched the young man living as Latoia's twin in the current life. He had not yet been able to forgive himself and was still afflicted with the self-loathing that had led him to overdose on drugs in this lifetime.

She knew that Latoia's soul was striving to achieve a peaceful resolution and advance to a wiser understanding. This was to be her mission before she could achieve the money and fame that she desired in this life.

The village and the suffering faded to a dark coolness. Courtney could hear someone breathing. She reached out and touched the unconscious form. She knew instantly that it was Latoia.

"I'm here," her thoughts whispered, "We are going to find you and help you."

The vision faded. Courtney lifted her head and once more stared at Caitlin's painting. The telephone was ringing.

CHAPTER TWENTY

Hattie was restless. She was happy to be going on this trip, but something was gnawing at her. She squirmed in her seat yet again. She sensed unrest. She made a mental list of everything that should have been done before she left. One by one she checked off each item. She sighed with relief as she leaned back in the seat and closed her eyes. She had completed everything and she had packed everything she wanted to bring with her.

As usual some of the passengers had already begun to nod off. Excited chatter had quieted to occasional muted conversations. The readers were fully engrossed in their books and others worked knitting needles or crochet hooks.

Hattie calmed herself and sent up a prayer first of thanks and then a special request to be shown who was in trouble for she was now sure that was what she was feeling. Then she added one more request and that was for guidance as to how she should lend her assistance.

Within a few seconds the blue light appeared and the vision opened. She saw Courtney standing in the sunroom looking at a frightening picture. Her sister was seated nearby in the rocking chair. Hattie knew that the one in trouble was Latoia, Courtney's friend. The vision closed suddenly as if a camera lens had closed.

Another blue light appeared before Hattie could open her eyes. Large dark eyes filled with strength and peace stared back at her. The vision moved back revealing satiny dark skin covering high cheek boes. Aeonkisha spoke in sure strong tones. "Cease your worry. When you raise your voice with the others you will summon legions of angels. Destiny is fulfilled. "

Hattie smiled as she drifted into a light doze. Her seatmate happened to look up from her knitting in that moment. She envied the happy dream her friend must be having. Tullie Mae was never able to sleep in the van on their choir trips. She did get a lot of baby clothes made to sell at the church bazaar though. She smiled at the thought of how pretty this little white baptismal dress was going to be.

***

Latoia regained consciousness as she felt herelf being lifted out of the trunk of the car. Her eyes were covered by something but she realized that her feet were no longer tied together. She gathered her strength and tried to kick out viciously with her legs. But her hopes were shattered as she found that her legs were bound at the knees. She was placed upright on her feet but she lost her balance and fell hard on dry rocky ground.

"Get up. You have to walk," a gruff male voice commanded. "I'll help you so don't worry Martita. You're strong. I'm just going to keep you safe." The voice had lost the rough edge and was now kind and whispery.

Latoia felt strong hands pulling her to a standing position. She was weak and dizzy. The man shoved her forward and she was forced to shuffle along with short steps due to the restriction of her knees. A wind blew but the August hot sun bore down causing sweat to quickly drench her clothes. Rivulets ran down her forehead onto the tape that covered her eyes.

If only she could open her mouth to breathe. They were moving up. She could feel panic stirring in her stomach as she struggled to breathe. Her captor stopped suddenly and the tape was brutally ripped from her mouth. She frantically gulped in air between whimpers of pain and fear. Something was pressed against her mouth and tepid water poured in so fast she choked and sputtered. She did manage to take a few gulps before the tape was once again pushed against the raw skin of her lips.

"C'mon girl, keep walkin'. We got a ways to go yet. Pretty view from up here. If you behave yourself we could maybe build us a house up here. I bet you'd like that," the man's voice had grown soft and dreamy, as he drifted into his fantasy for a few moments.

The water and brief rest revived her enough to fight down the panic. She started to organize her thoughts. She had escaped a life threatening situation only months before. She told herself she could do it again. Her head was throbbing painfully. She wished for some aspirin. It was even worse than the hangover she had after she and her brother got into the champagne punch at their cousin's wedding.

She squeezed her eyelids under the tape while she fought to keep her sobs under control. Something warm touched her cheeks and streamed downward. Tears were rolling down her face! She focused on trying to open her eyes against the strength of the tape. The tape had loosened and God be praised she could see a sliver of light.

She pushed against her lips with her tongue until she felt the fabric of the tape. Next she worked on pushing saliva toward the unrelenting sticky surface. She could breathe a little through her mouth. She was nearly overcome with relief and gratitude, for the small victory.

They had been moving slowly upward for what had seemed an eternity. She could feel the painful chafed skin between her knees. Sweat continued to drip from her body and she could feel the sting of the salty secretion as it reached her eyes. She told herself that was good news because at least the tape was loose now and she could see the dry brown dirt of the path they traveled. She found a measure of comfort in that as well as being able to keep her balance better.

Zeke had begun to mumble. Latoia was not sure if that was a good or bad sign regarding her chances of surviving this ordeal. She had already determined that the person leading her up the path was utterly insane. He was calling her by another name and he was mumbling bible verses. She remembered the strange verses that had been written on the walls of her studio apartment. Methodically she tried to work her way through the events that had led her to this moment. The last thing she could remember was the security guard that had come to the door of Stephanie's condo. Something stirred in her memory. She remembered seeing the same guard working in Stephanie's office building and again at the guard shack at Stephanie's apartment complex. It was the same cold expressionless face that had shaken her the day that Raeford called. A little sob came up out of her throat as the realization dawned on her. The man had been following her all along! She wished now that she had said something to Stephanie about it.

Without warning she was shoved hard. Her body pitched forward and she felt herself falling. There was no time to even feel fear but she knew her life was surely over. He had pushed her over a cliff and now she was going to die. The free fall ended abruptly as her body slammed against rocky hard packed earth knockng the breath from her lungs. She rolled through dry weeds and sharp twiggy bushes, hitting her shoulder on small rocks and scraping her skin bloody on scorched gravel. When she finally rolled to a stop on level ground she could hear the man sliding downward in a rush of loose gravel and dust. The noise stopped as he came to a halt nearby.

"We're here. Get up now but watch your head, low bridge," he jerked Latoia to her feet and shoved her forward. His voice was now lilting in a higher pitch nearly child-like.

Her nostrils flared as a suffocating musty smell rode the cooler air currents of their new destination. The sliver of light at the edge of the tape disappeared and they were in darkness. She could hear a click and she knew that the man had turned on a flashlight. She was so exhausted. Her entire body ached and the raw skin of her arms and legs burned with every stumbling step she took. She tried to wiggle her fingers but her wrists had been wrapped so tight that her hands were swollen and numb.

Another mighty shove toppled her face down onto something soft. She was so grateful that her sensitive skin was not being scratched again that she could only feel relief. She listened to the man moving around mumbling. He sounded as though he was talking to someone.

"Okay, now let's move over. You have been very patient waiting here for me haven't you," he spoke in a kind soothing voice. "Now don't worry I've brought someone to keep you company."

Latoia's heart skipped a beat. Someone else was here! She was overjoyed. As soon as this lunatic went away then they could work together to escape. She willed herself to stay calm and lay still. She would make contact with that other person soon.

***

When Stephanie walked through her front door she saw the broken glass. A drop of dark fluid stained the pristine tile floor. She knew it was blood. Fear and panic overwhelmed her in those first few seconds. She was sick to her stomach and her brain literally could not function.

Latoia had been forcibly taken!

Stephanie's knees turned to jelly and she sagged against the wall. "Latoia," she sobbed out the name though it was barely more than a whisper. Her lungs constricted and she tried desparately to gulp in some air. She slid slowly down the wall as her knees completely buckled.

"It's my fault," she whispered through blinding tears, "I thought I could keep her safe. I've failed her, oh my God," she wailed as the reality of the situation hit her along with the unthinkable possibilities.

"Police," her chest heaved with great sobbing gulps of air, "Police!" She crawled forward still unable to stand. "Police!" she sobbed and shrieked as she scrambled across the floor on her hands and knees toward the telephone.

Forty-five minutes later Stephanie sat sobbing again in her living room while two plain-clothes detectives questioned her about Latoia. Black and whites were parked at odd angles in the parking lot while their lights flashed a warning to stand clear.

Uniformed officers questioned neighbors and the little crowd of curious onlookers who had gathered in small clusters around the perimeter of the activity. A representative from the Proguard security company pulled up and a tall uniformed guard got out and strode along the concrete walkway toward the entry door and disappeared inside as he spoke to one of the officers. He pushed the button for the elevator and stepped inside.

Two hours later a team of communications experts set up a telephone monitoring system in Stephanie's living room. They thought maybe the abductor might call for a ransom.

Agent Murphy and his partner Ted Swann of the FBI suspected that this was not going to be the type of case where someone called and demanded a ransom. Murphy had that prickling sensation on the back of his neck. There was not going to be anything normal about this at all.

Captain Martin 'Marty' as his friends called him stretched and yawned as he sat at his kitchen table. He enjoyed his early morning coffee but it was lonely now since his wife had died. He glanced at the floor near the kitchen door. She always left her gardening shoes there on a little mat so she wouldn't track mud into the house. He liked seeing her shoes there. He could imagine that she was still nearby getting ready to spend the morning tending to her beloved flowers and vegetables.

The ringing telephone startled him.

"For the love of….who is calling…aw shit, I'll bet some idiot didn't show up for his shift. Yeah," he growled into the receiver.

Marty grumbled all the way to his truck. "I don't understand why they don't fire his ass and get some reliable replacements. We've been short-handed for months now. You ask me I think these people are just a buncha damn cheapskates!"

He had decided to take a short detour before heading in to pull the extra shift. He had looked up Darmon's home address the last time he had failed to show up. This time he was going to pound on the guy's door and see how he liked being disturbed.

He stomped down on the accelerator as he crossed Sepulveda Boulevard, still muttering and swearing under his breath. Even at this early hour traffic had begun to pick up in North Hollywood and Van Nuys.

He easily found the address and slowed his faithful truck. He pulled into the driveway of the little two-story house and sat for a moment looking around. He marveled at the incongruity of the tall four-story apartment buildings crammed into the neighborhood like predatory animals wedging the older home in on all sides.

The blinds were closed on all of the windows. The tiny patch of grass on each side of the entry walk was over-grown and unkempt. Marty shook his head in disgust as he marched up the steps to the front door.

He pounded loudly and waited for a response. There was no sound but the passing traffic behind him on the street. Marty wrinkled his nose as an unpleasant odor floated in the vicinity of the front door. The smell overpowered even the exhaust fumes from the passing cars. He was undecided whether it was leaking gas or rotting garbage.

"Hey," he called to a young man who had just come out of one of the apartments. "You know the guy who lives here?"

"No, he's kinda weird. I saw him leave about two nights ago like he was goin' to work. He was dressed in his uniform. Haven't seen him since."

Marty waved his thanks and mumbled, "Weird is right!"

He walked briskly around the house and let himself into the gated back yard. Junk was piled next to the fence, rusted buckets, some shovels, tarps and scrap wood. The longer Marty stood there, the less he liked it. The smell was stronger back there away from the street.

He climbed the back steps and pulled open the screen door. Then he pounded on the door and hollered for Darmon to get out of bed and answer the door. Still there was no answer so he pounded again. This time the door opened. It had not been locked.

Captain Martin was not prepared for what he found in that house. When he saw what was left of Zeke's father he was sick to his stomach. He went downstairs and used the telephone to call the police and then the Proguard home office. He was sure Zeke Darmon should no longer be employed as a guard with that company...or anywhere.

Courtney lay sleepless for the second night. Even Storm Cat's presence on the bed with her failed to give her comfort. She had called Hattie's hotel in Myrtle Beach and left a message. Hattie had called her even before the front desk had given her the slip of paper. She had promised Courtney that she and her choir members would form a prayer circle and try to help keep Latoia safe. It was comforting to know that Hattie and those wonderful men and women would be supporting her friend with prayer but the terror still held her in a heart-pounding grip.

The sisters had been communicating almost non-stop with their unique silent whisperings. At last their tired minds quieted and each fell into a fitful sleep.

At three thirty in the morning something awakened Courtney. She looked at the clock and then was startled to see a softly glowing light at the foot of her bed. The top of the light was rounded as though it were a doorway. A hooded monk stepped through the light and bowed. Then he stepped aside as one by one, young girls stepped forward from the light door and allowed Courtney to see their lovely faces. Then each one turned and went back into the light. There was no sound, no word spoken just profound silence in which the viewing of these spirits was communication enough. Finally the monk stepped forward and bowed low in Courtney's direction. The message had been delivered. He opened his arms and pulled the door shut and the room was once more draped in the early morning darkness. Courtney knew that Latoia was still alive but there were others who were not.

Courtney glanced over at Storm Cat. He was staring at the place where the monk had disappeared. "You saw it too didn't you," she whispered. Storm Cat stood up and arched his back. His tail was fluffed to twice its normal size. He shook himself vigorously before making a little circle and curling up once again. He was careful to position his head so he could keep an eye on the place where the monk and the girls had appeared. He didn't want to miss anything else that might happen in the night. Courtney lay back against her pillows with a sigh. Her life was certainly going to be different than anything she could ever have imagined. Her eyes finally closed and she slept more peacefully for a short time.

A scraping noise in the hall outside her bedroom door alerted her to the fact that Caitlin was up and headed for the stairs. She glanced at the clock, five-thirty. It was time to get up. She knew without a doubt that she had to go to California.

Theresa was in the kitchen by the time Courtney had showered and dressed.

"I bet you'll never guess what Caitlin is doing," Theresa pointed to the sunroom door with a grin. "Oh, by-the-way, your man is going to call you," she raised one eyebrow and tilted her head to one side.

"He isn't my man, he is Caitlin's doctor and if he doesn't call me I'll call him. I have to get permission to take Caitlin to California. I would like you to go too if you can. I'll need your help with her while we try to find Latoia.

I plan to pay all of your expenses and I'll pay you for your time as well. Please say you'll go with me."

Theresa's eyes grew large and her mouth dropped open. "You don't have to ask me twice! I'm gonna go pack right now! California!"

The sunroom was bathed in soft early morning light. Caitlin sat hunched over her drawing table while she worked with her watercolors. Brown was gripped under her left arm as usual as she painted.

Upon closer inspection Courtney could see that the wound from Caitlin's fall was miraculously nearly gone. A tiny frown creased her forehead and Courtney was fascinated as the new picture took shape. A red convertible with a female driver was unmistakeable. Her blond hair streamed out behind her. The darkenss followed this girl just as it had with Latoia.

"Oh my God," she whispered, "He's going after somebody else!"

"Somebody else," Caitlin echoed.

The telephone began ringing at seven o'clock. It was indeed Doctor Baylor. He made excuses claiming emergencies and being over loaded with work. Courtney could hear the truth of his words but she could also sense that he had deliberately refused to take the time to call. She didn't really want to think about that at this moment so she broke in on his rambling explanation and quickly outlined what she needed. He thought for a few seconds and then promised to call her back as soon as he could with the answer.

Courtney had just hung up when the telephone rang again. It was Stephanie. She explained that upon her insistance, Latoia's mother, grandmother and aunt Pearl would be coming to stay with her during the search for Latoia. She felt that all of them would find comfort in being together. Stephanie wanted to make the ladies as comfortable as possible during this terrible time. They had not been easy to convince but when Stephanie told them that the FBI wanted them there in the event that the kidnappers might call they agreed without hesitation.

Courtney told Stephanie that she and her sister planned to fly out there on the earliest possible flight. Stephanie insisted that they all stay with her. She had plenty of room for everyone and she needed to feel as though she were helping in some way.

The next call was from the detective who wanted her to speak with an agent Murphy. He was very interested in the psychic gifts that Courtney described to him, but he was also filled with a skeptisim that would need physical proof in order for his doubts to be dispelled.

Stephen called again to say that he was able to get the release for Caitlin to travel.

"Thank you so much, we have to leave as soon as possible. Latoia's life is…" her voice broke.

"I understand that you need to help and that the two of you will find your friend by using your extraordinary gifts. It's a lot for anyone to handle…me included, but I believe you are more than capable. Please keep yourself safe and your sister."

"Thank you Stephen. That means a lot to me and I do believe that we *will* be safe," Courtney had regained her composure and her voice was soft but filled with strength.

"I'm hoping that we can have a lot more talks and I'd still like to take you to dinner when you get back," his tone was hopeful.

"I would like that." Courtney replaced the receiver as a mixture of emotions swirled around in her head like confused bees. She felt the little thrill of anticipation of the time she would spend with Stephen but it was mixed with the fear she felt for her friend.

The telephone rang again and she jumped, jerking her hand away from the receiver as if it were hot

Agent Murphy spoke in clipped official dialogue. He told her that two agents would be arriving to help her pack up her sister's paintings and then drive Courtney to the airport.

"Now you have to understand agent Murphy, that my sister and I work as a team and I am bringing a nurse along to help with my sister. There will be three of us traveling. I was planing to travel on a commercial airline and use an airport limo to get us there." Courtney spoke firmly and her tone was cool.

Agent Murphy spoke with someone nearby and soon he came back on the line.

"Miss Hammond it won't be necessary for you to go to all of that trouble. There is a car on the way to you now. You and your companions will be taken to a private plane and you will be flown to LAX. I will be there to meet you."

"Thank you agent..." he had already disconnected.

Courtney called out to Theresa and briefly explained what was happening then she hurried upstairs to pack for both her sister and herself. She filled two small bags and as an afterthought, she grabbed Caitlin's blue backpack and carried everything downstairs.

Theresa was just answering the front door when Courtney reached the bottom of the staircase.

"If you will pull around to the kitchen door it will be easier to load up everything," Theresa directed. The tall thin man nodded with a half smile and turned to carry out her instructions.

Courtney hurried to the telephone and placed a call to her grandmother's caregivers and another call to her parents. She left a message at both places. Then she took a deep calming breath and walked into the sunroom.

Caitlin worked quietly, sitting where Courtney had left her the last time. She extended her energy toward the girl and silently called her name. Before she could get a response the tall agent and his female counterpart bustled noisily into the room.

"Are we supposed to pack up all of those paintings and drawings?" The woman was a good deal shorter than the man but her voice was deep and husky.

"Yes, but,..." Courtney had wanted to speak with Caitlin first to prepare her for what was going to happen. She was not at all sure what her sister's reaction would be.

It was too late. The pair marched past Courtney and began gathering up Caitlin's work.

As soon as Courtney heard the moaning, she knew there would be trouble. Before anyone knew what was happening Caitlin started to scream. She hurled her painting water at the tall young agent and the brush flew through the air hitting the woman's pale gray jacket.

When the bedlam subsided the two agents had splotches of paint on their clothing and their perfectly groomed hair stood out at odd angles. Theresa was able to quiet Caitlin with a tootsie roll pop. Courtney took that opportunity to send a silent message explaining that her paintings would travel with her and would then be used to help find Latoia and the man who had taken her. Caitlin rocked silently back and forth as she placidly sucked on her candy. The paintings and drawings were packed with no further outbursts.

The ride in the limo was quiet but when they got to the airport Caitlin became agitated. "Get me a chopper now! Yes sir. Upside over and get out Roger! Get in that chopper private, do it now!" Caitlin made her voice lower as she spoke. She had spotted a helicopter formation and was craning her neck to watch their flight pattern.

"They watch a lot of old movies at The Oaks," Theresa shrugged as she suppressed a giggle. The two agents simply looked at each other then stared straight ahead.

The private jet was cool and comfortable. Theresa sat with Caitlin and Courtney sat across from them. They were served iced tea and small sandwiches. The two agents who were escorting them had attempted to clean their clothes in the washrooms at the back of the plane. It was a futile attempt but they did look less disheveled.

Courtney leaned back in the seat and allowed her body to relax. Her breathing slowed and deepened and in a few seconds the blue vision began to form in her third eye.

A beautiful young woman was getting into a bright red convertible. Her long blond hair floated around her shoulders and softly framed her face. She backed her car slowly out of a parking space and drove through the parking lot of an apartment complex. She drove past a guard shack and turned onto a tree-lined street. A dark colored car pulled out as she passed and began to follow a short distance behind her.

The vision skipped to another scene. The sports car had pulled into a gas station and the blond was putting gas in her car. The dark car pulled up at a nearby pump and the driver proceeded to do the same thing.

The man wore some sort of official uniform. He was average height wearing glasses and short-cropped gray hair. Courtney's heart rate quickened. She knew that this was the man who had taken Latoia and he was getting ready to take someone else.

The vision suddenly changed. The bright blue day blinked out and she peered into the darkness at a barely discernable shape. A faint glow brought the shape into focus. A woman's body! Her eyes and mouth were taped shut. One side of the tape had come loose but her lips were still tightly secured. There was movement. Her mouth was working the tape loose! A dark substance oozed down the side of the girl's head. Blood!

"Latoia!" Courtney's mind called her name. "I am coming to find you. Show me where you are." Latoia's head turned slightly and frown lines creased her brow, then she lay still. The vision ended.

"Miss Hammond?" the agent touched her shoulder. "We will be landing soon.

The pilot has told us to fasten our seat belts."

Courtney was stunned that the time had passed so quickly. She must have fallen asleep after the vision ended. She did feel more rested and that was good. She would need all of her strength and energy for what was to come. There was more than just a little turbulence to cope with.

CHAPTER TWENTY- ONE

Zeke had no particular plan in mind as he followed the blond girl. He just knew that he had a commandment to fulfill and that the way would be shown to him. He was completely unaware of the chaos and destruction that his actions had caused. His mind had left behind the rules of normalcy that most of mankind follows. His was now a world made up of the macabre meanderings of the criminally insane.

His father's voice ordered him to carry out his commands with ruthless precision. Sometimes, like now, all thought of precision and care were abandoned for the sake of accomplishing the task without delay.

Tamara was feeling sassy. She was positive she would get a call back for the toothpaste commercial. She just had a good feeling about it. Her teeth were perfectly straight and white. Her parents had spent a fortune to make sure they had no flaws. She tossed her gleaming blond hair out of her eyes and squinted at the gas pump. Ten gallons would do nicely. She replaced the knozzle and tightened the gas cap, then went to the cashier to pay for it and to buy some gum.

A man in a rumpled uniform was standing near the driver's side of her red convertible.

"Looks like you got a low tire miss. If you'll pull over to the the air pump I'll fill it for you."

"I don't have any spare change," she stated flatly, thinking he might just want a hand out.

"I don't want any money, I just wanted to help you out. His reply was polite and his smile seemed friendly.

"Okay thanks."

The man gestured to the air pump located near a large old tree away from the gas pumps. He got into his car and called out to her to pull her car under the tree.

As soon as she was parked she jumped out of her car and walked over to the air hose. She thought she really should be able to do it herself. How hard could it be anyway? She yanked on the hose and pulled it toward the low tire. The man pulled his older model Buick near the front of her convertible effectively blocking her view of the station and her exit.

"I got a pressure gauge in my trunk. You don't want to over fill it," he pulled the trunk release and hurried to get the gauge out. He hadn't expected the girl to try to do it herelf. He had watched her coming and going from the same exclusive complex as his Martita. The difference is that this girl was wanton. Young men came to see her, deceived by the devil's beauty. She had a vile tongue, cursing and taking the Lord's name in vain.

"Oh Christ it's hot. How do you make this damn thing fit…are you bringing that thing or…." She broke off mid-sentence as she abruptly stood up from her crouching position near the tire.

Zeke moved up close behind her. He had an iron bar in his hands. Her head connected sharply with his chin. His teeth clamped down on his tongue and blood spurted in his mouth. The force of the blow knocked him back a step but he raised the bar again and brought it down toward Tamara's head.

Years of tennis and track events from high school through college, had built strong muscles and quick reflexes in her young body. One dainty foot caught Zeke squarely in the mid-section. The bar came down on the side of her head with only enough force to break the skin and cause a painful bump.

Zeke doubled over as the air whooshed out of his lungs with a surprised grunt of pain.

"Fire, fire," she shrieked at the top of her voice. "Car's on fire!" She kicked at Zeke's knees as hard as she could, causing him to fall to the ground. The metal bar clanged loudly as it hit the dark gray pavement. Then she turned and ran as hard as she could toward the gas station.

A customer had heard her screams and alerted the cashier. He grabbed a fire extinguisher. Both men were running toward the two cars prepared to do battle with a flaming vehicle until the fire department arrived. Instead they found a middle-aged man struggling to his feet. The right lens of his glasses was cracked and his lips were pulled back baring his bloody teeth. The men halted as Zeke shouted at them spraying spittle with every word.

"My God, what is that?" the cashier spoke never taking his eyes off of Zeke as he ranted and waved his arms.

"Looks like a demon if ya ask me," the customer was backing up. "No wonder she yelled fire. I betcha he's coming up straight from hell!"

Zeke picked up the metal bar and began swinging it hitting the windshield of Tamara's convertible.

"He's no demon he's a frigging nut case," the cashier was backing up. His face had paled and his long slender fingers were white where they gripped the red fire extinguisher.

Tamara reached over the counter in the store and picked up the telephone to dial 911. She was shaking but she managed to tell the dispatcher that she needed the police and that she had been mistaken about the fire. She knew that screaming about a fire would bring help more quickly than just yelling for help, especially at a gas station.

Distant sirens wailed. As soon as Zeke heard them he limped to his car and sped off. His father's voice had been silenced in the wake of his own rage. The relief of the blessed silence was exquisite. He felt so good. He must have

212

done everything right. His father might even be proud of him. That is when the laughter started.

***

Agents Murphy and Swann were waiting with a large black airport limo when the jet landed. They said very little beyond cursory introductions and went straight to work loading up Caitlin's artwork and the small bags that each of the travelers had packed. Caitlin clutched Brown as usual and she refused to let anyone take the blue backpack.

Murphy looked at the paint-splattered clothing of the two Charleston agents. He never changed his expression. "Colorful," was all he said.

"I have to tell you Miss Hammond I do not believe in psychic hoodoo voodoo. The detective here tells me that you came up with some facts that matched up with a case that began a couple of weeks ago".

Courtney listened to everything they said as she fought back her rising anxiety. At first she was patient with their probing questions and answered them with quiet dignity. After an hour she was beginning to feel uneasy and she longed to take action.

"Look, to tell you the truth, I have never done this before myself. I know very little about the workings of any type of law enforcement agency. I don't understand your investigative methods any more than you understand mine. I just feel as though we're wasting time," Courtney's voice rose as her patience came to an end.

"I understand Miss Hammond, but we need to be thorough..."

"Then you need to add this new information," Courtney broke in and proceeded to describe what she had seen in her most recent vision.

"Ah, okay thanks. Our experts are studying your paintings."

"My sister's paintings." Courtney corrected him.

The agents glanced over at Caitlin, who sat near Theresa on a worn brown leather couch. She was licking at another sucker while she rocked her upper body, bouncing gently off of the cushions behind her.

"She's autistic but she has unique gifts."

"A savant?" the agent queried.

"Yes, she's psychic and paints what she sees."

"Ah, hmm," Murphy lapsed into silence.

A woman entered the room and handed a note to agent Swann.

"Ms Mills is here. She says you're staying with her. Why don't you go with her for now? As soon as our experts come up with anyting I'll let you know. Stay near the phone and if you ...uh...see anything else just call me at this number." He handed Courtney his card and the agents filed out of the room.

Stephanie was waiting for them on the ground floor. Courtney had never met her before, but she instantly knew who she was from Latoia's vivid description.

The women introduced themselves and shared a warm hug which brought each to tears. They exchanged greetings and engaged in brief conversation, then loaded up their suitcases and climbed into Stephanie's car. She lived only about twenty minutes from the FBI office.

Stephanie's housekeeper and Latoia's grandmother were in the kitchen, preparing a light meal. Latoia's mother and Aunt Pearl were just coming downstairs when all of them arrived.

There were more hugs and tears and conversation. Courtney could feel Mary's grief and fear during their embrace.

"I know that Latoia is alive," Courtney looked deep into her dark eyes as she spoke.

"I know she is too. I've been prayin' night and day. I know she's alive, I can feel it," she spoke with absolute conviction. When Courtney felt that strength rise up in Latoia's mother, she was relieved. She was sure that the tall stately woman would be able to cope with everything…at least for now.

***

A large red fire truck roared into the parking lot of the gas station. Tamara was pacing in agitation as she looked for the police car that would soon follow. As soon as she saw one threading through the heavy Friday evening traffic, she ran out of the station waving her arms.

"He's getting away," she kept screaming over and over. The cashier had gone over to speak with the firemen and the helpful customer was telling the story to the station manager who had just arrived. A small crowd of people had started to gather to watch all of the commotion.

The policemen pulled into the lot and tried to calm the agitated young woman. She gave them a brief outline of what happened including a decent description of the attacker, his car and a few numbers from his license plate. One officer radioed the information to any units that might be nearby.

Tamara repeated her story again while the officer made notes of everything. He walked with her to her damaged car and wrote down everything he would need for his report.

Another police car pulled in with his lights flashing. The uniformed policeman leaped out of his car and spoke in low tones to the officer who was interviewing Tamara. She couldn't hear what was being said but from the expressions they wore she knew something big was happening.

Captain Martin had been badly shaken by what he found at Zeke's house. None of the law enforcement team who had been there that day would ever forget what they saw. Marty had arrived late to his post after undergoing extensive questioning by police and detectives and it had been difficult to focus on the job that day. After his shift he arrived at his home, his sanctuary, but his thoughts were too full of the horrors of Darmon's activities for him to feel safe and relaxed. He climbed into bed with the lights on in every room of his house. No matter how he tried, sleep elluded him. At five he finally got up and started the coffee and took a shower. Then he poured himself a cup even adding some sugar and milk and turned on the television to watch an early morning news show.

The news anchor was reporting on the macabre discovery made by a security guard and suddenly his own square-jawed face filled the screen.

"Well I'll be damned," he almost laughed. It was the last thing he ever expected. "Well I just hope they catch that lunatic freak," he muttered.

He arrived on time for his shift and other than being tired, the hours passed uneventfully until his lunch break. There was a small lounge on the second floor that sported cold drink machines, a candy machine, a sandwich machine, a small table with four uncomfortable chairs and a television set which was always turned to a news program.

No matter how long he studied the contents of the machines nothing ever looked appetizing. Finally he settled for a candy bar and a soft drink. Then he walked slowly to an empty chair and sank heavily into it. He placed the soft drink can on the table and opened the paper around the candy bar. He glanced at the television set. Latoia's beautiful face flashed up on the screen. The news story explained that she had been abducted from the home of a friend and police were asking for people to call if anyone had any information about where she might be.

"Holy crap!" Marty knew that girl. He knew too with every nerve in his body that Zeke Darmon had something to do with her disappearance. He hurried back to the guard's station to make some calls.

***

Zeke was not aware of the fact that he had become the object of an all points bulletin. The angry voice in his head demanded his full attention and diminished all outside activity to nothing more than an irritating blur. Without realizing it he slipped away from his pursurers when a catering van and a flower delivery van collided behind him, creating a nasty traffic jam which, effectively halted any further pursuit.

The crunch of metal and honking horns triggered the sounds of battle in his damaged mind. He heard the voice of his commander, guns being fired in the distance and more terrible than anything else the agonized cries of fallen and injured soldiers all around him.

Time slid forward and tumbled back warping in on itself then stretching far into the distance as he viewed everything as though he moved through a horrific fun house of mirrors. He fought the war once again and his weapon was empty. He ran to fallen comrades and seized the guns and grenades that they would not be able to use then ran deep into the jungle to hide and attack the enemy from the dense foliage. He was in the Viet Nam jungles again fighting for his life.

Emergency calls began to come in to local dispatchers as citizens reported a crazed man leaping from his car to snatch odd items from the outside of homes or stores. They reported that he screamed ominous warnings that someone named Charlie was coming and they would surely be killed.

Zeke made it to Topanga Canyon Road and drove as fast as the treacherous curves would allow. He found his familiar side road and turned right following it to the dirt road then turned left. He jammed the accelerator to the floor spraying gravel and dust as the Buick fishtailed down the seldom-traveled road. When he arrived at the pile of boulders, he turned the wheel hard swerving left and came to a stop behind a collection of shrubs and small straggly trees.

The sun was setting and long dark shadows crept across the hills and valleys of the uneven terrain. Zeke knew he would have to find the cave before it got too dark. The path was steep and in daylight it was dangerous but at night it would be much worse even with a flashlight.

He always kept some supplies in the wheel well. He jumped out of the car and opened the trunk. In a short time he had gathered everything together, including a knife, rope and flashlight then crammed all of it into the backpack that he had ripped from the hands of a startled child walking along a quiet neighborhood sidewalk.

Zeke ducked low when he saw a light twinkle in the gathering dusk. He knew the enemy was close. He would have to be careful. After thirty minutes of hard fast travel on foot he jumped, slid and rolled down the steep embankment until he was at the entrance to his cave.

Latoia was weak and dehydrated. She had no idea how much time had passed. She was always so grateful when unconsciousness carried her blissfully away from the horror of her circumstances into lovely dreams of comforting voices and most recently conversations with Lawrence, her deceased twin brother.

Her hands and feet were numb but she continually pulled and struggled against the tape and rope. Her face was raw from scrapping her skin against every surface she could reach with her head in an effort to loosen the tape on her eyes.

Sometimes she forgot that her head ached. She only knew that there was pain somewhere in her body. She had managed to free one side of her mouth and she enjoyed the precious freedom of gulping in air and licking her dry lips.

Something moved near her head and she screamed. Her throat was so dry that she only succeeded in making a parched rasping sound, but it was enough to send the field mouse running. She jerked her body intermittently in hopes that the other creepy crawlers might be frightened enough to look elsewhere for a new perch.

It was growing cooler again. It must be getting dark. She tried to think how many times that had happened. This could be the third night. She dreaded the long hours of shivering. Well maybe she could just die and be done with it all. She took a breath and tried to relax. "I'm ready to go Jesus, please take me home. I'm sorry I didn't get to church more often," she felt the darkness pulling her under. She let go and floated into it.

Zeke had twisted his ankle in his rush to get down the slope to the cave. He dropped to his knees and belly-crawled through the entrance. Martita was forgotten. Latoia was now a prisoner who would be interrogated. Charlie was no match for him and his men.

The mutterings of the crazed man reached Latoia's ears. She had been alone for so many hours that it was almost a relief to hear him nearby, but she was filled with terror at the thought of what he might do.

She lay quietly listening to her own heart pounding as Zeke moved around ranting about someone named Charlie. Her senses were on high alert as she tried to figure out what was going on. She was sure that hours passed. She was cold and shivering again. Her own mind was wandering in and out of delirium.

Zeke was getting worked up. He started shouting in Vietnamese. He knew his prisoner was not going to give him the information he needed. It was time to use some persuasion. He picked up his knife and limped toward the filthy rotting mattress where Latoia lay.

A figure stepped out of the shadows startling Zeke so much that he stumbled back putting too much weight on his injured ankle.

A tall young black man stood protectively in front of the prone shaking figure on the mattress. His eyes stared like burning black coals into Zeke's mind.

"Get back!" Zeke shouted and he sliced through the air with his knife.

The young man's mouth simply curved into a mocking smile. The knife did no damage and he took another step toward Zeke.

Something wasn't right and even in his confused state Zeke knew it. An unseen force was pushing him back. He pushed back as he tried to maintain his position and figure out where the kid had come from. His ankle collapsed again as pain shot up his leg every time he tried to ease his weight down on that foot. The kid had weird eyes. He must be battle crazy.

They were at the entrance to the cave now. The sky had grown dark and Zeke's flashlight seemed insignificant in the vast night shadowed landscape. Still he was able to see the young man very clearly. Zeke scrambled and stumbled backward along the uneven ground. He was near the edge of a steep drop off.

"You shouldn't have hurt my sister. She's a good person. She deserves a good life," the young man's voice roared through Zeke's head as he fell back into empty space, then plummeted into the black void. His body thumped against the rocky earth far below.

Latoia heard Zeke's hysterical cries. She knew something had happened to him but she was too tired to care. She was cold and her stomach hurt from hunger and her throat hurt from thirst.

"Rest baby sister, everything's gonna be fine now." That sounded like Lawrence. She must be dreaming again. Warmth slowly crept through her body and the shaking stopped. Her eyes closed. She heard Courtney's voice again. They were coming. She would be fine just fine like Lawrence said.

Saturday morning the sun rose slowly over the eastern rim of the canyon, pushing back the shadows that would only dare return at nightfall. Zeke's body was badly broken but he was still alive. He opened his eyes with a clear mind for the first time in months. For a few seconds he enjoyed the warmth of the sun. Then the memories of his actions hit him like poison darts as his emotional pain kept pace with his physical pain.

Something shook nearby. The madness returned as the rattlesnake coiled and rattled a warning.

Zeke knew that this was a test of faith. He was certain that the snake that had come to taunt him straight from Eden was tempting him to lose his faith in what was right. "Get thee behind me Satan!" He cried out as loud as his weakness and pain would let him.

"I am not Satan. I am not evil," the snake spoke to him in a hissing rasp. "It is the evil in your own heart and actions that brought you to this end. I am the symbol of healing and transformation. You must transform by leaving this earth." The snake struck swiftly.

***

Caitlin had slept well, but she was up early working with her sketchbook. Courtney had not slept well at all but she realized she must have drifted off for three or four hours. She was resting on the living room sofa when she drifted off. The sun was up and someone was making coffee in the kitchen. She stretched and yawned pointing her toes and tightening the muscles of her calves. A painful cramp brought her to a sitting position abruptly.

"Oh you're awake. The coffee is nearly ready," Stephanie's housekeeper smiled as she walked into the living room with a plate of finger food for Caitlin.

"Thank you for doing that," Courtney said through a grimace as she massaged her feet and coaxed her toes out of the spasm.

"Hmm, too much stress and not enough bananas and liquid." The housekeeper disappeared into the kitchen again and returned moments later carrying a tray filled with food. There was a bowl of sliced bananas and strawberries floating in cream, coffee and a warm sliced blueberry muffin with two pats of melting butter on top.

"Thank you so much. This looks wonderful. I just don't know how much I can eat." Courtney's eyes felt grainy and her stomach was unstable.

"Well, start with the bananas and cream, then try a bite of muffin. You might be surprised with how much you really can eat."

Courtney followed her suggestions and *was* surprised at how good the food tasted. Her stomach even settled down and stabilized.

Caitlin's sketches were strewn around on the chairs and tables. Courtney began examining each one. She saw the blond girl at the gas station, the same one she had seen in her vision.

Caitlin had drawn the first clear picture of the assailant's face. His features were twisted in an ugly scowl and his mouth was open. He stood with his arms poised over his head as he prepared to bring down a heavy stick on the girl's head. Courtney felt sick again and she hurried to pick up the other pictures.

She saw that the girl had escaped, but the man did too. She was intrigued with the strange images that floated around the man's head. She realized that Caitlin was trying to say that the man was driven by other influences and maybe voices.

Other pictures showed winding roads and mountains. They were unfinished and unclear. There was another one that showed Latoia lying on her side. She was bound at the ankles and knees and her arms were secured behind her back. Her eyes were taped shut.

Courtney shuffled through the remaining sketches, desparate to know more. In one drawing Latoia's abductor was on his knees looking up at a tall dark figure that Caitlin had not filled in. It appeared to be a man but his body was just an outline.

Caitlin suddenly put down her charcoal pencil and moved to another chair where she began nibbling on the fruit and small squares of toast, left there by the thoughtful housekeeper.

Courtney looked at the drawing she had been working on. The man was lying down. His arms were flung out on either side and were bent at odd angles. His legs too were bent in unnatural positions. Nearby a coiled snake held up a tail full of rattles. Above and to the left the strange war-like images were fading. In the right corner far above the fallen man lay Latoia. Her mouth was open but her eyes were still taped shut. Her hands and feet were still tightly bound but Courtney knew she lived.

"Telephone for you," the housekeeper announced.

"He's dead," Courtney said softly.

"Ding dong the wicked witch is dead," Caitlin sing-songed between mouthfuls.

Courtney hurried to the kitchen to take the call. It was the detective she had originally dealt with. He relayed all of the information that had come in and they now believed that a security guard was responsible for Latoia's abduction. They knew his name and background but the man had slipped away and there had been no further sightings since the previous evening.

"I think he might be dead," Courtney spoke softly. "Detective, my sister has created a series of drawings that will help you find your man and Latoia is close by maybe in some sort of cave. She's tied up but alive."

"I'll be there in twenty minutes," he disconnected without another word.

By the time he rang the doorbell Courtney had scooped up the drawings and hidden them behind the sofa. Stephanie, Latoia's mother, aunt and grandmother had come downstairs. The women stood shoulder to shoulder behind Courtney as she faced the powerfully built older man.

Courtney explained in a firm strong voice that she had no intention of showing him the pictures until he promised to take her and her sister to help find Latoia.

He sighed with great annoyance but nodded his head in agreement.

Courtney knew too well that he may be inclined to change his mind, but she was ready. She slipped quickly into a light trance and allowed the waiting spirit to speak through her. "Now you listen to me Alby, it's not nice to tell lies. You tell your mother who put the grasshoppers in the cookie jar?" Courtney's eyes had glazed just slightly as she spoke.

The detective's face paled and his eyes widened. "Ok, that…that was below the belt, but okay you can both go."

"I am going too," Theresa announced firmly as she joined the group in the foyer.

The detective rubbed his hand over his face and rolled his eyes. "Let's have a look at those drawings," he said gruffly. The women moved aside and Courtney led him to the living room. "The FBI people are going to have to be notified. They're technically running the show now", he grumbled.

CHAPTER TWENTY-TWO

The police radio crackled as dispatchers spoke through the static in short terse sentences filled with code numbers and official jargon. Courtney sat in the front seat with the detective driving the unmarked car. Theresa sat with Caitlin in the back.

They were reasonably sure that Latioa was hidden in one of the canyons. The problem was in narrowing the choices. The FBI missing persons division and the local law enforcement had agreed to cooperate in the search. Volunteers from various organizations generously offered to help along with local compassionate civilians.

Courtney had carefully considered all of the possibiities. She felt no urgency at the mention of Mulholland Drive or Laurel Canyon. When Topanga Canyon was mentioned it caused her heart to flutter and her stomach to clench. She knew that was where the search should be focused.

Their progress seemed agonizingly slow, but Courtney forced herself to be patient and remain calm. She knew she had a better chance of sensing something from Latoia if she could keep her mind still and receptive. The enormous job of putting together a search of this magnitude had come about with amazing ease. There had been media coverage for the three days since Latoia's abduction. There were already a large number of professionals who had been working diligently to find her friend.

Courtney closed her eyes to shut out the view from the car windows as they rushed forward. She allowed her mind to quiet and her thoughts to lift.

"I've been waiting for you," Caitlin's familiar voice filled her mind. "This is our purpose you know."

"What?" Courtney thought back.

"This. Finding people. Helping people. Working together."

"We haven't found her yet," Courtney's silent tone was peevish.

"We will," Caitlin replied soothingly.

"Courtney, do you uh, see something?" He struggled to find the right words as he waved one hand in circles in front of his face.

"No, not yet, but I hear something," Courtney smiled.

***

Hattie stood with her choir as the director signaled for them to begin their group warm up scales. It was a small group compared to the choir from Columbia and the one from Greenville. Those groups had either rented or owned large buses to bring their members to the competition.

The little church choir from Charleston shuffled their feet nervously while they warmed up their voices. Hattie felt their nerves. She was nervous too. She knew there was a lot going on today and not just at this choir competition. She had been praying non-stop for the safety of Latoia and everyone involved. She had received phone calls from Theresa updating her on everything. She had also enlisted the help of the choir members and they had willingly formed a prayer circle. They held hands and brought their open hearts together in a powerful plea for help to find Latoia.

The intermission was over and everyone was anxious to perform. It was seven o'clock but Hattie's choir was not scheduled to sing until seven thirty. The auditorium was filled to capacity. The next choir filed onto the stage and the director raised his hands and led them through their performance.

***

It was four o'clock as the unmarked car finally turned onto Topanga Canyon road. Courtney was feeling highly agitated. The detective had insisted on traveling across the other canyon roads first. He felt it was smarter to eliminate each one and since they were closer to Mulholland to start with, he wanted to begin there. He stopped to check in with various search teams and occasionally got messages from the two helicopters that were methodically combing the canyons from high above.

Caitlin kept up a constant stream of movie dialogue every time she saw or heard a 'chopper'. The detective's face had taken on a reddish tinge as his jaw muscles worked and his scowl deepened.

Finally, he turned on to Topanga Canyon Road. The road climbed, dropped and twisted its way through the golden-brown hills, dotted with the occasional dark green tree or gray boulders, brindle cows and small wildlife.

Then she felt it, the tug from her solar plexus. This was the right way. Courtney sat up straighter and grabbed the dashboard.

"What?" detective Denton barked.

"This is the right road. Keep going."

They were all silent including Caitlin. Courtney's heart raced and the pull grew stronger. They streaked past an unmarked road to their left and Courtney felt a stab of fear in her mid-section.

"Stop, go back we have to go down that road!"

He braked as fast as he could. The two agents following them were hard pressed not to rear-end the car as tires squealed and a few yards of black rubber burned into the pavement. Both cars swung around and headed back to the small road. Courtney felt the pull again and it was growing stronger.

Ruts and cracks in the eroding pavement made for a bumpy ride. The road was obviously seldom used. They jounced and jerked for nearly a hundred yards then the road dropped down sharply only to rise up again immediately.

Caitlin began to murmur. "Up we go and down we go," she repeated the phrase three more times and suddenly hurled the undigested portion of her lunch on the back of Denton's neck.

"Aaagh" swearing profusely Denton brought the Crown Vic to a jerky halt.

Theresa grabbed tissues and wet wipes from her large bag and worked to clean up the mess.

Courtney got out to stretch her legs. She noticed a large black butterfly with a touch of blue on its wings. It flew around the dusty trees then over a cluster of rocks.

"This way!" Courtney pointed to what they could now see was a dirt road turning off to the left.

Courtney sprinted the few yards to the turn off. The dust and rock had been disturbed by tires and left well-defined impressions in the loose dirt, as it must have swung wide and fishtailed. She followed the tracks with her eyes. Something glinted in the brush. She trotted toward it, careful to avoid the deeply etched tracks. When she rounded the curve she saw Zeke's abandoned car.

"Stop. Stay back!" The agents had their guns drawn and had fanned out approaching the abandoned car with great care.

Courtney's heart pounded furiously. She truly had no idea what to do next. She knew Latoia was not in the car but where was she? Her gifts had always come to her spontaneously. Until recently she had no need or desire to try to use them. That business with the detective's deceased mother was unexpected. Somehow she had sensed that all she had to do was open her mouth and the words would spill out

"God, please help me find Latoia", she prayed silently.

When the men had searched the area and found there was no apparent threat Courtney walked over to the car and bowed her head. She immediately saw dreadful images, young women being brutalized; an older man molesting a little boy; mummified bodies in a dark place. She was sickened as the images persisted. Sweat beaded up on her face and dripped down her chest and back. The magnetic force was so strong that her hands were plastered to the car as though they were being sucked into the metal. She could not pull away and she was at the edge of panic.

A bolt of light shot through the offensive images shattering them like a puzzle made of glass. Then blessed peace flowed through her as she realized she was looking into Hattie's beloved face. She was singing. It was *The Lord's Prayer* as only Hattie and her choir could sing it. Courtney sobbed with relief. The terrible suction on her hands released and she pulled away easily. The choir continued to sing.

Courtney turned unaware that Caitlin and the others surrounded her. She had no idea that only moments before her slender fragile twin had morphed into a growling snarling dynamo that kept anyone from touching Courtney while she was consumed by the visions, or that she became her usual docile self the moment her sister's hands were released from the car.

The black butterfly flapped erratically near the edge of the unkept road. Caitlin lifted her good right hand and pointed to it. Courtney was already running.

Suddenly everyone was in motion. Orders were shouted into radios. More officers were called and given their location. An ambulance service was ordered on standby. Radios crackled with voices talking through static. Courtney heard none of it. She heard only the choir and her inner urgings. Miraculously Caitlin could keep up with her and was only a few steps behind with Theresa, one of the agents and detective Denton.

***

Hattie's choir segued into a rousing gospel number. They were hitting high notes, blending their voices and singing from their hearts like never before. Members of the audience took up the rhythm swaying and clapping. First a few people stood up and a few more until everyone in the audience was standing, smiling, crying and clapping. The emotional electricity filled the auditorium touching hearts, reaching the angels and the power grew. As palpable and real as a tornado of healing energy it spun into the singing choir and lifted to arc across a continent and found its way to the search party.

***

The black butterfly stayed far ahead bouncing along through the dry late afternoon air. It flew in a straight line, taking the shortest route while everyone else was forced to follow the narrow rocky path that wound down and up around the canyon.

Courtney was single minded in her purpose. She hardly noticed when she or someone else slid on the treacherous loose gravel. Everyone was out of breath now and sweat dampened every brow.

Hattie's choir director was caught up in the ecstacy of the moment. He couldn't believe what was happening, but he did not question the power of the Almighty. He signaled to Tullie Mae, the pianist and she rolled a magnificent arpeggio of her own composition and quieted everything for Hattie's solo in *His eye is on the Sparrow.*

As Hattie's powerful voice began the first verse, choir and audience alike, felt their hearts open and tears rolled down many a cheek.

***

Courtney had set a blistering pace, but now she slowed as the choir in her head assured her that a gentle loving deity cares for everyone.

The butterfly disappeared over the edge of a particularly steep drop off. Courtney hurried to the edge and stopped. She could see a fairly wide ledge below and the bushes and dry grass had been torn up. She could see skid marks where someone had slid down.

Caitlin was close behind Courtney and she was dragging the blue backpack. Courtney looked around for another way down. There was none. The pull was strong here. The butterfly had settled on a clump of shrubbery a few yards below.

Hattie's voice had just hit the final note of that song when a little brown bird darted so close to Courtney's head that she had to duck and lost her balance. Caitlin threw her backpack down the embankment and then she threw the beloved Brown right after it. Courtney's feet lost purchase and she was sliding on the backpack with Brown clutched in her hand taking the brunt of the scrapes and bumps.

***

The auditorium was silent for only seconds as the tone died away. Tullie Mae, carried to the heights by the glory of it all, pounded out the chords to the next song. The choir belted out Hallelujah and the audience was on their feet again. Tears rolled, hands waved; it was an experience none of them would ever forget.

As soon as Courtney slid to a stop on the ledge, she saw the entrance to the cave. Heedless of the calls and warnings of the officers and agents coming behind her she dashed headlong into the cool gloom. She ran as quickly as she could, calling out Latoia's name. She saw Zeke's discarded flashlight lying on the ground and she scooped it up as she ran. The cave opening was small but once inside the ceiling was surprisingly high. Courtney was able to stand easily. She was aware of only one thing and that was finding Latoia. She shouted her name and searched the cave with the weak beam of the flashlight. Then she saw her.

Latoia lay, much as Courtney had visualized. She was bloody, limp and her hands and feet were tied behind her. The visible parts of her skin were covered with insect bites. Her breathing was labored. Courtney knew her friend was in trouble. She placed one hand gently on Latoia's throat and another over her heart. Courtney closed her eyes and drew in energy. Then she sent it straight into Latoia's body. The cool blue light around her throat took the swelling down and her breath flowed more easily. The bright pink and green lights that entered the weakened heart added strength to her heartbeat and Latoia's chest rose and fell with a normal rhythmic breathing.

"I'm here Latoia, can you hear me?"

She moaned and then "Girl yes I can hear you. What took you so long?" The voice was no more than a raspy croak, but it was strength behind the words and there was no doubt about it, it was definitely Latoia's style.

A helicopter arrived and disrupted the distant birdsong with its loud whup-whuping roters. It hovered far overhead so the dry dust covered ground would not be lifted into the air thus blowing away any possible useable evidence.

Detective Denton stood at the scene taking it all in. He looked out at the canyon as the shadows lengthened with the setting sun. This was normally a peaceful place of changing light, and small wildlife just as the creator intended. Men dressed in dark uniforms went about their work with serious efficiency as they processed the scene. Flashes of light appeared in sudden bursts as the crime scene techs took endless pictures of Zeke's broken swollen body. Lights flashed inside the cave as they photographed the bodies of the many long dead girls. It was going to be a long night. Denton scratched his head as he reflected on the events of the last few days. He was baffled and shaken as he thought about Catlin's paintings. They had actually told the whole story. He was reasonably certain that the bodies of the dead girls would turn out to be the missing persons that Caitlin had painted. No telling how far back it all went, fifteen maybe twenty years. Forensic specialists would have a good old time figuring out all of that. He wished they could also figure out how the twins, who lived on the east coast would know what was going down on the west coast. Of course there was the added puzzle of one of the girls who was afflicted with autism.

The puzzled man shook his head. He was disappointed that the FBI would be the group to unravel the case but on the other hand it was a secret relief. There were some things about it that he was sure no one could explain. He took a deep breath and tried to relax his shoulders. His knees felt weak. This case, he knew would change his life and alter his thinking. One thing was certain, he would *never* forget it! His glance was drawn to the top of the embankment where Caitlin stood rocking back and forth. With no warning she started to moan and then to scream. Theresa appeared beside the distraught girl.

"Detective, would you please bring up her back pack and teddy bear?" She smiled sweetly.

His reply was an unintelligible growl, but he grabbed up the two items and started the slippery climb to the top, muttering, cursing and sweating. When he got there Caitlin's tantrum ended abruptly. He held her possessions out and when she took them, he gave a little bow. Caitlin rewarded him with a rare gift; the merest hint of a smile.

ONE WEEK LATER

"Whooee, that Raeford is one hot hunk-a-burnin' love honey," Stephanie winked at Latoia.

"He is a good friend," Latoia did her best to suppress the grin that hurt her still cracked lips.

"Unhuh," Stephanie did not pursue the subject. Latoia was still fragile on every level. She was still walking with a slight limp. The scars from the thirty stitches in her scalp would be hidden in her hair, thank goodness. The hundreds of insect bites were fading and barely visible. On the outside Latoia was healing quickly. Even the broken ribs were not nearly so painful. She had little memory of what took place and that could be a blessing in Stephanie's opinion.

"This place seems empty now that everyone has gone home."

"Isn't it heavenly," Stephanie rolled her eyes. "But the truth is, I miss that warm family feeling. Now don't get me wrong I love my privacy, but I love people too, especially your mother. My housekeeper loves your grandmother. I have a feeling they are going to be frequent guests here."

Latoia chuckled softly, but the sound died away quickly and the lost faraway expression crept back all too easily.

"Now listen Latoia, I want to talk business for a minute."

Latoia frowned as if she was not sure what Stephanie was talking about.

"I've been in contact with New York," she paused to watch Latoia's face, but there was no change in her expression.

"What happened to you has been all over the news…the National news."

A small frown appeared above her dark brown eyes as they widened slightly.

"I have kept everyone away from you so that you could recover in peace."

"Thank you so much," Latoia murmured.

"Now don't even worry about that. I did it because I care. Now the thing I want to discuss with you is the contract with Frazier Inc. Fragrances. I spoke with Bryson Marsh, the CEO if you remember, and he is perfectly willing to wait one more week. He was especially interested in the advertising campaign I outlined for him."

"Oh my God…I …I think I actually forgot about all of that. How could that happen?"

"You went through an unspeakable trauma, honey child. It's over now and the rest of your life is going to be beautiful."

Tears poured down Latoia's cheeks. "I look terrible. I'll never be able to measure up to an ad campaign for the most prestigious company in the world."

"Never say never sweety. Let me explain why," Stephaine's grin was huge and self-satisfied. She had a winning idea that could bring everyone big, big bucks by the coming spring. Life was good.

Two weeks later

Latoia's heart fluttered nervously as she stood in the lavish dressing room of the New York fragrance company. She took a deep breath and waited for Stephanie.

The elegant gold mask covered all of the healing scratches on Latoia's face. Only her eyes and lips were visible, and they were covered with gold make-up. The mask accentuated her high full cheekbones and covered the front portion of her head, successfully hiding the still healing wounds.

Stephanie placed Latoia on a stool in the presentation room. She draped a shimmering gold fabric around her and told her to close her eyes. One of the secretaries lowered the lights.

Men dressed in expensive suits and skeptical expressions filed in. When they were all comfortably seated, the lights were taken down further. Spotlights blinked on.

"Awaken," Stephanie's low husky voice whispered mysteriously.

Latoia's eyes opened slowly. She moved with a slow sensuality until she was standing upright. The gold fabric slipped away. Latoia was clad in a nearly sheer body stocking. Her long exquisite dark-skinned body was clearly apparent but the ugly healing scratches and wounds were invisible. Blue-black silk fabric was attached to her arms and when the fan was switched on it billowed out behind her as she slowly arched her back and held her arms gracefully away from her body. Her golden mask tilted skyward showing off her elegant profile.

"Butterfly Noir whispers mysterious elegance." Stephanie's voice was a perfect addition to the mood.

The room was silent. The executives were mesmerized. Then they applauded.

ANTIQUES AND SWEETS

Alyson, Babette and Abigail were draped across various chairs and settees in their newly completed store. They were exhausted from their labor over the past few weeks. The smell of fresh paint mingled pleasantly with the peculiarly distinct odor of antique furniture.

Babette had just brewed her favorite espresso in the tiny coffee shop adjoining the antique store. The women sipped from Limoge demi-tasse cups and tasted samples of the rich desserts that Babette had selected.

"Mmm, the chocolate meltaway is to swoon for," Alyson closed her eyes as she savored the flavor.

"No, no this cherry liquer cheesecake is the best," Abigail declared.

"Well this version of Southern key lime pie is the best I've ever tasted," Babette's words were slightly obscured as she spoke with her mouth full. She licked her lips trying to capture a bit of cream that stuck to the corner of her mouth.

"Have you ever visited the South?" Abigail raised an eyebrow.

"Oh yes. I love it. Atlanta, Savannah, Hilton Head Island, Charleston. They are such gracious lovely people. In fact, you might consider going there on a buying trip. There are amazing antiques to be found at estate sales and auctions all over the south."

"Hmm. Sounds nice. I've actually already done some investigating. Once our shop opens and we work out the knots I may very well plan a trip there."

The blue stone that Abigail wore continuously on a chain around her neck seemed to heat up. She put her hand to her chest as if she were in pain.

"Are you feeling sick?" Alyson cried out thinking that her friend might be having a heart attack.

"Oh, I'm fine, really," Abigail reassured her, "just a little heartburn. Too much stress and espresso." The stone had already cooled down and she was sure that it had been her imagination. The incident had left her a little breathless.

"Have I told you how much I positively adore every color you have chosen for this shop?" Abigail deflected the attention to her friend. Alyson flushed with pleasure at the compliment.

It was a new experience for Abigail to have friends that she actually counted as friends. It felt good to sit around with them, work with them, drink with them and best of all was the shared laughter. She had always kept an emotional distance from people, especially since her chosen line of work was a bit out of the ordinary. She smiled slightly; yes, at the very least, it was a bit off the path.

"What is that smug grin all about?" Babette's eyes had narrowed and she regarded Abigail shrewdly.

"I was just thinking how lovely it is to have friends."

"You never had friends before?" Alyson knew what it was like to have very few people to share friendship with. Her husband had made sure of that.

"Not close friends," Abigail cast her eyes down.

"Well here's to friendship," Babette lifted her empty espresso cup. "Uh," she grimaced, "What say we toast our friendship with the good stuff," she gave a sly wink and headed toward the back of the store.

Abigail walked slowly behind them as she began planning her trip to the south. She conjured scenes of willow trees; old plantation homes filled with antiques and of course jewels that might be hidden away in someone's attic. Not only that, but she wanted to meet…the blue stone began a slight pulsing on her chest. She nearly jumped. This was mysterious. She had never encountered a stone that *spoke* like this one did. Was it haunted do you suppose? The stone cooled and quieted, but the quiet, she knew, was more of a waiting. The day would come when it would speak again and she would do her best to solve this intriguing puzzle. But today… she would drink champagne!

None of the women noticed a change in the air as they trouped to the back of the store. A faint glowing orb had formed in the area where they had just been sitting. A small being stood in the center of the light and watched them in silence. A male figure short in stature smiled at them, his eyes riveted on Abigail. His round face wore an expression of satisfaction. He felt good now that his assigned task was nearing completion. It had been so many lifetimes in the making and he had grown tired of the efforts that were required of him. He knew though that it wouldn't be too much longer. He was feeling quite proud of himself for arriving so close to the end of his journey.

Yreva had set aside the anger and thoughts of revenge that had plagued him and condemned him to the terrible karmic situations that he had faced for hundreds of years! It was good to feel at peace with himself and to be looking forward to a brighter future. It would be soon...very soon. Avery/Yreva had lapsed into an unconscious state as his spirit traveled into the state of spirit. It felt so good to know that his karmic journey would soon be easing and that at last he was close to finishing that journey of his soul. It would be so wonderful to start anew and finally be released from the rigors of learning his many serious lessons. He looked forward to doing good deeds and to seeing his family again.

When you go back and look at it—
        Your eyes become darkened.
When you speak of it—
        Your voice drips bitterness.
When you think of it—
        Your mind trembles in pain.

Release the unbending past,
That shows no sorrow.

Break out of the bondage,
And become accustomed to freedom.

Learn from it yes.
Learn—

                to let it go.

By Roger Ludwig

Yreva/Avery thought blissfully, "Let go of the past and embrace the now then move toward a beautiful future!"

ABOUT THE AUTHOR

Award winning ballet teacher and choreographer, Jimelle Suzanne began dancing at the age of seven and performed in her first ballet company at the age of twelve. At fourteen, she went on to join the Sacramento Ballet Company under the artistic direction of Dean and Barbara Crockett. While in grammar school, she enjoyed storytelling and writing plays.

She was the editor for the Roseville Union High School newspaper and wrote inspirational essays as librarian for Job's Daughters, a Masonic based organization for young women. As a young adult, she performed for the Los Angeles Regional Opera Ballet Company. Jimelle formed her own dance studio in Roseville, California and later she created the Golden West Theater Ballet Company. There, she was responsible for the artistic content including music selection, costume design, choreography and production. After becoming a homemaker and mother, she developed her own psychic abilities.

Her psychic knowledge was increased through the study of Edgar Casey's work and books authored by Rudolph Steiner. During yoga meditations, Jimelle began having visions which led to the enhancement of her abilities. In 1985, while living on Hilton Head Island, South Carolina, she facilitated group meditations and mediumship classes. In 1994, she created and published a meditation tape, *The Rainbow is You*, which was distributed by New Leaf.

For the past twenty years, Jimelle has been a ballet instructor, choreographer and professional psychic while making her home in Apex, North Carolina. She volunteered at the 1994 Maui Writers Conference to gain insight into story development through lectures by well-known authors, agents and publicists. Jimelle Suzanne's passion is to author the stories that come to her through her experiences and psychic abilities. She has written *Blue Vision* and is currently writing the third book of the series.

Made in the USA
Columbia, SC
02 December 2023

27601781R00140